Sex In The Title

A Comedy about Dating, Sex, and Romance in NYC
(back when phones weren't so smart)

Zack Love

SQ Publishing

SQ Publishing

ISBN: 978-1494812119

Contents

Acknowledgement

This book is dedicated to the women of the world. Without you, there would be no muse.

*****

Special thanks are owed to some individuals who joined my book adventure and made the arduous journey far easier than it would have been otherwise. These virtual friends (known only through our Facebook and email interactions) were my book's guardian angels and provided some much-needed help with this third edition of *Sex in the Title* and with my other releases. And, yes, they are all women!

Author Ker Dukey, for her early and boundless support — unparalleled in its loyalty, generosity, and depth, and truly humbling; for managing my street team and sharing her keen instincts and advice from her own writing journey; for providing amazing graphics for my banners, teasers, and covers (humoring requested revisions with the patience of a saint); and for lifting my morale when needed and helping in countless other ways.

Myriam Judith Perkins, for providing so much industry experience and strategic advice (at times a la "The Wolf") and helping with promotions and introductions, including to Ena Burnette who did an awesome job organizing a sales blitz and blog tours for this book and my other works.

Anna-Maria Butucescu and Anita Viccica Toss, for being such loyal and hugely helpful fans who provided tremendous promotional support on Facebook, Goodreads, and other book forums, and were always ready with a helping hand on other projects.

Crystal Solis and Jennifer Pou, who constantly worked to build a buzz while offering extra help with researching promotional and partnership opportunities.

Author KM Golland, for her friendly advice (often delivered with amusing wit) and her impressive efforts to spread the word about my novel to new readers, including Jenna Hanson, who helpfully pointed out several editing errors.

Diane Dininno, for generously sponsoring so many giveaways and providing assistance with various projects, including the campaign I launched to support a little girl's cancer fight.

My street team, which has promoted my work tirelessly (on Facebook pages, blogs, and unsuspecting foreheads) and includes: Jennifer Cothran, Abby Porter Cook, Kathy Coopmans, Jessica Lynn Leonard, Sarah Mae Zink, Colleen Farrell, Lisa Dale, Veronica Sloan, Lisa LB Johnson, Verna Mcqueen, Isa Jones, Renee Dyer, Kiersten Riley Funcheon, Eileen Robinson, Jacy Goodwin, Misty Hinton, and Liz Stephenson.

Thanks are also owed to my test readers who reviewed the draft of this novel from 2003 and/or the polished and updated 2013 e-book version: Eugenia, Steve, Carolina, Guy, Alex, Leah, Adam, Max, Donna, Sarah, Debbi, Victoria, Sophie, and Mia. Their feedback encouraged me to press forward with this book and often helped me to refine the manuscript.

My mother and her grandmother deserve special credit for instilling in me a respect for women – by their incredible life examples and their progressive thinking about the role of women in society. Providing a somewhat complementary perspective, my uncles were the first to show me the pleasures of pursuing women and, more importantly, the joy of having a woman in one's life. And I am eternally grateful for my funny, kind, and wise sister, who has been a lifelong friend and advisor – on women and life in general.

I am also indebted to my male friends for the many years that they have served with honorable distinction as wingmen, strategists, therapists, and jesters. Our shared adventures – with the laughs and lessons learned – made it that much easier for this novel to come to life.

Lastly, I am especially grateful to every woman who ever went on a date with me — not only for tolerating me through a coffee (or more), but also for unwittingly providing some form of inspiration and/or insight into the ever elusive female psyche.

Preface

In case the title of this book somehow left any doubt, those who are easily offended by sexual content (or profanity) should probably avoid reading this novel. For everyone else, I salute your thicker skin and/or adventurousness, but a brief note about vulgarity and salacity is still warranted. The first and only time that I submitted this work to anyone in the publishing industry was back in 2003, after sharing it with about a dozen (mostly female) test readers who thought it was hilarious. The book was conditionally accepted by two reputable literary agents. One agent offered to represent the book if I made it more outlandishly raunchy, while the other agent asked me to do the exact opposite. Both agreed that — despite centering on male misadventures — the comedy avoided misogyny, which was key because most fiction readers in 2003 were female (and, in 2014, clearly still are). But I was puzzled by what to do with the agents' diametrically opposed comments.

In the end, rather than write three different versions of the same novel (more raunchy, less raunchy, and as is), I concluded that maybe I had struck the right balance, and so never bothered to do anything more with the book other than let it clutter up my hard drive. But over the years, my original test readers encouraged me to publish this novel, and — for better or worse — I finally listened. Of course, there's no pleasing everyone — as the reactions from those two agents illustrate. Nevertheless, if you're one of those intrepid readers who haven't been scared away yet, I genuinely think (and hope) that you'll be more amused than offended.

It's also worth commenting on the era depicted in this novel (1993 through the spring of 2001). Life seemed simpler in many ways — a conclusion produced by nearly all nostalgic reflections on prior decades. The Twin Towers still majestically decorated the Manhattan skyline and terrorism was rarely mentioned as a national concern. Calling the main phone number of a business generally still yielded a human being rather than five minutes of robot-voiced call options. Cell phones weren't nearly as smart or ubiquitous as they are today, so people were as likely to write a phone number on a piece of paper as they were to enter it into a mobile phone. Au Bar was still a midtown watering hole for the rich and/or beautiful. Home video was still normally watched on VHS video tapes that were inserted into VCRs. Music was listened to on the go with a portable tape or CD player like the Walkman (a comically bulky device compared to today's options). People carried paper calendars and address books. Computers were still using floppy discs. Smoking was allowed in New York restaurants, bars, and clubs. The city's iconic yellow cabs still didn't have interactive digital displays planted in front of the back seat for passengers to view or silence.

When I reread *Sex in the Title* for the first time, about a decade after writing it, these outdated details struck me as quaint relics from a narrative time capsule – and worth keeping because they help to define an era and the way people interacted in it. So, rather than revise the manuscript to replace outmoded technologies with smart phones, social media, and other present-day realities, I thought it best to preserve the original details and release the novel as a kind of period piece.

One final note about this book's genre, which was surprisingly hard for me to pin down. The novel is arguably some form of "lad lit" because it's mostly about five men, but it's decidedly not "fratire" because, as mentioned, it's not sexist and there is plenty of material about relationships (rather than just the sexual adventures and mishaps that are the focus of fratire). The book is definitely a comedy because it describes some extremely comical situations and often employs humor in descriptions and dialogue. But the work is also "literary" to the extent that it indulges social, psychological, and philosophical musings, and embraces a relatively advanced vocabulary. The story also has elements of romance in it. So maybe it's a "literary romantic comedy." Critics should have a field day with that one.

1. Evan's Journey from Bad to Worse

"Your employment is terminated. I'm out of the office this morning for meetings but you should pack up your belongings by 1 p.m. today. Your last pay check will arrive in the mail."

That was the first email waiting for Evan on Monday morning, May 29, 2000, at the office where he had worked for the last two years. ChocaChump.com, the Internet-based, chocolate home delivery company, was another dot-com whose days were numbered. About six weeks earlier, the NASDAQ had dropped more than twenty-five percent from its peak in a single week.

The tech crash would continue, and Evan's boss, a mercurial CEO who closely managed his twenty employees, grew increasingly bitter and difficult as his company faltered. After Evan read the email terminating his employment, he recalled their curt discussion from the previous Friday.

"Tell me the real reason why you were gone so long yesterday."

"It's the reason I gave you: my grandma had a bad fall and needed to be taken to the hospital. She called me for help because my parents were out of town."

"You were gone for six hours."

"Well, I had to go to Queens, where she lives. She needed a bunch of medical tests. And I wasn't just going to leave her alone in the hospital. She's a seventy-five-year old widow, so I had to be there to comfort her, and help her deal with insurance forms, doctors, etc."

"Evan, everyone's got problems. You don't think I have a grandma who needs me just as much? Do you think our competitors care about our grandmas? It's war out there! And we're losing. Things used to be much better, but our operating budget no longer covers middle-of-the-day-grandma-emergencies."

"But this is the first time I've ever done that. And I told you before I left that I had a family emergency. I can come in this weekend to make up for the lost work time."

"Yes, please do that...I'll have to think things over."

As he promised, Evan spent much of his Saturday making up for his time away from the office. But there was no reversing a CEO desperate to trim his payroll.

Evan decided not to tell his girlfriend, Alexandra, about the fact that he was now unemployed. He would wait until after they returned from the Puerto Rican vacation that he had promised her a month ago, so that she could fully enjoy the experience, rather than feel guilty about the expense. The quality time with her would also help him to refocus on what really mattered to him, he thought.

Hoping for a fresh and positive start the morning after he was fired, Evan turned on his home laptop and purchased the airline tickets online. He then logged into his email account, so that he could forward the trip details to Alexandra. He noticed a new email from her in his inbox.

"Evan, Hun, sorry to tell you like this over email, but my plane's leaving soon, so I don't have time to do this in person. I'm leaving because I really need a break. From everything. Please don't start wondering what this means or what you did wrong or anything, because you've been great. And that means that I have to use that trite line about how this isn't about you. Because it really is about me…I'm twenty-four years old and I feel like I'm losing my youth suddenly. I just want to feel young and free for a few months. And I'm tired of this city. It's making me old. The routine, the stress, the constant competition. I just need to escape for a while. I know we were supposed to go away one of these weekends, but I need more than a weekend. Much more. I decided — in a totally spur of the moment kind of way — to go to Australia. I know this all seems crazy and surprising, but that's how these things go when you're young. Without planning too much. I'll be gone for six weeks. Maybe more. I'd ask you to wait for me, but that wouldn't be fair to either of us. And I'm just not sure we're right for each other, even though you're really a wonderful guy…I think a clean break would be best for both of us. By the time you read this I'll probably be on a plane. I'm really sorry, Evan, because I know this will hurt, even though that was never my intention. Call it a crazy and selfish impulse, but I just need this change right now. You've always been a sweetheart and I'll totally miss you. Postcards will follow! Kisses, Alexandra."

*****

Evan stared at his laptop screen, in speechless disbelief.

For the lonely three months that followed, he struggled with the loss of a job he had mostly enjoyed, and a woman he had begun to love after almost five months of dating her.

2

On the few occasions when he could motivate himself to go out and act like a single man again, Evan crashed and burned with every woman he approached. Julia, a sexy, thirty-two-year-old therapist, was the only exception, but there were too many issues for that prospect to go anywhere. She couldn't resist psychoanalyzing Evan whenever they met, which he soon realized was just her way of avoiding her own doldrums. Julia was clinically depressed and desperately seeking marriage and children (which Evan didn't want for another four or five years), so his conscience forced him to nip things in the bud, even though she seemed open to a fling with him.

Thus, Evan continued stumbling along his losing streak, learning just how much being down is not particularly appealing to anyone — especially the attractive women of New York City, clad in their heels or hipster boots, looking for a good time.

Evan Cheson was actually a charming and good-looking man. He had a full head of thick, black hair; blue eyes; an athletic, six-foot-one build; smooth, dark eyebrows; and facial features suggestive of his French-Italian ancestry. And for most of his adult life, he had been a confident and successful man, from school, to work, to women.

But several major failures in rapid-fire succession can inhibit good judgment, and thereby invite more failure. For Evan, losing a job and a girlfriend, each via email, one day after the next, was too much to avoid the absurd downward spiral that would ensue. He even avoided checking emails for a while, but that didn't help.

On Thursday night, after a few months of fruitless rebound attempts and embarrassing faux pas with women, there was something perverse in Evan — maybe even carelessly self-destructive — that wanted to know just how laughably low he could go.

So he put on a new pair of dark slacks and a collared, button-down, sky blue shirt just snug enough to suggest his occasional gym routine. His clean look — with a dab of cologne, a gargle of mouthwash, and freshly polished leather shoes — was calculated to minimize the entrance hassle into Manhattan's clubs. But had Evan fathomed just how hard he would end up crashing that night, he would have surely stayed home in his T-shirt and boxers.

2. Evan Runs Full Speed into the Wall Ahead

It began in a bar. The Bowery Bar. It was the end of summer – an auspicious time for an unattached twenty-nine-year-old male in Manhattan. Scattered sparingly about the spring, summer, and fall, there are about fifty days of perfect weather in New York City: zero humidity, clear skies, and seventy-five to eighty degrees fanned by a light, cool breeze. During such days, smiles sprout more readily, clothes pronounce rather than protect, and the sweet scent of promise wafts everywhere in the air.

The last day of August 2000 was one of those perfect fifty days. And it was a Thursday, which meant that most of the Manhattanites leaving the next day for a weekend in the Hamptons were still in the city, and that meant more female prospects for Evan. Indeed, that Thursday felt so promising that Evan thought he might finally reverse a dry spell that somehow felt longer than his postpubescent years. But Evan's new insecurity, which resulted almost entirely from his recent bout of bad luck, made him somewhat desperate to prove himself any way he could. And as his desperation led to ever greater and more frequent fumbles, he began to question the quality of his goods, as even the most steadfast traveling salesman does after enough slammed doors. He lost his touch, hesitated with his humor, and forgot some of the tactics that had served him so well in the past.

So when Evan spotted a woman across the bar who easily qualified as a "9+ hottie" in his book, he broke one of the most important rules of the pick-up: never wait more than a minute to make a move. A longer delay after initial eye contact suggests a lack of interest or — even worse — a lack of confidence. It also converts the interaction from the flowingly spontaneous to the self-consciously calculated. Evan's five-minute delay before approaching a woman who absolutely attracted him was, in this case, attributable only to his three-month string of prior botches. To exacerbate matters, when he finally gathered the gumption to approach her, he allowed some form of autopilot to take over, in the hope that luck alone might produce some good results.

She was wearing body-tight, silk white shorts, and a pink wife-beater undershirt with no bra. Her perky, full breasts looked to Evan like two deliciously firm, cherry-topped cantaloupes, daring him to look anywhere else. The woman oozed sex and her name was Tina, although Evan would never actually come to learn this basic fact about her. He would instead remember her only as "the soft porn babe I massively underestimated."

As Evan arrived next to her at the bar, he realized that the only thing about her that he had observed was that this sultry, petite blonde in his crosshairs had the figure of an exotic dancer or a soft porn actress. Evan's autopilot skills were reliable enough to avoid a disastrous opener like, "Say, did anyone ever tell you that you could be a great exotic dancer?" But they were sufficiently lacking in foresight and imagination to realize that asking Tina what she does for a living might be just as bad, if she was, in fact, an exotic dancer. So when Tina turned and noticed that Evan had squeezed into the small space at the bar next to her, all Evan could say when she looked at him was "So…What do you do?"

Tina, who had noticed Evan hesitate for several minutes before walking up to her, just shook her head with a mockingly disappointed look on her face. "Couldn't you do any better than that?" she replied.

As Evan's continuing bad luck would have it, Tina had already been approached by four conversationally unimaginative men during the last two hours. All four had started with a similar question, and they were each clearly interested in Tina only as a sexual object. So by the time Evan came by, Tina was more than ready to dish it out.

"Well I realize it's not a great opening line," Evan began excusing himself, "but you've gotta start somewhere, right? So why not with what you do?"

"Because that's probably the worst question you can ask a woman you don't know."

"Why?"

"It's about as original and sincere as a flight attendant greeting."

"Is it really that bad?"

"Guys ask me that question all the time. You think any of them actually cares what the answer is?" Tina perked up her chest a little, as if to emphasize what they really care about.

"But I do care."

"I'm sure you do," she replied. "Which is why I'm sure you stopped to consider the possibility that I might not like what I do, or might not want to discuss it with a stranger."

Evan realized that he had to get off autopilot fast, because the young beauty in front of him was far sharper than he had estimated. He feared that he would soon be adding her to the list of females who had abruptly walked away from him in the middle of his attempt to "make a new friend," as he liked to think of his bungles.

"So," he began, "should I have started by asking you what you don't do?"

"Maybe." Tina released a slight, reluctant smile at the question. "At least it would have been more original."

"All right," Evan started anew. "So tell me. What do you not do?"

"I don't tell guys I don't know what I do."

"OK. What else do you not do?"

"I don't play basketball."

"How funny! I also don't play basketball," he said, forgetting his love of the game.

"I don't approve of how the city government handles New York's solid waste problem."

"Couldn't agree with you more about solid waste," Evan replied, despite his complete indifference to the issue.

"And I don't particularly like your outfit."

"Really?" Evan smiled with some embarrassment. "It's actually refreshing to hear a woman say what she really thinks, at my personal expense…"

"At least you don't have to wonder what I really think."

"I actually spent four hours in the store, consulting with every female in the area, before I bought it."

"That just goes to show you that your shopping time isn't helping the quality of your shopping decisions."

"I hate shopping."

"It shows."

"Say, can we restart this conversation at some point where I was doing better?"

"There is no such point," she responded with a playful half-smile. "You were always doing this bad."

"So I should probably quit while I'm ahead?"

"Probably," Tina replied, mysteriously. "But I'll let you crash and burn for a little longer by telling you what I do for a living."

"Thank you...I guess." By now, Evan was at once intrigued, intimidated, and otherwise totally at a loss with respect to how he should proceed with this woman.

"I actually don't know why I'm going to share this information with you..." Tina paused for a moment, to give the value of her confession the respect and seriousness that it deserved. "Because I ordinarily don't tell this to strangers, but for some reason I trust you." Tina suddenly seemed vulnerable and exposed to Evan, who now felt awkwardly unworthy of whatever it was that she was about to disclose about her job.

"You know, we really don't have to talk about what you do," Evan said, trying to match Tina's tone. "I mean, people start there because it can tell you a lot about someone's choices in life, and what their day to day life is like, but sometimes it can be very misleading. I mean, look at me. I'm a computer programmer."

"Really?"

"Yeah. I'm another survivor of a dot-bomb," Evan explained, putting the best spin he could on things. "My company went bankrupt two months ago, and I've been freelancing as a software development consultant. But that has nothing to do with my real passion, which is writing."

"What do you write?"

"I've been working on a novel for the last five years. And I've written a bunch of screenplays as well."

"You write screenplays?" Tina's interest rose for a moment. "Have you written anything that was made yet?"

The only thing Evan hated more than that follow up question was the answer that he had to give to it. "No. Not yet...Why do you ask?"

"I work in film too," she replied.

Given Tina's original reluctance to discuss what she does, Evan concluded at this point that she was either 1) a disgruntled actress who was stuck at the bottom of the totem pole, grunting away on some low-budget film production with the hope that her travail would someday pay off in the form of a film job that would be less embarrassingly exploitative than her current one; or 2) a soft porn actress who bore her flesh in those late-night cable TV films that had too little sex to qualify as true porn and too little story or character to qualify as true cinema. Either way, he thought it best to change the subject.

"You know, I don't even know your name yet," he tried.

"Well if I tell you what I do, then I certainly won't tell you my name, so you'll have to choose: my name or my job."

Now he was almost positive that she was a soft porn actress, and knew that a discussion about her job should be avoided at all costs. "Your name. I don't need to know what you do. But I do need to know your name."

"That's too bad, because I've already prepared myself to tell you what I do, and now I'm feeling the need to share it with you."

"Because I write screenplays?" he said, trying to feign ignorance and still hoping to change the subject.

"No. Because I trust you for some strange reason. There's something honest and reassuring about you."

"There is?"

"Yeah…Like you mean well — even if your delivery needs work…So here's what I do." Tina looked away for an awkward moment.

Evan felt even more uncomfortable now. He knew that this conversation had grown too serious too fast and there was no recovering from it now. There was only a graceful exit strategy to be devised as quickly as possible.

"I'm an actress…" Tina started. She made eye contact with Evan for a moment, and then looked to the side a little. "I work mainly in skin flicks…I mean, I work in skin flicks right now…Nothing really hard core…There's no actual intercourse involved and it pays really well…"

Tina tried a forced smile at Evan, and Evan looked at her acceptingly.

"I ran away from home when I was sixteen, and I needed something to pay the bills and then get myself through college…Then, I guess I just kept doing it…But I want to get involved in other films — you know, normal films — one day soon, I hope…"

Evan sighed at the end of her confession, and — still clueless about how to respond but painfully aware of the need to say something — he reverted once again to autopilot. "I think that's really cool that you can admit to that. I mean, it makes you real. Someone who knows her issues and has dealt with them."

"I guess," Tina replied distantly, with a self-reflective gaze that suggested she might not have even heard what Evan just said. Evan hoped this was the case because he had no idea what issues he had just referred to in his compliment.

"And I think it's really cool that you're so comfortable with your body and with your sexuality…I mean, not everyone can look natural on camera…And a lot of people are very inhibited about their bodies and their sexuality."

"Are you?" she asked, suddenly focused on this question.

"Well I could never…" He tried to think of a polite way to describe what Tina does, but preferred to stay away from that topic. "I mean, I'm very comfortable with my sexuality, but…Well, I don't know…Women tell me that I'm definitely comfortable with my body sexually. And I've never really felt uncomfortable in bed, so I guess – "

"Women tell you that?" she asked, somewhat intrigued. "So have you been with a lot of women?" There was a genuine curiosity in her question that gave Evan some hope.

"Actually, I've been with my fair share, for my age."

"And you're what – twenty-seven years old?"

"Thanks. But I'm twenty-nine."

"So what's the body count?"

"The body count?"

"You know: how many women have you slept with in your twenty-nine years?"

Evan wasn't sure whether to overstate the number to look sexually impressive to a soft porn star, or whether to understate the number to look less promiscuous and more like the responsible, clean cut, solid-boyfriend type. Since he still hadn't quite figured out what Tina was looking for or who she really was, he decided just to tell the truth.

"I've been with about sixty-seven women."

"What do you mean 'about sixty-seven?' You say 'about sixty' or 'about seventy.' But not 'about sixty-seven.' You're obviously keeping track." Tina looked amused at another opportunity to toy with Evan.

"All right. You got me," Evan conceded. "I've been with precisely sixty-seven women."

"Unless, of course, you said 'about' because the total depends on how you define 'being with a woman.' For example, if you just got a blowjob and nothing else then maybe you don't count that."

"OK. To be more precise, I've had sexual intercourse with sixty-seven women."

"All right, so then you've probably been with many more women than sixty-seven?"

"Yeah. But I don't keep track of those." Evan suddenly wondered why he didn't bother to keep track of anything but consummation.

"I see...So when did you get started on these sixty-seven women?"

"You mean, how old was I when I lost my virginity?"

"Yes."

"Twenty."

"So you've slept with sixty-seven women in just nine years."

"Well, actually I've had six serious relationships that together took up about two years."

"Serious? Let's see...Six serious relationships in two years...So each one lasted an average of four months. You call that serious?"

"Well, it was an intense four months. And I wasn't seeing anyone else. You know, that's kind of a big deal in New York," he added ironically. "Dating someone exclusively for four months in New York is like four years in Anchorage."

Tina chuckled at Evan's joke. "All right, so not counting the serious relationships, you've slept with..." She crunched some numbers in her head. "You've slept with sixty-one women in just seven years... That's an average of almost nine per year...A new woman every forty days." Tina seemed impressed, which suddenly made Evan feel rather promiscuous.

"Do you think that's a lot?"

"You probably have a few STDs by now, right?"

"None that I know of, thank God."

"So you've been tested? I have to get tested before each of my films."

"Yeah, I actually just got my AIDS test last month. And I'm clean."

"But were you tested for herpes, gonorrhea, and hepatitis?"

"No."

"And you might have chancroid, crabs, HPV or molluscum contagiosum."

"I hope not."

"What about scabies, chlamydia, syphilis, or Trichomoniasis?"

"I don't think so."

"But you were only tested for HIV."

"Yeah."

"Do you have genital warts?

10

"Nasty! No, I don't have warts."

"They're actually not all that bad. An actor who used to work on my films got them and couldn't work anymore until he got them removed. But they're really just a cosmetic nuisance."

Evan was feeling overwhelmed by this sex education class.

"You sound really knowledgeable about this stuff…Do you have any STDs? I mean, with your line of work, you've probably slept with a lot more people than I have." After Tina's grilling, Evan felt emboldened – and relieved – to turn the microscope onto her.

"I told you that in my line of work, which is soft porn, I don't need to have actual intercourse with any of the actors."

"But you said that you have to get tested before each film."

"We do. The producers don't want to take any liability risks, in case there's some kind of accident…And certain scenes do require quite a bit of skin-to-skin contact, even though there's no actual intercourse or head involved. So if anyone has anything that could spread by accident, it could slow down production – particularly with STDs that don't look good on camera…So our producer is extra careful about these things."

"Oh."

"There's something else I should ask you."

"What?"

"Are you comfortable with homosexuality?"

"What do you mean?"

"Well, I do a lot of scenes with other women, and I've had some sexual relationships with women, and I just need to know that you're comfortable with that sort of thing."

This question gave Evan some hope. Tina had just asked for explicit reassurance on a personal and sexual topic – something that she wouldn't have done if she had absolutely no interest in him.

"Oh, well, I'm totally comfortable with it."

"Have you ever had sex with another man?"

Evan was again faced with a conversational dilemma: should he lie and try to impress her with just how comfortable he is with homosexuality by claiming to have had at least one experience, or should he honestly report the truth because Tina prefers her men to be unflinchingly straight?

"No. I've never had sex with another man…I mean, I just never really had the urge."

"Oh. That's what I figured. That's cool. So now I just have two more questions before I can reach a decision."

"A decision?"

"Yeah. A decision about you."

"About me?"

"Yeah. You know, whether you're someone I'd want to date." She grinned mischievously. "Or just have a fling with."

Evan's face broke into a huge blush of relieved optimism. He didn't have a clue where the conversation had been going, and now he finally received a clear signal that things had actually been going quite well.

"Sure. Bring on the questions."

"Now this may strike you as a bit forward and vulgar, but we've talked about quite a few intimate issues, and I'm feeling very comfortable with you..."

"Ask away."

"Are you hung? All of my men have been really well endowed. So I'm a bit spoiled in that department. And I always need to check."

"I'm very well hung," Evan replied, proud to be answering such a promising question from such a sexy woman.

"But all the boys say that."

"Well I can prove it," Evan replied, blushing a little.

"All the boys say that too."

"But not all of them can."

"True...Do you know why that is?"

"Because not all of them are hung," ventured Evan.

"Nope...Because not all of the boys who are hung are uninhibited enough to prove it. Which brings me to my second and last question."

"What's that?"

"I'm a very sensual and uninhibited person, so it's very important for me that my man be equally sensual and uninhibited."

"I think I probably am."

"Well, the way to find out if you are, in fact, as uninhibited and well hung as you say is really quite simple..." Tina seductively licked her lips and suggestively looked down with interest at Evan's groin area. He suddenly realized where she was going with all of this.

"So your next question is whether I'm uninhibited enough to prove to you, right here, that I'm well hung?"

"Right here. In the Bowery Bar."

Evan was dumbfounded because he had never before encountered such a request, and felt genuinely torn about whether to grant it. He looked at the inviting, azure eyes in her ravishing face, and then passed over her sultry, perfectly curved body, as if to weigh carefully the certain humiliation he would experience upon publicly revealing himself against the joy of a potential "score" with one of the sexiest women he had approached in years. He remembered that he hadn't come this close to succeeding with anyone, much less a stunner like this, in a painfully long time. Evan imagined how he would later think himself a coward and a fool for having walked away from the opportunity. He looked around the bar quickly and didn't notice anyone in particular paying attention to the two of them. He calculated that he could probably drop his pants quickly and then pull them back up before anyone could see. "Hell, I'm still young and crazy," he thought. "At the very worst, I'll just have a funny anecdote to tell everyone," he told himself.

Evan tried to look Tina in the eyes with complete cool, but he started blushing as he fumbled awkwardly with the button at the top of his pants. Tina just stood there, propped up against the bar, looking mildly amused but slightly unimpressed with how long Evan had taken to reach his decision and implement it. She glanced at her watch. It was 12:50 a.m. Evan thought she might actually begin timing how long it would take him.

He finally unfastened the top button and quickly unzipped his pants. Tina still looked unimpressed. He knew he had to be more adventurous about the whole thing if he was going to prove to her that he was as uninhibited as he claimed to be. So, after tucking his thumbs under the waistband of his underwear, he looked her straight in the eye again, smiled for a moment, and then pushed everything down with a confident and unreserved extension of his arms.

As he stood there exposed, Evan became acutely aware of the many people in the immediate vicinity who – up until that moment – had seemed oblivious to him. Evan noticed the thirty-something barman in black trying to sneak in peeks while serving some customers at the bar. He noticed an attractive young couple that had stopped making out by the bar to watch. He looked at them for a moment, and they laughed self-consciously, returning to their tongue lock but occasionally angling themselves for another view. Out of the corner of his eye, he noticed four slick-looking guys in their mid-twenties, joking amongst themselves about this guy just twenty feet away whose pants

13

were dropped in front of this babe. "Now that's what I call balls at the Bowery Bar!" one of them yelled. Evan pretended not to notice this group or hear its heckles only because there were too many of them for a threatening stare to do anything but goad them into even more obnoxious behavior. The only thing to do now was get it over with as quickly as possible, and walk out with the gorgeous prize that would vindicate virtually anything he had done in public. Who could argue with his manliness or his judgment if, after he pulled his pants back up, Tina gave him one of those triumphant, Hollywood French kisses, and then took his arm and walked out of the bar with him?

As he stood there with all of his manhood dangling in the cool, smoky air, he thought only of that glorious moment. He didn't see all of the people watching him with a mixture of fascination and repugnance. He focused only on Tina. He waited for her to acknowledge his courageously stupid act with some look of impressed gratitude and/or validation of his size. He waited for her to signal in some way that he had gone well beyond the call of duty, and that he could now pull his pants back up and receive his reward. But he saw none of this in Tina's face, which just looked slightly amazed that he had actually gone through with the whole thing.

So Evan ended up holding his pants down for longer than he had originally planned to, and lifted everything back up only after realizing that he would receive no instruction from Tina to do so. As he zipped his pants back up, he heard some ornery howls from the crowd of guys, and saw the couple quickly resume their kissing with another you-caught-us-staring blush. He couldn't tell how much the barman had seen.

"So?" Evan asked, looking expectantly at Tina. "Did I pass your test?"

Tina looked unmoved by Evan's Bowery Bar boldness. Somewhat reluctant to answer his question, she replied, "Well...To tell you the truth...I don't think you did."

"Really?" Evan felt a devastating humiliation barreling his way, but – in what was to become a pathetic pattern that night – he felt perversely determined to confront it head on. "Why not? I'm not hung enough for you?" he asked, preparing himself for the worst.

"No. I actually think you're probably hung enough."

Upon hearing this confirmation, Evan exhaled a small sigh of relief, but was still waiting for the bad news.

"So what is it? I mean, I'm obviously uninhibited, right? I mean, you weren't expecting me to dance on the bar naked, were you?"

"No, please. Spare us."

"So what is it? Why didn't I pass your test?"

"You really want to know?"

"Yeah. I do."

"Do you really think I would take home someone who drops his pants in public just because I asked him to? I need a man with a little more self-respect than that."

"Are you serious?"

"Absolutely."

"But you get naked in public all the time. Hell, you even simulate sex for the public."

"No, I don't."

"What do you think being a soft porn actress is?"

"It's definitely getting naked and simulating sex in public, but I'm not a soft porn actress."

"What do you mean?" Evan asked in dismay.

"I develop swaptions, derivatives, and other hedge instruments for the futures markets at Morgan Stanley. Princeton grads generally don't go into soft porn."

"But...But you..."

"I know that's what I told you. But that's just my screener. I get hit on by a lot of guys, so I like to filter out anyone who's really promiscuous, bisexual, infected with an STD, or willing to drop his pants in public...I'm too busy to waste a bunch of dates finding out deal-breaking data that I could have uncovered from the get-go...Life's too short not to cut to the chase, right?"

And when Tina finished that reply, 104 anvils, each carefully crafted and weighed in the best metal workshops of the American heartland, came crashing down onto Evan's head.

3. Desperately Seeking a Rebound

Escape. That was the only thing that Evan could think of. What was the quickest way out of the Bowery Bar? He saw an opening and navigated a focused path to the door, blurring out of his mind the obnoxious jokes and comments trailing from various areas near Tina. He shuffled past the glam squad and various hotties piling in, and didn't say goodbye to the doorman or bouncers as he usually did, hoping that if he looked down and moved quickly enough, they wouldn't notice his emergency evacuation.

He jumped into the nearest taxi and said "Just drive!" – as if he were in the midst of some dramatic, high-speed getaway. As he sailed away from the disaster area, with the soft, summer night breeze blowing against his face through the open window, he slowly began deliberating about his options. "I should just quit while I'm ahead," he thought.

Ignoring his own advice, he pulled out his cell phone and a printed list of phone numbers.

Back in autopilot mode, he called a cell phone number off the list.

"Can I speak to Sayvyer, please?"

"Who the fuck is calling here after one in the morning?"

"I'm returning a wallet that she lost."

"You have the wrong number."

He tried the next number on the list.

"Can I speak to Sayvyer, please?"

"You're looking for the savior? At 1:15 a.m.?"

"No. Her name's Sayvyer."

"There is no savior here. Especially not at 1:15 a.m."

Evan shook his head in frustration and wondered for a moment whether the comely brunette had given her real name to Evan. "It had to be her real name...She knew way too many jokes off the top of her head that involved her name," he recalled. "And she told me how – when she was young – she thought her hippy parents were cruel for giving her such a weird name and how later she thought the name made her hip and distinctive...And two of her friends called her 'Sayvyer' that night...So it's definitely her name..." Evan crossed out the two numbers he had just dialed and shook his head in frustration. "But why couldn't she have had a more normal name?" he thought.

In Evan's world, Sayvyer was an "8.5 hottie," which would be more than enough of a consolation prize at this particularly low-spirited moment. Unfortunately, there were four digits separating Evan from his savior. He thought about how cruel and absurd it was that something as trivial as the knowledge of four particular numbers could keep him from a potentially delightful encounter with a woman who could salvage his miserable night.

He had met her six weeks ago at Au Bar. The posh nightclub on East Fifty-eighth Street drew "Euro-trash," cigar-smoking bankers, and attractive women vying for trophy-wife status. After his fifth drink, Evan had shared all of his woes with Sayvyer at the bar. "Do you have any idea how much talent it takes to lose a job and a girlfriend in just two days, and all via email?" he began. "It's really pretty difficult, and I'm thinking of starting an evening workshop for people who aren't as talented as I am in that regard."

Evan's charm and sympathetic misfortunes grew on Sayvyer during their thirty-minute chat, and she tried her best to lift his spirits. "I think it's great that that asshole boss fired you," she said. "You needed to get out of there. You're way too good for a place like that."

"I heard they're about to go bankrupt soon anyway."

"You had no business working there in the first place."

"Why do you say that?"

"You're one of those guys who's too smart to be working for someone else."

"Do I really seem that geeky?"

"You're a total geek."

"Oh great."

"But you're a hip and handsome geek. I mean, how many computer programmers out there look like you and write novels and screenplays on the side?"

Evan felt truly lifted for a moment. He was starved for this kind of validation. After some good laughs and playful conversation, the two ended up dancing, and eventually grinding, on the dance floor, where they made out briefly among a room full of swaying, tightly pressed bodies.

But their momentum was interrupted when Sayvyer's friends came up to her and insisted that she come with them to an exclusive party in the VIP section of another club. She couldn't refuse the gorgeous group or convince them to let Evan tag along. But she did stall them long enough to explain her departure to Evan and give him her phone number.

"Why was I such a bonehead?" he thought, as he recalled their concluding banter, and how he had foolishly tried to show off his memory and knowledge of psychology.

"Now I'm giving you my number only if you absolutely promise to use it," she said. "I'm sick of guys not calling when they say they'll call…"

"There are actually guys out there who promise they'll call you and then don't?"

"Yeah. And some think that email is just as good. But it's a very bad sign…I mean, if the guy doesn't call you before you've slept with him, he sure as hell won't call after."

"Well, I hereby unconditionally and absolutely promise to call you if you give me your phone number. And I do this on behalf of every negligent male, in every mammalian species," Evan said, in the geekiest tongue-in-cheek he could muster.

"So you're now representing every non-calling male in every species?"

"Even the he-goats that didn't call the she-goats. And the dogs that didn't dial the digits of bitches…"

"So if you break this promise, I can truly write off all males, and just become a lesbian?"

"Yes. But if I keep my promise to call, then you have to forgive all of these males, and start giving them all the benefit of the doubt — from the dogs to the dudes."

"And why is that?"

"Because – contrary to all appearances – I'm as bad as they get, and if I call when I say I will, then there really is hope for all the other males out there."

"Well that's very reassuring to hear," she replied. "So are you going to get something to write down my number with?" she asked, as her friends waited impatiently for the two to end their encounter.

Evan drew nearer to her and whispered into her ear, "Just tell it to me…A dog like me doesn't need to write it down…"

"Why not?" she asked, resting her hand on Evan's lower back.

"I can remember it. Trust me," he replied, letting his hands find their way to her firm and round behind.

"Why are you so sure?" she said, placing her lips just above his neck and below his ear.

"Because I can. Most people can...You know, phone numbers have seven digits in them because memory experiments showed that this was the maximum number of digits that most people can retain."

"You are a geek, aren't you? A yummy-looking geek," she said flirtatiously, as she slid her waist between his legs a little.

"A geek who will definitely call," he replied, emboldened and aroused by the physical contact.

At this point, Evan felt so good about his odds with Sayvyer that he suddenly wanted to avoid taking any chances with his memory – particularly because he had imbibed one too many vodka cranberries and had already crammed his head with four other names and numbers from earlier that night.

"Well, geeks run the world...And that's sexy," she replied, grabbing Evan's butt and grinding into him until she could feel something harden a little more. And with that statement, she made it impossible for Evan to backtrack on his offer to memorize her phone number, because resorting to the safer pen and paper approach after that statement would defrock Evan of his geeky godliness. He also feared that Sayvyer's increasingly impatient friends might drag her off while he foraged about for a paper and pen.

Fortunately for Evan, when Sayvyer whispered her 212-phone number to him, while continuing to arouse him on the dance floor, he did manage to notice that there was a sixty-nine in the last four digits – a mnemonic fact for which he was quite grateful.

"See that? There's a sixty-nine in your number, so there's no way I can forget it now!" he pointed out.

"True. But that number won't mean anything to us if you can't remember the rest," she replied suggestively.

"Don't worry. I'm more likely to forget my name," he said, just as Sayvyer was pulled away by her friends. He caught one last wink from her as she moved towards the exit with her gang and then disappeared behind a large crowd.

The next morning, as his Saturday afternoon hangover subsided, he realized that he could perfectly recall only two of the four numbers he had taken before meeting Sayvyer, and – worst of all – he could recall only that the first two digits of Sayvyer's phone number were ninety-four and that there was a sixty-nine somewhere among the last four digits. No matter how many times he replayed his dialogue with

Sayvyer, Evan couldn't remember what the third digit was, or even where among the last four digits the number sixty-nine appeared.

He thought about his monumental misstep from the previous night while shaving, which was in itself a mistake because each time he thought about his error, a spontaneous, self-flagellating headshake occurred that produced a minor shaving cut. But a little later, as he popped two frozen waffles into a toaster and heated up some coffee, it dawned on him that his sexy geekiness could still save the day.

Given the facts of which he was sure – a seven-digit number beginning with ninety-four and containing sixty-nine among the last four digits – Evan calculated that there were exactly three thousand permutations of possible phone numbers for Sayvyer. He quickly wrote a computer program that generated for him a print out of all three thousand permutations.

He figured that if he tried one phone number permutation per day it would take him a maximum of roughly eight years to get the correct number. He then thought about what it would take to call Sayvyer within the optimal wait period, as most women he knew defined it (i.e., no more than two days later). To conduct some ballpark research, Evan timed a random call and realized that it took fifteen seconds to dial one phone number and let it ring at least three times. Assuming a conversation that lasted only long enough to establish that the number dialed was incorrect, Evan concluded that it would take approximately thirty seconds per phone number. He calculated that if he worked assiduously for twelve and a half hours per day, which still gave him some rest time between calls, he could cover one thousand five hundred numbers per day. At that rate, working for two days, he could call her in no more than two days after she gave him her number.

Satisfied that it was actually feasible to reach her within the optimal two-day period, he set about trying to dial every permutation on his print out, crossing out wrong numbers as he worked his way down the list. He applied himself to the task rather diligently for about five hours, and eliminated six hundred incorrect numbers. At that point, however, his fingers were tired, his ear was sore, his neck was stiff, and he was wondering whether the tedium and physical fatigue of nonstop cold calling were really worth the brownie points of calling within two days.

He took a dinner break — consisting of leftover Chinese food — and settled on a compromise solution that struck him as far more reasonable. There were now two thousand four hundred permutations left, and he would try forty per day on average, so that it would take him no more than about two months to dial the correct number for Sayvyer. This meant that he would have to spend only about twenty minutes per day dialing numbers, and if bad luck brought him to Sayvyer's number only in month two (rather than, say, in a week or two), then he would just need to invent a good excuse for waiting so long to call her.

"If only Sayvyer could know how committed I've been to meeting my obligations to the female gender," Evan thought to himself, as he sat in the back of the taxi, that last Thursday night of August 2000, where he reflected for a moment on how he had voluntarily exceeded his quota of forty phone number permutations for that day. But then he admitted to himself that – after what had just happened to him at the Bowery Bar – he was prepared to do almost anything to save the night, or at least soften its sting.

But Evan needed a quick fix now, and dialing more random phone numbers from a list of seven hundred remaining possibilities in the hope of reaching a woman he had met about six weeks ago at Au Bar was hardly going to help. A better solution suddenly dawned on him. He would call up Alexandra, who had returned from Australia four weeks ago.

Evan leaned forward and finally gave his getaway cab driver a more specific destination: "Can you head to the Upper East Side?" The Pakistani cabbie shook his head a little, slightly annoyed, as he turned the next corner to drive in the opposite direction.

Evan had seen Alexandra each day of her first week back in New York, and had tried in vain to get back together with her. But she had made it clear that they were through. On her tenth day back, when Evan showed up with a bouquet and dinner from her favorite Thai takeout, she gave him what she sarcastically dubbed "your last charity fuck." A few days later, Evan decided to check in with her on another whim, at around midnight, just to see if she still hadn't met another guy and might therefore be ready and willing to indulge one more spur-of-the-moment tryst, if not a fuller restoration of their relationship. She invited him up.

As they removed their last articles of clothing, she remarked playfully, "This really is your last charity fuck, Evan."

"Alex, as long as I can keep coming back for one last charity fuck like this, I may eventually come to terms with the idea that we're breaking up."

She laughed and pulled him towards her.

They impatiently attacked each other with sexual desire, and made their way towards her bed.

But when Evan called her the next day, she reminded him in a more serious tone that it really was over between them.

Three weeks later (but this time at around 1:30 a.m.), Evan decided to resort to the same desperate measures, even though Alexandra wasn't the kind of woman who stayed single for more than a few weeks.

From the back seat of the cab, he called Alexandra on his cell phone. As her phone rang, Evan rehearsed in his head a slew of opening lines and excuses for why he was now calling her, at 1:30 a.m., on a Thursday night.

After eight rings, she finally answered.

"Hello?" She had been sleeping.

"Hey Alex."

"Who is this?"

"It's Evan."

"Evan?"

"Yeah, it's Evan. Remember me?"

"What's going on?"

"I…uh…What's up with you?"

"You called me."

"I know…I thought maybe…"

"Maybe what?"

"Maybe we could, uh. You know, maybe, uh…"

"Evan, are you stoned?"

"No, I…Uh…"

"Have you lost some brain cells?"

"No, I…I was just riding in the back of this cab, thinking about how great that last charity fuck was, and I thought I'd call you to see if you're feeling charitable."

"You're waking me up in the middle of the night for a charity fuck?"

"Basically."

"How about a charity abstention?"

"I've already had three weeks of those."

"Well this abstention really would be charitable, if you know what I mean…"

"What do you mean?"

"Evan, you're calling me at…1:30 a.m."

"I figured you'd be up…"

"I am up…Now that you called…And thanks to you, Tito's up now too."

"Who's Tito?"

"My Samoan boyfriend…"

"Samoan boyfriend?"

"Yeah, you know those guys from the Pacific Islands who are about six-five and three hundred pounds?"

"Is he really Samoan?"

Evan heard a stentorian voice in the background say "Gimme that phone."

"Listen fuck-face," the Samoan began. "If you ever call this number again, day or night, I'm gonna find out from Alex where you live, and if you've moved, I'm gonna have my cousin at the FBI track you down. And then I'm gonna find you, and then I'm gonna personally pound your face into a rare burger patty. And you know what I'm gonna do then? I'm gonna feed your face to your asshole. Nice and slow. You got that? Now say your last words to Alex."

Evan heard the phone being passed back to Alexandra.

"Evan…Sorry about that…He's actually really nice once you get to know him…But I think I should go now."

"Yeah…It's been nice knowing you."

"Good night, Evan."

His cab was at East Fifty-sixth Street and Third Avenue when Evan realized that he was headed in the direction of – rather than away from – the scene of his latest disaster. He leaned forward to redirect the cab driver.

"Actually, can you head back downtown again?"

"Where do you want me to go? Can't you make up your mind?" The cabbie's heavy Pakistani accent somehow magnified the exasperation in his voice, and he had clearly forgotten that he was profiting from Evan's indecisiveness.

Evan concluded, incorrectly, that he had hit the nadir of his evening and could now go back to his studio apartment in Gramercy and privately lick his wounds.

"Let's go to Twentieth and Park," he instructed.

The cab driver shook his head impatiently as he made a left at Fifty-seventh Street.

But Evan suddenly remembered two buddies who were often awake late and possibly still looking for a good time at 1:40 a.m. on a

Thursday night. On a whim, he called each friend. The first call went to voicemail. "At this hour, he's probably getting laid or dancing in some club that can't get cell phone reception," Evan figured. But the second friend he called answered his cell phone.

"Dude, let's meet up," Evan urged. "It's beautiful out, and there are babes everywhere."

"Tell me about it. Where are you?"

"My cab just hit Fifty-seventh and Park."

"Funny, I just came from that area."

"So where are you now?"

"On Forty-third and Eleventh, about ten feet from my futon and TV."

And with those words, Evan knew that getting him to come out was a lost cause. Evan had once coined the term "The Law of Subjective Progress" to describe the psychological aversion that prevents any New Yorker from retracing a path just taken. He recognized that this psychological allergy afflicted humans everywhere, but because New York was so compact and relatively easy to navigate, it always struck him as doubly irrational when – for example – someone who had just crossed from Midtown East to Midtown West would rather go to a slightly farther destination in a different direction than return to Midtown East. Evan's psychological theory posited that humans subconsciously associate their geographical location with their overall life progress, so he knew that it would be impossible to convince his friend to come back to the area he had just left. The Law of Subjective Progress was too powerful – especially after 1:40 a.m. and with a New Yorker over the age of thirty who was steps away from his futon.

So Evan wished his friend a good night, leaned back in his cab seat, and finally resigned himself to calling it a night.

But about ten minutes later, when Evan's taxi was waiting at a stop light at the intersection of Thirtieth and Park, a boisterous bevy of babes playfully waved at him. The scantily clad college students seductively beckoned him to follow.

Despite the lingering suspicion that he was on too serious a losing streak for this omen to be a good one, Evan decided to get out and follow them.

"Actually, I don't need Twentieth and Park. This is fine," he said to the cabbie, who was just as happy finally to rid himself of the most fickle passenger he had had in the last year.

Evan paid his fare, got out, and closed the cab door, at which point he heard one of the four young women exclaim, "Oh my God, he's actually coming over!" As he looked over at the group, he saw them giggling immaturely and scurrying ahead of him a little faster, as if to escape the very adventure they had provoked.

"Hey wait a sec!" Evan hurried up after them, but this only made them move away faster. Evan followed briskly in their direction, alternating between a fast walk and a run, not sure if they would be amused or frightened when he finally reached them.

At Twenty-eighth and Park, he caught up to them, and tried to catch his breath and introduce himself, but they were all giggling too hard, as they exchanged accusations.

"You called him over here!" said a tall redhead in a tight mini-skirt and a black silk top that barely managed to cover her bouncy breasts; she seemed to be the leader of the pack.

"You did!" protested a shorter brunette in a similar outfit.

"No I didn't! Liar!"

"You both did," Evan began. "But don't worry," he said between breaths, "I don't bite…I just come when I'm called."

"Can you roll over and play dead?" the redhead asked, as her sophomoric gang broke into laughs.

"Only if I've got someone to roll with," Evan replied. It was the best answer that came to mind, but he knew it wasn't great.

"You're way too old for us to roll with you!" the shorter brunette quipped.

"How old do I look?" Evan replied, suddenly more concerned about the true answer than what it would ultimately mean for this particular encounter.

"At least twenty-eight," opined the redhead.

"Why twenty-eight?"

"I don't know. You can just tell…"

"Well, I'm twenty-nine."

"That's even worse."

"Why? How old are you?"

"We're all nineteen."

"Oh." Evan could sense that he was about to start desperately grasping for straws. "Well don't you want to know what it's like to be a decade older?" he asked.

"Not really," replied the redhead.

Because Evan's question assumed that these women were profounder than they actually were – at least at the age of nineteen – it only succeeded in highlighting just how much older he was. Evan, of course, was not in any state to appreciate this paradox.

"But aren't you curious about my wise perspective on life?"

"We've got the rest of our lives to learn what it's like to have a wise old perspective," replied the redhead, on behalf of her clan. The others all laughed in agreement, as she hailed a taxi.

Evan shook his head in frustration as the college girls all loudly piled into the back of the cab and drove off.

4. The Painfully Unforgettable Brandy and Bonnie Encounter

Evan started down the eight-block walk back to his apartment, assuming reluctantly that his night was over, but occasionally looking around with the faint hope that someone – a lone female or even a few men headed for a nearby party – might somehow salvage, or at least extend, his pathetic night.

At the corner of Twenty-third Street and Park Avenue, Evan's hope was suddenly realized. A giant, shiny white SUV pulled up next to him. Its dark windows were shut but Evan could hear hip-hop beats blaring inside the vehicle. The rhythmic thumping grew louder as the SUV's backseat window slid down slowly, exposing a beautiful black woman with a seductively tough, no-nonsense expression on her face.

The window opposite the driver's seat whirred down, so that Evan could see the entire plush interior of the SUV. He looked at the delicious driver, an olive-skinned woman with an enticing smile. She winked at Evan as she lowered the music volume enough to permit conversation. He smiled at her self-consciously and then looked back at the black woman next to him, catching a glimpse of her tempting cleavage – two firm, pendulous mounds tucked under a skimpy, leopard-skin bikini bra.

"Where you goin'," she asked, her head moving slightly to the faint beats in the background.

"Home," he replied, realizing that she was definitely a prostitute. Evan had always thought himself above paying for sex, but this woman looked positively delectable and Evan desperately wanted to save the night somehow. So he decided to see if he could somehow talk her into a freebie.

"It's too early to be goin' home, sweetheart."

"Oh yeah?"

"Yeah…You wanna blowjob?"

Her segue from casual conversation to commercial negotiation caught Evan by surprise.

"Well…Is it on the house?"

She turned to the sexy driver and reported in amusement, "Bonnie, the fella wanna know if this one's on the house."

Bonnie looked at Evan for a moment, checking him out.

"Why not?" she replied, "He's cute enough."

The backseat prostitute turned back towards Evan and eyed him up and down, sizing up his physical appearance a little more. "Yo' dick best not be stanky," she warned. "Because you sexy enough for a freebie but I charge extra if you stanky. So if it's on the house and you stanky, you still gotta pay."

"No. I'm not stinky – I showered a few hours ago...So is it on the house now?"

"Yeah, you kinda tasty-lookin'...Come on."

Bonnie, who had been listening in, flashed a smile and returned the stereo to its former booming volume. She hit a button and a dark window separating her from the backseat area rolled up, creating more privacy for her partner and Evan.

With an excited and slightly nervous grin, Evan climbed awkwardly into the hip-hop-filled SUV, stepping carefully over the young woman's long legs as she shut the door behind him. The side windows rolled up and the large vehicle drove off.

"So what's your name?" he began, awkwardly.

"Since you ain't payin', you ain't namin'," she replied, tongue-in-cheek. "Only payin' customers get to pick my name."

But Evan could barely hear her because the music was so loud.

"What did you say your name was?"

"It's Brandy."

"What?"

Brandy leaned forward towards the front of the SUV and tapped on the dark window separating them from Bonnie. The tight, white miniskirt around her waist accentuated her hourglass figure. Bonnie slid the window down.

"Whassup gurl?"

"Turn down the music," Brandy said.

"What?" Bonnie asked.

Brandy leaned closer still and repeated the request into Bonnie's ear, and then whispered something else. Bonnie nodded an "OK," and lowered the volume, as the dark partition window hummed back up and Brandy moved back to where Evan was waiting.

"That's better, now isn't it, sexy eyes?" she said with a seductive smile.

"So what did you say your name was?"

"Brandy, to your cheap ass…But don't worry: I still think you sexy."

"OK Brandy…Hey listen, I'm not cheap – I mean, I don't mind buying you drinks or taking you out to a nice dinner and a Broadway show…I'm just opposed to the idea of paying a woman for sex…"

"And whatchyu think buyin' dinner and theater tickets is? That shit cost more than I charge for a blowjob."

"You're trying to tell me that when I take a woman out to dinner and the theater I'm paying for sex?"

"Look, if yo' ho won't fuck you unless you take her out to dinner and the theater, she makin' you pay for that shit." Brandy's large brown eyes lit up with interest, as if she had spent many hours considering this issue. "I don't care what you wanna call it, but that's just another form of payment...Me personally, I prefer cash."

"But I can't just pay you cash. That would be paying for sex."

"Well, what if you gave me all the money for our date upfront, so that I could pay for our dinner and theater date for you and me? 'Cept that I wouldn't spend no hundred and fifty dollas on no front row seat for me, and I wouldn't eat no food at no five-star restaurant where they charge you forty dollas for a slice a cucumber'n shit? Instead, I just watch yo' ass eatin' forty-dolla cucumbers, and then I read about the play in a newspaper, so we could still talk about it after we fuck. How 'bout that?"

"But that's not the same thing. I mean, that's not really a date then…That's back to prostitution."

"Don't gimme that bullshit, fella."

"My name's Evan, by the way."

"Evan, eh? That's a pretty sexy name you got there, Evan…In fact, I think I'm goin' call you Sexy Evan. Is that cool?"

"It's cool," Evan replied, amused.

"Aight…So lemme repeat my last point, Sexy Evan. You tryin' sell me some serious bullshit. You know damn well that if you hit on me in some bar and I went straight home with you – without no date – then you wouldn't think of that as prostitution."

"No, that would be a huge score. But I wouldn't be paying you the equivalent of a date afterwards."

"So what if you just hit on me at some bar and we made out a bit, and then I told you that I wouldn't sleep with yo' ass unless you took me out on some really expensive dates? Caviar'n shit. 'Cuz I'm old-fashioned and I need lotsa winin' and dinin' 'n shit, befo' I remove my panties fo' anyone...And that if you wine and dine me for at least four dates, at one hundred dollas per date, then you was pretty likely to get some."

"If I was really interested, I'd probably go for it."

"You mean if I was a really-frickin'-fine-lookin' woman, you'd probably go for it."

"Yeah, probably."

"Well do you think I'm really frickin' fine-lookin'?"

"I'd say you're somewhere between frickin' fine-lookin' and really frickin' fine-lookin', which means that I'd probably hold out for three $100-dates, but not four."

Brandy looked appalled at Evan's qualified endorsement of her good looks: "In that case, you betta get yo' cheap ugly ass the fuck out my car." Brandy started to move towards the driver area, about to knock on the window to tell Bonnie to pull the SUV over, when Evan grabbed her arm and tried to save the situation.

"No, no. I'm sorry. I meant you're really frickin' fine. I just...I just..."

"You just what?!"

"I just didn't want your good looks going to your head... Because...Well, because you already seem confident enough about the fact that you're really frickin' fine-lookin' so there's no need to dwell on that point."

"Nah, nah, nah. You got somethin' all wrong there, sweetheart. You can never say or understand that truth enough. So you need to repeat it again, after me: Brandy, you are the most really-frickin'-fine-lookin' woman out there and I am thankin' the lord that you still talkin' to me at this moment...Say it."

Evan had lost any hope of controlling the situation, and now felt bound to do as Brandy said.

"Brandy, you are the most really-frickin'-fine-lookin' woman out there and I am thanking the lord that you're still talking to me at this moment."

"That's what I thought...See, I was tryin' to make a point, Sexy Evan. Don't you understand that you was killin' my point with that last ugly comment you made?"

"I understand and I sincerely apologize."

Brandy started undoing one of her high-heeled sandals. "I wanna see if you really mean it."

"What do you mean?"

"If you really sorry, and you really think that I'm really frickin' fine-lookin', then you goin' suck on my big toe, just like you want me to suck on yo' big dick."

Evan tried to conceal his mixed feelings about this latest challenge, and attempted just to flow with the events of this ever more unpredictable encounter. Ostracism from Brandy's SUV, he thought, would probably still feel worse than sucking on her big toe and then possibly getting some action.

As she raised her foot to his mouth, he caught a peek of her matching, leopard-skin thong and regained some motivation for the toe-sucking operation before him. Evan carefully inserted Brandy's toe into his mouth and began bobbing up and down on her big toe, wondering whether a blowjob was worth a toe job...As his head moved up and down on Brandy's toe, he began to concentrate on its somewhat calloused texture, and then noticed that it tasted like a blend of shoe sweat, leather, nail polish, and cheap perfume.

"That's good...Now you can just keep on goin' like that while I finish up my point...Now what was I sayin'? Oh yeah: let's just say that I'm some really frickin' fine classy lady who's mo' old fashioned than yo' mamma's mamma, and who therefore needs to be wined and dined – caviar style – fo' at least fo' nights, at a hundred bucks a night, right? And only then you goin' get some ass...Now would that be prostitution if you just paid me the four hundred dollas up front, and we just went on some cheap ass McDonald's dates fo' times in a row, and then I let you get some?"

Evan was still bobbing up and down on Brandy's toe.

"OK. Tha's enough." Brandy took her foot back. "Answer my question." Evan straightened himself out, wiped his mouth a little, and reflected on the fact that he was now, without a doubt, at the lowest point of his entire history as a sexual being. He had just finished sucking on the toe of a prostitute and was following her every command because he was afraid that she might banish him from her SUV and thereby bring him to an even lower point. His last shred of dignity consisted in not paying her for any sexual favors, and he wasn't going to buckle on this principle.

"Well, I still think that would be prostitution, because I would be paying you for sex that's guaranteed after four dates...If it was a normal dating situation, there'd be no guarantee that I'd get any sex after four dates, no matter how much I spent. You know, it's the uncertainty of getting laid that makes it such an interesting challenge."

"You a stubborn one, ain't ya', Sexy Evan?"

"When it comes to certain principles, I am."

"Well, if it's the uncertainty of the booty that's so important to yo' ass, we can just agree that if you pay me four hundred dollas, I might fuck you, but I might not. No guarantees for Sexy Evan. You just goin' have to take yo' chances."

"But if I'm going to spend four hundred dollars, I'd like us to at least have some nice dinners and entertainment."

"Why you gots to impose yo' ideas of entertainment on my ass? Can't I spend the four hundred dollas the way I want to spend them?"

"Well why should I even give you the four hundred dollars in the first place?"

"So that I might let you fuck me in four dates. 'Cept that we won't actually go on four dates, unless they be like McDonalds dates."

"And what if you decide not to fuck me after date number four and I want to see you again?"

"You know, you a funny bird, Sexy Evan. Most guys pay my ass so that they can walk away. But you already gettin' attached to me...Which is understandable because I'm such a – what am I again, Sexy Evan?"

"The most really-frickin'-fine-lookin'-woman out there."

"That's right. And what are you thankin' the lord for?"

"That you're still talking to me at this moment."

"Thas' exactly right. See why you gettin' all attached to my ass? Now we can arrange for you to see me more than four times, but each date is goin' cost yo' ass, and I ain't promisin' you no booty either. 'Cuz we can't have no pimpin' goin' on here."

"And you can't see anyone else while we're dating?"

"Now you askin' fo' my premium services. If you want unlimited dates and exclusivity, that's goin' cost yo' ass a very pretty penny."

"As long as it's not prostitution, I'm cool with it..."

"So we have a deal, Sexy Evan?"

Brandy leaned forward across the seat, so that she was looking into Evan's lap.

"As long as I'm not paying for it. Think of it this way: you could give me a blowjob now for free, as a way to get our dating relationship off to a nice start."

"I like your stubborn style, Sexy Evan, but ammo' give you one last chance to pay fo' yo' blowjob anyway..."

"Oh yeah?" Evan said, in an intrigued but sexual tone produced entirely by the way Brandy eyed him up and down. "And what's your pitch going to be this time?" he continued.

"Just remember that you get what you pay for…"

"So you're trying to tell me that the blowjob will be better if I pay for it?"

Brandy nodded her head lasciviously.

"I've never met a blowjob that I didn't like…So I think I'll take my chances."

"You know, Sexy Evan. If you wasn't so sexy, I wouldn't still be talkin' to yo' cheap ass."

Brandy seductively looked up and down from Evan's groin to his face.

"But all this talk with Sexy Evan has made me kinda hungry."

Brandy began rubbing her hand against Evan's inner thigh.

"You still got yo' pants on, Sexy Evan!" she said, letting her hand drift upward to Evan's crotch.

Evan's excitement intensified – particularly when Brandy slid the bikini leopard cloth downward off one of her breasts, and let her soft brown nipple brush up against his left cheek and down across his lips.

"My titty ain't been sucked by a sexy man in a long time, Evan. If you want me to give you a blowjob, you goin' have to suck ma titty a little."

Evan was all too happy to oblige her. He was completely open to this kind of quid pro quo transaction. The SUV gradually slowed down.

"Aight Sexy Evan. Take off yo' pants. 'Cuz ammo' give you a blowjob like you ain' never had and you ain' never goin' forget."

The SUV pulled over and parked in a darker section of the street.

Evan began nervously fumbling with his trousers, all too excited by Brandy's moves and words.

The minute his boxer briefs were down far enough, his Johnson (as he liked to call it) was involuntarily catapulted upwards, with almost embarrassing vigor and bounce, and – before Evan could even blush – Brandy was on him, devouring him with a zeal that he had never before witnessed. As her head worked its way up and down on his Johnson, her uninhibited technique and concentration – even conviction – was so perfect and practiced that Evan thought he was experiencing the very pinnacle of physical art. Brandy's strong yet graceful head thrusts produced a moist and warm blend of rhythm and blues that brought Evan ever closer to the gates of paradise.

And then all of the sudden – in mid-thrust, halfway up Evan's Johnson, when he was within seconds of what he thought would be the greatest orgasm he had ever had – the pleasure abruptly turned into an excruciating pain.

"Aaaaarrghhhh!!!!" he yelled, as the soft fellatio turned into razor sharp teeth digging into his Johnson with a force that he had never before imagined could be applied to his member. It was nothing short of sheer torture.

The pain was so focused and so intense that Evan didn't even notice Bonnie get out of the car right on cue and approach the back seat area (the hold-up strategy involved using the victim's scream as the signal for the driver to go over to the backseat area and state the demands of the robbery).

"Stop! What – what the fuck are you doing?!" Evan stammered.

Bonnie opened the passenger seat and brandished a small gun, pointed it at Evan's torso and, with her partner in crime holding all of Evan's manhood snugly between her incisors – broke the full extent of the bad news to Evan: "Now you goin' be overcharged for the blowjob. Gimme your wallet."

"What?" Evan was shocked at the realization that he was being held up at blow point. Evan looked over at the gun and then back down at Brandy's mouth, firmly clenched around his Johnson and poised to nip it off in a second. He looked back at Bonnie. The gun in her hand, with the black high heels, tight black miniskirt, and stylish black sports bra together made her look like a James Bond woman.

"You heard what I said: gimme your wallet or she goin' bite yo' lil' white dick off. Just like if it was a hot dog…She done it before. You know, she make Lorena Bobbit look like an amateur."

The mere thought of having his Johnson bitten off was so horrific, and felt so imminently possible that Evan began desperately blundering through his pockets for his wallet. Brandy loosened her grip a bit as she saw that Evan was trying to cooperate.

Bonnie looked like she was just beginning to have fun.

"What's yo' name, mister?"

"Evan."

"Evan, we ain't even talked about the extra charge for dick stankiness…Brandy, was Evan lyin' about not bein' stanky?"

34

Brandy didn't bother trying to answer orally but started to nod her head to answer Bonnie's question. Evan yelped in response to the additional pain that her head movement created.

"Don't!" was all Evan could cry out in reaction to Brandy's nod.

"You don't expect her to talk with her mouth full now do you, Evan?" Bonnie couldn't conceal her amusement anymore and broke into a smile. "Where yo' manners, Evan? Now that's very bad news that you was lyin' about yo' dick not bein' stanky. And I know that you want to pay the surcharge for stankiness, because Brandy has a really big appetite for white frankfurters, and I know that she wouldn't mind keepin' yours as a souvenir…You know she got a whole collection at home. In this little jar of pickles…So repeat after me, Evan: I really wanna pay the surcharge for dick stankiness."

"I really wanna pay the surcharge for dick stankiness," Evan blurted out, in helpless terror.

As he awkwardly tried to get a good enough grasp on his wallet to pull it out, he caught a glimpse of Brandy looking up at him, mid-Johnson, with the intense but cool eyes of a Doberman ready to deliver the salami-slicing bite at the slightest sign of resistance.

"It's on account of dick stankiness that Brandy and me have to alternate responsibilities. 'Cuz it wouldn't be right if one of us always got stuck with the stankiness…And tonight she's on dick detail and I'm on pistol patrol, which means you could be outta luck, Evan…I remember this one time, Brandy bit it off and held it as collateral until the customer paid up…He finally agreed to pay up, but then had to get it stitched back on…So I'm really pleased to see that you'd rather skip the whole dismemberment portion of this story." Bonnie moved a little closer. "But I don't understand something."

"Wh…What?!" Evan was entirely freaked out at this point. Bonnie, on the other hand, was enjoying complete control of the situation and no longer even felt the need to point her gun, which casually dangled from her index finger.

"How come you still ain't given me yo' wallet if you wanna hang on to your lil' white dick tonight?"

"I…I'm…I'm lookin' for it…"

"Aight. Take ya' time." Bonnie took a step back and patiently watched Evan struggle to find his wallet. She calmly began to share some additional musings with Evan and Brandy: "You know, I never did understand why they call it a blowjob. Do you, Brandy?"

Brandy started to shake her head, in agreement with Bonnie's ponderings about the etymology of the term.

"No, no! Don't move your head," Evan pleaded, "I'm lookin' for it," he said, frantically trying to get into his pants pocket, which was all the more difficult to access because the slightest movement by him could hurt more than a head nod from Brandy. "I just can't seem to..." he struggled desperately to push his hand into his pocket but to no avail. "I just can't seem to get it out of...my...my."

"I mean, there's really no blowin' involved in a blowjob," Bonnie continued, oblivious to Evan's distress. "Wouldn't you agree with that statement, Evan?"

Evan's fidgety hands, uncontrollably nervous about the possibility of a sudden penectomy, couldn't seem to make their way through his trouser pockets, which – because of how he was sitting – were folded in a rather constricted way that blocked access to anything that was lodged deep inside them. In desperation, Evan asked for a little bit of maneuvering room: "I...I can't get to it without moving a little."

"So move a little, Evan. Ain't nothin' about a blowjob that prevents you from movin' a little."

"But...But I can't move with her on me like this."

"You know, I always thought that it should really be called a 'bite job' 'cuz the lady – I don't care how good she is – the lady basically has to bite you, but without using her teeth...Now the really great blowjobs make you think the lady ain't got no teeth. I've given a few of those myself. But those are the ones you gotta pay for...The free ones carry a little extra risk, as I think you've come to learn. But even with the best blowjobs there really ain't no blowin' involved. I mean, I guess as a kind of a thank you to the customer, you could throw in some blowin' at the end...Specially if the customer's dick be really raw and sore and shit. You know, from too much use...Then blowin' on his dick might actually feel like a nice little courtesy. But like I said, that's special treatment that don't normally come with your standard blowjob."

Evan began to panic at the thought that he couldn't get to his wallet, and that there was no telling when the guillotine might fall on his Johnson. His future as a sexual being was at the mercy of an apparent psychopath who could order a jaw-clenching death for him at any moment. Evan began to hyperventilate.

"I mean, the last customer who got the Brandy Blowjob Special – you know the one that's free, like the one you enjoyin' right now – he insisted that we change the name of the service to – you know –

somethin' more precise. Like the 'Brandy Bite Job Special.' But then Brandy and me, we was havin' a marketing meeting last Tuesday, and we discussed the possibility of changin' the name and all. And we just decided that the 'Brandy Blowjob Special' still has a much more appealing sound to it. You know, you wanna entice the customer. That's what marketing's all about, right Evan?"

Mercifully, Evan finally managed to pull the wallet out of his pocket. With one last desperate yank, it fell out and rolled down the seat and onto the ground in front of where Bonnie was standing. She picked it up and began going through its contents.

Brandy unlocked her dental mousetrap and released Evan's traumatized trouser snake.

He fell back against the seat. The pain, shock, and hyperventilation were too much.

Evan had fainted.

When he came to, he was in an ambulance with gauze bandages around his Johnson.

5. Lucky Chucky and Heeb

Unlike Evan, Carlos Fuentes lived a thoroughly charmed life. Carlos's family beat the odds twice by not being caught during their illegal border crossing from Mexico to California, and then winning the naturalization lottery a few years later. In school, if the gifted student had made a strategic choice not to study certain material while cramming for an exam, it would conveniently not appear on the test. At cards, he consistently had the best poker face, and if it was raining, he always had an umbrella. In a high school car accident that left the vehicle totaled, a tree mangled, a fire hydrant overturned, and passengers injured and drenched in water, Carlos somehow emerged dry and unscathed.

But it wasn't until the fall of 1994, at the start of his senior year at Harvard College, that Carlos was dubbed "Lucky Chucky" by his new roommate, Sammy Laffowitz. The nickname was inspired when Sammy, a short, balding, heavy-set, bookish type from the suburbs of Philadelphia, became enviously dumbstruck at the female fortunes that constantly graced Carlos. Ironically enough, Carlos remained single and regularly complained of having no luck with women. But most men with his attributes would be unattached for a small fraction of the time that Carlos would stay single. Standing six-one, Carlos had the slick, Latin look of a telenovela star. He dressed with impeccable style, maintained a great physique, and easily charmed with his silver tongue. He was considered a mega-catch even before "dropping the H bomb" on women.

"Dropping the H bomb," as he and his friends referred to the tactic, involved any ostensibly nonchalant, circuitous attempt to mention the school they were attending in the hope of impressing a girl. The trick was to say something that induced the female to ask, "What school do you go to?" (for example: "In my college, we don't have majors, we have concentrations"). Then, when she would ask, "Where do you go to school?" the artifice involved avoiding the actual name of the school, so as to appear modest (for example: "I go to school in the Boston area").

Sammy, on the other hand, had absolutely no luck with women, no matter how many times he dropped the H-bomb. While his baby face had pleasantly benign features and a cutely compact nose, there were several liabilities that made it difficult for him to get anywhere (at least by his own estimation): the hair on the top of his head had thinned so much that his scalp seemed far more prominent than the thin brown layer of hair combed over it; his pudgy frame rose only five feet and seven inches; his breath sometimes took only an hour to beat the most potent mouthwash; and he absolutely loved to discuss quantum mechanics, epistemology, and topological algebra – in no small part because it was his acumen at math that enabled him finally to lose his virginity to a homely and promiscuous sophomore who got into Harvard because of her father's connections and who desperately needed Sammy to take her final exam for her. Despite numerous indications to the contrary, Sammy continued to operate under the illusion that what got him laid once could get him laid again, and that if he just displayed his knowledge of higher mathematics to enough women, one of them might declare herself willing to barter some sex for his math skills.

Sammy and Carlos were so different in looks, style, and personality that they would have never become such close friends were it not for the random housing lottery that made them roommates after Carlos returned from his junior year abroad in Brazil. Living together in close quarters for their last year of college forced each to embrace the crazy quirks and neuroses of the other, usually after some extensive badinage. And Carlos was unquestionably the perfect roommate for Sammy, because – since the age of sixteen – Carlos had easily attracted pretty females, and therefore carried absolutely no insecurities about his desirability as a man. Hence, he wasn't the least bit concerned that Sammy's ineptitude with women and his dramatically less attractive looks might harm his ability to interest women when the two were together.

So while most men with Carlos's looks would snobbishly shun someone like Sammy, Carlos decided to embrace the oddball, and make him a regular partner in his outings. Carlos never fully realized that such social altruism actually made him even more desirable in two respects: 1) his good looks were even more pronounced in the company of the far less handsome Sammy, and 2) his tolerant and good-natured character shone through, as he was clearly above the superficial snap judgments that led most "cool" people to summarily dismiss anyone like Sammy.

Sammy didn't really have any reliable "good friends" besides Carlos and Titus. Titus was an African-American man in his late sixties who checked into a Boston clinic for the blind after losing his sight to glaucoma during Sammy's freshman year. The two of them met on Sammy's first day as a volunteer at the clinic.

"Why you spendin' your fine days as a young college student with a blind old fart like me?" Titus asked, in his characteristically blunt and playful manner.

"Well, after twelve years of Hebrew school, I really remember only one thing: thou shalt not place stumbling blocks before the blind."

"Is that right? Is that all they taught you in twelve years?"

"It's the only thing that really stuck with me. I don't know why. There's just something so cruel about the idea of people placing stumbling blocks in front of the blind that – ever since I heard that – I've always wanted to do something to help them."

"Well, that's mighty kind of you, Sammy."

"I guess so…I can't have my parents thinking that twelve years of Hebrew school was a complete waste."

"You mean you didn't learn any Hebrew after twelve years of Hebrew school?"

"I know how to say 'I don't eat pork.'"

"Now that's the most ridiculous thing I ever heard!"

"Why is that?"

"Because the only people who are ever gonna understand you when you say that to them in Hebrew are people who would never try to serve you pork anyway."

"True. But I was never very good at foreign languages."

"I thought you said you go to Harvard."

"You know, that's the problem with telling people you go to Harvard. If they're dialing some phone number in Tajikistan and they forget the country code, they're shocked if you can't spit it out for them."

"I'm not talkin' about country codes for Tajikistan. I'm talkin' 'bout the language your parents paid good money for you to study for twelve years."

"Well I got into Harvard on math and science. Not foreign languages. I can barely speak English, much less a language with a different alphabet that's read in the opposite direction."

"But you're Jewish!"

"Yeah, but I'm a bagel Jew."

"What's that?"

"You know: for me it's more about the food, the culture."

"Well, you oughta know how to say a few things in your own language. Looks like I'll have to teach you some things."

"You speak Hebrew?"

"I worked on a kibbutz for a summer when I was in college, so I learned a few phrases that were useful with the honeys over there. And boy, lemme tell you. They definitely got some honeys over there."

"Maybe that's why it's called the land of milk and honey," Sammy joked.

And ever since that day, Sammy made weekly visits to see Titus, to help him with his errands or any paperwork he had to take care of, or just to describe the day for him with as many adjectives as he could conjure to satisfy Titus's visual curiosity. After a few years of Titus's persistent tutoring, Sammy even learned how to get through a very basic conversation, and conclude it by saying "You're a beautiful woman. Can I kiss you?" in Hebrew.

Back at school, Sammy always had a few friends during any given semester. But once the class that brought them together ended, so did any need for Sammy's perfect notes and understanding of abstruse issues, and these "friends" would soon disappear. Indeed, Titus was Sammy's only friend from freshman year who would last more than a semester. And Carlos was the first roommate in Sammy's college days to nurture a real friendship beyond mere cohabitation. Naturally, Sammy didn't know what he had done to deserve a roommate like Carlos, but he felt eternally grateful for the godsend and tried to reciprocate with math and science tutoring services whenever Carlos needed the help.

Carlos emboldened Sammy and made him feel like he was cool. During one of their first nights out together at a college dive called the Bow and Arrow, Sammy was unable to gather the gumption to approach a cute college student at the other end of the bar.

"She'll never talk to me, Carlos. I'm a year away from baldness."

"You're not a year away from baldness."

"I'm a year away, and it's killing me."

"Are you seriously worried about it?" Carlos asked.

"I'm obsessed."

"Why don't you try one of those hair loss treatments?"

"I have. Nothing works on me. Minoxidil is the most effective treatment and it works on only forty percent of men."

"Forty percent?"

"Yeah. Do you know how many doctors, scientists, and multimillionaires are bald?"

"So?"

"So do you really think they'd be bald if there were a scientifically established cure out there for everyone?"

"Well what about the stuff you haven't tried?"

"The other stuff out there is even less effective and could cause reduced sex drive or even impotence."

"Are you serious?"

"Yeah. Isn't that absurd? The same product that I'm taking to help me get laid ends up making me impotent!"

"That is absurd. But you'll never get laid if you stand here all night and complain about your bald spot. You have to go up to her and charm her."

"But it's an objective fact that she'll never go for me. Not in a thousand years."

"How can you be so sure?"

"It says it all over her face."

"Why is that?"

"Because she's really cute."

"So?"

"So she's thinking: I look good and therefore I should prefer good-looking men. Bald men are inherently less good-looking than men with hair. Therefore, I should prefer men who aren't bald. QED."

"I'm sure that's exactly what she's thinking. Especially the QED part."

"I just analyzed her thinking into its component parts for you, but it's all there."

"You know what you need?"

"What?"

"You need to think about what a badass bald man would do in this situation."

"There are no badass bald men. By definition."

"What about Dwight D. Eisenhower?" Carlos suggested.

"President Eisenhower?"

"Doesn't he qualify as a badass?" Carlos insisted.

"Look, he may have been president, but he doesn't exactly come to people's minds when you ask them to think of a badass."

"All right. How about Kojak?" Carlos asked.

"That police detective show with Telly Savalas?" Sammy asked.

"Yeah, Kojak. He was a badass. Always cool under pressure."

"All right," Sammy replied. "Let's just say, for the sake of argument, that Kojak was a bald badass. So what?"

"So you have to imagine how Kojak would deal with this situation we have in front of us. He wouldn't be worried about whether this girl digs bald guys. He would just walk right up to her, knowing that he's a badass and just take care of business. You see, it's all in the delivery."

"The delivery?"

"Yeah, the execution. I learned that in my sophomore acting class. And from just watching people in action…How you say something is often more important than what you say. If you have the world's slickest line and you deliver it pathetically, it's doomed to fail. And if you have a really cheesy, unoriginal line that you deliver in the slickest, most confident way, it has a pretty good chance of succeeding."

"And Kojak never delivers a line poorly," Sammy concluded.

"Exactly. Because he's Kojak. Now go over to that girl, and show her where Kojak learned his stuff."

All pumped and ready to go, Sammy walked towards her, but by the time he was close enough to say anything, two football players had already begun talking to her. Sammy stopped in his tracks and thought to himself, "Why does that never happen to Kojak?"

While that was Sammy's first and last attempt to approach a female on his own that night, several important concepts were born: "Kojaking" a situation; being a "Kojak"; and possessing "Kojak." These terms would be regularly invoked by Carlos whenever Sammy needed some psychological fortification.

Despite all of Carlos's best intentions and efforts to prop Sammy up, there was no helping the fact that Carlos also made Sammy's physical handicaps (shortness, baldness, plumpness and plainness) stand out more by the stark contrast that was created when the two were together. And, as if Sammy's odds of attracting a woman weren't already bad enough, Sammy studiously avoided Jewish women, even though they were consistently the only ones who would even consider talking to him.

Early in their friendship, Carlos quizzed Sammy about this paradox.

"But if you're proud to be a Hebrew, and you're determined to marry a Hebrew woman some day, why won't you date any?"

"Because then I'll have to actually take her seriously. If my parents find out, they'll be asking me about her all the time, hoping that

I'm planning to marry her some day. I'll have to have a real relationship. And if I can't sow my wild oats now, in college – which is supposed to be the best time of your life – then when can I do it? When I'm married with two kids and have even less hair?"

"You got a point there, I guess. I mean, if I completely distort the rules of logic."

"I don't know what it is. Call me crazy."

"No. I think I'll call you Heeb."

"Heeb?"

"Look, if you're gonna call me Chucky, which is a gross Americanization of my name – "

"Lucky Chucky sounds much better than Lucky Carlos."

"But Chucky sounds nothing like Carlos."

"It's an approximate derivation. Charles is the American version of Carlos. And Chucky is a familiar version of Charles. Therefore Chucky is a familiar American version of Carlos."

"Well, you're Heeb. You're a dweeby Heeby who explains nicknames with syllogisms."

"How is Heeb anything like Sammy Laffowitz?"

"Because it's completely laughable that a Hebrew who wants to marry another Hebrew can't date any Hebrews, because he'll sleep around with only non-Hebrews."

"That's not funny. I haven't slept around with anyone in two years."

"Well maybe if you stopped discriminating against your own kind you'd have better luck."

"Can't do that, Lucky Chucky."

"Whatever you say, Heeb."

Fortunately for Heeb, Lucky Chucky was impossibly selective, and the women he rejected left Heeb with a far greater number of opportunities to strike out than he would otherwise enjoy. In fact, if Heeb wanted to go out and look for women, he would just follow Lucky Chucky around – even if Carlos was just headed for the library or the grocery store, rather than some bar in Boston. Women just seemed to gravitate towards the Latin stud, sometimes with far-fetched pretexts ("Didn't I see you in some Spanish movie?") and sometimes with more brazen approaches ("Where are you going, and do you mind if I tag along?"). But no matter how perfect the girl looked to the rest of the world, Carlos always had some very particular reason for graciously rejecting her, and his reputation for extraordinary selectivity only made him that much more desirable to the women who knew of him. These women saw him as possessing a certain mythical, celebrity-like status and were intrigued by the challenge of trying to seduce a man whom no woman – no matter how stunning and brilliant – had succeeded in snaring. There were even occasional speculations that Carlos was gay, but those who knew him could see that he was clearly interested in women and unequivocally indifferent to men – including the many handsome homosexuals who regularly approached him.

A peculiar constellation of Puritanical beliefs, severe standards, paranoia about germs, and a hesitation about developing intense emotional intimacy prevented Carlos from indulging in the only gender that caught his attention. For Carlos even to consider straying from his strictly celibate norms on behalf of a particular woman, she first had to meet the Carlos requirements that Heeb and others could at least understand if not endorse. The woman had to be:

1. strikingly beautiful;
2. "intellectually dangerous" (as Carlos liked to put it);
3. fluent in Spanish, so that he could feel comfortable reverting to his native tongue with her;
4. an ex-Catholic so that she would naturally understand his neuroses and cultural traditions; and
5. a staunch environmentalist who was a non-smoking vegetarian with a Buddhist outlook, so that their worldviews and healthy lifestyles would be compatible.

Carlos was an eco-Nazi who excoriated anyone he caught throwing away recyclable goods, thanks to a crush he had had on his English teacher, back when he was a fifteen-year-old fawning after the brunette by the blackboard whose wardrobe always managed to show some leg. The busty Buddhist pedagogue was eight years his senior, but she shared her ideology with the pimply and precocious Carlos as if he were her peer. In time, Carlos became increasingly health-obsessed, eating only organic foods, exercising regularly, and avoiding all unnecessary environmental hazards (from excessive sun exposure, to X-rays and microwave ovens, to cell phones, when they became more popular during his late twenties). By the time Lucky Chucky got to college, his body was a temple to be zealously guarded from all elements or forces that might degrade its quality or shorten its life, and that included women with unhealthy lifestyles, germs, or worldviews.

But it wasn't enough for Carlos to find a gorgeous, intellectually brilliant, fluently Spanish-speaking, ex-Catholic-turned Buddhist, who is a non-smoking, strict vegetarian and a staunch environmentalist. The woman had to meet an additional set of bizarre requirements (or "crazy Carlos criteria," as Heeb called them) that disqualified even the rare women on the planet who made it past the first set of "coherent Carlos criteria":

1. She had to be able to name at least five great Latin American writers, at least two of whom had to be Mexican.
2. She had to possess a European passport, so that he could get European citizenship in the event that they got married.
3. While not an absolute requirement, if her name began with the letter "C," it was a superstitious "bonus" for Carlos. His only two prior loves had names starting with that letter and – in true schoolyard love fashion – Carlos wanted to be able to write "C+C" everywhere, once he did meet his dream woman.

It was no wonder that, at the age of twenty-two, despite the hundreds of otherwise attractive and high-quality women who had made passes at him over the previous six years, Lucky Chucky was still a virgin who didn't feel nearly as lucky as Heeb made him out to be.

One time, just before spring break, Heeb and Lucky Chucky crashed a Harvard alumni party in Boston, where Carlos was accosted by a woman who satisfied 4.75 of the five "coherent Carlos criteria" (she was a smoker, and so failed a quarter of the fifth criterion). She even met one of the three crazy Carlos criteria (she had a European passport). Carlos was devastated at having met someone who came so close but would not get his cigar. And Heeb was appalled at Chucky's intransigent commitment to the irrational.

As they rode the subway ("the T" as Bostonians call it) back to their dorm, Heeb began to mourn the loss of what was undoubtedly the last great hope for Chucky: "But how could you?" he began, in offended astonishment. "How could you? I mean, she was…She was perfect…Absolutely perfect, Lucky Chucky — "

"Would you stop calling me Lucky Chucky? Call me late bloomer; or lame bloomer. Call me destined to virginity. Call me choosy Chucky. But don't call me Lucky Chucky…I don't feel very lucky right now."

"I can't believe the crap you're trying to feed both of us. I mean, you're a freak of nature – a statistical anomaly. No matter what you do or say, you've got hot women throwing themselves at you every other minute. The fact that you're too insanely picky to take any of them suggests that your name ought to be 'Dummy Chucky' but there's no way that you're not going down in history as the luckiest man alive."

"I told you that I don't look at women like you do. I can't just bone someone who's not good enough to marry."

"How about just boning someone who's good enough to divorce?"

"Huh?"

"This is where you've still got major Catholic issues, Chucky."

"It's not about that. I know plenty of Catholics who enjoy premarital sex…Don't you realize that each time you sleep with someone, you're potentially making your body more impure? More exposed to bacteria, diseases, viruses? The common cold? The dust and dirt off the street? I mean, don't get me wrong, I do have my fantasies."

"Yeah, they all take place in an incubator."

"I just don't think it's worth it. The thought of getting down and dirty with all of those fluids – that sweat and odor…"

"Wait a second. How did you spend your junior year in Brazil, studying how to protect the Amazon if you're so worried about dirt?"

"That's different. That's natural dirt."

"So is sex."

"No. Sex is different. Sex is a sinfully dirty act…And it's probably very crude and imperfect in reality."

"What do you mean?"

The T stopped and some passengers filed out while some new people boarded. Sammy and Carlos made some room for them.

"I just doubt that the reality of sex can compete with my fantasy of it," Carlos continued.

"At the rate you're going, it never will."

"I'm just not ready to give myself up, Sammy. I mean, there's something perfect about virginity, and I haven't found someone who deserves to take that perfection away from me…"

"You're loco, Carlos. Insane. Totally crazy…Most guys think they're imperfect for still being virgins past the age of seventeen."

"Well, they may have a point…But the way I see it, you get only one body in this life, and I'm not going to risk exposing it to impurities for just anyone. She has to be worth it, and I'm just not ready to settle."

"You mean you're just not ready to come up with a set of requirements that anyone can actually satisfy?"

"I didn't say that. Now you're putting words in my mouth."

"Are you suggesting that your standards aren't too high?"

"I'm suggesting that you think they're too high only because your standards are so low. It's all relative, you know."

"I've got very high standards."

"Yeah, she's gotta chew her cud and lactate."

"You've gotta stop with that cow joke. I told you I was too drunk to notice her mass."

"Even when she was riding the Hebrew National?"

"I was on top."

Lucky Chucky was still playfully rejoicing for Heeb who, a week earlier, finally broke his two-year celibacy spell after successfully Kojaking a bovine chemistry student at an MIT frat party.

"Look, my point is that your standards don't deserve to be called standards because any non-Jew with the requisite anatomy qualifies," Carlos pointed out.

"If I'm excluding the only ethnic group that will talk to me, that makes me a very picky guy. I don't see how you can argue with that."

"I guess. But there are still about three billion women who meet your standards."

"Yeah: look how much good it's doing me!" Heeb rejoined.

"At least you're not a twenty-two-year-old virgin."

"True, but if I ever become famous, there are going to be a lot of nasty-lookin' women telling television talk show hosts that they slept with me."

"That'll be a problem only if you become famous."

Heeb was about to protest such wry skepticism when he noticed that a foxy female student wearing a Wellesley sweatshirt had boarded their train car. With tight white spandex and a white headband, the bouncy, energetic redhead looked as if she was returning from a modern dance class. Her head moved to the beats blaring in her headset as she surveyed the train car for the best place to stand. There were plenty of spots but, once her eyes crossed Carlos, she chose the space across from him that offered the best, apparently nonchalant view of the dark, virgin Adonis in the blue navy coat, wearing dark gloves. (To avoid exposure to germs, Carlos always wore gloves while riding public transportation).

Carlos didn't notice any of these details and was just waiting for Heeb to say whatever it was that he was going to say in defense of his prospects for fame.

"It's just not fair!" Heeb protested abruptly, after seeing enough of the redhead looking over at Carlos.

"What's not fair?" Carlos finally looked where Heeb was looking and understood. He smiled in resignation and let Heeb finish his rant.

"I mean, why can't I just accept that I'm always going to fly in economy? Why do I insist on trying to upgrade into first class when I don't have enough miles?"

"That's not Kojaking it, Heeb. Let me see you Kojak this one."

After several playful glances, and two train stops, the redhead allowed the large crowd that had just alighted the train to serve as her pretext for moving up close to the Latin heartthrob, and the mostly invisible, heavy-set nerd ogling her.

With a slight blush, and a little short of breath, she removed her headset and attempted her opening line with Carlos: "This train's gotten so crowded." Carlos just smiled politely and looked at Heeb. That Carlos could be so indifferent to her suddenly made the cute student seem approachably vulnerable. Heeb felt the Kojak coming on strong, and let it loose without any hesitation.

"Look, I know you're hot. And I know that you know that you're hot. But you don't have a chance with this guy," Heeb said, gesturing towards Carlos.

"What are you talking about?" The redhead looked slightly embarrassed — even insulted — that the man talking to her was Heeb rather than the hunk she had addressed. She looked at Carlos, hoping that he would rescue her from the impudent intrusion by this geek, but — to her disappointed surprise — Carlos was focused intently on Heeb, as if Heeb were the only thing worth observing at that moment. Lucky Chucky was genuinely interested in the evolution of Heeb's Kojak.

"I'm sorry. That probably wasn't such a nice way to introduce myself. My name is Sammy Laffowitz and this is my friend Carlos."

"Hi," she said, moving to offer Carlos a handshake.

Carlos acknowledged the introduction with a half nod and a slight smile, and then looked back at Heeb. Trying to conceal the fact that her offered hand was just subtly rebuffed, the redhead awkwardly tried to move her hand to a pole, as if she had intended all along to brace herself from the train's occasionally jerky movements.

"So what I was trying to say is that we're coming back from an alumni party where I just watched Carlos reject the woman who was Miss Spain three years ago and is now getting a PhD in astrophysics. I mean, I don't know if I'll ever meet someone like that again in person

49

unless NASA decides to send a *Playboy* bunny into space and I somehow get hired as a consultant…This girl – she was – she was beyond perfect. And she was practically stalking us – I mean Carlos – until she had him cornered…And Carlos somehow – somehow found it in his heart to turn her down."

"What are you trying to say?" The redhead looked around awkwardly to see if there was an easy way to slip out of the situation, but – to her dismay – the train had become too crowded for a fast and discreet getaway.

"I guess what I'm trying to say – if you really want me to get the point – I'm saying that you should probably talk to me, because your odds will be significantly better with me."

"But I'm not really interested in you." She looked over at Carlos, but he was still completely focused on Heeb.

"I know you're not really interested in me because – well – you're not interested in me at all…I understand that…In fact, I would be completely shocked if that weren't the case. But perhaps we can just discuss an issue that's been on my mind all night. You know – just as friends…"

"What do you mean?"

"Well, I hate to the use the F word with a pretty woman I just met, but I'm feeling like we've achieved some comfort level with each other here."

"It takes a lot longer to become friends in my book…What do you want to talk about?"

"Nothing that will change your opinion of me. But something that I just need to get off of my chest – and which could change the universe for the better."

"What do you mean?"

"In a totally mechanical universe determined by the laws of physics, everything affects everything, including even my taking a moment to vent my frustration and make an anonymous confession – I mean, you would never give me your number and you'd never call me if I give you mine, right?"

"Right."

"So this is definitely an anonymous confession because I'll never see you again. But I'm going to share it with you because it might just affect your behavioral patterns in some small way, which could have significant results for how the planet evolves and thereby lead to an improvement in the universe over the long run, if you take chaos theory to its logical extension, that is."

Carlos spoke for the first time in the redhead's presence: "Sometimes Sammy gets really deep. You're getting a rare treat here, so listen closely."

"Really?" she replied, trying to increase her interest in whatever it was that Heeb was about to say.

Feeling fully empowered, Heeb declared, "I just want to point out how this is not the best of all possible worlds."

"What do you mean?" she asked.

"Do you think it's fair that I was born wanting women like you with no chance of ever having them? Do you think that's really fair? Just be honest with me for a moment."

"I guess not."

"Clearly this is not the best of all possible worlds. I mean, why couldn't I have been born to find women like you unattractive? And that way I wouldn't care if you find me unattractive, or if you ignore me, or blow me off. Why couldn't I have been born to find women like you ugly? Or why couldn't you have been born to find guys like me hot? Life would have been so much better. So much easier. So, you see, there's definitely something wrong — something cosmologically unfair — with our universe."

"Hmmm…That's deep. In an adolescent sort of way. And how is this anonymous confession of yours going to improve the universe?" she replied.

"Because the next time you see someone like me who belongs in economy but is trying to upgrade into first class, you might actually look beyond his assigned seat and remember that you have the power to make the world seem like a dramatically more fair and happy place to this guy."

The train came to a halt. Carlos and Heeb exited, with a departing smile at the redhead. She looked back at them, perplexed. Carlos was proud of Heeb's Kojak. Even if its results weren't yet consistently there, its spirit had tremendous promise.

Heeb's senior year in college was his best year ever in terms of fun, self-worth, and success with women (although, by his own admission, fun and self-worth were really just a function of success with women). He even managed to date a pretty girl for about three weeks. Heeb thought she was arguably seated somewhere between economy and business class, and was therefore somewhat baffled that she had nevertheless taken some interest in him. His only explanation was the metaphysical speech he had given to the redhead on the T (and, of course, the slow but steady improvement in his Kojak).

"Chucky, the world is infinitely interconnected," he theorized, as they lounged around in their Adams House dorm room, the night after his second date with Debra. "And everything you say or do affects the entire universe. That's the only way I can explain why Debra agreed to go on a third date with me."

Then, four days into their courtship, he discovered what he thought was the only real explanation for why she had taken an interest in him (Kojak and chaos theory notwithstanding): she was half-Jewish. At first he struggled with this bad news, but – considering that this was the best-looking female Heeb had ever managed to interest – he decided that half-Jewish was acceptable.

"I knew you'd eventually compromise on that stupid rule of yours," Carlos pointed out, as if he was finally vindicated.

"Look, she's not technically Jewish according to Orthodox law, which follows matrilineal descent."

"Are you Orthodox, Heeb?"

"No. But still. She's not really Jewish in my family's book."

"So what?"

"So that means that if I married her it would cause heart attacks in both of my parents and all three of my living grandparents. Now I'm not so crazy about my paternal grandfather, but I am worried about the others."

"So you wouldn't have to take her seriously because there was no chance that you could marry her?"

"Right."

"And this is because half-Jewish doesn't really count in your family?"

"Yeah. She probably celebrates Chanukah for only four out of the eight days."

"You can't be serious."

"Or even worse: she fasts for only half of Yom Kippur."

"Do you always fast for all of it?"

"Not always. But I will when I have kids."

"You're completely crazy, Heeb."

"Why?"

"How do you expect to have kids when you can't even date a woman seriously?"

"I'm still sowing my oats, Chucky. Especially now that you've helped me with my Kojak."

"Great. So now you're just going to be a bachelor, exploring the reaches of Kojakdom for the foreseeable future?"

"Until I'm twenty-eight. Then I'll give myself two years to find a wife."

"Why twenty-eight?"

"That gives me about six years to fool around and two years to find a wife."

"You've really got your priorities straight, Heeb. You're willing to spend six years fooling around on women you'll never see again, and only two years looking for the woman you're going to spend the rest of your life with."

"Look, how much time you give yourself is ultimately arbitrary. I mean, some guys find their wives in high school. Others don't find their wives until their forties, no matter how hard they look. It comes down to luck really, so how many years you give yourself is essentially arbitrary. At some point you just have to call it quits and pick someone."

"And for you that cutoff point is thirty?"

"Yeah. Anyone in my family who's still a bachelor at thirty is viewed as some kind of alien curiosity. I might as well show up to holiday dinners as a unicorn."

"I submit to you – as a matter of scientific and irrefutable fact – that you are completely whacked, Heeb. A real meschugana, as your people would say. But that's why I love you."

"We'll see who's a meschugana. With your crazy Carlos criteria, it's guaranteed that you'll still be a bachelor at thirty…A virgin bachelor."

"The sad thing is that you're probably right."

Heeb and Chucky could not have been more mistaken.

6. Chucky Gets Lucky in New York

In June 1995, after the commencement ceremony, the packing, and the goodbyes, Heeb left for DC to start his work as an actuary for a major life insurance company. He would be paid well to use his prowess with statistics, and within two years, would be promoted to oversee a team of twenty actuaries and researchers.

Carlos decided to seek his fortunes in New York City. But unlike most of his college buddies who headed to the Big Apple, he didn't go with any concrete plan, having decided during his senior year that he had no interest in any of Manhattan's coveted corporate positions – in management consulting, investment banking, and public relations — available through on-campus recruiting. The reputedly long hours and conservative culture of such jobs were enough to persuade him to seek his fortunes in some alternative career path. Carlos figured that in a city as large and diverse as New York he was bound to find the right workplace for himself.

Two days after graduation, Carlos took the five-hour bus ride from Boston to New York City with a college friend whose sister lived in the city. The sister was away on vacation until Friday evening, which gave Carlos exactly three nights to crash on her living room sofa and three days to find an apartment and a job.

In New York City, capital of the enviously malcontent, it is virtually impossible to find and keep all three of the following for more than two years: 1) a good enough apartment, 2) a good enough job, and 3) a good enough mate. That's why, when Carlos found all three of these things during his first three hours in the city, he finally and completely embraced the nickname that Heeb had given him nine months earlier. Shortly after dropping off his four large bags and taking a cool shower, Carlos boarded a local bus to midtown, where his destiny awaited him.

Meanwhile, Carolina, a ravishing Italian woman with cocoa-colored hair and long, dark lashes, joked on the phone about how hot and muggy her office felt, even though the air-conditioning had just been upgraded in the entire building.

"It's as if God is trying to prove that technology will never keep up with a Manhattan summer."

"We're all in this sauna together, Carolina."

"That's irrelevant, Ann. The fact that others share my problem only makes things worse."

"Why?"

"Because then there are more people in the city spending more of their time bitching about more things because they're grumpy and uncomfortable."

"So you'd rather be the only one feeling this muggy heat?"

"Well at least I'd be interacting with more pleasant people."

"I guess," Ann replied.

"Except then people would be less empathetic to my bitchiness because they wouldn't understand the discomfort that was causing it."

"Very true."

"So maybe they wouldn't be more pleasant."

"Was Greg more pleasant?"

"Greg?"

"You know, the guy who gave you the bouquet on Third Avenue."

"Oh, that Greg. No. It was all downhill after the bouquet."

"Why?"

"He was boring like the others…I'm sick of dating, Ann."

"So is every other woman I know in New York."

"Again, the fact that others share my problem just makes things worse."

"Why?"

"It's just a reminder of how much competition there is for the few good men out there."

"You have no competition, Carolina."

"That's very sweet of you, Ann. But I need results, not a support group."

"But I'm serious. You turn every sidewalk into a movie set with your looks and charming style. And you're only twenty-five for God's sake. You've got plenty of time."

"Your flattery is too kind, Ann. But I've been single for seven months now, without one fruitful encounter besides the lesbian masseuse who offered to give me weekly massages at no charge after I told her that I'm straight."

"It's not like no one's interested…What about that guy, John, who started dancing with you when we were out last Saturday?"

"Very nice. As long as he doesn't talk."

"What about that grad student, Eric, from your comparative literature class?"

"He's great. As long as he only talks."

"But I thought great conversations turn you on."

"They do. But he just doesn't do it for me. He's too much of a pencil-head. And his nose comes up to my breasts for God's sake. I need a little more height than that."

"How about that tall venture capital guy you said wants to invest in your company?"

"He just wants to invest in my pants. And I think his portfolio is already diverse enough without me."

"What about that guy your parents set you up with?"

"Please."

"Really?"

"Any question that consists of the words 'What about that guy your parents set you up with?' has already answered itself."

"What about getting back together with Hal?"

"Hal? Are you joking?"

"What would be so bad about that? You Europeans are famous for your environmentally enlightened ways. Why not recycle a little?"

"He was far too middle America for me."

"What do you mean?"

"He spent his entire life in Missouri before we met at Stanford. He had American flags on his underwear for God's sake."

"You know he'd fly out here for you in a heartbeat."

"I know. He's a real sweetheart. But too provincial for me. I need someone a bit more worldly. Looks and brains alone aren't enough. I spent two years realizing that."

"So what are you looking for exactly?"

"A virgin Latin lover with manners, culture, and a brain. Is that so much to ask?"

"A virgin Latin Lover? That's an oxymoron! I think you're being way too picky, Carolina."

"Maybe."

Carlos opened the front door to Arezzo Properties Limited, a midtown real estate brokerage firm advertised in the newspaper that he had scoured during the long ride down from Boston. He walked into a superbly stylized yet minimalist office with black and white photos of great Manhattan architecture, marble floors, white walls, and a black leather couch positioned next to a splendid window view of the city, twenty-eight floors below. A pretty receptionist told him that a broker would be with him shortly and that he could take a seat on the sofa until then.

Through the closed circuit camera transmitting images of the waiting area to Carolina's large computer screen, Carolina noticed Carlos take a seat. She zoomed the camera in for a closer look at his face. He sat there, cool and in his element, as he waited for a broker. His thick black hair, still moist from his shower, blended with his chocolate eyes and his golden dark skin.

"Why don't you try letting go a little?" Ann suggested.

"What do you mean?"

"Why don't you just go with the flow? Guys come up to you constantly. Why not just start dating the first one who looks remotely appealing?"

"Now there's an idea." Carolina zoomed in some more and adjusted the camera's focus a bit.

"Just try suspending all judgments for a while. Let go and have some fun."

She moved the camera down a little. His broad shoulders and strong dark arms were subtle suggestions under the curves of his loosely fitting beige T-shirt. His firm thighs filled out the khaki trousers that ended just above his stylish, Italian-made leather sandals. A flood of warm and nervous tingles erupted in her gut.

"Listen, I have to take care of something. Let me call you back."

"Cheer up, Carolina. Your life can change in an instant."

"I know," she said, with a smile. "You're a sweetheart, Ann. I'll call you tonight."

Carolina hung up the phone and then called the receptionist to tell her not to pass the customer to any brokers because she would handle this client herself.

"But you haven't shown an apartment to anyone in almost a year."

"That's precisely what I was thinking today…I'm very out of practice. Every business is in danger of failing when top management forgets the bread-and-butter work – the essential goods and services that actually produce revenue for the company."

She hung up the phone, picked up a folder of properties, and – for a moment – gazed out at the inspiring view behind her corner office. On her way to the door, Carolina looked into the full-length mirror by the door. The mirror stared at her slim figure – a poised, five-nine sculpture of grace and elegance shrouded in loose-fitting white cotton pants, and a beige, unbuttoned long-sleeve shirt, fluttering open to reveal a white cotton undershirt snugly covering her firm breasts, with the shirt sleeves rolled up to expose her long, smooth, tan arms.

She walked out into the reception area and approached Carlos, who was looking out the window, admiring the picturesque view of the city.

"So you need an apartment?" she began, looking him over with a nervous smile.

As Carlos turned towards her and saw her for the first time, he hesitated with an almost reverent awe at what was undoubtedly the most breathtaking woman he had ever seen. He stood up in a bit of a daze, still looking at her, and then looked away for an awkward moment.

When he returned to her hazel eyes, he realized that he had forgotten what it was like to try to be smooth with a female he found so attractive. For the first time ever, he was genuinely unsure as to whether he had enough Kojak.

He awkwardly approached her a little more, so that he could say something to her without the receptionist hearing. Their newfound proximity produced a potently mixed scent of cologne, perfume, sweat, body odor, and Manhattan mugginess.

"Is there any way you could get another broker to show me around?" he whispered coyly.

"Why?" she asked, intrigued.

"Well, I don't like to mix business with...I mean, I'd really just like to find a good deal and not get fleeced on the rent or anything..."

Carolina smiled and led him out of the reception area and towards the exit.

"It's good to look at these things objectively, if you know what I mean," Carlos continued, as they approached the main door. Never had the prince of confident equanimity felt so uncertain about how to proceed with a woman; never had he wished harder for some Kojak. "And it's my first time looking at New York apartments...Which is why I'm probably going about this all wrong, telling you all of this now..." he said, holding the door open for her. Carlos feared that he was sounding increasingly naïve – even infantile – and had no idea that Carolina actually found this bit of innocence to be endearing and reassuring. It gave her the confidence to press forward with her impulsive attempt to learn more about the first man ever to leave her so nervous and breathless.

As the office door shut behind him, Carlos kept bumbling for a little longer, not really knowing what his verbal strategy was any more but praying that it would take a turn for the better soon: "I guess what I'm trying to say is that I'd just feel more comfortable with someone else showing me apartments…" He hesitantly followed her towards the elevators.

"I'm sorry but I'm the only one available right now, and the first rule of the brokerage business is: never turn away a customer. Besides, honesty is a hallmark of our professionalism. It's one of the things that sets our company apart from the competition." She turned around for a moment so that he could catch up a little. "But don't worry. We'll figure out a way for you to get fleeced on the rent anyway."

Carlos loved her style. He loved everything about her. The way she walked with unstoppable vigor. The way she pushed the elevator button as if she owned it. The way she whipped out her sunglasses and brought them to her eyes with the grace of a ballet dancer who divided the unfolding circular motion of her arm into equal segments of movement timed to conclude exactly as the two of them entered the sunlight. He loved that her every answer felt two steps ahead of whatever he said or asked.

And yet all of this grace and confidence belied the fact that she had no idea which apartments to show, how many to show, how long to show them, or what her ultimate plan was for Carlos. The only concern guiding her from moment to moment was how to steal another look at this unprecedented specimen of a man and how to learn all about him while maintaining a veneer of detached professionalism. Her utter lack of a coherent apartment-touring program would have been obvious to any real estate broker, and even to Carlos, were he paying attention to anything other than Carolina.

The first three apartments were spellbinding experiences for Carlos because they were walk-ups. Carolina had chosen the first walk-up purely out of absent-minded convenience (it was the first apartment listing in her folder), rather than out of any calculated expectation that the walk up portion of the visit would intoxicate Carlos. But the opportunity to climb stairs a few steps in front of Carlos and feel her hips swaying rhythmically, no more than three feet ahead of his face was enticing enough for her to take him to a few more walk-ups after that first one, despite the hot and sticky weather.

All of these apartments – and the three elevator-building apartments that followed – were too noisy or too small for Carlos. But there was a tacit conspiracy between Carlos and Carolina not to discuss any specifics that could bring their tour to a premature conclusion because he had never mentioned his budget or general criteria and she had never inquired about these basic details. Carlos just kept feigning an almost academic interest in each apartment without ever explaining why they needed to see the next place on the list (he might as well have been saying, "Hmm…So this too is an apartment, isn't it?").

But the seventh apartment that Carolina brought him to was a particularly well lit one that made Carlos finally express, for the first time, an actual preference. Of course, he didn't tell her that the only reason he wanted an apartment with large open sky views was because when he followed Carolina into a sun-drenched room, the light illuminated her pants into a gossamer hovering over a silhouette of her long, gracefully sculpted legs. He just had a preference for natural lighting, he told her.

The eighth apartment was very well lit by sun, but it was so impressive — a twentieth floor penthouse on Park Avenue — that Carlos actually spent a moment admiring the place rather than the person who brought him there. And in a carelessly naïve and silly moment, he asked a question that suddenly highlighted the absurdity underlying their entire tour of apartments up until that moment: "This is really nice. What's the rent like?"

"Six thousand a month," Carolina replied, now embarrassed about the open acknowledgment that there was really no business purpose to viewing any of the residential properties they had visited.

"Wow. I guess I'll have to get a job soon," added Carlos, still dazed by their apparently pointless, two-hour tour of Manhattan apartments – particularly now that he may have inadvertently brought it to an end.

Carolina sensed that the tone might awkwardly change for the worse if she didn't somehow resurrect the previous energy that had pervaded their time together.

"I could always hire you," she said, breaking into a playful smile.

"You could hire me?" Carlos asked in skeptical amusement.

"Why not?" she insisted.

"Well…I just didn't think that brokers had the authority to – "

"It's my company."

"Your company?"

Carolina blushed a bit, realizing that she hadn't even introduced herself properly.

"Yes. My name is Carolina Arezzo. Pleased to meet you."

Carlos reddened a little as he extended his hand to meet hers. "The pleasure has been memorably mine."

They looked each other in the eye, as her hand fit snugly into his firm but gentle handshake. The tension was too much. Carolina turned away and started leading him out of the apartment, gradually letting go of his hand. He followed, feeling somewhat dizzy.

"I'm serious," she continued, trying to keep an even keel. "It's not every day that I meet a bilingual Harvard graduate with a sense of humor and charming people skills. And we do need some help."

"What about an apartment?"

"Did you like any of the ones I showed you?"

"I liked a lot of them…I mean, yes, they were all nice, but I'm not sure if any of them was quite right for me."

"Let me show you a few more."

"OK."

In the cab ride to the next apartment, Carlos tried to process everything that had happened. Carolina sat quietly next to him, looking out the window while trying to calm the churn in her stomach, but stealing occasional glances, as she wondered what exactly was on his mind.

Like a detective who has been reluctantly avoiding a difficult conclusion, but who has an overpowering suspicion that compels him to return to the evidence and review the overall meaning of all of the separate and unrelated clues before him, Carlos mulled over all of the facts that he had discovered about Carolina during their two hours together – two hours that felt as rich and varied as two weeks, yet had passed like two minutes. She was born and raised in Italy but spent ten of her formative years in Spain and Portugal. She speaks fluent English, Italian, Portuguese, and Spanish. In just three years, she graduated from Yale College at the age of twenty, and finished her MBA from Stanford by the age of twenty-two. She's been in New York since then. In three years, Arezzo Properties Limited grew from one to twenty employees and made a net profit of 1.4 million dollars last year. Carolina Arezzo is the founder and owner of Arezzo Properties Limited. In her spare time, she has been earning her PhD in comparative literature from Columbia University. Carolina Arezzo is by far the most beautiful woman Carlos has ever met. She was born Catholic but no longer practices the religion. Her name begins with the letter C. And she is sitting next to him in the cab.

"Carolina, do you have a valid European passport?"

"Yes. From Italy. Why?"

"And can you name at least five great Latin American writers, at least two of whom are Mexican?"

"Why?"

"It's too crazy to explain to you right now, but I just need to know."

"OK," she said, taking it all in humorous stride. "I'll give you five great Latin American writers with two from Mexico. Miguel Angel Asturias is from Guatemala and he won the Nobel Prize for literature in 1967. Pablo Neruda is from Chile and he won the same prize in 1971. Gabriel Garcia Marquez is from Colombia and he won in 1982. Octavio Paz is from Mexico and he won in 1990. And Juan Jose Arreola is from Mexico; he never won the Nobel Prize, but he's definitely considered a great writer."

Carlos was blissfully mystified.

Carolina was just one criterion away from being the perfect woman, but it was the fifth – and arguably most difficult – of the "Coherent Carlos Criteria." He still didn't know if she was a non-smoking vegetarian with a Buddhist worldview and environmentalist values. As he thought of how painful it would be to have to walk away at this point, he struggled with his longstanding, tenacious commitment to the Carlos criteria – an unyielding fidelity that had always baffled Heeb. He suddenly wished that Heeb were there so that he could consult with him, even though he knew exactly what Heeb would say.

"Are you crazy, Carlos?!" Heeb would exclaim. "You deserve to be castrated if you blow this one because of your idiotic criteria!" The imaginary Heeb looked particularly agitated as his scalp flushed.

"But my whole life I've respected these criteria…I've never compromised on them for anyone – I mean, in terms of giving up my virginity…Can I really be sure that no one will come closer to satisfying my standards?"

"Carlos, the odds of someone else coming closer are so bad that if you stall on this for another second I'm personally going to castrate you myself and then you won't have to worry about how and when to lose your virginity anymore."

"I'm sorry, I'm just —"

"Carlos, this woman is heaven. You probably don't even deserve her. Especially with these completely irrational doubts you're having about details that are stupider than stupid."

"But I've respected those stupid details my whole life. There's something to be said for consistency about one's convictions."

"Especially if they're stupid convictions."

"I guess I could compromise on the Buddhist environmentalist bit. I mean, she could always evolve into that over time, right?"

Heeb exhaled a sigh of exaggerated relief: "I see a light of reason at the end of a very dark and celibate tunnel...But you're not done. I mean what about the vegetarianism? Don't even think about asking her if she eats meat, because I can tell you right now that she loves a good filet mignon, and if that's a deal-breaker on this woman, then you deserve to die alone on a vegetable farm."

"OK, that's gone too. I guess we just won't be able to share our food all the time."

"So you're ready?"

"Well there's still one thing. One deal-breaker that I do have to ask her about."

"What?" Heeb's patience was at its limit.

"She can't be a smoker...And I'm worried, because Europeans tend to be smokers." Heeb appeared frustrated like never before. Carlos continued, defensively: "Look, that's a health issue. I just can't be breathing unnecessary impurities, or kissing someone who breathes them."

"Now don't budge, Lucky Chucky. I've got the surgical knife right here. Your new name is Castrated Carlos. It's time to end everyone's misery." Heeb took the scalpel out of his shirt pocket and started moving towards Carlos, who was paralyzed by indecision.

Carolina spied another look at Carlos, who appeared as if he were watching a television embedded in the cab seat in front of him. She smiled in amusement and decided to interrupt the broadcast. But preferring to avoid an improper intrusion, she rummaged through her purse a little and then resorted to a harmless pretext that had proven its efficacy on countless other occasions.

"Carlos, do you have a light?" she asked, with a cigarette between her fingers.

Carlos felt the knife neuter him forever.

He groaned aloud and then released a moaning wale.

"Nnnnooooooooo!" He couldn't contain the anguish of his disappointment.

"What's wrong? Are you OK, Carlos? What happened?"

Carlos leaned against the door, dizzy. He saw a blurry image of Carolina moving closer to him, with the unlit cigarette trailing in the air, as if in a slow motion film.

"Please…Please don't…"

"What? What is it? The cigarette?" That was the only explanation she could surmise for his unexpectedly dramatic reaction. "Are you allergic?"

In Carolina's considerate inquiry, full of concern and sensitivity, Carlos suddenly regained most of the hope that he thought he had just lost. With a tremendous sense of relief, he grabbed hold of the lifesaver that Carolina had inadvertently thrown him and began trying to elaborate on his newly discovered allergy.

"Terribly allergic…I…I've had some awful reactions…I'm sorry…I shouldn't have reacted that way…My body has just grown instinctively repulsed to even the sight of cigarettes…After…After so many bad experiences."

It was the best he could do to parry Heeb's castration threat. There was no explaining to Carolina that his aversion to cigarettes was actually just a small example of a much broader and more complex neurosis. That was another talk for another, safer time. For now, a medical allergy was a far simpler and more palatable explanation for the perfect woman who had taken so long to arrive in his life.

"I'm sorry…I didn't know," she said with a gentle smile, as she dropped the cigarette into her purse.

The cab pulled over. Carolina passed the driver a ten-dollar bill and the two got out.

"Thanks for being so considerate, Carolina."

"Don't be silly. Actually, I've tried quitting many times, but it's hard to drop a habit that you started at the age of twelve."

That didn't sound encouraging. But Heeb was right there, ready with the scalpel, so Carlos needed to change the topic.

As he followed Carolina's lead up Fifth Avenue, he noticed that they had traveled all the way to Eighty-second Street, near the Metropolitan Museum of Art.

"Is this where the apartment is?" he asked, genuinely intrigued, as they walked into an impressively large and ornate lobby.

"I think you're really going to like this one," she said with a wink. "It's nicer than anything I've shown you so far."

"When you were offering me a job, I didn't think the salary you had in mind was so good."

"That's because you don't know just how much responsibility I have in mind for you. That's what happens when you raise expectations, Carlos."

"Oh," said Carlos with an irrepressibly curious grin.

"You'll like the light in this apartment," she added. "And the views of the park are incredible."

They got out of the elevator on the fifteenth floor, and, as Carlos followed a few steps behind Carolina's enchantingly graceful figure, he wondered about the purpose of this particular apartment visit. He doubted that she would really pay him enough to rent a place like this, but was happy all the same to return to the familiar pretext of viewing apartments together.

Carlos agreed that this was the nicest apartment she had shown him. It was a two-bedroom penthouse with a balcony and a spiral staircase leading to a roof deck.

"Why don't you walk around a little?" Carolina said, walking into the large kitchen.

Carlos took a moment to tour the space on his own. Its elegantly simple style, stunning park views, high ceilings, and airy feel were extraordinary. But he suddenly noticed that the apartment wasn't vacant.

"Someone's stuff is here," he observed. "Are you sure it's available?"

"It's available for the right tenant. Come and check out the marble kitchen."

Carlos walked over to the kitchen.

Carolina was leaning against the marble sink area, drinking a glass of red wine.

"I'm sorry. It's just such a hot and muggy day, and this seems like just the right drink now."

"Do you always raid the fridge of your client's properties?" he asked in amused surprise.

"I'm on very good terms with the landlord here."

"Really?"

"Yes," she replied, offering Carlos the glass. "Do you know why?"

"No." Carlos took the glass in his hand. "Why?"

"Because I am the landlord."

Carlos couldn't contain his pleasure at her artful ways. They shared a mischievous smile.

"Take a sip."

He hesitated for a moment. Carlos regularly indulged in a single daily glass of red wine after reading that the practice promoted cardiac health. The problem was that Carolina's germs were on the glass.

But as he looked at her standing there – a portrait of perfectly poised pulchritude – he realized how the last two hours were nothing short of one continuous miracle whose germs he was ready to swim in for the rest of his life. He thought about how it had been years since he wanted to kiss a woman so badly, and how the kiss would surely involve more exposure to her germs than the shared wine glass.

And so he took the wine glass and – rather than lift it to his lips – he moved it to the side and set it down on the marble counter, so that his hands were free to float down to her hips as his lips moved towards hers.

And what started as gentle caresses and slow kisses against a marble kitchen counter gradually grew more firm and vigorous, until it became urgent and frenzied — like so much water boiling on a hot summer day in Manhattan.

7. C+C

Any relationship with long-term potential has a honeymoon period, however brief, marked by the happy illusion that one's lover might be uniquely perfect. This fool's paradise is sustained by the elaborate deception artfully employed in every courtship: the diplomatic dodging of difficult issues, the careful concealing of unflattering flaws, and the strategic stressing of charming virtues. But as trust increases and each person grows weary of maintaining this initial beguilement, the blissfully blurry lens through which the other is perceived eventually refocuses to a clearer picture.

Accordingly, at some point after the honeymoon period, in a relationship of equals, there will be at least one dramatic dispute – one moment of tremendous tension – when the whole relationship is called into question because a raw difference has been fully exposed for all of its import. For Carlos and Carolina, this moment occurred about two months after they first met. It began with a perfectly simple and innocuous question.

At a tender, twilight hour, when the couple finally stopped quaking from the intensity of their lovemaking, Carlos asked her gently and wistfully, "How did you do it?"

Despite his inexperience, he knew intuitively that his new girlfriend was much more passionate and free in bed than most women were.

"Do what?"

"Lose your guilt about sex…It's as if you never had any," he explained, hoping to find some inspiration or direction in her answer.

Carolina smiled for a moment at the answer. "I confronted it head on. At the source."

"How?" Carlos asked, genuinely intrigued by the complex and mysterious woman next to him.

During their honeymoon period, Carolina would have surely evaded the question or supplied a misleadingly incomplete answer. But now her guard was down, and in a moment of exceptional intimacy, she decided to share a story from her secret past.

"I've always been too ashamed to tell anyone," she began hesitantly. "But…You're different…And this is different."

Carlos caressed her, patiently waiting for her to muster the courage to continue her story.

"I was seventeen at the time, studying in Madrid, when I met Father Vegas…It's uncanny how much you look like him," she added. "You have the same deep, dark eyes, the same — " Carlos removed his hand from her back and adjusted his position in the bed.

"I'm sorry." Carolina reflexively covered her mouth in regret. "I shouldn't have compared the two of you like that."

"Don't be silly."

"Do you want me to continue?"

"Yes. Please."

*****

Soon after joining the Madrid parish, the handsome, twenty-five-year-old priest from Valencia took notice of Carolina, not only because she came to confession so frequently, but also because she was clearly an exceptional girl. After hearing eight of Carolina's confessions, Father Vegas realized that she was precociously perceptive and insightful, and remarkably articulate in a language that wasn't even her native tongue.

But none of these private observations, nor any of her previous sessions with him, had prepared Father Vegas for her ninth confession – which would be the most memorable of his career as a priest.

"Forgive me, Father," she began nervously. "For I have come here to sin."

"What do you mean?" Father Vegas asked, his voice rising in alarmed confusion, hoping that he had misheard something through the thick black curtain that temporarily replaced the wooden lattice barrier, which had been removed for repairs.

"Don't be angry with me, Father."

"Speak freely, my child."

"Father… To be truly open and honest with you…I have been sinning almost every night since you became a priest here. Every night before I'm due to make my confession. And every night after too. I come to confession for only one reason, and that is to be near you and talk to you."

"You mustn't say such things, my child. These are all terrible sins that can blemish your soul."

"Am I an immoral person for having such thoughts, Father?"

"Temptation is a natural part of every journey, my child. We must all struggle with it. But it is precisely in that struggle that we define our moral life."

"But Father, this passion is not one that I have chosen. Rather, it has chosen me. It has consumed me. Nobody ever asked me if I wanted you to become a priest here. You just appeared one day. And now I have this passion burning within me…So how can I be less moral for having these feelings if I never chose to acquire them? If they thrust themselves upon me, as I now wish to thrust myself upon you?"

"Please child. You mustn't say such things!" he admonished through the curtain separating them. "You are speaking sin!"

"How can it be wrong to act upon my most natural of impulses, which is to share this passion with you, even if others may judge me severely for it?"

"Please, my child. Stop talking like this. Say ten Hail Marys for each time that you have had any thoughts like these."

"Father, if I do that then my grades in school will suffer."

"Why is that?"

"Because then I couldn't do my homework. There would be no time for anything but repeating the Hail Marys."

"My child, you have to stop this madness…Immediately."

"I know, Father, but I couldn't take it anymore. I had to talk to you. And I had to ask you if you can play any instruments besides the organ…"

"What do you mean, my child?"

"Every chance I get, I listen to you playing the organ, Father. You don't see me because I'm always standing in the entrance farthest from the organ. But I see your broad shoulders and long arms dominating the organ with such graceful force and elegance…You play so beautifully…"

"Thank you, child, but music is a pleasure for the senses and right now we must focus on the work of the soul."

"But Father, my soul is housed within my senses."

"Let us focus on the spiritual edifice, rather than physical adornments of that dwelling."

"Please just tell me if you play any other instruments. Can't you tell me that much, after I have told you so much about myself?"

"That is not relevant to the cleansing that you are here to accomplish."

"I have opened my soul to you, and countless personal questions and struggles. And you can't now tell me if you play any other instruments?"

There was a silent moment, as Father Vegas weighed the value of building and rewarding trust in this penitent against his reluctance to start divulging any personal details or otherwise lose control of the confession.

He finally broke the silence. "I can play the guitar."

"Have you ever played it for a Flamenco dancer, Father? Do you know that I can dance Flamenco? I have been studying it for the last four years that I've been living in Madrid."

"Child, why do you insist on diverting us from our duty here?"

"Because you can't call me child any more. You can only call me Carolina. And I can't call you Father Vegas any more. What is your first name?"

"I…I can't…I can't do this, my child."

"Tell me your name!"

"You mustn't ever call me by it."

"Just tell it to me once, so that I may know who has heard so many of my confessions – including this most humiliating of all confessions…This stubborn display of my affection despite your steadfast resistance and rejection. Tell me your name! It's the least you can do in return before I plunge into despair and try to forget that I ever met you."

There was something so desperately true and irresistibly pure and undeniable in Carolina's plaintive voice that Father Vegas couldn't refuse her.

"It's Fernando."

"Fernando, pull this curtain aside."

"You mustn't call me by my first name!"

"I need to see you."

"We mustn't speak like this."

"No. We must. Because I will keep coming back here like this. Until you leave this church and disappear without a trace. I will return. Either that or I will have to leave Madrid. But there is nothing we can do now but deal with what is between us."

"What are you doing?"

"Only what feels pure and natural to me."

"This is too much. You mustn't do this."

"I realize that this may require a vocational change for you, but that's why I asked if you play any other instruments. I know of a few pubs that are looking to hire some musicians. And there's always room for a good guitarist in Madrid...I can introduce you to my Flamenco teacher too. He may also be able to use a guitarist."

"Carolina...Please...Don't..." he began. The young virgin priest became dizzy from their exchange, as he recognized his own weakness and the overwhelming power of temptation – a temptation that he had managed, with substantial effort, to evade or resist for his entire life.

"Fernando, I'm sorry for being so brazen and forward. I just had to be true to my feelings. I've made my confession to you and now I can go. I have been honest with myself and with you. If you can't love me, then I will leave Madrid and never see you again...But please move this curtain aside and let me see you one last time. One last time, and then I will leave you forever."

There was a heavy silence, as Fernando tried to absorb the full meaning of the stark options suddenly laid out before him.

Carolina faced the curtain separating her from Fernando and moved closer to it, eagerly waiting for it to be pushed aside.

Another quiet moment of solemn reflection passed.

Fernando finally drew the curtain open in an impulsive flash, where he saw Carolina's luscious lips waiting for him.

He kissed the priesthood goodbye.

*****

"That certainly is confronting your guilt about sex head on, at its source!" Carlos noted in amusement. "And where is Fernando now?"

"I don't know. He's probably still in Spain somewhere, making his living as a Flamenco guitarist...I haven't spoken to him in almost three years, mi amor, so there's no need to be jealous...He was too attached to Spain to follow me to New Haven, where I had to start college about four months after that first kiss...Sometimes I wonder what became of him..."

Carlos replied facetiously, "Well, I can see why you wonder... Most career counselors like to follow up with the people they advise."

Carolina laughed — mostly out of relief at how tolerantly Carlos had received her confession about confession.

In reality, however, the story somewhat offended Carlos's vestigial Catholic sensibilities and, to his surprise, made him rather jealous. The enthusiasm and longing with which Carolina recounted the story of her first truly passionate love – a love for another Latin virgin whom Carlos resembled – and the idea that she and Fernando had united under circumstances that were equally charming and magical (sacrilege aside), all made Carlos feel unexceptional and replaceable, at least in theory.

This festering jealousy soon made Carlos more aware of details that he had overlooked or that Carolina had concealed during their dating honeymoon. Lately, her breath revealed that she had been surreptitiously smoking a few cigarettes per day. He recalled how she had recently ordered a veal dish, despite the lengthy ethical and environmental explanation for his vegetarianism that he had shared with her just a few days earlier. These minor disappointments conspired with the jealousy ignited by the Fernando story to make Carlos irrationally demanding. Carlos needed to test her love for him and see if Carolina was prepared to fulfill exacting requests just to prove to him that he still meant more to her than anything else did.

Two days after the Fernando story, Carlos finished showing a potential buyer an apartment downtown, and then walked over to Spring Street to meet Carolina for a Sunday SoHo stroll. Carlos greeted her with a kiss and immediately frowned upon realizing that her breath was nine parts mouthwash, one part ashtray. "I told myself that I would never date a smoker," Carlos began, noticeably irritated. "I thought you were going to quit."

"Carlos, I've been smoking since I was twelve. It's going to take time. And it's not like I've been smoking in your presence."

"Not yet. But in another month or two, I'm sure that'll be next. I mean, our first month together I couldn't tell that you even smoke. But by the second month, I could tell that you're a smoker with a great mouthwash. So what does the third month hold?"

"Why are you being so harsh on me? Don't you realize how hard it is to quit?"

"Don't you realize what a big turn off it is for me?"

"Turn off? And what if I asked you to get over your mysophobia in just a few months?"

Carolina's tone had just enough punch and sting to make her rejoinder feel painfully personal.

They began their eastbound stroll in an awkward silence.

Early in their relationship, Carlos had explained to Carolina all about his mild anxiety disorder involving an abnormal and irrational fear of contamination or defilement – particularly from publicly handled objects. Initially, she humored his bizarre quirk, but over time found it strange – especially when he would put gloves on before boarding any public transportation or opening the doors of public establishments. In the late summer, shortly after their dating honeymoon had expired, the two were returning from a business lunch in midtown when Carolina mischievously tried to loosen him up on the issue while also indulging the sudden impulse to kiss him. As she held his right hand with her left hand, she pretended to notice something strange in the phone booth to her right, making Carlos lean towards it for a better view, and then she playfully pulled him off balance into the booth with her. She laughed hysterically at how silly Carlos looked trying (unsuccessfully) to avoid hand contact with any part of the phone booth. To indulge her romantic impulse, she then tried to kiss him in the booth, but he was clearly too uncomfortable there and just wanted to find some water with which to clean himself. Later, when he remained sour over the incident, she began to question their compatibility a little.

Carlos's mysophobia also affected his sensuality. There was always a moment of hesitation before he would make his lips or body accessible to Carolina, who had always been accustomed to fending off oversexed men (other than Fernando). Carlos's tentative physicality usually had the effect of teasing Carolina and making her even more aroused, but she sometimes wished that he could be the first to make a move. She knew from their searching talks, his fervidly held views, and his emotionally profound reaction to art and poetry that he was a man with tremendous passion and soul. She knew that – while Carlos had little sexual experience – he had all of the potential to be the best lover she had ever had, after some training and the elimination of his paranoia about germs. But she also knew that it would take time. On one occasion, she even suggested that he go to therapy to resolve the issue more quickly, but he grew angrily defensive at the idea.

With Carolina's simple question ("What if I asked you to get over your mysophobia in just a few months?"), all of these issues were instantly conjured in a way that alienated Carlos and suddenly made him feel insecure. He finally broke their strained silence.

"That's not a fair comparison. My mysophobia doesn't affect your health like your smoking affects mine. It doesn't taste bad in your

73

mouth. It doesn't expose you to impurities…On the contrary, it encourages you to avoid them."

"Carlos, your mysophobia does affect my health. I feel freer – more alive, more vivacious and, ironically enough, healthier – if I'm not constantly made to worry about germs and unhealthy choices. Whether it's for a moment of spontaneous kissing in a phone booth or eating an occasional hamburger…Obsessing about your health doesn't actually make you healthier. The fact of the matter is, Carlos, our bodies are decaying at every moment, regardless of what we do. Living is bad for your health."

"It doesn't have to be."

"Maybe if you live in an antiseptic bubble specially designed by the CDC it doesn't. But in a place like New York City, you're fighting a pointless battle. You can either embrace the dirt and the germs as part of the risky joy of living in an exciting, overpopulated metropolis, or you can spend lots of mental real estate obsessing over whether you touched a few extra microbes when you got on the subway."

They walked in silence for a few more minutes. The powerful logic behind Carolina's arguments only aggravated the mix of embarrassment and insecurity that he felt. These emotions were in addition to the very jealousy that spawned the whole exchange. Now that Carlos felt self-conscious about his mysophobia and theoretically replaceable by someone like Fernando, it became all the more crucial to assert his dominance in the relationship. He had to test her devotion to him. And he had to prove that he was above all of these issues – that he could just walk away from the whole thing if she wasn't willing to accede to his demands, no matter how unreasonable they were.

Carlos finally broke their silent walk, after mustering the courage to state his ultimatum. "I can't date a smoker, Carolina."

"What are you trying to say, Carlos?"

"I…I…It's…It's really important to me…"

"This is because of Fernando isn't it?"

"No! It has nothing to do with that!" Carlos angrily denied. "Before I ever met you, before I ever knew about your trysts with the church, I always knew that I would never be with a smoker. Period. Don't try to complicate this….Because….Because it's really simple….It's me or the cigarettes."

"You're not saying what I think you're saying."

"Carolina, I'll give you a month to quit…But that's it."

She stopped walking. He stopped after her.

She looked him in the eye. "Are you serious?"

"As serious as lung cancer," he replied.

Carolina's brow became crinkled in a torrent of confused emotions.

"Well in that case I don't need a month," she began. "I'll quit right now." A tear rolled down one of her cheeks and she turned around and ran.

For a few minutes, Carlos's wounded pride prevented him from running after her, and he just continued walking stubbornly in the same direction at the same pace, watching Carolina get farther away by the minute.

Suddenly, his memory of the tear on her face jolted him into an apologetic sprint.

By the time he got within earshot of her, her fluttering summer dress was rapidly descending the entrance stairs of the Spring Street subway station. As he ran towards the stairs, he pulled out his anti-germ gloves and put them on just before he reached the handrail. As luck would have it, when Carlos bolted down to the bottom of the stairs, the train was already there and Carolina was boarding it. His only hope of getting on and catching her was to accelerate and jump over the turnstile rather than stop long enough to get his metro card out and swipe it through one of the potentially uncooperative turnstiles.

Praying that there were no police around, he opted for the risky route and flew over the turnstile, with all of the grace of a cheetah on the hunt.

"Get away from me!" she cried in tears, as the subway train's slamming doors barely missed Carlos's back. As he approached her, out of breath, she began walking from train to train, figuring that the germ-filled passage between cars and the dirty tunnel air would surely deter Carlos from following her.

But Carlos was too focused on her to think any more about germs and dirt.

"I'm sorry, Carolina," he said, following behind her, still catching his breath. "I was wrong."

The passengers turned their attention to the unfolding drama of a lover's quarrel.

"Go away!" she replied, crying even more and dodging some passengers, until she got to the door and moved to the next train.

This chase continued until Carolina had exhausted all of the train cars and was in the first car of the uptown six train. By now,

Carlos had caught his breath and was about ten steps from cornering Carolina.

"Leave me alone!" she said, still crying. "Go look for your fucking non-smoking, perfect girl somewhere else."

"I'm sorry, Carolina. Really, I am...I'm so sorry," he said, getting within just a few steps of her. "It was about Fernando. I got really jealous. In a totally idiotic and irrational kind of way. Please forgive me."

And with that, Carolina gushed a fresh set of tears, and Carlos went up to her and cradled her in his arms. "I'm so sorry, mi amor."

He sat her down on the subway seat, and she cried some more on his large, built chest, with his strong, tan arms around her graceful, feminine figure. When she finally looked up at Carlos, she could tell from the embarrassed look on his face that they had an audience.

Eager to add some levity to the situation, Carlos addressed everyone looking at him with heartfelt, sappy smiles. "Go ahead. I know you want to clap. You might as well," he said as the passengers around them erupted into self-conscious laughter.

"Let's just turn this into that cheesy, tear-jerking, Hollywood mush scene that it already looks like," he added.

By now, Carolina was laughing too. "Come on. Put your hands together. I'll help you out."

Carlos began clapping, and soon everyone – including Carolina – was clapping with him.

When the clapping finally stopped, a seventy-year-old man sitting next to his wife across from the reconciled lovers launched his directorial debut of the Hollywood sap scene. "Sunny, that was great, but you've got to kiss her now. You know, Casablanca style."

"You're absolutely right," Carlos said, as he and Carolina shared another laugh and then kissed to some more applause.

*****

The distress of nearly losing Carolina made their reconciliation almost more blissful than their initial honeymoon. Carlos and Carolina remained lip-locked for the next six subway stations, by which point they had an entirely new audience on the train with them.

After the sixth station, none of the people riding the train with them had witnessed any of the drama leading up to the passionate kissing that Carlos and Carolina were still indulging. So when the two finally came up for air, they became acutely aware of the many people in

76

the world who are enviously, sadly, or bitterly not in love. They suddenly felt enveloped by some warm and mystical energy that protected them from the cold faces of the alienated passengers surrounding them. Yet they were still aware of these passengers who seemed to resent a couple that was so happily together in the presence of individuals so miserably alone.

As if in deference to the ever-present possibility that they too, at some point, might end up like the unhappy people standing around them, Carolina asked Carlos, in an irresistibly childlike way, "Do you think we'll always be in love, Carlos?"

"Yes," he replied, with the resounding certainty of scientific fact.

"But...But what about the cigarettes?" she asked, smiling at how absurd the whole issue now seemed.

"We'll work it out," he replied, with the same self-conscious smile. "In fact, I figured out a whole compromise while running after you."

"You did?"

"We'll go on a two year plan."

"What do you mean?"

"In two years, you won't be smoking cigarettes and I won't have mysophobia."

"Really?" she asked, her face full of wonder and hope.

"Yeah. I'll see a therapist. I can beat this thing if you can quit smoking."

"You can?"

And with that, Carlos smiled at Carolina, and gave her another kiss. He then removed the anti-germ glove from his right hand, inserted his index finger into his mouth just enough to wet the tip. Carolina watched in awe as Carlos turned around and drew a small heart shape on the dirty, dusty subway train window behind them, and then, in the middle, wrote "C+C."

She smiled dreamily, and the two kissed again as Carlos discreetly wiped his finger against his pants, trying to remove the dirt.

8. Evan's Bad Trip to the Hospital

From the moment Evan passed out to the moment he regained consciousness, his mind drifted like a lifesaver bobbing about on a stormy sea of surreal hallucinations. His strange and oneiric thoughts shifted about in this twilight zone of illusion with the same rhythm as the occasional bumps of the ambulance conveying him to the hospital.

First, he saw his parents sitting next to him in the ambulance. They looked very disappointed.

"Victoria, I told you we should have had another child. Just in case this one turned out to be a letdown."

"Oh stop it, Frank. He's a good boy…Aren't you, Evan? If you would have just listened to us. We told you never to bring girls to the house. This isn't a playground. This is a respectable Upper West Side apartment, and we can't have our neighbors getting the wrong idea about our family."

"Victoria, that's not the point. He shouldn't be starting with girls in the first place. Not before college anyway. Evan, high school is the time to focus on getting into college. Girls are a waste of time right now. Just like all of that creative writing you do. You have to focus your energies on more practical things. Focus on finding yourself a solid career path. Like accounting or law or medicine."

"Evan, you're father's right. Now look what's happened to you."

The ambulance slowed down as the cars in front of its whiny siren gradually cleared out.

"Frank, we have to get out of here because I've got some spaghetti on the stove."

Evan's parents moved to the back of the ambulance and his father opened the rear door for Evan's mother. She stepped out and his father followed with these parting words: "Sorry to leave you like this, son. But dinner will get cold. We'll come visit you in the hospital. Victoria, make sure you save some spaghetti for Evan. We'll bring it to him in the Tupperware."

As the ambulance began to move again, Evan saw himself surrounded in the back of the vehicle by all of the major characters of that disastrous night: Tina, Sayvyer, Alexandra, her giant Samoan boyfriend, and Brandy and Bonnie.

78

"Now do you see why I played you like that?" Tina said to him. She turned to the others and continued. "I have to screen guys carefully so that I don't take home anyone like this."

"Why didn't you just write down my phone number, Evan?" Sayvyer asked. "We could have been happily dating by now, instead of sharing this ambulance ride."

"Don't be so hard on him, guys. I'm really the one responsible for this mess," Alexandra began. "None of this would have happened to him, had I not dumped him...I'm so sorry for all of this, Evan. You're really a great guy, but I just wasn't feeling it...I needed a change..."

"You should have quit while you were ahead, Evan," her Samoan boyfriend added. "She said no more charity fucks. That means go home and jerk off. And if you call her again, what happened to you tonight will feel like a bubble bath massage."

"You shudda just paid fo' yo' blowjob, Sexy Evan," Brandy said. "It wudda been so much better fo' both of us...You think I liked bitin' down on that shit?...I kept tryin' tell you that you get what you pay fo', but you wouldn't listen..."

"Forget it, Brandy," Bonnie said, flipping through Evan's wallet. "In the end, we got paid with some fat-ass interest. Come on. Let's get back to the car. I see a payin' customer waiting for us."

Bonnie led the way, followed by Brandy. The others filed out of the back of the ambulance, until everyone but Alexandra had exited from the back of the vehicle. She gave him one last word of advice.

"Evan, you really should make up with your buddy Narc. You let a good friendship end over something stupid. And if he had been with you tonight, none of this would have happened."

She blew Evan a kiss goodbye and then left.

The vehicle remained empty for a few moments, until Delilah Nakova appeared, all alone, in front of Evan, with a bright halo around her.

Delilah Nakova was universally adored as a charming, intelligent, and stunning starlet. Born in Prague to a Czech father and an African-American mother, the exotic, green-eyed, mocha-skinned, five-foot-six actress was discovered at the age of thirteen in the luggage pick-up area of JFK airport, when the Nakova family had arrived in New York City for the first time that Delilah would call it home.

Given Delilah Nakova's fame, much of her biography was common knowledge. But after randomly running into her at a party about a year and a half earlier, Evan fell obsessively in love with the celebrity and researched virtually every publicly available fact about her.

In the ambulance, floating in front of Delilah Nakova's angelic face, a hologram-like film of her remarkable life story played for a few moments. Evan witnessed the moment when the female forty-something talent scout first found the teen actress while walking next to the Nakova family at JFK airport. The agent marveled at how charismatically and convincingly the little girl was imitating some of the rude airport personnel, and how easily Delilah slipped from Czech into perfect English. She followed Delilah and her parents to the taxi area, and then persuaded them to let her share their cab and pay for it. During the cab ride, she convinced Delilah's parents to entrust their daughter to her professional management and to enroll the young girl in acting classes.

The hologram then displayed a montage of memorable performances by Delilah Nakova, showing her evolution as an actress taking on ever more important, challenging, and high-profile roles. The mini biopic concluded with a televised interview that had particularly struck Evan, in which the eighteen-year-old A-list actress was asked about her acting plans during college.

"I've decided to cut back on my production schedule so that I can get the most out of my time at Brown…What good is fame and wealth without knowledge and perspective?"

The hologram flickered and then vanished. Delilah Nakova was still sitting in front of him, enveloped by the halo. She moved closer to Evan.

"I'm so sorry about everything that happened to you tonight, Evan. You really didn't deserve any of this."

"I know," Evan replied. "And now there's no way that you'll ever be with me…I'm even more below your level than I was before…"

"Don't say that, Evan," she replied warmly.

The ambulance doors in the back of the vehicle swung open and some of Delilah's college friends climbed in. "Come on, Delilah! We're late. What are you still doing talking to that loser?"

"Wait…Let me just make sure he's OK."

Evan was dumbfounded by the goodness of her soul.

"Evan, are you OK?" Delilah asked.

The image of Delilah dissolved into an indistinguishable blur, and then materialized again into the face of the female ambulance staffer next to him.

"Are you OK?" the staffer asked again.

"Yeah, I think so," Evan said, shaking his weary and confused head a little. "What a bad trip!"

"Nah. Traffic was nothing. If it was the middle of rush hour — that's a bad trip," she replied. "But we're here now. We'll wheelchair you over to the emergency room."

9. Narc

Narc, Evan's freshman-year roommate at Brown, was quite the "bad boy" compared to Evan. Yet even Narc could not have imagined what would one day happen to Evan in the back of an SUV. But because the two longtime friends stopped talking a few months before Evan's fang-filled-fellatio, Narc wouldn't find out the crazy details until the two reconciled, several months after the incident.

Narc embodied a complex composite of cultural contradictions. At home with his traditional Chinese parents, he was Yi Wang, the respectful, responsible, and disciplined eldest son who lent a hand around the house and helped his younger sisters with their homework. But outside of the home, his high school buddies nicknamed him "Narc" for always being the first to procure and consume whatever new narcotic constituted the dare du jour. At age fifteen, the exotically handsome and precociously smooth-talking Narc was also the first among them to lose his virginity.

While Narc was still a "model minority" whose grades consistently ranked among the top five percent of students in all of his classes, he had a wild edge to him that most of his fellow Asian classmates seemed to lack. He also felt physically different from them. At six-two, he always stood among the tallest students in his high school class, and he would grow another inch by graduation. He was in love with the NBA and hip-hop culture, and would much rather hang out with high school dropouts "from the 'hood" who could match him in hoops or rhymes, than discuss the physics problem set or history reading with the other high achievers in his honors classes. He had hundreds of NBA trivia and scorecard statistics memorized and would regularly debate the virtues of various players and teams with anyone who challenged his predictions about any particular game. Narc was also the only non-black member of the basketball gang with whom he regularly played ball on the court near the Newark, New Jersey home where he grew up. Indeed, the other members fondly dubbed him the "Chinese Niggah," which they soon shortened to "Chiggah." Narc embraced the term as a token of respect and acceptance from his basketball "brothas." Whenever the tall, gold-chain-sporting-gangsta athletes ran into him, they greeted him with a wide-armed, high-fiving, "'Sup Chiggah?" To which Narc would reply: "Jus bein' cool, yo."

"You catch that tight Nets game last night?" one of them might ask.

"It was off the hizzle for rizzle my nizzle," Narc would reply with wild gesticulations, to indicate that the game was truly something to behold.

"Word," they would say, in agreement, with a high five.

Yi Wang artfully lived what was essentially a double life. His parents knew nothing about "Narc," his gangsta/hip-hop friends, his recreational drug use, or his promiscuous lifestyle (by age seventeen he had already slept with eight females in the area, including two from his high school). They knew that Yi loved basketball, since he was one of the star players on his high school team, and they knew that he didn't have nearly as many Asian friends as they would have liked, but that was all they knew of his rebellious side. Likewise, Narc's friends knew almost nothing of Yi Wang, his desire to go to a top college primarily to please his parents, or the dutifully serious person he became while helping with his family's laundry business. Narc kept the laundry business secret to prevent his friends from showing up and meeting his parents or seeing how humble, soft-spoken, and respectful he was around his family.

As a result of his double life, Yi effectively spoke four languages. Whenever he was in the presence of family and other Cantonese speakers, he spoke Cantonese. If he was with family and non-Cantonese speakers, then he spoke polite and proper – even subdued – English. But on the street with his basketball buddies, or in his high school clique, Narc spoke a street English that combined hip-hop vernacular with copious profanity. If he was writing a term paper or an exam, or delivering some oral presentation to his class, then he switched to high academic English.

His friends did have the impression that Narc was strangely protective of his identity and his family. On one occasion, in the eleventh grade, one of Narc's high school friends learned of Narc's sexual exploits with a particularly attractive girl in their class, and jokingly exclaimed, "You wanged her?!"

"Don't disrespect family," Narc snapped back, with a seriousness that was not to be questioned. Narc was not at all amused by the pun, which he viewed as a sacrilegious defamation of his family heritage.

His sensitivity to the issue began at age twelve, when he was regularly harassed by some fifteen-year-old students in his junior high school. The four adolescents regularly addressed him with racial slurs and taunted him about his last name until he confronted them about it one day. Narc was on the school basketball court with two friends when three of the four members of the gang appeared and began their racist insults. Two of the three kids were bigger than Narc, so they were hardly deterred when Narc threw his basketball aside, walked straight up to the largest member of the group, and said, with a cool, angry voice, "That was the last time that you make fun of my name or my race." Emboldened by his bravado, they just sneered and shoved him.

Narc's two friends standing nearby were too afraid to jump into the fray but ran to notify a teacher. By the time an adult came to break up the fight, Narc was badly beaten up but the three older kids who had harassed him looked just as thrashed. The school principal suspended everyone, including Narc, for two days and called everyone's parents with a stern warning. But it was the last time that anyone ever maliciously mocked Narc about his race or his last name.

Narc's acceptance of the nickname "Chiggah" was the only exception to his sensitivity about race, and it wasn't until college that he would lighten up about the issue. Early in Narc's first year of college, in the fall of 1989, Evan accidentally caught a glimpse of Narc's eight inches of manhood and blurted out, "Wow!...Now I understand the origins of the Wang family name..."

"That's not funny," Narc snapped defensively at his roommate.

"Whoa, Narc. Don't take offense, man. You're representin' as they say. Next time I hear anyone say that Asians are small, I'll have them see you."

With that exchange, Narc became less protectively paranoid about his name, and started to take pride in the fact that he could personally undermine the stereotypical notions that people had of the Asian physique. When he and Evan went out together, he sometimes even referred to himself jokingly as a "Wangman," if he was doing a particularly good job of making Evan more appealing to the women they approached.

Nevertheless, he stuck with the nickname "Narc" throughout college and afterwards, after growing attached to it. Evan and Narc's other college buddies welcomed the name because it seemed short for "narcissist," which – in their view – aptly described the stylishly dressed, mirror-obsessed college student. When he spent too much time getting ready for a night out or admiring himself in the mirror, they would pronounce his name "Narse" to tease him about his vanity. Narc in turn nicknamed Evan "Libby" as shorthand for "Evan the libido" and – when Evan was particularly out of control – Narc would call him "Whiplash Libby" to describe the neck injuries Evan suffered any time an attractive female passed by.

Although Narc had the grades and test scores to enroll in Princeton, he chose the slightly less prestigious but more liberal Brown because it was farther from home and struck him as a less WASPy environment. It was a difficult choice for him, given how much his parents wanted him to stay local and go to a marginally more prestigious college, but he ultimately won them over with a promise to study pre-law or pre-med and get into a good graduate school.

While college provides a time and place for many people to rebel and explore their values, it had a certain moderating force on Narc, who had already done quite a bit of exploring and rebelling in high school. At Brown, Narc dabbled in drugs less often and became more intellectually and academically inclined (although he still regularly fantasized about the NBA and played for the college basketball team). In high school, hanging out with the gansta folks was a way to rebel against all of the myopic nerds of his class, but in college, he found that there were plenty of rebels among his intelligent classmates: students with crazy haircuts, whacky political views, unconventional post-college plans, and a drug record much worse than his. There were also plenty of Asians who broke the ethnic stereotype he so actively resisted in high school. Consequently, the need to rebel seemed less urgent, and being at Brown rather than Princeton was, in his mind, already a rebellion of sorts.

During college, Narc didn't entirely abandon his "Chiggah" status; he still checked in with his gangsta friends at home during summer and holiday visits to Newark, and he had one friend and teammate from the Brown basketball team who was culturally identical to them, but with a high school diploma and stellar SAT scores.

Narc became even more of a "playa" in college, as he discovered how easy it was for him to attract women with his good looks, his mastery of pop and hip-hop culture, his impressive performances on the college basketball team, and his reputation for being extraordinary in the sack. By his senior year, several happy customers fondly referred to Narc as "Big Everlast" after learning from firsthand experience that his body was truly proportional and that he could perform as well in bed as he did on the court. Narc's "scorecard," as he liked to call it, improved substantially in college. And Evan, who was equally addicted to and skilled at pursuing women, made for an excellent wingman.

One vice that Narc acquired in college was collecting and consuming pornography. This bad habit actually became a point of contention between him and Evan, who was – despite his oversexed libido – somewhat opposed to the practice, for a variety of idiosyncratic and ideological reasons. Evan had enrolled in a women's studies course thinking that he would meet enough women there to start a harem, but ironically ended up being influenced by certain feminist ideas – particularly once he started dating Zoe, a fellow student in the class.

Quite apart from any feminist objections, Evan also thought it was embarrassingly tacky to have a pornographic film playing on their living room television. He viewed masturbation as a personal activity, and considered pornography a mindless, masturbatory aid that should be viewed only privately, if at all. He was also somewhat squeamish about the possibility that someone – particularly Zoe – might come over unannounced and notice that there was a porno playing.

One time, when Evan was in the shower, Narc went out for some errands without turning off a porno that was playing in the living room. Narc had left the door unlocked and, a few minutes later, Zoe showed up unexpectedly early. When she loudly demanded an explanation from her shower-dripping date, Evan managed to convince her that he was doing preliminary research on a possible paper concerning the degradation of women in pornography.

Later that night, after she had left, Evan confronted Narc about the issue.

"What's the big deal, yo?" Narc said passively, from the couch. "Watchin' porn is part of my freedom." His feet were propped up on the coffee table as he followed a basketball game blasting away on their TV. "It's something I could never do at home. And the shit is cool. The porn professionals are smokin'."

Narc looked over at Evan, who was sitting in the comfortable beanbag chair notorious for prompting armchair discussions and wildly speculative theories in anyone who sat in it.

"How can you call them professionals?" Evan objected. "They're glorified prostitutes for God's sake. And it's totally demeaning to women, this porn crap."

"If it's so demeaning to women, why do you watch it?" Narc asked, looking back at the game.

"Only because you have that shit playing in the living room, so it's hard not to notice it. But I would never go out buy a porn flick. And if you'd stop leaving those tapes lying around the house I swear to God I'd never plug one into the VCR."

"Where's your self control, you big hypocrite?" Narc asked derisively but lightheartedly.

"Look, I'm a little curious, but I'll admit that it's wrong, and I'm ready to swear off porn entirely if you'll just help me to implement the decision."

"I can't believe this sanctimonious bullshit you're tryin' to feed me! You don't think you're demeaning women every time you go out and try to get laid?"

"That's totally different."

"Why?"

"Because there I have to deal with women as people, not sex objects."

"You are so full of it, Evan! You're dealing with them as people only so that you can ultimately deal with them as sex objects."

"No. I'm dealing with them as people only so that we can deal with each other as sex objects. It's a mutual exploitation. Whereas with porn you're just exploiting them."

"They're exploiting my fuckin' pocketbook, Evan! They're profiting from my masturbation, so it's a mutual exploitation. And it's a free market system. They don't have to become porn stars. Clearly, they like it on some level, or maybe the money makes it worth their while. But they freely chose that shit. Just like if you charm some babe into bed, she freely chose to go there with you."

Evan got up from the beanbag chair and stood up, as if to make his closing argument.

"Look, even if you can come up with some convoluted capitalist justification for pornography, there's no denying that it reduces women to their sexual anatomy...Imagine if you discovered that your mom or your sisters were in a porn!"

What started as a casual theoretical debate suddenly hit a raw nerve in Narc. He jumped to his feet, walked over to Evan and moved right up into his face, which was two inches below his, and said, "Don't you ever bring my family into a conversation like this." Narc looked as if at any moment he might use his lean and muscular arms to give Evan a facelift.

"Whoa. Whoa. Calm down, man," Evan said, backing up a little.

"My family has nothing to do with this, OK?"

"Of course not. Of course not. Bad example. I think we need a beer for this conversation," Evan said, backing away from Narc and moving towards the kitchen. "Let's take my family," he continued, pulling a six-pack out of the fridge. "Imagine if you discovered that my sister — "

"Take families out of this, OK?" Narc replied, this time less stridently.

In Narc's mind, family was sacred and not to be combined with the profane, the sexual, or the morally dubious. As far as Narc was concerned, no man could ever go near his sisters unless he was prepared to be the most loyal, faithful, loving, caring, and providing husband of the best fairy tales he had ever heard. And, as far as he was concerned, his parents had had sex only three times — once to create him, and two more times to create his younger sisters.

While Narc's parents seemed to him almost mechanically assiduous and asexual, particularly when it came to their laundry business or keeping the house in order, they were very much in love with each other. But their absolute devotion to each other and to their children expressed itself entirely in deeds and almost never in words or physical gestures. Only on a few, exceptionally rare occasions had Narc actually seen his parents become physically affectionate with one another.

When Narc's youngest sister turned ten, and he was a sixteen-year-old who had more than proven himself capable of managing things in the house, his parents instituted a rule that they followed religiously ever since: after 11 p.m., their bedroom door was locked and they were not to be disturbed unless there was a bona fide emergency in the house. Narc always assumed that this was just their private time to sort out family issues, discuss private matters, and spend time alone, without the pressures of their children. It was unthinkable to Narc that anything sexual took place after 11 p.m. in their bedroom. And so Narc developed an idealized, consecrated sense of family as an impregnable, asexual unit of trust and support.

Evan had only an intuitive inkling of Narc's complex feelings about family, but he realized that he needed to try a different tack if he was going to get anywhere with Narc on the pornography issue. Once they had each downed two beers, Evan tried a direct appeal to self-interest.

"Narc, the real bottom line is that you should drop porn because it's bad for your scorecard."

"How so?" Narc asked, in amused skepticism.

"Because it'll make you develop totally unrealistic expectations about the women you can have, what it takes to seduce them, and what they'll be willing to do with you sexually."

"Why do you say that?"

"It'll destroy your pick up skills…After watching enough porn flicks you'll soon forget that 'bend over' isn't a good opening line."

"That's ridiculous," Narc protested. "It's just a friggin' movie."

"Yeah, but movies have a subtle and powerful influence on the mind. After enough porn exposure, you'll think that you can go in for a doctor's appointment, tell the hot doctor you want a complete physical examination and twenty seconds later start fucking her and her hot assistant in the patient room."

"You've gotta drop that women's studies class, Evan."

"It has nothing to do with that, Narc. I'm telling you, I've thought about these issues on my own before."

"Then whassup' wit' you reading *Playboy Magazine* and those other rags if it ain't cool for me to watch porn?" Narc said, slipping playfully into ghetto mode.

"The magazines I look at are totally different. They just celebrate the esthetics of a woman's body – not its subjugation to a man's sexual will."

"I'm not seein' the difference, yo."

"Magazines like *Playboy* show the art of a woman's body in a classy and artistic way. It's art. Porn flicks are just plain obscene. There's no artistry whatsoever. No plot. No originality. Just women being fucked. And the camera angles are all from the male perspective, which only confirms that porn is really just another form of male domination."

"Oh and there's no male domination when the male photographer tells the woman how to pose for the males like you reading *Playboy*?"

"That's totally different."

"Evan, you're feeding me so much bullshit, that I'm thinking you're the one who should go to law school. Forget that computer programming crap."

"I'm serious. The magazines I look at never portray sex itself. Only beautiful women. There's a big difference there."

"Evan, what face exercises do you do?" Narc asked, in a calm, matter-of-fact manner.

"What do you mean?" Evan replied, confused.

"You know, those face muscle exercises that you do each night in front of the mirror…"

"What are you talking about?"

"You know, the ones that enable you to spout bullshit like this with a straight face."

"I'm being totally honest and serious, Narc."

There was no changing Narc's mind about porn. Although Evan did manage to win a compromise out of him: there would be no porn tapes lying around the house, and there would be no pornography playing in the living room unless Narc was alone in the house and Evan was expected to be away for at least six hours.

Despite Narc's good intentions at honoring their agreement, there were a few more accidents. Evan was convinced that these events contributed to the demise of his brief relationship with Zoe.

"Don't blame that shit on me, yo!" Narc said, after Evan suggested that his porn habit was to blame. "You know damn well she dumped yo' ass because of that Whiplash Libby fiasco two days ago."

Narc was referring to an incident in which Evan was supposed to pick up Zoe at the library. Evan was about fifteen minutes late so Zoe impatiently spotted him approaching and began walking towards him. He hadn't yet seen her since he was looking to the side while walking. A few moments later, when Zoe was about thirty feet away from Evan, she tried to wave to him. But Evan was too busy blatantly checking out a gorgeous girl in spandex jogging by, just as he was crossing the bike path. Whiplash Libby's diverted attention caused an oncoming cyclist to have a minor accident and set Zoe off into a rage.

"Look, it didn't help that she kept stumbling across porn when she came over. And maybe all of that porn is what makes me check out other women so much! It gets me all horny," Evan replied.

"Evan, did you ever consider that you were just born horny? I can't believe the kind of bullshit you try to feed me. You should really look into farming. Or lawyering. But not computer programming."

*****

90

Evan ultimately decided against being Narc's roommate beyond their first year of college. Despite their various differences, however, the two remained close friends throughout college, as both wingmen and basketball partners.

Towards the end of their senior year in college, Narc trounced Evan on the basketball court in the final and heavily wagered match of their "nine-game, one-on-one playoffs." The two left the outdoor court, toweling off their sweat and catching their breath. Narc continued dribbling the ball as they headed home.

"You know in college you've had an unfair advantage, since you were on the team," Evan began, explaining his three-six defeat. "But I really see this is as an ongoing competition. Like with any top team. You don't just look at one season. You look at their performance over many seasons."

"Are you trying to challenge me even as you lick your wounds?" Narc asked.

"I'm just saying that next year, when you're studying your ass off at Columbia Law School, you're going to be badly out of practice. Whereas I'll be improving my game every weekend. So then we'll see what's what."

"Aight. You on, mo fo'," Narc said, breaking into an elaborate dribble routine, as if to accept the challenge with all the more bravado. But just as he began, he caught a glimpse of a college student in a white tennis skirt, with a racket slung over her back, riding past them on a bicycle. Narc lost control of the ball, which bounced off in another direction. The two friends stopped, frozen in their tracks.

"Did you see that?" Evan asked, in a daze.

"In-fuckin-credible," Narc replied.

Once they recovered enough to resume their walk, Narc ran over and picked up the stray ball. He began dribbling it again, slowly. As they continued their walk, a hypothetical problem occurred to Evan that required some consultation with Narc.

"Now I know this is a sensitive topic with you," he began, "but if you had to choose between chasing tail and chasing balls, which would you take?"

"You can't prejudice the question by phrasing it in a homosexual way like that: tail versus balls. You gotta ask it as tail versus hoops."

"OK. Fine. Tail versus hoops. Like if that girl on the bike were with you on sports Sunday and she wanted to get it on, but you had the Nets playing the Knicks, what would you do?"

"That's a really tough question…You're saying that there's no way that she'll wait a few hours?"

"She wants to get it on right now. I mean, she's hot and horny and ready to go, and if she has to wait a few hours, she'll be looking elsewhere…"

"That's a really fucked up situation."

"But you have a VCR. You could always record the game and watch it afterwards."

"Now why isn't there a VCR trick like that with women? Why can't we just record that horny state of mind and play it after the game?"

"That would be nice. But the reality is that it's now or never with this babe."

"But you know that watching the game just isn't the same if it ain't live…"

Evan refused to modify the hypothetical.

"I can't watch no recorded Net-Knicks game, yo! That's just not right. I gotta be there when it's happening. You can't be askin' me unfair questions like that, bro…What would you do?"

"I'm not like you when it comes to this question."

"Are you saying that you would rather go for the babe and watch a taped version of the game later?" Narc asked, in disbelief.

"I wouldn't hesitate for a second. Tail trumps everything else for me. Even hoops."

"I'm not saying it's not a really close fuckin' call. I'm just illin' about the fact that there has to be this conflict…I mean, what about some kinda compromise solution?"

"Like what?"

"Like she blows me while I watch the game."

"I guess that could work," Evan replied reflectively, as if he hadn't thought about the possibility.

They walked for a moment in silence, which gave Evan the opportunity to consider the compromise solution some more.

"But she'd probably want more afterwards," he said, suddenly breaking the silence.

"Well that would have to wait."

"I think you might lose her then. She could get really pissed off about that scenario."

"Evan, I don't like these impossible dilemmas you come up with. There just aren't really any acceptable answers to them. Women just need to understand that some things are sacred and not to be disturbed."

"You're crazy, Narc. It really is a shame that you're not in the NBA."

"Why do you think I dream about it all the time? It's not just that those guys get whatever smokin' hot ladies they want. They also get smokin' hot ladies who will watch the NBA games with them, and have even more respect for those games than the players do."

"And those guys make serious coin."

"And they don't have to sit through no three fuckin' years of law school. They got the life. No question."

"Do you think anyone has a better scorecard than the NBA stars?"

"Porn stars."

"You and your crazy porn star fantasies," Evan said, shaking his head in amused disapproval.

"There are no male Asian-American porn stars out there," Narc noted. "I could be the first…"

"So why don't you do that, instead of law school?" Evan dared.

"If I knew for sure that my family would never find out, I might actually have the balls to go for it. But I can't. It's juris doctor time for this Wang. Gotta represent the family, yo."

10. Trevor

Throughout his three dismal years at Columbia Law School, Narc struggled with the temptation to drop out and pursue the unconventional careers linked to his two recurring fantasies: trying out for the NBA and becoming a porn star. The only force that kept Narc in graduate school until commencement was his familial superego: his parents would absolutely delight in his graduation, and they would suffer epic, multi-generational shame if he, instead, become a failed NBA wannabe, or – even worse – a porn star.

Narc felt very out of place in law school, even though he performed well in his classes and had at least one thing in common with most of his classmates: he was there because he didn't know what else to do with his life. During orientation, when everyone appeared to hail from diverse life experiences with varied perspectives and goals, Narc thought he might actually befriend some interesting people. But within the first two months, virtually all of his classmates transformed into obsessive-compulsive competitors who brownnosed even the most despised professors in hopes of better grades or recommendations. Classmates who once seemed so intriguingly different began sounding tediously similar. His fellow students were now interested in discussing only the facts and holdings of legal cases, the legal doctrines likely to be tested during finals, the law professors revered or hated, the law firms recruiting on campus, the smart or dumb things said by other law students, and the various opportunities – like the law review and Moot Court competitions – to improve one's standing in the class hierarchy. Despite all of the frenzied peer pressure from high school-style cliques, Narc just couldn't get himself to care about the law school experience, or any of the people sharing it with him. He was there just to please his parents, collect his diploma, and move on.

Consequently, Narc spent as little time as possible among his classmates, and rarely attended classes after his first semester. He found much greater satisfaction volunteering as a tutor and older brother to underprivileged youth in the neighboring Harlem area. He also spent three days out of every week going back to New Jersey to help his parents with their laundry business, chip in with household chores, and offer whatever big brother help his younger sisters needed.

Contrary to Evan's bold predictions, Narc's basketball game actually improved during his time in law school, since Narc never let school pressures interfere with regular practice. It was also on the basketball court where Narc met Trevor Bediako, his only close friend from law school and a formidable hoops rival.

Trevor, like Narc, was not particularly fond of law school or most of the people he met there, but stayed happy with the help of basketball and the Manhattan nightlife. Those shared pleasures – in the stiflingly narrow and conservative law school environment – were enough to bond the two men, despite their considerable differences.

At six feet seven inches, Trevor was a human skyscraper. Narc enviously nicknamed him "Tower." Trevor's dark African complexion, handsome physiognomy, English accent, and immense stature gave him an almost mesmerizing presence, despite his soft-spoken style.

Born in London to parents who had emigrated from Ghana, Trevor was raised with a European mentality and a simultaneous admiration for and suspicion of American culture. Even in the heat of a basketball game, Trevor spoke like a British aristocrat, with flawless grammar and articulation, true to his undergraduate education in history at Oxford. He was marked by gentlemanly mannerisms, reserved speech, and – by comparison to Narc – Puritan sexual mores. Trevor's impeccable grooming always included perfectly cut nails, three sprays of cologne, meticulously removed facial and scalp hair, and exceptionally neat and stylish attire. His shiny clean scalp accentuated his handsome looks and the strong, symmetrical shape of his head.

Trevor's parents had spent ten years slowly building what would become a lucrative family business, importing fine crafts, rare masks, and high-end paintings from Africa. Their financial success enabled them to give their three children a refined upbringing that was far more privileged and comfortable than any they had ever enjoyed. Their humble beginnings, however, ensured that Trevor and his younger brother and sister were each made to earn any spending money from the age of ten, and were all regularly reminded of the multitudes living in far less fortunate circumstances.

Despite his polite and gentle graces, Trevor secretly loathed the superficiality often required by his polished upbringing. His favorite shirt for working out or playing ball said simply, "Boycott small talk." Indeed, making meaningless chitchat was, for Trevor, the most indigestible ingredient of the urbane character he was raised to have.

Narc discovered this fact about his friend when Trevor announced one day that he was never going to go on another blind date.

"Was she nasty-lookin'?" Narc ventured.

"No. She was actually a fairly fit bird," Trevor replied. "But we had absolutely nothing in common. So we were forced to sit there, over a two-hour dinner, pretending to be interested in each other so that the people who set us up with the best of intentions wouldn't feel slighted. And there's nothing more torturous for me than having to make small talk for two hours."

"Couldn't you just talk about yourself for two hours?"

"The only thing more tiresomely banal on a first date than exchanging polite niceties is recapitulating the essential facts of my life, with which I am already far too familiar and which I find utterly boring to recount, after so many years of repeating the story."

"What about current events? Couldn't you talk about the news or something?"

"That's just the problem. Politeness requires avoiding any topic that people actually care about, such as politics and religion, unless of course the two people are of like minds on the religious or political issue at hand."

"Well, were you?"

"Not at all. She comes from a family of radical communists who vehemently deny God's existence, so there was no way to discuss politics or religion without spoiling the pleasant dinner ambiance."

"What about pop culture?"

"We have completely different tastes. She fancies folk music and everything else that came out of the sixties and seventies. And she thinks of hip-hop only as a form of social protest rather than an important innovation in music. She even suggested that I enjoy classical music only because I was raised as a member of the bourgeois."

"What about the weather?"

"That's what we were left with for eighty percent of the dinner. Do you have any idea how bloody painful it is for me to spend even a second comparing the climate of New York with that of London?"

"But the weather is the greatest topic out there, yo!"

"You can't be serious."

"Can you find any other topic that affects everyone, that everyone can relate to, and that everyone has something to say about?" Narc persisted, more out of amusement than conviction.

"The weather doesn't affect me in any way that is significant enough to justify the breath involved in speaking about it. I find it difficult to relate to people who enjoy discussing the utterly uninteresting and unchangeable facts of life. And I have absolutely nothing to say about those facts," Trevor replied urgently, as if he were finally given the chance to correct a tragic mistake being committed every day all over the world.

Narc generally saw Trevor as an assemblage of oddly comical contradictions. Trevor liked hip-hop music, but always felt uncomfortable repeating the often racy lyrics. He appreciated the esthetics of women but would never get graphic in describing what precisely he admired about a particular female. Trevor relished the challenge of trying to attract a woman's attention, but – unlike Narc – he always seemed too shy or dignified to make the first move. And while Narc could very nonchalantly describe how exactly he had managed to "score" with a particular female and what they did together, Trevor — to Narc's considerable frustration — always remained fairly tight-lipped about his exploits, as if additional disclosure to anyone might make him less chaste and proper.

Nevertheless, the twenty-three-year-olds worked well together as wingmen in a club. Trevor's redwood perspective in any crowd enabled him quickly to find the part of the club with the greatest potential "play." He would then nudge Narc, raise his eyebrows with a boyish enthusiasm, and Narc would know that it was time to follow the Tower radar. Once they were within speaking distance of the females in question, the women would ordinarily make some joke amongst themselves about Trevor's remarkable height, at which point Narc would jump into the conversation with something like, "If you think he looks different, wait until you hear him speak!" This line worked like magic, making the women naturally curious to hear Trevor speak. Trevor would always refuse initially, by bashfully shaking his head, but eventually Narc would say something that would get Trevor speaking. And as soon as the women heard Trevor's deep voice and disarmingly suave and sophisticated British style of speaking, they became even more intrigued by the pair of tall, exotically handsome men. Narc particularly enjoyed the moment when he and Trevor were asked the inevitable "What do you do?" question, because the answer they gave would only further impress the women, making Narc temporarily value the prestigious education he ordinarily dismissed.

Thanks to his dapper dress, charmingly debonair manner, and strikingly good looks, Trevor had no difficulty attracting women. But his Puritan superego, particular esthetic standards, and impossible height requirements together restricted his "cumulative scorecard" to just a handful of women. Trevor was happy to flirt with any attractive woman who showed an interest in him, but, for a variety of practical and psychological reasons, Trevor would almost never consider dating her – particularly if she was under six feet tall.

"Don't you realize how much that limits your game?" Narc remarked, when he first learned of Trevor's requirement over a dinner of ramen soup at Tome, a Japanese restaurant near the Columbia University campus.

"I know. It's a bloody curse, being six-seven," Trevor explained, in his British accent. "But what's a man of my height to do?"

"Learn to stoop."

"You're expecting me to stoop down to your level?" Trevor quipped. "You know my upbringing wouldn't permit that!"

"I'm not talking about upbringing, Trevor. I'm talking about downbringing. To a normal female height. For God's sake, the average American woman is about five-five. If you expect at least seven more inches, you're basically limited to the female basketball players in this country."

"And what would be so tragic about that? At least I'd have one more thing in common with the lady."

The waiter took away their bowls and left them the check.

"But I'm not even talkin' about a serious girlfriend here, yo. What about having a short fling? Literally."

"You know I don't believe in those, Narc."

"All right, how about a long fling with a short woman? Just to see if you might like it."

"Narc, you telling me to consider women under six feet is like me telling you to consider women under five-eight." Trevor knew that Narc, at six-three, preferred women who were between five-nine and six feet.

"That's bullshit, Trevor."

"It's not bollocks at all. Why should seven inches mean any more to you than to me?"

"Trevor, seven inches shorter represents a much larger percentage decrease for me than it does for you."

"I have to concede that that's a legitimate rebuttal."

Trevor checked the bill and put his ten-dollar share on the table.

"Shouldn't you try going below six feet at least once?" Narc insisted, putting down his ten dollars on top of Trevor's.

"But I have, Narc. I dated one woman who was substantially below six feet tall and it was bloody awful. My flatmate at Oxford had introduced me to her. And she was a really fit bird, so I overlooked the fact that she was only five-seven. But dating her was an unmitigated calamity."

"What was so bad about it?"

"First of all, she was one of these marathon kisser types, who loved kissing in public, and – "

"I thought you hate PDA."

"I do. But she bloody loved it. She would try to kiss me in the bloody loo if it were a unisex. And after her five-minute kisses I'd start to get these neck cramps, especially if I had just finished a few hours of fitness and it was parky weather out."

The two put their winter coats on and headed out of the restaurant.

"What the hell is 'parky?'"

"That's British slang for cold. Like this bloody weather we've got now," he said, as they ventured into the snowy New York winter outside.

"Please, Trevor. Don't use anything but Oxford English around me," Narc said mockingly.

"I try to, but on occasion you cause me to slip into more vernacular speech because of your own fondness for informal colloquialisms. Anyway, besides the physical discomfort of kissing her, it was also a bit embarrassing to be with someone who looked so much shorter than me."

"That can definitely look funny."

"Funny? She was a foot shorter than me and it looked completely awkward. At times, I even feared that others seeing us from afar might think that I was engaged in some sort of illicit relation with a minor."

"You crack me up, Trevor."

"What's so funny about that?"

"Everything about you. How you think, how you speak. You're a total character, bro."

"I'd thank you for your remarks if I thought that I could take them as a compliment."

"See what I mean? You're the only guy on the whole fucking planet who would say something like that. Which is why I love you!"

And in a rare moment of spontaneous fraternal affection, Narc effusively threw a bear hug around his giant friend's chest. Trevor fended him off in squeamish amusement, saying, "Stop that now!" Trying to wrest Narc off his body as they both stumbled into a pile of snow, Trevor added, "Even close friends should avoid the appearance of homosexual affinities between them." The comment made Narc laugh too hard to maintain his grip, and he eventually fell off.

Trying to resume a serious conversation, as they brushed the snow off themselves, Trevor continued: "It isn't as though I didn't make a good faith effort to make the relationship succeed. We dated for a respectable six months."

"So you shagged her?" Narc asked playfully, in a feigned British accent. He loved watching Trevor get embarrassed at a pointed question about his sexual history.

"No comment," Trevor replied, unmoved. He had grown accustomed to Narc's games.

"I'm just trying to see whether height matters for you in bed."

"I will say this much: height is a factor whose importance can surface in a variety of areas in life."

Narc knew that that was Trevor's way of saying that height does, in fact, affect sexual compatibility.

But the gentlemanly giant was also saying much more. He really wanted someone who could relate to the psychology of being a physical misfit in a world designed for shorter people. He preferred a person who understood what it's like always to be the tallest one in the group. He wanted someone who could relate to the daily problems he had with things that most people take for granted, like finding sufficiently large clothes or fitting into spaces made for a smaller populace – from subway trains and elevators to taxis and planes.

11. Heeb Gets Hurt in DC

Five years after shopping for an apartment and losing his virginity in a marble kitchen, Lucky Chucky was defying every statistic about the longevity of jobs, flats, and mates in New York City. Not only was he living in the same apartment with the same woman and working at the same company, he was now happily married to Carolina and serving as the number two executive officer of her company.

Heeb, of course, was not so lucky. Everyone he met in DC was a political lobbyist, a political consultant, a political lawyer, a political journalist, a political pundit, a political staff member, or just plain political. The math and science geek who never quite found his crowd in the intellectually more diverse city of Boston found it all the more difficult to find his place in DC – particularly without Carlos around. Heeb made good money in what he considered a prestigious job, but he had a hard time finding women in DC who were impressed by the title "Deputy Chief Actuary."

He got along well enough with his colleagues, and with Jerry, the CEO of the company, who bore an uncanny resemblance to Heeb. Both men were five-seven and roughly 170 pounds, with fleshy figures, and a similar physiognomy. Thus, they appeared strikingly similar – except for the fact that Jerry still had all of his hair. Jerry was five years Heeb's senior, but – much to Heeb's chagrin – people who thought the two were brothers always assumed that Heeb was the older sibling. Eventually, Heeb learned to deliver his sarcastic clarification in increasingly good-humored form: "No, he's older and he's not my brother. But I donated my hair for his toupee so that he'd give me the job."

Heeb worked long hours and many weekends supervising complex group projects and preparing for the seemingly interminable series of stressful actuary exams that were a part of his profession. But he earned good money and enjoyed a relatively flexible schedule that enabled him to get away for a four-day weekend every month or so. For his first two years after college, he alternated these weekend trips between family visits to Philadelphia; Boston trips to see Titus, with whom he regularly spoke on the phone; and stays in New York City, where he would visit Carlos.

When Heeb first met Carolina (about six months into her relationship with Carlos), he was flabbergasted by her beauty and brains, and how Carlos had ended up with her so fortuitously.

"You see why I nicknamed him 'Lucky Chucky?'" he asked her.

"I used to hate that name," Carlos chimed in.

"Until the day you met her, right? Then you finally came to accept your Lucky Chuckyness."

"Chucky?" Carolina repeated skeptically. "I think it sounds awful."

"But don't you think 'Lucky Chucky' sounds better than 'Lucky Carlos?'" Heeb ventured.

"Maybe," she conceded. "But Carolina Carlos sounds even better. And it's not because I prefer alliteration to rhyme."

"She's got a point there, Heeb. I didn't get lucky. I got Carolina."

"I guess so."

Fortunately for Heeb, when Carolina first met her husband's former college roommate, she correctly concluded that there wasn't a safer man with whom to let Carlos go out without her. And she was happy to use the time alone to work on her dissertation or catch up with her girlfriends. So for Heeb it was just like the good old days – except with a much bigger playground at their disposal. Carlos, who was hopelessly in love with his wife and not at all interested in meeting any other women, was still the perfect wingman for Heeb. Just as in college, Carlos never competed with Heeb for the many women who gravitated towards the Latin heartthrob. Instead, he always directed them to Heeb, whom he would praise and build up as effusively and charmingly as ever.

At the start of his third year in DC, Sammy met a cute, twenty-four-year-old, Japanese exchange student at Georgetown, studying international relations. At five-three, her petite figure, tiny porcelain hands, and light steps seemed to complement her culturally bred habits of profuse politeness. When she laughed, her face lit up and she quickly covered her mouth, as if to quell any improperly excessive mirth. She had long dark hair extending to her mid-back, and eight tiny freckles splashed about her small nose and soft, narrow cheeks.

Her name was Yumi, which Heeb affectionately mispronounced as "Yummy." When they first met, her English wasn't good enough for her to catch the pun or to bother trying to correct what she thought was his poor pronunciation of her name. She was by far the prettiest female Sammy had ever dated and he couldn't quite explain why she had taken any significant interest in him. The real reason was a fairly simple one: timing. Heeb had serendipitously sat next to her on the flight from New York to DC, and – upon arriving in DC – they shared a cab from the airport. So Yumi's first day in the U.S. consisted of several hours of continuous conversation with a man who ended up paying for her cab, helping her with her three enormous suitcases, translating her broken English into something that the housing and university officials could understand, and generally assisting her with settling in. He gave her his phone number and encouraged her to call him whenever she needed any help, which she regularly did. He was all too happy to drive twenty minutes at midnight to help her locate a drug store that was still open.

Two weeks into her stay, Yumi had found her prince charming and his name was Sammy Laffowitz. And after a month of dating her, Sammy finally ended his eighteen months of solo pleasure (his last climax that wasn't self-induced had been in New York City, when Chucky brought out Heeb's Kojak). It was also the first time in his life that Heeb had slept with an Asian. He was helplessly attracted to her and enthralled by the quality and frequency of their sex together. And because she appeared to be falling for him as well, he would occasionally indulge the thought that he might actually retire from being a bachelor, regardless of what his family might think or how many additional women he had always assumed he would date before settling down.

Yumi was also the most sensual person Heeb had ever intimately known, and she immensely enjoyed introducing him to a fetish that he would virtually obsess over forever after: toe arousal. Yumi so masterfully employed a technique of licking and sucking Heeb's toes that he became dizzy with pleasure and the desire to climax through his toe tips.

After a few months of such terrific touching and a genuinely interesting and loving companionship, Sammy began to dismiss his initial feelings for Yumi as mere infatuation, and gradually came to acknowledge that he had fallen in love for the first time in his life. He respected her intelligence and was drawn to her person. He saw Yumi as an irresistibly adorable woman who really understood him, despite the charming Japanese idiosyncrasies that culturally separated her from him but that Heeb had come to cherish. He became so convinced that Yumi brought out the best in him that he was prepared to break all family rules and prior plans, in order to stay with her. Within four months,

Yumi moved into Sammy's spacious two-bedroom apartment and Sammy refused to accept any rent money from her.

She had tremendous leverage with Heeb — particularly as her English improved — because he was absolutely smitten by her, and spared no effort or expense to please her. Early in their relationship, he took great pleasure in helping her with all of the logistical and practical problems that she faced as a foreigner with broken English visiting the U.S. for the first time. He enthusiastically assisted her with any issue that she brought to his attention or he anticipated in advance. She was also devoted to him, and would happily cook Japanese meals for him, take him shopping for more stylish clothes, teach him how to dance to hip-hop music, and humor his excitement about some obscure statistical innovation he had proudly devised for a work-related project.

Yumi was a gifted and assiduous student of the English language. By her tenth month in DC, her English was good enough to sustain personal and introspective discussions that were some of the most profound and satisfying that Heeb had ever had with a female. His relationship with Yumi made everything about DC — and life in general — seem infinitely better, and this worried Heeb on occasion. A latent concern lingered in his mind: how could a single person exert so much influence on his overall wellbeing? His gut told him that he was too vulnerable.

And his instincts were right. Heeb made the mistake of bringing Yumi to his company's annual banquet ball. It was the first time that he had even opted to attend the black tie gala, and he was so proud to be involved with a woman like Yumi, and she had become such an integral part of his life, that he couldn't imagine going without her.

Yumi was all too honored to be invited. She had always been intrigued by his firm — given its impressive international stature and scope (including an office in Tokyo) — and she was curious to meet Jerry, the CEO mentioned in so many of Heeb's funny work anecdotes. Excited to dress up for the occasion, Yumi wore a shoulderless, velvet crimson gown that seductively hugged her petite figure and (unbeknownst to her) made Heeb feel strangely inadequate at the event — as if he wasn't worthy of such an attractive girlfriend.

The night commenced uneventfully, with Sammy making the rounds and saying all of the hellos that he politically needed to say to solidify or improve his ties with all of the executives above him. By his side, conducting parallel conversations, Yumi learned that Heeb's colleagues all considered Jerry to be a witty, brilliant, and visionary man. She also learned that he had recently gone through a bad divorce.

A little later, Jerry walked in fashionably late with Nadine, a former swimsuit model. Virtually everyone present regarded her as the sexiest female of the night, but Jerry was immediately taken by Yumi – a fact that made her feel like the star of the evening. Sammy, however, was too busy politicking to discern the fast evolving energy between his girlfriend and his boss. When he finally noticed that Yumi was talking to Jerry, he began to walk towards them. But before he could get any closer, Nadine approached Sammy and chatted him up for another fifteen minutes.

Yumi caught a suspicious look from Sammy and tried to end her conversation with Jerry. "I should probably get back to Sammy now," she said. "But I'm glad that I got to meet you, after hearing so much about you."

"What you've heard is all lies! I'm a ruthless, capitalist taskmaster looking for more slaves," he replied playfully.

"So you like to play master and servant?" Yumi asked, amused.

"In the Tokyo office I have to play servant because no one understands my commands. But here I usually play master."

"I don't understand," Yumi replied mischievously.

"So the Japanese beauty banters with me for a little role reversal," Jerry remarked. "I'm intrigued."

"Intrigue is good," she replied, with a slight blush, before bowing goodbye and walking over to Heeb.

After the gala, all of Heeb's insecurities blew up into a huge fight.

"What the hell were you doing flirting with my boss?"

"I wasn't flirting."

"The flirting was all over your face. And his."

"Don't be so jealous, Sammy. We were just talking. He was there with a date."

"She was an escort. No other kind of woman would talk with me for so long while her so-called date spends all night flirting with you."

"And why were you talking to her for so long if you were getting so jealous? Maybe I'm the one who should be jealous."

"Jealous of what? Did you see us exchange information the way you and Jerry did?"

"He wanted to stay in touch. I didn't want to be rude. Especially since he's your boss."

"You could have just said that the two of you would get in touch through me...You obviously like him."

"You're just being jealous."

"You like him because he's more successful, more powerful, and more hairful."

The hair bit was the most painful part of all for Heeb, because it was the one difference that immediately and dramatically distinguished two men who otherwise bore an uncanny resemblance. It was as if Jerry had been marked "genetically superior" on the top of his scalp.

Unfortunately for Heeb, things just weren't the same after that night. A week later, Yumi decided that she wanted to move out of his apartment and end her eleven-month relationship with him. A few weeks later, Heeb learned from a co-worker that she had moved in with Jerry.

Heeb was crestfallen.

He sought solace with an abrupt trip to Boston, where he hoped that Titus would help put things into perspective. Initially, Heeb didn't mention the Yumi situation, hoping that his close and familiar routine with Titus might get his mind off her for a while. As usual, Heeb helped Titus with all of the various tasks that were difficult for the blind, like dealing with accumulated letters and bills that didn't arrive in Braille, and Titus quizzed Heeb to see how much of his Hebrew he had forgotten since their last visit. But Sammy couldn't snap out of his funk, and he finally interrupted the Hebrew quiz with a desperate question: "Titus, have you ever had your heart broken?"

"Oh, son. How could you ask a man who used to play the blues a question like that?"

"How long does it take to go away?"

"A broken heart?"

"Yeah."

"There's no precise formula, Sammy."

"Just give me an estimate."

"A good rule of thumb is at least half the time that you were in love. Or twice the time. It all just depends."

"I was afraid you'd say that."

Sammy ended up staying with Titus for a few months, after deciding to quit his job. There was no way he could go back to his workplace and see Jerry again. The thought of seeing either him or Yumi made him feel homicidal or suicidal, depending on his mood.

During his time in Boston, he purposely avoided his alma mater, even though he had always stopped there for a visit during his previous trips to the Boston area. Now it felt too melancholy to roam a campus where he was just a sentimental visitor peering into an idyllic world where he obviously no longer belonged – a world that had passed from him to the next generation of students.

Fortunately, Heeb had saved plenty of money from his well-paying former job, and decided that he was in no rush to jump back into the working world. After three months in Boston, Sammy returned to DC, broke his lease, packed up his life, and moved back to Philadelphia, where his parents could spoil him a little, and he could complete his emotional recovery while figuring out what to do next. He stayed in Philadelphia for about nine months, volunteering his time at a local clinic for the blind and doing other community service work.

Heeb concluded that DC was definitely not the place for him, socially or otherwise. Were it not for the coincidence of sitting next to Yumi on a plane, he surely would have remained single for his entire four years in DC, he conjectured. He decided it was time to move to New York City while he still had three years left in his twenties to enjoy. His long weekend trips there (before Yumi) had always been memorably adventurous and had proven how much easier it was for him to meet women in Manhattan than in DC. Not that Heeb was so successful in New York, even with all of Lucky Chucky's support. But Manhattan offered so many people from so many backgrounds doing so many different things, that even his odds, Sammy reasoned, could improve significantly if he just lived in the Big Apple. And probability means everything to an actuary.

Besides, jumping back into the fray was the only way for him to get over Yumi – according to Carlos and everyone else he talked to, including himself.

So, in the late spring of 2000, at the age of twenty-seven, Sammy relocated to New York City, where he quickly landed a new job as an actuary.

12. The Charlene Incident

While Narc and Trevor were getting through law school, Evan spent his post-college years working for a few different software start-ups. Evan's social life suffered a bit, but he always managed to find some time for "the chase" – particularly with Narc living in the same city. Narc introduced Evan to Trevor in the fall of 1993 and the two quickly became good friends. The three men regularly met up for a bachelor's night out or a game of weekend basketball.

In the summer of 1996, when it came time for Narc and Trevor to study for the New York Bar exam, the three musketeers lost their steam. Narc and Trevor disappeared into a two-month abyss of legal rules and multiple-choice exams. Their extended period of voluntary self-torture involved little daylight and lots of trick questions about the rule against perpetuities, and culminated in the two-day, pressure-filled, test-taking experience that is the New York Bar exam. The day after, the two friends cast aside their doubts about whether they passed, and went traveling together down the Latin American continent for two months.

Once they returned to New York City to begin legal careers that had virtually nothing to do with what was tested on the Bar exam, Narc and Trevor rarely saw each other. Both men worked at top, high-powered, corporate juggernauts where seventy-hour weeks were commonplace and boasted of with pride among the five hundred attorneys there. Narc joined the firm of White, Schue, & Krep, and Trevor joined Bartles, Arp, & Polka. Work at their respective law firms would occasionally slow down to a more humane forty hours per week, but Murphy's Law always seemed to ensure that such a slowdown never happened to Narc and Trevor simultaneously.

Thus, for the first few years that Trevor and Narc worked as lawyers, they got together with Evan only a handful of times each year, although the three friends did enjoy a few vacations together. While Evan seemed overworked as a computer programmer, his exuberant optimism about early retirement in the New Economy kept him going – particularly in 1999. The twenty-eight-year-old lawyers, on the other hand, were distinctly miserable with their jobs, but handled their respective situations rather differently.

As Narc became busier at work, he developed a bold new dating philosophy. His idea of a perfect first date was doggy-style, followed by a cup of coffee. He just didn't have the time or patience for anything resembling conventional courtship patterns and felt too depressed to be the charming smooth talker that he had once been. Consequently, he didn't interact with females much during most of his law firm years, and – after a string of failed pick-up attempts – resigned himself to an ever-increasing reliance on Internet porn. Narc was patently bitter about the career and lifestyle choices he had made just to please his parents and saw the months of his precious twenties just passing him by in a blur of legal documents and late-night deal closings. With a new junk food diet that suited his sedentary desk-life, Narc put on weight and had an ever-harder time getting out of bed every morning in exchange for the paycheck that was supposed to sustain him through the long hours and tedious work. Narc managed his chronic malaise only with fleeting forms of escapism: occasional marijuana or ecstasy, shopping sprees for designer clothes or fancy electronic gadgets, junk food binges, and marathon sessions of surfing Internet porn.

Trevor, on the other hand, used the little free time that he had to explore yoga, socialize, and research alternative careers. By the middle of his fourth year as a corporate associate, he had decided that he wanted to transition into an organization focused on African economic development. Trevor had also been steadily dating someone for a few weeks and was ready to introduce her to Evan and Narc.

At six feet two inches, Charlene Smith was the tallest female – and only the second of African origin – whom Trevor had ever dated, although he hadn't yet had "intimate relations" with her, as he put it. Trevor seemed particularly pleased about her height. "I submit to you that it has made all of the difference," he said to Narc, when he first told him about Charlene over the phone. "I feel more comfortable with her than I've felt with any other woman. And it's absolutely brilliant how intuitively she understands me on an everyday level." Charlene had essentially picked him up at a SoHo art gallery, after Trevor walked in looking somewhat lost, in the middle of a rare Saturday out of the office. A child of the South, the twenty-five-year-old African-American had moved to New York at the age of nineteen to launch her career as a theater diva and part-time fashion model. Four years later, she also began developing her own clothing line while working as a part-time receptionist in various art galleries. Charlene closely followed the latest female style trends and was constantly consulting a mirror to ensure that she looked just right. Her cramped apartment resembled a hall of mirrors populated by newly purchased women's wear, fashion magazines, perfumes, plants, cosmetics, and cabaret memorabilia.

On a pleasantly cool Saturday night in April 2000, Evan and Narc met at the posh Pangaea club, a favorite among New York's twenty-something model crowd. It took thirty minutes and several Andrew Jacksons for the unaccompanied males to get past the doorman and bouncers and into the chichi lounge. Once inside, it didn't take long for Evan and Narc to spot the towering Trevor by the bar with his new girlfriend.

Throughout the night, Evan and Narc shared the vague conclusion that something wasn't quite right about Charlene. Evan had met very few females taller than he was and so couldn't stop thinking about how odd her height seemed. Narc, who was two inches taller than Evan and had been with a woman almost as tall as Charlene, was focused more on her behavior. Her playful enthusiasm in trying to get others in the lounge to flirt with Evan and Narc seemed slightly aggressive – even for an unusually confident and theatrical woman.

As Evan sat at the bar trying to convince Trevor to leave his miserable firm job and join him in the promising tech economy, Charlene took Narc around Pangaea saying, "What about her? Do you think she's hot? I'll make sparks fly!" Narc would smile out of surprised amusement at Charlene's style, but she took this as an unequivocal green light and proceeded to accost or grab several target females and try to arrange a match.

When they went back to meet Trevor and Evan at the bar, Charlene then offered her pushy matchmaking services to Evan. Her success rate was as poor with him as it was with Narc.

Meanwhile, Trevor took advantage of the private moment with Narc to share his concerns about Narc's appearance. "You don't look so good these days, mate. You seem a bit depressed...And you've put on some weight since I last saw you," he said, gently.

"I know. I know. The firm's killing me."

"That makes two of us, Narc. I don't know how much longer I can take it. In fact, I've decided to apply for a job with the United Nations Development Program."

"Hey, that's dope, bro!" Narc said with a proud smile. "I could see you likin' that kind of work. And it's a good cause."

"Indeed...But what about you, mate? What's your exit strategy?"

"I don't have one. My parents would freak if I left a six figure salary at a prestigious firm."

"But you went to law school for them too…I know they're very important to you, but how much of your life are you going to live for them? Are you still helping them out with their laundry business?" Trevor asked.

"About once a week tops. I feel like they never have enough help."

"But you're bloody miserable and you barely have time for yourself. Don't they realize that you're working full time now?"

"They don't expect me to help. But I want to. All of their kids are out of the house now and they're getting too old to run that business on their own. Especially with their broken English. Someone has to help them with all of the bills, legal documents, and business issues that go into running that place. What am I supposed to do? I'm their only son. I'm keeping this shitty job because I'm basically their retirement plan…But let's change the topic…This is just gonna depress the fuck out of me and – " He was interrupted by the abrupt arrival of Evan and Charlene.

"Hey guys!" Charlene said ebulliently. "Come on, Trevor!" She playfully pulled Trevor away and into the crowd that was grooving to the hip-hop beats playing in the lounge. Trevor charmingly and helplessly shrugged his shoulders as if to apologize, but Narc and Evan just smiled understandingly and gave him the thumbs up.

Narc was actually relieved to have a private moment with Evan, as Trevor and Charlene moved out of earshot.

"Tower's girl is really buggin' me out," he began.

"I think she's a man," Evan replied, matter-of-factly.

"Word. I've been thinking that myself. We gotta save Tower."

"But how are you gonna break it to him? I mean, he looks like he's really into her. Or him. And we've gotta be one hundred percent sure…I mean, she does have a nice body."

"Those tits actually look a bit fake," Narc opined.

"Plenty of women get fake boobs."

"And her shoulders seem kinda broad," Narc persisted.

"That's just because she's so tall…Did you see an Adam's apple?"

"I'm not sure," Narc replied, suddenly unsure of himself for a moment.

"Well we should see if there's an Adam's apple, because – if there is – that would answer the question."

"Right."

"But if there's no Adam's apple, we'd still need to dig further."

"Why's that?" asked Narc.

"I read somewhere that you can get your trachea shaved off as part of a transgender operation."

"What the fuck were you doing researching transgender operations?"

"It was for a screenplay idea I had."

"Oh…So if there's no Adam's apple, how can we tell if it's a guy?" Narc asked.

"I think it's a guy. Look at the height. How many women have you seen who are that tall? And look at the mannerisms."

"Yeah. They're way too forward for a woman…I'll bet there's an Adam's apple," Narc said.

"Well, let's check first," Evan said. "We should really get whatever evidence we can, because if we say something to Trevor and we're wrong, it'll be really bad," Evan said.

"Not as bad as if we're right and we don't say anything to him," Narc replied.

"True."

When Trevor and his new girlfriend finally returned from dancing, Narc followed the plan he had hatched with Evan. Narc engaged Charlene in a conversation about the ceiling of the club, so that she would look upwards and he could get a closer look at her throat area. Meanwhile, Evan discreetly asked Trevor if the male trio could enjoy some quality time alone, just for old time's sake.

Narc pushed the limits of his artistic observation skills, as he kept trying to generate new esthetic comments that would prompt Charlene to look up at the ceiling. After remarking on the club's tall ceilings, he asked her to estimate their height; then he asked her about the precise color and texture of the paint, about the particular style of the roof beams, and about the decorative elements near the upper parts of the walls. But he found it difficult to discern whether Charlene's slightly raised throat area constituted an Adam's apple. He glanced at the throats of various men and women nearby, but they were each too far away and moving too much for Narc to make any useful comparisons. The need to remain subtle and avoid arousing any suspicion in Charlene was paramount to his investigative efforts, and so – when he had thoroughly exhausted all possible observations about the rather unremarkable ceiling above them – Narc gave up.

About twenty minutes later, Trevor began negotiating an early end to his night with Charlene. As she protested vociferously, Narc whispered his inconclusive findings to Evan, but insisted that he still had serious enough doubts about Charlene's true gender that they had a duty to confront their friend with the issue. After some deliberation, Evan agreed.

Charlene finally and reluctantly agreed to leave the boys alone for the rest of the night. Trevor apologetically put her into a cab, and the three friends jumped into a separate cab. Narc instructed the driver to take them to Chinatown, where he knew of several small Chinese restaurants that effectively offered perfect privacy as long as the three friends spoke in English.

Narc picked out a small, circular table in the restaurant and then translated everyone's orders into Cantonese for the waiter, who seemed to be moving in fast forward, like everything else in the place. Trevor and Evan were impressed with Narc's Chinese language skills. Narc's thoroughly American style and his fluency in both academic English and ghetto talk made his friends forget that he could still revert to an authentic Chinese mode. After the waiter left, Narc teased them for a few minutes about having the expression of bewildered tourists on their faces.

A few minutes later, an awkward silence settled in as Evan and Narc looked at each other, each hoping that the other would break the bad news. Trevor realized that something was amiss.

"What? What is it?" he asked, slightly amused by his friends' strange silence.

"There's really no good way to say this," Narc began, a little self-consciously.

"Say what?"

"We think," he continued, and then paused awkwardly. "We think that Charlene is a man."

"Or that she used to be a man," Evan quickly clarified.

Trevor did a double take, and looked at the two friends across from him, trying to perceive whether this was some kind of practical joke. But they appeared unquestionably serious – even concerned.

"Are you bloody barmy?!" he exclaimed.

"What's that?" Evan asked Narc, who — after spending considerably more time with Trevor — was much more familiar with British slang.

"It means crazy…Trevor, we're bein' totally serious. We've both been trippin' on your girl, or your guy, or whatever."

"This is pure bollocks. Some kind of joke, right?" Trevor replied, in amused disbelief. For someone incapable of openly and unequivocally admitting that he had slept with a woman, nothing could be more inconceivable or disturbing than the possibility that he was dating a man, or a former man.

"I know it's not easy to think about," Evan began. "And we really didn't want to say anything unless we were absolutely sure that you need to look into the matter."

"And unfortunately, we're both absolutely sure," Narc added. "So we felt that it was our duty to tell you. As your friends."

But Trevor would have none of the idea, no matter how earnestly and seriously his friends repeated their concerns. After Narc tried wrestling in vein with Trevor's blindly closed-minded denials for another ten minutes, Evan tried a more intellectual approach.

"Trevor, let's just say that Narc and I have this working hypothesis. And it's completely contrary to your working hypothesis. And until we assess all of the evidence, we really can't say who's right and who's wrong."

"But that's precisely my point," Trevor retorted. "I have so much more evidence than the two of you have."

"But did you score?" Narc asked pointedly, as if he were deposing Trevor.

"No comment."

"Will you at least confirm that you've closely inspected her anatomy?" Narc persisted.

"I am definitely more familiar with what she looks like than the two of you are."

"The trouble is that after transgender operations, it can be very difficult for the untrained eye to notice the traces of the surgery," Evan added.

"What authority are you on this subject?" Trevor asked, appalled at the suggestion of a sex operation.

"Evan's our de facto resident expert on transgender operations. He wrote a screenplay on the topic."

114

"Actually, I just researched it. I never wrote the script. The topic just freaked me out too much."

"Listen mates, I really don't want to talk about this anymore," Trevor said, somewhat impatiently.

"We don't really want to talk about it either," Narc persisted. "But we just thought that – as your friends – we should say something. It's obviously a ball-breaker of a subject. And it's not even something you can really discuss with Charlene."

"Yeah, even if she wouldn't take offense to the question," Evan added, "you can't be sure that she'd give you a straight answer."

"You have to explore the issue subtly," Narc added.

"How do you explore that issue subtly?" Trevor asked flippantly, as if to humor their ludicrous assumption.

"See how she reacts to certain things," Evan suggested. "Like tell her 'I saw the most disgusting show about transsexuals last night on TV. I can't think of anything more nauseating and repulsive than a transsexual.'"

"How would that tell me anything?"

"Because you'll see how she reacts," Evan explained. "I mean, if she really cares about you and having a relationship with you, it wouldn't be in her interest to hide such a basic part of who she is from you."

"Or maybe it would," Trevor rejoined. "Maybe she's so in love with me and so determined to stay with me that your strategy would only cause her to be all the more careful about hiding certain facts from me."

"You've got a point," Evan conceded. "But what about seeing how quickly she'd be willing to have anal sex?" Evan paused for a moment. The Chinese waiter had arrived with their food. The waiter's rushed movements and indifferent expression confirmed that they had perfect privacy, so Evan continued: "Most real women don't like receiving anal sex, whereas most gay men do."

Trevor, who had also noticed how clueless the waiter was about their conversation, launched into his rebuttal: "I would never want to have anal sex with any woman, so that's a preposterous question."

The waiter finished transferring the last dishes to their table and left in a flash.

"He just means asking her hypothetically, to see how she reacts," Narc chimed in. "But you could still get false positives from the few women who like it, and false negatives from the few gay guys who don't. So it's not really a good test."

"I've got it!" Evan said. "Go into her bathroom some time and see if she has any tampons or pads anywhere. And if you can't find them in her apartment or her purse or anywhere else, see how she reacts when you ask her whether she has menstrual cramps and how she deals with them."

"Word. That's it! Evan got it," Narc said, excited about the strategy.

"And I have another one," Evan said. "At some other time, so she doesn't get suspicious, ask her whether she wants kids. Most women want kids at some point. Tell her that you can't get serious about any woman who isn't open to bearing your children some day, and see how she reacts."

"I like that one too!" Narc said, high-fiving Evan, who was clearly pleased with his own cleverness.

"You blokes have a very fertile imagination. Or you've been watching way too much of that Jerry Springer bollocks. All of this talk is completely barmy."

But no matter how much Trevor tried to dismiss their suspicions as wild and baseless speculation, a haunting doubt lingered in his mind during the weeks that followed, until he finally gave in and began investigating the matter.

Each time Trevor collected some new piece of data, the results either failed to reassure him or they actually troubled him a bit. Charlene didn't seem to keep any tampons or pads in her bathroom or purse and claimed not to suffer from menstrual cramps. She didn't want kids because it would interfere with her artistic ambitions too much, and she was happy to have anal sex any time Trevor felt the urge. Her throat seemed slightly raised, but not enough to qualify as a "smoking gun Adam's apple" — particularly since Trevor doubted his expertise on such matters (although he did develop a minor fixation with throat shapes).

By the second week following his Chinatown dinner with Narc and Evan, Trevor needed a final and accurate answer to the question. He was too squeamish about the subject and too Puritan to confront her about the issue directly. He was also unsure whether she would tell the truth, and he was afraid of saying something inappropriate, if her answer didn't fully eliminate his festering suspicion. So he decided that the most natural way to find out the truth was simply to do that which she had been wanting to do since the day they met: get fully naked and have sex.

Trevor purposely planned to see Charlene on a weeknight when he would be working late, so that she would try to convince him to spend the night. Because he had never agreed to her prior attempts to have him stay over, he feigned reluctance initially, so that she wouldn't suspect his true purpose. After this initial resistance, Trevor agreed to go over to Charlene's place at around 11 p.m. and spend the night. She excitedly began preparing her place for Trevor's visit. Charlene meticulously cleaned her apartment, made a bubble bath, put out wine glasses and candles, and arranged her condoms and sex toys in discreet but easily accessible hiding places.

Immediately upon his arrival at her place, Trevor began imbibing far more wine than he normally consumed in a single night in order to calm his anxious nerves. By 1 a.m., he felt unusually light-headed and giddy. In fact, he was so inebriated and lost in the pleasure of Charlene's passionate kissing and highly skilled fellatio, that he almost forgot his original purpose for that night. But at one point, after Charlene had swallowed his man-juice and was proudly lying atop him, he let his hands run over her blouse, which she still hadn't removed for him. He was too drunk and happy to notice her breasts, but Charlene – in a moment of self-conscious insecurity – thought that Trevor had felt their true shape and blurted out a self-deprecating admission: "I know, Baby…They're really flat…The fillers are just temporary, I promise… I'm getting implants in two weeks…And the rest of the operation a month later…It'll look so much better, Baby."

Trevor tried to shake his intoxicated lightness enough to inquire further, but Charlene saw his questions coming and effectively stopped them by starting to kiss and arouse him again. During the renewed fondling, Trevor did manage to get his hand down towards Charlene's groin, and she finally let him explore the area. There was no hiding that Charlene was aroused.

Because there was no hiding that Charlene was, in fact, a man.

"No…Please, Baby," Charlene protested feebly, "just give me a few more months…"

But Trevor now felt inevitably propelled down a course from which there was no returning, and he needed to confront the full reality of the situation, no matter how shocking it turned out to be. Charlene soon recognized a somewhat familiar look of anxious curiosity and discovery in Trevor's eyes, and let him finish coming to terms with the situation.

Trevor's hands continued exploring every inch of Charlene's body, and the two eventually resumed their kissing.

One hour later, they were asleep in Charlene's bed.

*****

The next morning, Charlene messengered to Trevor's office a black envelope wrapped in a pink ribbon. Afraid that his officemate might catch some glimpse of the contents or his reaction to them, Trevor took the sealed envelope with him to the bathroom. He locked himself behind a stall, sat down on the toilet seat with his pants on, and nervously opened the envelope, realizing that this might be the single most memorable and momentous package that he had ever opened.

In the envelope there were playbills featuring Charlene, old photographs, a photocopy from a high school yearbook, and other assorted memorabilia, along with a handwritten note. For a moment, it was all a blurry set of disjointed pieces, until Trevor finally focused on a few key details that he had initially glossed over in denial. Charlene's original legal name, as it was listed below the Texas high school yearbook picture, was "Charles Smith."

He then read the hand-written note that Charlene had included: "Trevor, dear, you were delicious last night...I hope this isn't too strange for you...I've never felt so attracted or so close to someone before...So I wanted to share some of my past with you, in the hope that you might understand where I've been and where I'm going...And embrace my future with me...As you can see from the photos, I look so much better as a woman...And I've never really felt right as a man...I'd really love to see you again and I just hope that – "

Trevor stopped reading, as a feeling of nausea suddenly overcame him. The envelope, note, and photos fell to the bathroom floor as Trevor's hands went limp from shocked disgust. With only a slight hangover pounding away at his otherwise sober head, Trevor now had to acknowledge unequivocally that he had engaged in sexual relations with a man – and enjoyed it.

The queasiness in Trevor's gut became overwhelming. He dropped to his knees, turned around to face the toilet, and vomited.

13. Narc and Evan Fall Out

Trevor quit his job that day. He knew that it would be weeks, maybe months, before he would be able to concentrate again on any kind of work, much less painfully tedious legal work. He felt unshakable embarrassment and lingering disgust.

Trevor's conservative upbringing involved virtually no reference to the existence of homosexuals and made it far too difficult for Trevor to recognize his own attraction to men. Thus, he had always pursued androgynous women as the next best alternative. Being away from home, of course, made it easier for Trevor to entertain homosexual ideas, but because he had no gay friends and had never quite felt free enough to "come out," the Charlene incident surprised and unsettled him profoundly. An overpowering need to cleanse his body and his mind settled into his conscience. He had become increasingly interested in yoga during the last few years and now felt the impulse to explore Eastern religion more seriously.

Trevor felt deeply embarrassed about misidentifying Charlene's gender and about the resulting confusion surrounding his sexual identity. He was too mortified to say anything to Narc, Evan, or any of his other male friends, all of whom were unquestionably heterosexual. Instead, he abruptly and quietly left the city for an ascetic ashram in upstate New York. Trevor took a vow of celibacy, ate only two vegetarian meals per day, and practiced meditation every day.

A week later, Narc tried to call Trevor at his office but was informed that Mr. Bediako no longer worked at Bartles, Arp & Polka and that he had left no forwarding information. Narc tried calling Trevor's home and cell phone numbers but they were all disconnected. The next day, he got out of work early at 10 p.m. and took a cab to Trevor's one-bedroom apartment in Gramercy, where he learned from the new tenant that Trevor had sublet his place for six months. To Narc's relief, the new tenant had a phone number for Trevor.

Trevor's ashram had one public phone for three hundred disciples. After twenty-three rings, someone finally picked up. Yes, he would look for Trevor and tell him that Narc was on the phone, but it could take a few minutes to find him. About ten minutes later, the same voice came back to the receiver and informed Narc that Trevor didn't want to receive any phone calls or visitors for at least a few months and asked that his friends respect his wishes. The man apologized and Narc thanked him for his help.

The following Sunday, Narc had lunch with Evan in Chinatown. They talked for a while about Trevor and whether they should visit him or try to bring him back. Narc was concerned that Trevor might be getting involved in some strange cult, but Evan finally persuaded him that they should respect Trevor's personal decision – at least for the time being – and check up on him in a few months. They discussed competing theories about what might have prompted him to make so many radical changes in his life, and Narc concluded the cause was probably discovering that Charlene was a man or an ex-man.

"But you don't know that for a fact," Evan replied. "We never found out what he learned about Charlene…I really think he was just fed up with the corporate life that you complain about all of the time." And with that remark, the focus of the conversation changed, both because they had exhausted the Trevor topic for the moment, and because Evan had touched upon a raw nerve.

"I don't complain about it all of the time," Narc objected, reflexively.

Narc's favorite gripe about life was his job. He hated his job with a boiling passion. He hated it more frequently and more vocally than he hated anything else. Every morning – without fail – he woke up at 7:30 a.m. almost cheerful to be alive another day, and by around 11 p.m. that night, when he typically left his office, his throat was stiff with frustrated fury at the world and his particular place in it.

The waiter took away their empty dishes and left them the check.

"All right, I do complain," he conceded. "Because I fuckin' hate every minute of it."

"Sounds like you need to vent again, Narc."

"Yeah. Just last night my parents asked me, for the 429th time, what's so bad about being a corporate lawyer. They're calling me at 11 p.m. at the office on a Saturday night, as if that fact alone wasn't enough to answer their question. But then again, they're workaholic immigrants who don't know anything but working hard seven days a week, so what can I tell them? So for the 429th time I lied to them and just said that sometimes the high-pressured responsibility gets stressful and that that's the only thing that I'm really complaining about. But the fuckin' truth of the matter is that everything's wrong with being a lawyer!"

"Everything?" Evan repeated.

"Yes, everything. The question is, what's good about being a corporate lawyer? Besides the pay, of course. The work itself sucks ass, because – like city sanitation – it's the shit work that no one else wants to do, so the poor bastards doing it need to be paid well enough to ensure that they keep doing it."

"But lawyers make four times as much as garbage men," Evan replied.

"That's because lawyers work four times as many hours. Why the fuck do you think that for the last four years I've barely had the time to have a meal with you, much less play basketball, or go out and meet women? If you had those sanitation guys taking away the trash three thousand hours a year, you better believe you'd have to pay them a six figure salary."

"Yeah. And imagine how clean the city would be."

"Seriously."

"But how can you compare what you do to what a garbage man does?"

"It's the intellectual equivalent. It's shit work for the brain. It's the most friggin' tedious, comma-chasing, minutiae-oriented shit work you can possibly imagine. It's all that damn fine print in our society that nobody wants to read, but some poor soul has to draft or dissect."

"Give me an example," Evan said as he started to look at the bill. Narc snatched it from him, put his credit card on top, and called the waiter over in Cantonese. The server, who was taking an order nearby, signaled that he would come over in a bit.

"Thanks, Narc."

"Don't mention it. So last night is a perfect example. Last night was even worse than fine print."

"What happened?"

"Until 2 a.m., I spent six hours circling every number that I found in a two-hundred-page prospectus. Why six hours, you ask? Because the financial numbers in the prospectus were adjusted three times during those six hours, and each time, I needed to circle the numbers so that the accountants could give us comfort on the circled numbers."

"Circling numbers?"

"It's called doing a circle up for the accounts."

"What's that?"

"The accountants need to provide a comfort letter on the financial numbers in a prospectus. They need to comfortize the numbers, as we idiotically call it. And to know which numbers to comfortize, someone needs to tell them, because for some asinine reason, they can't make this judgment call themselves even though they're fucking accountants and any fucking seventh grader could provide the fucking accountants with their fucking circle up because all you have to do is circle every number that you see."

"Wow. That does sound bad."

"The hardest part is getting past the fifth hour of circling numbers, when you can't remember why on earth you paid 120 thousand dollars and three years of your life to go to law school so that you could one day spend your days and nights circling numbers."[1]

"I didn't realize your work was so riveting."

"Why do you think working at the firm made me vote Republican? If I have to put up with shit work all day in exchange for some bling bling, there's no way I'm giving up that bling bling for all the lazy fucks out there just waiting for some tax-subsidized government handout."

"Are you serious?"

"Of course I'm serious. Taxation is passive theft, yo. Don't get me wrong: I'm down with helpin' kids in the hood' but there's also a lot of government waste. And the more I'm taxed on income from a job I hate, the more I notice the waste."

"I hear ya'," Evan said, suppressing his urge to defend the Democrats to allow Narc his much needed ranting.

"Federal, state, and local taxes collectively take forty percent of my paycheck. I might be cool with that if I liked the work. But not if my paycheck represents days and nights of mind-numbing due diligence."

"What's due diligence?"

"That's just going through mounds and mounds of corporate data – memos and contracts and letters and documents and spreadsheets – looking for minutia that doesn't mean shit to you or anyone else you care about. Minutia that doesn't really mean shit to even the client, because they're some Fortune 500 company that can afford to

---

[1] About ten years later, the financial cost of a law degree from a top school has approximately doubled.

122

be needlessly thorough and will never question a nine-hundred-thousand-dollar legal bill that was, in fact, a complete waste of everyone's time and money, because nine hundred thousand dollars is just a rounding error to them."

The waiter came by to take the check with Narc's credit card.

"What about the people who work at these Fortune 500 client companies? What about your colleagues? Don't you at least enjoy your contact with these people?" Evan asked, hoping to find something positive.

"The firm's clients are a bunch of overly demanding, disorganized, and boneheaded corporate prima donnas. And my colleagues are, for the most part, a bunch of obsessive compulsive, conservative, anal retentive, phony yuppies who lack the courage or the imagination to do anything more interesting with their lives. So tell me what's good about my job, besides the pay check?"

Narc was really worked up now. Evan wanted to say something, but it was clear that Narc just needed to rage on some more.

"And you know what else I fucking hate?"

"What?"

"I hate the fact that the fucking partners in my firm are so obsessed with billing hours that while I'm standing there taking a piss in the firm bathroom, one of them will come up to me and start talking to me about what we're working on."

"What do you mean?"

"I mean, I'm standing there, dick in my hand, peeing into a urinal, and this partner I'm working with walks in still reading a draft of the document we're working on. He walks up to the urinal next to me with the document held up right in front of him, and then starts to piss."

"Maybe he's just trying to be efficient so that he can get out of the office earlier," Evan suggested.

"That's fine. I don't care about that. The problem is when he disturbs my private piss time to start grilling me about how far along I am in the circle up, and when I'll be distributing the next draft of the prospectus to the working group on the deal. There's no fucking reason why he can't wait five minutes to ask me that outside of the bathroom."

"I guess."

"What do you mean you guess? People want their fucking privacy when they're in the bathroom."

The waiter reappeared with Narc's credit card, and waited as Narc signed the charge authorization.

Narc continued his rant: "You know, the main bathroom on each floor at my firm has four stalls, and each stall has a paper toilet seat dispenser. Do you know which stall is always out of paper seats first?"

"No, I never really thought about that," Evan replied, amused by Narc's keen attention to strange details.

"It's the stall that's farthest from the entrance to the bathroom. Do you know why that is?" Narc asked rhetorically. "Because man likes to shit in peace. When man is shitting, man does not like to be disturbed by people coming and going or talking to him about corporate deals. Man is vulnerable when he's shitting. That's why he builds toilet stalls. To protect him while he's vulnerable. And so he wants to get as far away from the noise and the talking as possible and just shit in peace. That's why the stall that's the most hidden and peaceful always runs out of paper seats first, whereas the stall that's closest to the entrance always has paper seats left in the dispenser. Because everyone prefers to shit in the stall that's the most peaceful, and that's the stall that's farthest from the entrance."

"Interesting," Evan replied, trying to conceal his amusement.

A large group of Italian tourists arrived in the Chinatown restaurant and filled up the tables around Narc and Evan.

"I'm sick of this shit, Evan."

"Look, I'm sorry that you're so sick of your job, Narc. But I'm sick of hearing about how you're sick of it."

"What are you trying to say?" Narc snapped back, defensively.

"That after about four years, it's time for you to do something about it rather than just bitch. Like Trevor. The guy at least had the balls to make some dramatic decisions in search of a better life. And it's not like I haven't offered to help you move into the Internet space."

"You and your fuckin' Internet pipe dreams. Have you looked at the NASDAQ – or should I say the Nasdive – lately? It's over. Last week was the beginning of the end for that bubble."

"You don't know that for sure."

"You'll be unemployed within two months," Narc predicted (with prescient accuracy).

"At least I'll be happy until we go under. What gets you up every morning? You have nothing to hope for. Each time I see you, which is about twice a year, you just gain more weight and look more depressed."

"What the fuck am I supposed to do? I'm making good cash at a prestigious firm and don't have any better alternatives."

"What about your dream jobs?"

"You mean trying out for the NBA? Or becoming a porn star? My parents would fuckin' freak."

"Well then suck it up at work and accept that you're no better than your coworkers – 'the yuppies who lack the courage or imagination to do anything better with themselves,' as you put it. That's you, Narc. Face it. You're just like your colleagues. You're in good company."

"Fuck you, Evan."

Narc was fuming. He noisily got up from the table and left the restaurant brusquely.

The next day, Evan left an apology on Narc's voicemail, but he never heard back from his former college roommate.

14. Heeb's Brief Career as a Model

Soon after his arrival in New York City, in June 2000, Sammy concluded that there was no better place to be a single man. But he had to come to terms with the disappointing reality that Carlos was far less available to serve as his wingman than he had been in the past. Heeb would discover this frustrating fact a few days after his arrival, when they met for a sumptuous dinner at the Sanctuary, a vegetarian restaurant in the East Village.

"So this was just you exposing me to organic foods for an hour?" Heeb complained.

"Wasn't the food great?"

"I just ate seventeen different versions of tofu and veggies trying to taste like meat. Next time, let's eat carrots made of chicken."

"You're an incurable carnivore, Heeb."

"No, I'm an omnivore. An equal opportunity eater – which is how we homo sapiens were designed, by the way. Now are we going out on the town or what?"

"I can't."

"But you're one of the main reasons I moved out here!" he protested feebly.

"I know, Sammy. But don't try to guilt me into a divorce. I'm married now. To the most incredible woman on the planet who also happens to be my boss."

"You're all grown up now," Heeb said, almost nostalgically.

"Yeah. I've got a company to run. I helped Carolina triple her revenues over the last five years and we've got many more people on payroll now…"

"I'm still getting the check," Heeb said with a smile, as he passed his credit card to the waiter before Carlos could.

"I'll get you on the next one," Carlos replied, annoyed that the waiter had so quickly left before he could replace Heeb's card with his own.

"I just don't have as much time as I had during those first few years after college, Sammy," he continued. "I have a lot more responsibility now…I hope you understand."

"Carlos, for the last twelve months I've been more single than a one-dollar bill...For the last nine months I've been living with my parents, for God's sake."

"Ouch." Carlos had long ago forgotten what it's like to go without sex for more than three days.

"And even had I been in some ideal bachelor pad rather than my parents' place, I still would have been useless trying to start with women. I mean, it was hard enough for me on my own, in DC, before I met Yumi. But afterwards — I mean, you have no idea how she devastated me...You just don't know what it's like..."

"I hope I never have to learn."

"I hope so too."

"Has it really been twelve months?"

"Do you realize that last night I put a condom on for my nightly self-love session, just so that I don't forget the mechanics of putting on a raincoat? And it's a good thing I brushed up on my technique, because I'm badly out of practice. I mean, if it were the real thing I would have definitely fumbled it in some stupid, uncoordinated way."

Carlos tried to conceal his amusement.

"Don't worry, Sammy. You'll get your Kojak back...You've only been here a week. Give it some time. You'll soon discover how many opportunities there are to meet women in the city. Even without me."

"It's just not the same without you, Chucky."

"It will be. Trust me. You just have to put yourself out there. And I'll definitely join you when I can. But the next few months are going to be really busy for me. Carolina and I have some major business trips to Florida and California, and then we're going to Italy for a two-week vacation."

"You know that I have only one year left to play?" Sammy asked desperately, making one last attempt to evoke pathos in his audience.

"You mean you're sticking with the same crazy marriage timetable?"

"Well, when I was with Yumi that whole plan went out the window, but now I'm coming back to it. There's something comforting about consistency. And I really need some comfort these days. You know: just a familiar game plan that I can understand and follow."

"So you have one more year to date only non-Jewish women for casual play, followed by two years to date only Jewish women in search of a wife?"

"I know what you're gonna say. That I'm as crazy and immature as I was five years ago."

"No. You're actually more crazy and immature than you were five years ago, because at twenty-seven it's far more crazy and immature to be clinging to these notions than at twenty-two."

"Thanks, Carlos. I knew I could count on you to understand…"

"That's all right. Look, if I hadn't met Carolina, I'd be stuck in my own kind of crazy. I just got lucky."

"Finally, he admits that he's lucky. Now give me some advice about how to take full advantage of this city. I'm always looking to improve my odds."

"Just what I'd expect from a horny actuary."

"I'm serious."

Carlos reflected for a moment on the problem at hand. He actually had never needed or tried to take full advantage of the city in order to meet women, but he thought about all of his friends who regularly did. His face lit up as he thought of some helpful advice: "Get into the arts."

"The arts?"

"Yeah."

"But I'm not artistic."

"It doesn't matter. Many women are into the arts. Theater. Painting. Dance. They love that stuff."

"You want me to get into dance? Earthquakes have better rhythm than me…And can you really picture me in those tights?"

"Take an art history class. Learn photography. Get involved in a play or an independent film production. Get artsy, Sammy. I'm telling you, the senoritas dig that stuff."

"Really?"

"Yeah. You need to sign up for a bunch of artistic activities. But you can't let on that it's all just a pretext to meet women. You have to take a real interest in the subject or they'll quickly sniff out your game."

"I don't know…It's all so foreign to me…I don't know the first thing about being artistic."

"Heeb, this is the time to expand your horizons. And you're in the perfect city to do it. New York is all about reinventing yourself. Get out of your comfort zones. Become more of a Renaissance man. That's much more interesting to women."

Heeb broke into a smile. Just thinking about all the ways in which he could refashion himself was both exciting and liberating.

"I hate to admit it, but you're right, Carlos. I've become a unidimensional number cruncher. And there's a lot of exploring out there to do."

And with that remark, Heeb decided to go where no Heeb had gone before. His new job in New York left his nights and weekends free, and he decided to fill every available moment with a class or an activity, except for Friday and Saturday night, which he left open for dates. On Monday nights, he took photography. Tuesday and Thursday nights he took an acting class, hoping it would transform him into more of a fun and extroverted personality. On Wednesday nights, he took a hip-hop dance class. On Sundays, he learned how to inline skate with the Central Park crowd. And on Saturdays, from 1 p.m. to 3 p.m., he took the biggest risk of all, by embracing his chubby physique in a way that stepped well beyond the bounds of his "comfort zone": Heeb worked as a nude model for a beginning painting class comprised of twenty students, all between the ages of eighteen and forty, and twelve of whom were female.

It was undoubtedly the most absurdly surreal and embarrassing situation into which he had ever voluntarily placed himself – particularly since he found one of the students (a young Indian woman) attractive enough to qualify for "business class" seating. There was something unforgettably bizarre and ridiculous about walking into a large loft on a Saturday afternoon, getting undressed in the bathroom, putting on a kimono, walking out into the center of a large space surrounded by twenty easels, disrobing, and then assuming whatever laughable posture or position the German art instructor, Henrik, sternly commanded. The fact that the forty-something instructor spoke with a thick German accent, looked exceedingly Aryan, and conducted the class in a rather austere and militaristic way didn't make it any easier for the naked Heeb to take directions from him.

"Lean forv-ard and pick up your left foot so zet it is floating behind you," Henrik commanded. Heeb reluctantly obeyed.

"Come on zehn. Higher now! Like Nadia Comaneci. Show me some balance."

Heeb tried to raise his left foot higher and lean forward more but he quickly lost his balance and started hopping around moronically on his supporting right foot, with his shrunken wiener schnitzel bouncing about helplessly until he finally lost his balance and had to take an awkward stumble to the floor.

129

Several members of the class, including the cute woman, burst out into restrained laughs, until Henrik called the class to order.

"Come on, class! Zis is not komedy owar. Vee are here to paint, and painting is serious biz-nus. Laffovitz, pick up yourself and start vahnse again."

Heeb's face flushed red like a tomato, as he got up off the floor and moved back to where he had begun his pose.

"Zis time just stand zhere on bozh feet, but vis your vayt mostly on your right foot."

To Heeb's relief, he managed this easier pose without any difficulties, and the class resumed its business. Sammy stood there frozen, realizing that no posture could possibly make the task of posing naked in front of twenty strangers painting him seem any less preposterous. He began to wonder how people made a living at this sort of thing. "They must be exhibitionists," he thought. "I guess I was never meant to be an exhibitionist. Who am I kidding? I knew that all along…I'm an idiot for trying this…To hell with leaving your comfort zones…They're your comfort zones for a damn good reason: they feel comfortable…"

Heeb caught a glimpse of the cute Indian woman painting him. She seemed to be concentrating but he was afraid that she would catch him looking at her, so he looked at the floor again and resumed his monologue. "Can't I get out of this nightmare somehow? There has to be some plausible excuse I can invent for just getting up and leaving. Something like, sorry, I have cramps. That would work for a girl. Why can't it work for a guy? Is that gender discrimination? Or what about some disturbing medical excuse? Something like: I forgot to mention that I miraculously survived the Ebola virus but I can feel the onset of those same symptoms coming back now…Or how about: I just realized that my neighbor was counting on me to feed her dog and it's been four days since I checked up on the poor fellow…Or I could try the more honest approach: I've just been informed by my self-esteem that it's in serious danger of total annihilation. And it didn't come with any money back guarantee. So if you'll excuse me, why don't you, Henrik, get butt naked for the class and I'll take a stab at painting your Nazi ass?"

"Laffovitz, I said change zeh positions of your feet! Vaht are you still doing zhere in zeh first position?" Henrik exclaimed. "Zis is not a difficult job, Laffovitz!"

"Sorry…Sorry about that," Heeb stammered, as he snapped out of his head chatter and switched the positions of his feet.

His thoughts continued: "Well, if I do sit this one out, I'll certainly be able to handle any game of strip poker…And that short Indian cutie with the frizzy hair is just delicious-looking. I wonder what she's thinking of me right now. Probably something like, 'What a loser. He can't even find a self-respecting job. Why can't they at least get us body-builder types for models? Or at least someone with a hairy scalp. Or really well hung. That would be more interesting to paint.' That's what she's thinking. God, I'd love to tell her that I'm really an actuary who makes six figures. That would set her thinking straight, right? Yeah, right. Who the hell am I kidding? There's no recovering from the fact that I volunteered to publicly show my schlong so that she'd have something to paint. Especially if I didn't do it for the thirty dollars they're paying me."

He wondered whether looking in her direction again would cause him to break his pose enough to incur Henrik's ire. As his eyes moved from easel to easel, he again felt the surrealism of the moment, hearing the light tapping of brushes against canvas in the quiet loft, and watching intently focused eyes shift between him and their easel, with paintbrush ends popping up and down out of the sides of the easels, like the spear tips of cannibals preparing for their kill.

His eyes finally made it to her easel and, just as they were about to follow a collision course to the humiliatingly self-aware moment of eye contact, he saved himself the ultimate mortification and let his eyes shoot straight down toward the floor. There would have been something intolerably desperate about making eye contact with her at that moment, if only because she might interpret it as some attempt by him to make her pity him. Heeb spent the remainder of the first hour plotting his breach of contract with the art school that had hired him to model nude for another seven painting sessions.

There was a ten-minute break after the first hour, which seemed too short to get fully dressed again – particularly since Henrik and all of the students had filed out towards the bathroom area or near the elevators, so that there was no one left in the vicinity to make Heeb feel strange about walking around in a kimono. The brief freedom to pry suddenly possessed Heeb with an irrepressible curiosity and he urgently had to know what the various paintings of him looked like, particularly when it came to any representation of his Hebrew National.

As he quickly surveyed the twenty easels, he was dismayed to discover that virtually everyone had given him the short end of the stick, so to speak. Just as offensive, every painting had applied sufficient detail to his head so that the extent of his baldness was prominently and accurately portrayed. He also thought that the paintings tended to exaggerate the extent of his pudginess. Of course, the only paintings he could have possibly found both accurate and acceptable would have depicted a muscularly fleshy, well-endowed man with a thinning hairline, and so Heeb was inevitably disappointed. But he tried to take solace in the fact that most of the paintings were still in a rough, sketch form that could be corrected without too much difficulty.

When the class reconvened for the last fifty minutes, Henrik instructed Heeb to stand with his left hand holding his right elbow and his right hand contemplatively supporting his chin. Heeb – in mid-pose – couldn't stop thinking about how the class had cheated him on his manhood. He grew particularly vexed by the fact that the attractive Indian woman was no exception in this matter. To vindicate his masculinity, Heeb concluded that he needed to enlarge himself enough to force a subtle correction amongst all of the painters striving for realism and accuracy under the watchful and exacting eye of their instructor. The only way to compel this correction during the forty-eight minutes that remained, Heeb figured, was to fantasize enough to get himself aroused. He was initially concerned about going laughably and obviously overboard, but he realized that there were two powerful forces that would probably prevent him from getting overly excited: 1) he couldn't actually touch himself given the pose he had to hold, and 2) the pressure of having twenty people looking at him, with the risk that they might grow giddy upon noticing that he was at all aroused, was enough to check the effects of Heeb's rich and well-practiced erotic imagination. In fact, it was initially difficult for Heeb to concentrate on anything potentially arousing. But he eventually found a fantasy that suited him quite well, and he was confident that he could sustain it for just enough time to produce a dimensional correction in the depictions of his body.

He pictured all eight male students suddenly going bald, packing up their things, handcuffing Henrik, and leading him out of the loft and into a local prison, where they locked him up. He then imagined the twelve women, led by the cute Indian female, putting down their paintbrushes and forming a semicircle around him while he continued to hold his pose. The two women directly in front of him shed their clothing, article by article, and the other women caressed him and licked his body, while whispering erotic desires and flattering confessions into his ears. Once the two women in front were fully undressed, the semi-

132

circle would march clockwise so that two new, fully clothed women stood directly in front of him and began to strip. After about ten minutes, all of the women were naked, and they were all fawning on Heeb while caressing, kissing, and licking him all over his body. They played affectionately with his body fat, telling him how loveable yet manly it was, how brilliant his mind was, and how utterly charming and irresistible his personality was. And then they began to squabble over who had the privilege of sucking on Heeb's toes and who had the right to give him fellatio. Heeb, with his infinite wisdom and conflict-management skills, suggested that the labor be divided among the four prettiest women, including Miss India (she was now Miss India, and not just an attractive female of Indian heritage). He noted that they could even divide the work up into simultaneous shifts of two. And all of the women were so pleased at Heeb's Solomon-like solution that they started to laugh with delight and pride at their wise ruler, who was kept cool by giant, feathered fans waved softly by the two beauties standing next to him. The others continued laughing and touching each other and caressing him — as if they were all on some potent ecstasy drug — and two women sucked and licked his toes as Yumi had once done, while two other females began his fellatio and, as the laughter grew more unrestrained, Heeb realized that he had made himself much too erect and that the laughter he was hearing was from some of the nearer students standing behind their easels. Mortified, his face turned redder than a stop sign.

Much to Heeb's relief, the minute he snapped out of his fantasy and realized that the students standing closest to him had noticed a remarkable change in his shape and size, his frankfurter quickly shriveled up in a panic, just in time to avoid detection by Henrik. He couldn't tell whether the Indian girl had noticed what had just happened, but he desperately wanted the class to end.

When it finally did end, after what seemed like an eternity of curious conversations with himself, Heeb robed himself in the kimono and scurried over to the dressing room, where he quickly put his clothes back on. Meanwhile, Henrik gave his final remarks for the day by pontificating on Leonardo Da Vinci's biography and how nobody there, as far as he could tell from the day's work, was truly gifted as a painter. He nevertheless concluded by urging the students to spend their every free moment studying the life, work, and techniques of Da Vinci.

Now fully dressed, Heeb made sure to avoid Henrik as he moved towards the exit, behind a crowd of students shuffling out. He thought for a moment about trying to say something to the cute Indian woman, but he felt too ridiculous each time he got close enough for her to hear him.

"How would Kojak handle the situation?" he heard Carlos say in his mind. "You know that Kojak would go right up to her without the slightest hesitation."

"Even Kojak couldn't do it, if he went through what I just went through."

"Heeb, are you doubting the great Kojak? Are you doubting for a second that he would go right up to her as if he had done her and the rest of the world a major favor by modeling for them?"

"That's exactly what I'm doubting," Heeb said to the imaginary Carlos.

"Well you're wrong, Heeb. Because Kojak knows that he did them a favor that they are all eternally grateful for. A favor they'll forever remember and be influenced by."

"Only if Kojak were on crack."

"Wrong! Kojak wouldn't need crack because he wouldn't care about her reaction. Why? Because she's the one who should be trembling at the thought of being spoken to by the almighty Kojak."

"I can't do it!" Heeb protested.

"Why not? What have you got to lose?"

"My self-respect."

"You already lost that."

"Very true."

"You might as well try to get whatever upside there is from this situation, right?"

"I guess so."

"You're quitting this modeling thing anyway, so you'll never see her again. Might as well treat this as another opportunity to find the Kojak in you."

"Good point."

The imaginary dialogue empowered Heeb to press forward, and follow her until she was alone enough to approach. As luck would have it, she went into a nearby deli unaccompanied, where she walked over to the fruit section. Heeb discreetly followed her as she looked around at the various fruit options in front of her. Just as Heeb decided to deliver his opening line, she put her hand on a banana and began to wrest it from the bunch.

"So have you been painting for a while?" he asked. She looked up at him and – not expecting to find the nude model she had just been painting, as she gripped a fat and long banana – she could only smile in awkward surprise.

Heeb, subtly influenced by her grip on the banana and painfully self-conscious about how the two had originally met, thought to himself "She probably just wants to tell me what she thinks of my dimensions."

"Not long," she replied, finally pulling the banana off the bunch. Her darkish complexion turned beet red.

"What do you mean by 'Not long?'" he asked, fearing the worst.

"You know, like a couple of months." The girl was still embarrassed and clearly hoping this conversation would end soon.

"Oh. Well was this your first time painting a live model?"

She nodded her head, with an almost guilty look on her face.

"What's it like?"

"Hard," she replied.

15. Heeb Tries Online Dating in New York City

Sammy quickly cut short his career as an art model but continued enjoying the rest of his busy cultural and educational schedule — even if it hadn't yet yielded more than a handful of dates, none of which fructified. But nothing could discourage Heeb – particularly after the mettle he had acquired from his harrowing experience as an art model.

So, to take full advantage of the hyperactive New York dating scene, Heeb became an early adopter of online dating. Back in the early summer of 2000, when Heeb first joined Match.com, those who logged on for love were a slightly geekier, tech-savvier crowd who saw the phenomenon as an empowering adventure for the socially awkward rather than as a random new way to meet psycho-killers. Sammy discovered that he had a knack for witty online banter in chat rooms and was able to line up more New York dates in a week than he had in an entire year in DC.

Even more to Heeb's advantage, he started surfing for dates back when it was quite normal and acceptable not to have a picture posted. When women chatting with him online asked him what he looked like, he would often reply, "Let me put it this way: I've worked as a model before."

Because online dating – particularly back then – was somewhat predicated on deceiving the other person into an in-person rendezvous, women online responded to Heeb's dodge with varying degrees of tolerance. The worst rejection he had was with a five-foot-ten, Scandinavian ex-model who was now a web developer living in Williamsburg and curious about the online dating phenomenon.

She sent Heeb her scanned photo and was so fascinated by his online persona that she agreed to meet him sight unseen (since he, of course, had no digital photo, and she wasn't going to insist that he snail mail her a printed one). She was fascinated by this modern Renaissance man who studied acting and photography, understood advanced topics in mathematics and statistics, could inline skate and dance hip-hop, and had even worked as a model. She was so eager to meet him, in fact, that she showed up early to the agreed upon meeting place, in the book section on fashion modeling, in the Barnes and Noble bookstore at Union Square.

Heeb was so excited about the fact that a former model had actually agreed to meet him on a date (an historic moment for him), that he showed up late after spending an extra twenty minutes combing the strands of hair that formed the crown around his large bald spot, as if the additional grooming might actually make a difference. When Heeb spotted her across the store, he lost his Kojak as he excitedly went up to her with an outstretched hand and said, "Hi, I'm Sammy. The guy from Match.com. You know, the guy you're supposed to meet here at 8 p.m. for coffee. The café is actually on another floor, but I thought it would be easier for us to find each other in a specific section of the bookstore, so I picked the fashion modeling section because that's a topic that's of interest to both of us, which is good to have in case someone's running late. Have you been waiting here long? I apologize for running a bit late...I didn't mean to keep you waiting..."

"I'm sorry. I think you're confusing me with someone else," she said, genuinely convinced that some coincidental mix up of sorts had somehow inflicted itself upon her.

"No. No. It's me. I promise. You know, the math guy who studies photography and acting, and enjoys inline skating and hip-hop dancing?" Heeb busted a few imaginary and poorly executed hip-hop moves while clicking an imaginary camera and then pretending to inline skate around in a little circle near her.

"This is a joke, right?" she asked, dismayed by the absurd confusion unraveling itself before her. "Sammy must have sent you as a joke...You're his friend, right?"

"No, I'm Sammy. Really. I swear. It's me."

"He does have a clever sense of humor."

"I promise you. It's no joke. This is the real Sammy talking to you."

"No, it can't be. Don't take this the wrong way, but I would never agree to go on a date with someone like you. I mean, you seem nice, but – again, don't take this the wrong way – you're not exactly my type."

"But you were so much more open-minded online. What happened?"

"Well, I'm still very open-minded when it comes to Sammy. But not his friends."

Sammy decided it was time to pull out some official identification. He whipped out his Philadelphia driver's license and showed it to her.

She was impressed to see that his identity was, in fact, Sammy Laffowitz, and that he was from the same city as the Sammy she had been chatting with online, but she still couldn't accept the reality of the situation.

"Look, maybe he lied to me about his name and his background so that he could set me up with one of his single guy friends, but the man I chatted with used to work as a model."

"I did used to work as a model. In fact, I quit just a few weeks ago."

"You quit a few weeks ago?" she asked, with dismissive skepticism.

"I was sick of being objectified. Just like I mentioned to you in our chat. Don't you remember our whole discussion about that issue?"

"I didn't have that chat with you. I had it with your friend."

"No, you had it with me. I thought we really bonded over the evils of modeling and how you can get objectified as a model."

"Listen, I'm sick of this game. I've been stood up by this guy – and I don't like his sense of humor anymore. If he shows up late, you can have my date with him. And if he stands you up too – well, you can kindly tell him to fuck off from both of us." And with that, she stormed off, fuming over how the real Sammy had failed to show up.

Heeb observed that an online date's tolerance for his model ruse was inversely proportional to her physical beauty and to how conservative her humor was. Hence, after his experience with the Scandinavian ex-model, he decided that he needed to focus on women who were a bit closer to his own category of looks and who demonstrated an offbeat sense of humor.

A few days later, he knew he had found a promising candidate when he noticed this profile headline: "Cute, normal chick into fecal fetishes and threesomes involving pet animals." He clicked on her profile and saw some photos of a punk rocking goth-girl with purplish hair, braided on the sides like Pippi-Longstocking pigtails. As he clicked through her photos, Heeb was overwhelmed by so many distinctive details: dark mascara on her intense, beautiful brown eyes; cobalt lipstick on her thin lips; several piercings up and down her ears; dark blue jeans that still displayed a feminine figure; and a white, roughed up t-shirt saying, "If it's a law, I broke it."

138

He decided to send her an instant message — with a curiosity not unlike that of a zoologist exploring an unfamiliar species.

He knew he had to start with something sarcastic or quirky to engage her, so he commented on her headline: "That's always been my notion of a cute normal chick," he wrote to her. "But the real test of normalcy is whether you put on gloves when indulging your fecal fetishes. I've found that the most normal chicks have a preference for using their bare hands."

"LOL," she replied.

"LOL??? LOL has a lot of potential meanings…Losing Out Loud. Love Or Leave. Lots Of Laughter," he replied.

"LOLLOL," she wrote back.

"Now you've got me really confused."

"Laughing Out Loud at Losers Of Lust," she typed back.

"How did I become a loser of lust?"

"Cuz if you were a winner of lust, you wouldn't be here typing to me. You'd be indulging the lust."

"Laughing Out Loud at the good point. Hmmm…But it's a point that makes you a Loser Of Lust too."

"LOLs of the world unite! You have nothing to lose but your Internet connection!"

"The cute normal chick with a fecal fetish can quote Marx!!! ☺" Heeb replied; now he was having fun.

"Let me say it again," she wrote back. "Because this is what Marx would be saying right now, if he were still alive and single in NYC: LOLs of the world unite! You have nothing to lose but your Internet connection!"

"Hmm…But what if it was that very Internet connection that provided him with the conduit for the lust?"

"You mean if Marx and all the other Losers Of Lust were using chat rooms to have cybersex?"

"Yup."

"It's a notch better, but it can't compare to the real thing."

"So why are we still chatting online? Let's get to the real thing."

"Because I don't know anything about you."

"Oh right. I forgot about that detail…LOL…Well, I'm about five-seven, and – like you – I'm really into threesomes with pet animals."

"All right, so you're still buggin' out about the headline above my profile."

"It's certainly original."

"Look, it used to be 'Cute normal chick,' but then my inbox got flooded with emails from guys who claimed to be 'Cute normal guys.' Fifty emails a day from cute normal guys. That's just not cool. Especially when they were from fifty not so cute boring guys."

"You certainly figured out how to cut down on the fan mail."

"Yeah. Now I only get about ten emails a day…But they're all from guys with pierced peckers who work in an animal shelter."

"Ohhh….Ewww….You've ruined my computer!"

"Why?"

"You just made me throw up all over it."

"LOL…Because this is like the grossest exchange you've ever had with anyone."

"It's not LIKE the grossest exchange I've ever had. It IS the grossest. Period."

"Well. I'll take that as a compliment. I think."

"It was…because this gross exchange is also very very VeRy VERY funny."

"I'm glad to hear that someone's laughing about it…I guess you passed."

"Passed?"

"I'm screening out the boring, uptight guys."

"I'll take that as a compliment. I think."

"My, you're original."

"My, you're normal."

"You could say that. I guess. If you really wanted to insult me."

"All right, you're abnormal."

"That's more like it. Look, I'm just trying to liven up this online shit a bit, OK? (No pun intended). There are just way too many uptight geeks crowding my digital world."

"So why do you come to this digital world?"

"LOL."

"But of course! LOL. How could I forget?"

"And there's actually some truth to my gross headline. The dude who's clever enough to figure it out gets sex with me on the first night."

"Even if he's bald and short and named Sammy Laffowitz?"

"Especially if. That means he's getting dissed by a world that doesn't get his cleverness. And yes, I realize that I just complimented myself, but that's one of the privileges of being Melody."

"But arrogance is a malady, Melody."

"Do you like Oscar Wilde?"

"I just like being wild."

"Crack my riddle, and I'll let you play my fiddle."

Heeb was enthralled by their witty repartee, and now he was determined to wrack his brain all night if he had to, to solve the true meaning of her headline.

"Give me a hint. Just one hint. Pretty please…with dung on top?"

"LOL…OK, you've earned it. But the hint is another riddle about the same truth."

"I'll take whatever I can get."

"It's the same hint I give to everyone who earns it: Web designer chick gets laid off by a bizarre and failing company. Now she needs company. Or companies with cash flow. Because instead of an odd job, she has odd jobs."

"Ahhh. So now that you got laid off, you're hopping online to see if you can just get laid."

"LOL."

"Laughing Out Loud or Loser Of Lust?"

"Both!"

"That's what I figured."

"But if you solve my riddle then we'll both become winners of lust."

"And if I don't?"

"Then you're just a loser like everyone before you who's tried and failed. And I'll remain an LOL, waiting for the real man…The dude who can crack my code."

This only goaded Heeb on more, because he was now invited to compete with all of the other men in an area where he actually had a significant competitive advantage: intelligence.

"Hold on. I need to cogitate," he wrote. Heeb furrowed his brow a bit, as he repeated both riddles to himself a few times, and then the facts that they might imply.

"She's a web designer chick who got laid off by a bizarre and failing company," he began. "And now she needs company. Or companies with cash flow. Because instead of an odd job, she has odd jobs…Odd jobs…Hmm…And she's a cute, normal chick who's into fecal fetishes and threesomes involving pet animals…Pet animals… Threesomes…Company…Fecal…Odd job…"

141

Then all of the sudden he looked up in delight with an ecstatic sense of pride at his own sharpness. "I got it! Kojak got it!" he screamed spastically in his one-bedroom apartment, as if the computer in front of him could congratulate him. "Kojak Bay-Bee! Kojak got it!" Heeb got up and busted a few hip-hop moves to round out his victory celebration.

He finally sat back down in front of his computer and saw that Melody had written him several instant messages: "Wellllllll????????" followed by "If I could sing, I'd be singing that annoying Jeopardy music they play when the contestants are stumped." The line below that read: "Helllllooooo????"

In a fit of excitement, Heeb sat down and typed her back a message: "I'm not stumped. Because....I got it!"

"Let me see."

"Until a company with cash flow can hire you for a regular, full-time job, you'd like some company during some of your odds jobs... One of your odd jobs is being a dog-walker. And you want a guy to walk you while you walk the dog. That's the threesome involving pet animals. And you want a guy who will happily pick up the dog crap for you. That's the fecal fetish part."

"Holy dogshit!!!!!!"

"Am I right?"

"I'm speechless...I'm...I'm in psychedelic awe right now."

"So am I right?"

"Where do you live?"

"Why?"

"Because I'm yours."

"But you haven't even seen a picture of me..."

"I'm yours. Even though I'm not worthy of you."

"Are you serious?"

"Tell me where you live. It's time for me to worship you in person."

16. Sammy Meets Melody

As Heeb waited for Melody to arrive at his place on East Eighty-sixth Street, he began to worry a little about having invited her over to his apartment. What if she had posted fake pictures and was heinous-looking in reality? Or even worse, what if she was actually a man?

He should have at least called her and checked out her voice first, he thought to himself. But then he realized that in a phone call the spontaneous momentum they had built up might have been ruined as soon as someone felt awkwardly self-conscious or impulsively insecure about the whole thing. "Closing the deal" over the Internet created an implicit inevitability to their coitus: they had agreed to sleep together in honor of Heeb's genius and that was that. No further comment or discussion was needed or allowed. He just had to accept the concomitant risks of being so adventurous with online dating (as did she, he figured). And his gut told him that the Melody scheduled to show up at his apartment in forty-five minutes would be the same female Melody with whom he had chatted online. There was something disarmingly honest about her overall style that seemed inconsistent with the tactic of using a false identity.

In the time left before his doorbell rang, Heeb opened his CD collection and looked for the closest thing he had to punk music (The Cure). He cranked the music up as he ran about cleaning his bachelor pad, dimming the lights, taking out the garbage, putting away laundry, and – most importantly – fixing up the bathroom. He also combed the hair on the sides of his head, and applied some cologne and deodorant.

Melody made almost no effort to improve her appearance for the occasion, since – as far as she was concerned – their non-physical connection was so good that the rest would be irrelevant to the two of them (with the exception of offensive odors, to which she was quite sensitive). She wore no bra, so that her petite breasts culminated in two small, marbles under the white cloth of her T-shirt. Her rugged blue jean jacket gave her a sexy tomboy look and her baggy camouflage cargo pants obscured the shape of her long, spare legs. Melody's dark makeup, purple, hurricane-styled hair, and numerous ear piercings were true to her photo.

When the doorbell rang and Heeb opened the door, he felt a variety of intense emotions stirring within him: relief that it was, in fact, a female who looked substantially like the online photos he had seen; insecurity about being at least an inch shorter than her; nervousness about their plan to have sex that night; embarrassment at any regrets Melody might be feeling upon seeing what he actually looked like; excitement and intrigue about being with a goth-punk-looking woman for the first time; and uncertainty about what, if anything, to say.

Melody also felt a variety of emotions within her: nervous excitement about having finally found her soul mate, uncertainty about whether her breath still smelled like the falafel she had eaten a few hours before her online chat with Heeb, and restlessness originating in a strong desire to consummate their sexual bond and officially enter a deeply connected relationship.

"Nice place," she said, as she timidly stepped inside.

"Thanks."

"Can I use your bathroom?"

"Sure," Heeb replied nervously.

"Thanks," she said with an anxious smile, as she closed the door. In the bathroom, she scoured the medicine cabinet until she found some toothpaste. She put a gob on her index finger, which she planned to use as a toothbrush, but it fell off before she could raise her hand to her mouth.

"Shit," she muttered under her breath, as she turned on the faucet and pushed the fallen toothpaste down the drain. She eyed his toothbrush, tempted to brush her teeth with it. For a moment, she hesitated, guilty about not first getting his permission. But then she realized that she was about to pass all of her mouth germs to him anyway and proceeded to brush her teeth rather thoroughly with his toothbrush.

Meanwhile Heeb sat on the couch, trying to hit a relaxed pose for when she emerged from his bathroom, but thinking all along about the various excuses she might invent to try to back out of the whole thing. He was convinced that she was thoroughly disappointed. "She just needed the bathroom to regroup and plan her exit strategy," he figured.

Despite his initial instincts about her, his insecurities caused him to forget the extent to which Melody was, in every respect, a misfit with unpredictably quirky tastes – from makeup to music to men to just about everything else. So Heeb needlessly brainstormed for ways to

144

keep her at his place long enough to reestablish the charm and spontaneity that they had enjoyed online.

When she finally came out, he awkwardly tried to start a conversation on a safe topic but was braced for the worst.

"Do you like this music?" he asked hesitantly.

"Um, do you have any Johann Sebastian Bach?" she replied, anxiously.

"I have about seventy-five CDs of Bach...Why?"

"Bach is the only thing I listen to."

"Oh."

As Heeb went back to his CD collection, he suddenly felt as if the evening might still be on.

"Do you have Magnificat?" she asked.

"Yes. It's right here."

"Put it on."

"OK."

As he replaced The Cure with J.S. Bach, Heeb had his back turned to Melody and couldn't see that she had slipped out of her sneakers and taken off her jean jacket. His apartment was soon filled with the harmoniously uplifting horns and choral refrains of Magnificat. He turned around and noticed that she had moved quite close to him. The intense musical environment had an almost hypnotic power to it, and came to symbolize all of their shared quirks already known or soon to be discovered.

She moved closer still and — as Heeb was about to say something — she put her index finger on his lips, and then let her finger run down his chin, over his Adam's apple, down his chest, and over his chubby belly. As the music grew more solemn, she took off her T-shirt and began to undress Sammy as if participating in some holy rite one performs in the presence of one's long lost love. Sammy, on the other hand, thought he was in some sort of surreal film or wet dream. But the self-conscious monologue in his head faded into a purely physical concentration on the lanky body before him, as Melody pressed her body against his and kissed her way from his mouth to his neck. Between their caressing and kissing, they made their way to the nearby sofa, and continued discovering each other's bodies.

They had said nothing from the moment he answered her question about Bach until the moment they were lying in each other's arms on Heeb's couch, spent and ecstatic from their sexual exertions. The music had provided the dialogue for them. Anything else — any words before the sex itself – might have sounded contrived, awkward, out of place, or simply unworthy of the event that was to follow. And as they lay there, in their afterglow, they continued caressing each other while listening to the rest of the music.

When the CD ended, they were silent for a moment, as if in deference to the brilliant music that had just finished. But Heeb felt a potential awkwardness creeping in, precisely because they had said so little up until then, and because it now felt as if they could no longer postpone conversation. So Heeb resourcefully returned them to the playfulness of their online chat.

"So are we now Winners Of Lust?"

"Winners Of Love," she replied with a smile as she kissed his neck. "Put one of the Brandenburgs on," she instructed him. "Preferably the Fifth…And let's go to your bedroom. Under the covers."

"OK," he replied, dutifully getting up to take care of the music.

"Do you realize what you've gotten yourself into?" she asked lightly, as she made her way into his bedroom.

As Heeb approached the entrance to his bedroom, he saw that Melody was already under the covers.

For the seemingly interminable walk to his bed, during which her nakedness was covered but his was not, he slipped into a self-conscious moment of doubt again, bewildered at how she was still at his place rather than trying to flee the fact that she had just had sex with this fat bald guy. He abruptly quickened his pace to the bed, as if to minimize any chance that she might suddenly change her mind about him now that she could inspect his overall appearance more carefully.

But Melody was thinking nothing of the sort. She was preparing to deliver to Heeb the terms and conditions of the intense relationship that they had just embarked upon together. He would need to get a cell phone so that she could reach him if he wasn't at work or at home. He would need to accompany her on every morning and weekend dog walk (helping out with the dung cleanup would be a very nice gesture but certainly not an absolute requirement). He would need to speak to her no fewer than two hours per day, although phone calls and dog walks certainly counted towards this time. They needed to go to an art museum at least twice a month, and an independent art house film at least once a week. He needed to make sure that his breath and body odor were at all times perfectly fragrant (he had done a very good job thus far). And there were other things, but that was enough for now; the rest would be spelled out as the circumstances required.

Although Heeb intended to make a good faith effort to comply with Melody's long list of demands, they came as a peculiar surprise to him because Melody was still an enigmatic, total stranger to him. Melody, on the other hand, felt as if she could tell Heeb anything. In a leap of intuitive faith, she believed that he understood her at the core better than anyone else ever had. This intuition was based on their online chat, their shared humor and musical taste, and, most importantly, his unparalleled ability to decrypt her riddle.

The explanation for Melody's sudden intimacy was simple. Every person is a puzzle with a password. By solving the puzzle, the potential for emotional and physical intimacy is realized. There are two ways to solve the puzzle: 1) a lengthy courtship in which the pieces of the puzzle are gradually assembled, or 2) a brief utterance of that one password – unique to every person – that establishes the same level of legitimacy, comfort, and intimacy that can otherwise be achieved only through a methodical assembly of the various puzzle pieces found during numerous experiences together.[2]

Heeb had achieved instant intimacy by uttering Melody's password — a code that he had cracked through sheer cleverness rather than any deep and comprehensive intuition about who Melody was and what she really wanted. Thus, it was only with considerable effort and adjustment that Heeb could understand and accommodate Melody's many needs. But why did he bother? After all, when he had first started chatting with Melody online, the most he actually wanted or hoped for was an adventurous one-night stand with a sexy oddball. However, during their first night and morning together, he realized that he was

---

[2] Suppose for a moment that Melody had come from a Kurdish dissident family in Northern Iraq, and Sammy had been a leading Kurdish activist in Eastern Turkey, and the two had never met before their random encounter on a New York City bus. Upon correctly intuiting that Melody was also a Kurd, Sammy could utter a few sentences in Kurdish in which he praised the beauties of a town that happened to be Melody's village, which Sammy had visited in 1999 while on a political mission to negotiate the release from an Iraqi prison of a famous dissident, Mahmoud Ahmet — a man who, unbeknownst to Sammy, happened to be her father. These highly specific and personally significant sentences would effectively constitute a password that would instantly convert complete strangers into potential lovers. This password would have the same power to create intimacy as would an eight-month courtship between two strangers who have almost nothing in common. In reality, Sammy and Melody had far less in common than the Kurds on the New York City bus, but the specificity of Heeb's apparent knowledge about Melody produced the same net effect.

147

actually intrigued by her idiosyncrasies, and curious to understand her as well as she assumed he already did. He was also drawn to her — particularly when they showered together and her dark cosmetics and wild hairdo were washed away, leaving only traces of lilac in her dark brown hair.

The morning after their first encounter, a lazy Sunday, they ordered in breakfast and ate it on Heeb's bed. She had a fruit salad and he had lox and bagels. Between mousy bites, Melody shared some additional facts about herself that gave Heeb pause.

"Do you know why it's funny that my last name is Katz?"

Heeb felt a moment of alarm. "Your last name is Katz?"

"Yeah. Why? What's the big deal?"

"So...So are you Jewish?" Heeb had just convinced himself that he was sufficiently intrigued by and attracted to Melody that he wanted to date her for a while. But this new information threatened a premature end to his "play period." He had under a year left for "play," and he thought he could enjoy dating Melody for a month or two and then move on to the caddish project of cramming in as much additional play as possible before his two-year search for a Jewish wife began. But if she was Jewish, he might be tempted to extend that initial month or two into something longer. Why? Because if that something longer was good enough to last as long as say, eight months, he would already be so close to the two-year search period, that he might as well just stick with Melody, rather than start over and risk finding no one as good as her in time to be married by thirty. So Heeb was worried that, if Melody Katz was, in fact, Jewish, he might already be compelled, on their first morning together, to entertain the possibility that he would marry her. And that would be it: Heeb would have met his wife on the Internet. Equally discordant with all of his childhood notions of matrimony was the idea that his wife would be someone he had slept with on their very first meeting. Then he recalled Lucky Chucky's marriage story, and decided that this additional detail was acceptable, but still somewhat odd.

"I'm an atheist — or at least an agnostic," she answered. "But technically I'm Jewish. I mean, my parents are Jewish...Why?"

"Oh. Never mind."

"Are you?"

"Technically."

"Well, technically you didn't guess why it's funny that my last name is Katz."

"Why? Because you love cats?" Heeb ventured.

"Oh my God! You're brilliant."

"Am I right?"

"You should have been a tarot card reader or something. None of it's legit, but they do have good intuition. I can't believe you're wasting your talents as an actuary."

"So you really love cats?"

"Yeah. I have twelve living with me in my studio."

"Wow…How nice," Heeb replied with politic politeness, even though he had always harbored a passive aversion to cats – particularly in any quantity exceeding one.

"They're all very well trained, and I've developed a very good deodorizing system, so my apartment actually smells really good."

"I don't care how good your system is. There's no way I'm stepping foot into that studio," Heeb thought to himself. And then he said to Melody, "Sounds like you're the kind of cat lover they would feature in one of those human interest stories on the morning news."

"It's funny, because a journalist once offered to interview me for a story, but I'm really too shy for that sort of thing."

During the weeks that followed their initial meeting, the taxing process of adjusting to Melody actually made Heeb care more about making the relationship work, even if it meant the unplanned, premature end of his play period. The mere fact of having to accommodate so many of Melody's desiderata at his own expense made Heeb feel more invested in the relationship. The main requirement, of course, was his time – a demand that forced him to drop some of the very courses he had hoped would introduce him to women. After an extensive discussion, Heeb and Melody agreed that he would drop out of everything but photography, and that she would enroll in the same class with him — if they could persuade the instructor to let her join the class so late, based on her impressive portfolio of cat photographs taken over the last few years.

But despite Heeb's Herculean efforts, he always seemed to fall short of fully satisfying Melody's emotional needs. When he had to work late so that he couldn't meet her or talk on the phone, she quickly grew angry and frustrated at his unavailability. After working for nearly half a year as a freelance dog walker, babysitter, web developer, math tutor, and housecleaner, she had forgotten what it's like to have most of one's life consumed by a full-time, New York City job. She now had an erratic schedule with large periods of free time during which she assumed or wished that Heeb would be available as well.

Perhaps their most irreconcilable difference was her unbounded and apparently unavoidable love of cats, a fact confirmed by the reliable presence of at least a dozen bristles clinging to her clothes or shoes at any given moment. By her own admission, her feline fixation had cost her a few long-term relationships over the years.

For a while, Heeb managed to find apparently neutral and understandable reasons for them to go back to his place rather than hers: it was more spacious and better equipped with home entertainment systems, it had a better Bach collection and easier access to good restaurants, and it was located closer to his office and to most of her odd jobs. But after about three weeks, Melody correctly concluded that the only reason he wouldn't go back to her place – which he had never seen – was the prospect of being in a small studio with her and twelve cats.

As their relationship grew rockier, Heeb finally decided to call Carlos for advice.

Carlos was already aware of Melody's many eccentricities and needy psychology and asked Heeb to remind him of her virtues. "I know you guys have great conversations and great sex, but is there anything more to this whole relationship?" he asked.

"Does there need to be?" Heeb asked lightheartedly.

"I suppose not," Carlos replied in reflective amusement. "Well, let's not forget about friendship, taking care of each other – "

"We have that too. And she's probably the first woman who has ever unconditionally loved me."

"It sounds to me like she has a lot of conditions: two hours a day of communication, tolerating cats in ridiculous quantities, constantly keeping your breath and body odor in check, going to an independent film once a week, and – "

"But those having nothing to do with me, Carlos. Except the odors. And that's only because she's very sensitive to scents and my breath is sometimes bad enough to kill the roaches in my apartment."

"So you really think she loves you unconditionally?"

"Yes. It's really the first time that a woman loves me exactly as I am. I think Yumi loved me more because of how well I treated her and because she really needed someone to help her when she first arrived. But Melody genuinely loves me for who I am. She's not using me in any way. She needs me only on an emotional level…She's just a bit crazy and expects me to put up with it. But she would never in a million years pull a Yumi on me. She thinks we're perfect soul mates."

"Really?"

"If I gained fifty pounds, became homeless, and lost the hair on the sides of my head, she'd still be with me, as long as I could put up with her meshugas…There's something really compelling about that. The only problem is that we might just be fundamentally incompatible on certain things, including the cat issue."

"I don't know what to tell you, Heeb. Every relationship has its own rules. Had you asked me back in college if I thought that I could ever have a girlfriend who would take two years to quit smoking and who would expect me to sit in therapy until I overcame my mysophobia, I'd have told you that it was impossible. But Carolina and I confronted the impossible. And now we're both better off. As individuals and as a couple."

"So what are you saying?"

"That being in love can change almost anything: from your expectations and limitations to your very life plans. It's a completely unpredictable force. And how it operates within any particular relationship is a total mystery to anyone outside of that relationship."

"But I don't know if I'm in love with her…She's definitely in love with me, and on our good days, I feel like I might be falling in love with her. But on our bad days, I feel like if I stay with her we'll both end up institutionalized."

"It'll work itself out, Sammy. Just give it some time."

17. Love me, Love my Katz

On Sunday, five weeks into their relationship, Melody decided that she would confront Heeb about the cat issue the next time they spoke. The day before, the two had argued over the fact that she always came to his place. But because Heeb had had a lot of work to do at home and would need to wake up extra early the next morning, he acquiesced much more readily than usual when she refused to come over. The fact that he didn't call back after their fight to make up and charm her into coming over only further angered Melody, particularly since she hadn't seen him since Friday morning. Deep down she hoped that Heeb might get enough work done to accompany her on her Monday morning dog walk. But if he couldn't join her, she would also welcome the opportunity finally to excoriate him as needed, and air all of her accumulated grievances.

The exceedingly muggy Monday morning, towards the end of the summer of 2000, got off to a bad start for Sammy. In his frantic rush to get to the office by 6 a.m. so that he could finish a report expected by forty people, he quickly grabbed the many objects he needed to take but no bag in which to carry them: his apartment keys, an umbrella for the expected afternoon downpour, an assortment of documents and floppy disks, his cell phone, his walkman, his calendar, his wallet, some bill payments that he had to put in the mail, and the trash that was stinking up his apartment (his residence always deteriorated after any three-day period in which Melody hadn't been over).

To maximize his morning efficiency, Heeb had developed the habit of first calling the elevator, then dropping the trash in the building incinerator, and then locking his apartment door, by which time the elevator would arrive. As Heeb dropped the trash down the incinerator, while holding his keys, umbrella, phone, wallet, documents, calendar, mail, and disks, he thought about how bad it would have been had he accidentally dropped his only pair of apartment keys down the incinerator with the trash. This thought tempted him, as he was locking his front door, to run back inside and look for his bag, but the elevator arrived, and he decided just to opt for efficiency over convenient carrying. In the elevator, he organized the assorted objects as follows:

he put his keys, wallet, and disks into his various trouser pockets, his walkman onto his belt with the headset around his neck, his cell phone, and mail in his right hand, and the umbrella, calendar, and documents in his left hand.

As Sammy exited the elevator and began walking towards the train, he debated whether to call Melody and tell her that he wouldn't be able to join her 8 a.m. dog walk. If he called now (at 6:15 a.m.), he risked waking her up, if she had forgotten to turn off her ringer, and – even worse – he risked getting into a heated argument with her over the fact that he couldn't make their walk. On the other hand, there was a chance that at this early hour he would just get her voicemail, which would be ideal. Another consideration in favor of calling so early, during his walk to the train, was the fact that from the time he entered the train station until after his 11 a.m. meeting was over, he wouldn't be able to call Melody, and this might look to her as if he had just flaked on her dog walk.

Heeb was cranky from lack of sleep and stress related to his upcoming meeting, his hands and arms were uncomfortable from schlepping so many loose objects while walking at such a frenzied pace, and he was unsure of how exactly to manage Melody's potentially explosive reaction (particularly since they still hadn't made up from the previous night's fight). Nevertheless, he concluded that calling her during his walk to the subway station was the lesser of evils.

As Heeb dialed Melody's number, he prayed that his call would go straight to voicemail.

After a few rings, he heard: "Heh...Hello?" He had awakened her.

"Hi...It's me...I'm really sorry about calling so early."

"What...what's wrong?" she began groggily.

"I just didn't want you to think that I had forgotten."

"Forgotten what?"

"About the 8 a.m. dog walk." By now, Melody had seen that it was just after 6:18 a.m.

"Sammy, why are you calling so early?"

"Because otherwise we won't be able to talk until around 11 a.m."

"But we can just talk during the dog walk."

"No. That's what I'm calling to tell you...I can't make the walk today...I'm sorry."

And that was it. By this point Melody, who was a light sleeper, was awake enough to recall all of the simmering gripes that she had wanted to express since their last tiff, and decided that it was time to unleash her fury. "So this is how you make up for last night?"

"I'm sorry about last night. I just had a lot of work and didn't want to schlep – "

"Don't give me the schlepping shit. If I can schlep to your place every fucking time we meet you can schlep to mine once in a leap year. You don't like my cats. That's the only reason you've never been to my place."

"That's not true."

"Admit it once and for all or I'm hanging up on you. I'm tired of the bullshit reasons about better restaurants, it's closer to our jobs, you've got a better Bach collection, and blah blah blah. It all comes down to my cats. And that's it. Period. Admit it."

"Twelve cats is a lot for a studio."

"But you've never even seen the place."

"Look, four hundred square feet would be tiny for me without a dozen cats and another person…I'm just claustrophobic I guess."

"And you don't like cats."

"That's not true. I'm just not crazy about being in a cat farm."

"Admit that you don't like cats so that I can hang up."

"Did I just lose my right to dislike cats?"

"Love me, love my cats."

"I can't believe I just lost that right."

"Love me, love my cats."

"The right to dislike cats is an inalienable right."

"Not if you love me it's not."

"Look, can we just talk about this later?" Heeb really didn't want to suffer through this conversation just before an important business meeting and he felt very aware of three nearby yuppies who looked far too bored with their walk not to eavesdrop on his increasingly heated call. But deferring the discussion was unthinkable for Melody; she had finally mustered the courage to launch into a whole litany of complaints, and she wasn't about to lose her momentum.

"And you don't call enough," she continued, ignoring Heeb's plea.

"But we speak on the phone about eight times a day on average."

Heeb saw that he was stuck on this call and began to move away from the yuppies in the direction of a lone morning walker – a man in his fifties with headphones on, wearing shorts and sandals, and reading the paper while walking. He seemed too busy to tune in to Heeb's spat.

"That's not enough. And I'm always the one calling you."

"Yeah, during work, when I'm not supposed to be on the phone."

"You spend too much time in the office."

"Do you want to support me? You know I've always wanted a sugar mama. Or should we open up a dog-walking company together?"

Sensing that the conversation would only get more heated and irrational, Heeb glanced at the older walker next to him, just to confirm that he hadn't yet taken any interest in Heeb's conversation. He was still reading the newspaper with his headphones on.

"You're part of corporate America for God's sake. You don't have enough edge," she continued.

"What do you mean?"

"You wouldn't commit any crimes with me. Or even misdemeanors."

"You mean drugs? Or anal sex?"

They had had a fight over this issue about a week earlier.

"Either," she replied.

"I can't put my dick in anything that could contain parts of our dinner in it," he rejoined, without noticing the fifty-year-old look over at him in disgusted disapproval. "It just grosses me out, OK? It's against Biblical law."

"I told you I'm an atheist."

"Well maybe it's time to rediscover your religion," he retorted.

"I tried licking your toes once, like you wanted. Even though it was disgusting – especially with my sensitivity to odors."

"I washed my feet for twenty minutes first."

"Well you missed some spots. Anyway, that's not the point. You should be willing to try anything once," Melody countered. "Including a tongue enema, which I haven't even asked for yet, even though I love them."

"A tongue enema?" Heeb asked, in confused repulsion.

"Yeah. They're amazing. And I'd give you one back in return."

"A tongue enema?! I think that's the most nauseating thing I've ever heard of."

"How do you know you won't like it?"

"You and your anything-once-philosophy! Next you'll suggest that I make love to your cats." The fifty-year-old next to him continued his look of appalled eavesdropping.

"It would be nice if you could love them."

"See what I mean?"

"I was joking. You know that's not what I mean."

"Why not? Sodomy. Bestiality. Masturbating while skydiving on acid."

The fifty-year-old looked up at Heeb, shook his head vituperatively and muttered loudly to himself: "You sick fuck!" Then he sped up to get away from Heeb.

Heeb reddened for a moment and continued, trying not to lose his point: "I mean, where does the search for new experiences end? Everyone has limits. Mine start with the anus."

"You don't even do ecstasy for God's sake. How can you refuse to listen to Bach with me on ex? It's the most incredible experience."

"It's illegal. And they do random drug testing at my work."

"That's corporate America talking again."

"Would you stop with that corporate America crap? That's my job, OK? One of these days you may have to go back to having one too."

"Listen to what you're saying to me! Can you believe what you just – "

Heeb blanked out on Melody for a moment as he remembered that he needed to deposit his mail in the mailbox a few feet away because it was the last one before he entered the Eighty-sixth Street subway station. He had been looking forward to this moment, after uncomfortably holding his mail in a stack that was sandwiched between his fingers and his cell phone, which was held down on the stack by his right thumb and pressed up to the side of his head for the conversation.

He refocused on Melody's rant: "...not fair...I mean, listen to how you communicate with me! I feel like that's become our problem. That's really what this is about now: we just don't communicate like we used – "

And that was the last thing he heard Melody say. Heeb's painfully cramped and over-encumbered fingers were so eager to release the stack of mail from his right hand into the mailbox that they released his cell phone as well.

Heeb stood there for a moment, in dazed disbelief, looking helplessly at the sides of the mailbox.

Melody's continuing diatribe could now be heard only as a series of strangely muffled, barely audible noises, emanating from within the metal mailbox, like a transistor radio that falls into a manhole and just gives off a faint, chattering buzz.

In absurd desperation, Heeb tried cupping his hands to the mailbox for a moment, and shouting into it, hoping that she might hear what happened and that he really didn't mean to drop the phone in the mailbox just as she was complaining about how they don't communicate as well as they used to.

"Melody! Melody! I can't hear you! I dropped my phone in the mailbox! Can you hear me?! I'm sorry! It slipped!"

As several commuters walked by, looking oddly at this heavyset balding man in a suit and tie crouched down low and apparently talking rather urgently to a mailbox, Heeb felt that he may have reached the nadir of his follies in the New York dating scene. But it would actually get much worse.

Heeb was sure that Melody would call him at work that day and that the conversation would get even nastier because of how their last argument had ended. He had no promising strategy in mind for how to deal with her call at work, so it was with some measure of surprised relief that he reached the end of the day without having heard from her. He concluded that a Melody moratorium might do his nerves some good and decided not to call her that night. Sammy still couldn't quite understand how someone who had been so timid that first night they met could turn out to be so ferocious over what seemed to him such trivial matters (particularly the cat bit).

The next day at his office was so hectic that it wasn't until 7 p.m. that he even noticed that Melody still hadn't called. He decided to call her as soon as he got home and before he even went shopping for a replacement cell phone. He found her number in his address book and then called her from his home phone.

"Are you still mad at me?"

"No. Actually, I should thank you." There was a strangely amused and ironic tone to Melody's voice.

"What do you mean?"

"Well, I called you about two hours later, and guess who picked up?"

"The mailman."

"That's right, Kojak" Melody replied, complimenting Heeb's legendary detective skills. But – in the context of their quarrel – her

157

remark sounded to Heeb like an insult that cynically exploited his earlier confessions to her about his insecurities.

"Let me guess: he has lots of hair."

"He sure does. But you know I don't care about hair."

"And you know that I do! So you already went on a date with him?"

"We really hit it off over the phone. I mean it was a pretty hysterical situation, me calling a cell phone in a mailbox just as he opened it to collect the mail."

"Yeah, it's not too hard to come up with a few jokes about that one. But I'm sure you thought he was very witty."

"Maybe it was just fate."

"It was an accident for God's sake."

"And what's fate, if not a series of accidents that work out in just the right way?"

"I can't believe you went postal on me just like that."

"He's got a great schedule too. Lots of time for me."

"So you slept with him too?"

"No, Sammy. Don't be silly."

"So he couldn't solve your riddle?"

"God, you're quick. I will miss that about you."

"Miss? You mean this is it?"

"Unless you're willing to come over to my place."

"So you're going to take the mail guy over me because of the cat issue?" Heeb believed so strongly that he was in the right that, if this was in fact the end, he knew he'd be able to walk away with a clear conscience and relatively unscathed.

"He doesn't have any cat issues."

"But he has other issues."

"I'm ready for some new issues."

"I can't believe we're having this conversation."

"Well I'm lying here in bed waiting for you, if you'd like to be doing something else with me."

Heeb suddenly lost all of the fighting spirit fueled by his conviction that he was right in this dispute. With that invitation, he was ready to forgive her mailman date and just succumb to the twelve cats. As aggravating and stressful as Melody's moodiness and irrationality had been, Heeb was more than ready for some make-up sex.

18. Heeb Hits the Jackpot

During the thirty-minute commute to Melody's studio in Queens, Sammy tried in vain not to think about the dozen cats that would be there to meow around his feet, shed their hair all over his clothes, and step nimbly out of his way just in the nick of time. He convinced himself that this trip would at least give him a new argument in future quarrels about the cat issue. He would be able to say, in his own defense, that he had legitimately "tried it once": he had, in fact, tried to go to her place and the experience was so unpleasant that she should now understand if he doesn't want to repeat it.

As Heeb walked down the hallway of Melody's apartment building and got closer to the door of her studio, he could hear Bach's Tocatta and Fugue in D minor blasting from within. The dark and ominous organ sounds made the experience all the more strangely cinematic — as if Heeb were the gallant knight of some gothic horror movie who, after an arduous and dangerous journey, had courageously arrived at the stygian chamber of reckoning.

The door opened and Melody's lank figure appeared in a black leotard and dark tights. Atop her purple-streaked, brunet hair, pulled back into a chignon, sat black felt cat ears. In addition to her usual dark makeup, the tip of her nose was painted black and her cheeks were penciled with charcoal cat whiskers.

She simpered, and tilted her head towards the inside of her apartment, signaling him to enter.

Heeb stepped inside. The walls of Melody's studio were painted a tenebrous green, and the windows were covered by thick, black velvet curtains that ensured a total absence of light but for the scattered, plum colored candles burning in various corners and hanging from a small candelabrum. Crammed into the four-hundred-square-foot apartment were a kitchenette, a queen-sized bed, a tiny bathroom, a miniature table for eating and a large desk with a small stereo system, desktop computer, scanner, and printer for Melody's freelance design work.

As soon as the door shut behind him, Heeb felt crowded by the dozen felines roaming about the cramped space. A chorus of meows went off as soon as he walked in, though they were largely drowned out by the booming, intense, and ominous Bach music.

Heeb did his best to absorb this dusky and cramped cat cave, but he found the Tocatta and Fugue in D minor to be too much for the moment. "Do you mind if we put on something a bit softer or more serene? Maybe his Cello Suite Number One in G major?"

"How about the English Suite Number Two?" she replied.

"Even better."

While Melody searched for the right CD, Heeb continued to survey her place. He noticed that her cats came in three colors – black, grey, or tiger striped – and that they perched themselves anywhere they pleased. Three were lounging on Melody's bed, one of which – a large black cat – lay directly on her pillow. Two sat atop the desk with her computer equipment. Two were playing with a ball of purple yarn on the wood floor. One lay in the path to the bathroom, another obstructed the approach to the refrigerator, and another roamed about the front door area. Two others were running about somewhat wildly in the longest open space in the apartment. Each of Heeb's movements – whether it was a step of the foot, a swing of the arm, or an attempt to sit down – felt as though it barely missed a tail, a vibrissa, or a paw.

Cat hairs coated the floor and bedspread and clung to every piece of furniture. But the thick air in Melody's apartment had no offensive odors, and smelled like a subtle blend of burning candles, incense, and dried fruit. This was because, to accommodate her olfactory sensitivities, Melody had hired a contractor to build a "mini cat-room" out of specially scented pinewood, so that she could place all of the litter boxes and cat food into one well-sealed and custom-ventilated corner of her apartment.

Melody found the English Suite Number Two CD and began removing it from the shelf. But she stopped at the jarring caterwaul emitted by the tabby mouser that had been roaming about by the front door. Melody saw that Heeb had inadvertently stepped on the end of its tail as he continued trying to adjust to the small and surreal space.

"Hey! You just stepped on Vagina. Apologize to her!"

"Did you really name your pussy that?" Sammy asked, in surprised amusement.

"Yep."

"But isn't that a bit generic?"

"Well, sometimes I call her Vaj for short. Now apologize."

"Do you think she'll understand me? How's her vocabulary?"

"When talking to cats, it's all about the intonation and sincerity. So you have to mean it. Come on, Sammy."

Heeb crouched down to make amends with the irritated feline, using the most sincere voice he could summon under the circumstances. "Look, I'm really sorry about that. This is my first time meeting a Vagina with a tail, and I stepped out of line a bit. Literally. It was really an honest mistake. But I probably should have worn a condom on my shoe, just in case."

Melody laughed. She crouched down and, in a voice one would use with a baby, she called her cat over for some palliative petting. "Come here, Vaj! Sammy's really sorry. And very funny. Now come here and I'll make it all better!" The tabby ran over to Melody, who scooped her up and started petting her. "That's a good girl."

Melody eventually released the cat onto the edge of the bed, so that she could finish inserting the CD. The tabby approached one of the bed pillows, where the large black cat was still perched, watching Heeb walk over to Melody. As Vaj arrived at the edge of the pillow, the black cat moved off of it – not out of fear or deference to Vaj, but only because he was curious about Heeb. The fourteen-pound Bombay moved to the edge of the bed, and stared up at Heeb, as if to assess him. Sammy looked into the feline's yellow eyes, and then at his sleek black fur and sinuous body. The miniature panther eventually jumped down to the ground and circled around Melody's leg, like a furry ball of oil hovering over the floor.

After Melody finished inserting the new Bach CD, she knelt down to pick up the Bombay. She turned towards Heeb and, in a maternal and protective voice, said, "Jackpot's my favorite baby. Aren't you, Jackpot? Do you know why his name is Jackpot?"

"Hmm…A black cat named Jackpot…Oh, I got it! You wanted to correct the superstition that black cats bring bad luck, right?"

"You're a genius, Sammy," she said. "No one gets that on the first try. Isn't Sammy a little genius, Jackpot? Don't you just love that about him?" she said to her cat as she rubbed her face affectionately into his soft fur. Melody held the cat closely against her breast, and walked towards Heeb. Once she was within a few feet of him, she pursed up her lips coyly and seductively asked, "Do you want some pussy?"

"As long as you're not talking about Vaj," Heeb replied, pointing to the tabby that had taken Jackpot's spot on the bed pillow.

Melody chuckled, and then crouched down to let Jackpot drop gracefully to the floor. Emboldened by the affection that had just been showered upon him from the mistress of the house, Jackpot jumped back onto the bed to reclaim his throne from Vaj.

Melody stood back up and put her arms around Heeb and began kissing him.

She caressed him intensely and pressed herself up against him closely, as if a torrent of sexual favors might exonerate her from the mailman incident.

She slid her index finger up the length of his spine, until she could run her hand through the hair on the sides of his head.

But Heeb couldn't readily refocus his attention from the feline circus in the background to the erotic overtures of the cat-woman grinding up and down on him.

"Heavy petting in front of pets," he said, unable to keep the silly thought to himself.

Melody chuckled and whispered into Heeb's ear, "I missed your humor." She then proceeded to nibble on his ear as she undressed him.

But with eight of the twelve cats peering at him, it took about twenty minutes for Heeb to shake the idea that he was being closely watched. Even modeling nude for a room full of painters hadn't prepared him for sexual intimacy in the presence of so many mammals.

Heeb, who was soon naked, had to make a concerted effort to concentrate on the action at hand. Rather than flow naturally with Melody's physical movements, he was thinking about some National Geographic program he had seen a few years ago, in which the baritone narrator had declared that cats have the largest eyes of any mammal, in relation to body size.

Heeb finally returned to Melody enough to untie the knot of string in the center of her back that kept her leotard up. It unfurled gently off her torso and revealed her small breasts. She helped him to remove her leotard, so that she had nothing on except her black tights.

In a passionate frenzy, Melody moved them onto the bed, but Heeb abruptly stepped on the brakes, and got off the bed.

"What's wrong?"

"There's no way I'm lying on all that cat hair!" he exclaimed, brushing off the part of his body that had touched the bedspread and examining himself for any cat hairs that might still be stuck to him.

"Sammy, it's fine! Their hair is clean. I lie naked on that bedspread all the time."

"Why did you have to tell me that? I didn't need to know that about you."

"Really, Sammy. It's fine…Cats spend about thirty-four percent of their lives grooming themselves."

"You mean using their tongues to put cat saliva on themselves."

"And I bathe them once a week."

"Can we just get under the covers?"

"OK." Melody shooed the three cats off her bed and removed the bedspread. Heeb was relieved to see that the white sheets below were free of any cat hairs, but gave Melody a disapproving look as he flipped the pillows over so that the dirty, cat-used-side was no longer facing where they would rest their heads.

Melody blew out some candles and then joined Heeb under the covers.

She entangled her bare legs in his as their naked bodies approached each other. They hadn't seen each other in almost four days and were meeting on the heels of a protracted fight that resulted in a near break-up. They grabbed each other in restless anticipation of make-up sex, knowing that the tension from their spat wouldn't be fully relieved until its conclusion. The two unbridled libidos, brimming with the issues that had yet to be resolved, unleashed themselves under the covers.

Melody's dozen cats reacted differently to the whirlwind of sheets and legs and arms spinning around atop the queen-sized bed: some began to run around wildly while others just sat and meowed, as if in homage to the mating rituals of a friendly species. Undoubtedly, Heeb would have found any perceptible cat reaction to be both unsettling and distracting, because it would have made him recognize that he was effectively performing in front of a mammalian audience. But Heeb was too absorbed in the moment to notice the cats.

The rhythm of the limbs and the sheets finally reached its crescendo and Heeb collapsed atop Melody's sweaty body. Melody loved that coital moment more than any other: when a man's orgasm rendered his entire body flaccid and heavy – as if she had squeezed all of the vitality out of him and replaced it with some powerful sedative.

As they blissfully caught their breaths, they could feel each other's hearts pounding.

They shared a tranquil, reassuring smile, and all was forgiven.

The moment felt almost too heavy, and Heeb couldn't resist lightening the mood with a silly joke.

"Do you think the cats would get upset if we did it doggie style?"

Melody's face brightened in amusement.

"Not if I have you on a very tight leash," she quipped.

By 1 a.m., they had released a second bed tornado that ended more climactically than even the first. At 1:15, they were gradually slipping into an ever-drowsier state of dreamy lassitude. And by 1:30, Melody had dozed off and Heeb was close behind but still having occasional thoughts about how the make-up sex could have been even better had she sucked on his toes. But he reminded himself how asking her to indulge his favorite fetish would have surely exposed him to a litany of counter-demands that he simply wasn't willing to fulfill because they were too close to homosexuality, or too predicated on the use of psychotropic drugs.

By 1:45, Heeb's thoughts had gently faded into a garbled mumbling. By 2 a.m., there was total silence and Heeb was sound asleep.

Jackpot, and the other two cats that had been on the bed earlier, saw that the commotion there had stopped and that it was now safe to go back to their domain.

Jackpot lightly leaped onto the edge of the bed, and wandered about the thin strip of vacant bed to Heeb's immediate right, in search of an ideal place to sit. The other two cats, grey colored and somewhat smaller in size, jumped onto the bed next to Melody and began to approach the end of the bed where her head was resting. But after a few steps, they noticed that both pillows were occupied, and decided to turn around and head for the other end of the bed where there was more room.

The grey cats circled about the two pairs of feet positioned in contradictory ways at the end of the bed. After a few moments, at approximately 2:16 a.m., they began to take considerable interest in Heeb's feet — perhaps because his size nines were new to the area and carried with them a peculiar scent that intrigued them.

At 2:17 a.m., both grey cats began licking the big toe and index toe of Heeb's left foot. Their small, warm, pink tongues, rhythmically lapping up the sides and tops of Heeb's two toes were quickly and delightfully incorporated into Heeb's deep sleep. His dreaming mind easily transformed the cat tongues into those of Melody and Yumi simultaneously sucking on his left foot. After a while, Melody and Yumi moved to the next set of toes on his left foot, and worked on them with the same rhythm and indulgent patience as they had employed with the first set of toes, so that it felt as if this pedal pleasure might never end.

While Heeb had exerted himself rather intensely with Melody before collapsing in exhaustion, the titillation produced by the sensations at the base of his body and the dreamy fantasies they invoked aroused Heeb in a rather noticeable way. In fact, Jackpot, who had comfortably settled down immediately to the right of Heeb's hips, noticed something moving in that area. And at the height of Heeb's Yumi-Melody fantasy, when the two grey cats had moved over to the first two toes on his right foot, and began licking away with even greater gusto, Heeb abruptly became completely erect.

Now, at precisely that moment of Heeb's greatest arousal, Jackpot was sure that the object that had suddenly sprang up in the dark was a little mouse. Given how heavily fortified Melody's apartment was against rodents, it was with no small surprise or delight that Jackpot spied the first mouse ever to make it onto Melody's bed. In fact, Jackpot felt a certain amount of respect for the courageous little creature who could so brazenly wander into Jackpot's midst, with two of his formidable colleagues located just a few feet away, at the end of the bed.

Jackpot's evolutionary instincts were well honed and he knew not to underestimate the mouse's ability to escape. So, in a flash of hunter-like speed and precision, he pounced onto the object that had moved in the dark, so that the claws from both of his paws trapped the target for the second that it took Jackpot to get the prey between his sharp teeth.

But seconds after that moment of feline glory, when Jackpot caught between his teeth and claws that thing that had moved in the dark, the cat realized that a grave case of mistaken identity had occurred. Jackpot's realization happened just as Heeb's powerful blow sent the black fur ball sailing off the bed. Heeb's hysterical howl of pain had actually begun as a frantic yelp, and by the time he had sat up and swatted Jackpot off his Hebrew National, he was screaming at the top of his lungs – both from the psychological trauma and from the actual pain of the incident.

Some of Melody's neighbors were awakened, wondering what sort of domestic spat was underway next door. The matter was somewhat clarified when they heard Heeb scream "Call an ambulance!"

"Are – are you OK?" Melody stammered, equally shocked to discover what had happened.

"No, I'm not OK! Your cat just bit my dick! Do you think I'd be OK after that?! Now call a fucking ambulance!"

"OK. Right. An ambulance. 911," Melody said, scurrying about for the telephone.

The female emergency operator answered after the first ring: "This is 911. What is your location?" Melody was able enough to answer that question, but the query that followed left her stumped for a moment: "What is your emergency?"

Heeb's frantic cries could be heard in the background.

"Well, um…It's uh…an animal accident."

"What kind of animal accident?"

"You know, one involving animals."

"Miss, we need additional details, so that we can dispatch the proper emergency team to your area. Right now I don't know if you need an animal vet or a staff member with rabies expertise."

"Well…My cat bit my boyfriend."

"Where?"

"On his penis."

19. Misery Likes Company

To add insult to injury on that mortifying night, Sammy had to explain what had happened to him to six different people: the two ambulance personnel in the back of the vehicle, then the hospital insurance administrator, then the nurse, then his hospital roommate, and then the doctor. And because the story seemed so implausible on its face, none of the six people would accept the simple and brief explanation that Heeb initially offered: "A cat attacked my penis." Each of them interrogated Heeb about the circumstances preceding the bite, and had to be told exactly how a cat had managed to attack his penis.

Thus, Sammy had to repeat the following account six times: "My girlfriend keeps twelve cats in her studio apartment. Three of them were on her bed when I arrived. I asked her to shoo them away so that we could have the bed to ourselves. She did that, and then we got under the covers. We then had quite a bit of sex, and as far as I know, no cats were involved or on the bed at the time. But as I drifted asleep afterwards, some of the cats must have returned because I felt something licking my toes, which reinforced an erotic dream that I was having. That dream and the toe-licking sensation caused me to have an erection. And apparently, there was a third cat partnering with the toe-licking cats, and watching my waist area closely. And when he saw my penis move into an erection, he must have thought that it was a mouse because he pounced on it with his claws before taking a bite. Moral of the story? Wear steel underwear, if you're sleeping in a studio with twelve cats."

The worst follow up question came from one of the ambulance personnel, an Italian-American named Vinny, who was preparing various gauzes, disinfectants, syringes, and some antibiotics while his colleague read through some medical reference manual in the back of the speeding ambulance. "Adon' ahnderstand sumpin'," Vinny began in his thick, Italian-Brooklyn accent, "Why didn't you put ya undies back on after? I mean, just to be safe, you knows? With so many animals runnin' around and all?"

"Who the fuck thinks of these things?" Heeb replied in exasperation, his groin area still excruciatingly sore from the fresh wounds. "We had just finished having sex for the second time, for

Christ's sake. You drift off to sleep at that point. You don't start thinking about the anti-cat penis armor that you need to put on."

"I dunno, man...F'it was me, I'da put da' undies back on. Just to be safe. You don't wanna mess around wit' 'dat stuff."

Heeb knew that there was still some serious pain ahead of him, so he didn't want to argue with or in any way excite the people charged with his care. "You're right. I should have put the undies back on. I wasn't thinking," he said.

Heeb was glad that he had refused to let Melody accompany him. The fewer people who saw what he would have to go through, the better. And he had decided that a relationship with Melody was never going to work, that she was indirectly responsible for the catastrophe at hand, and that he never wanted to see her again. So he didn't want to give her any opportunity to gain back his affection by going with him to the hospital.

"Now this is gonna hurt a little, but we gotta clean out ya wound, or there could be complicashuns," Vinny said, as he approached Heeb with some disinfectant solution. Heeb knew that Vinny meant well, but the Mafioso accent was less than comforting under the circumstances.

Heeb's clenched knuckles turned white from the intensity of the pain, and he began hyperventilating between yelps, as Vinny washed away the blood, cleaned out the area, and bandaged the wound with fine mesh gauze soaked in saline solution. The needle prick of the tetanus shot that followed felt like a tickle by comparison.

The ambulance arrived at the hospital. Vinny and his co-worker helped Heeb out of the vehicle, put him in a wheelchair, and wheeled him towards the hospital's emergency admissions area. Along the way, Vinny couldn't help cracking a joke about how this had been revenge of the cats.

"It was like a conspiracy, you know?" said Vinny.

"I was just joking about the three cats partnering up," replied Heeb.

"No, but they did. It was just too puhfect. Like the JFK assassination. Look at how co-owdinated they was. I mean, two 'adem cats licked to get you hard, and then the third went in for da kill. Just like 'dat. I tell you, 'dem cats decided to make an example of you. They said, you people betta stop neuterin' us, o we's gonna show you what it means ta get fixed."

Vinny and his co-worker burst into laughs, which they managed to stop just in time to hand off their patient to the hospital staff.

By the time Heeb had been wheeled out of the emergency waiting room packed with at least a dozen traumatic injury cases and into a more private hospital room, he had been through a lot, he had explained a lot, and he wasn't exactly feeling social. He just wanted the doctor to arrive already so that he could get himself on a very private road to recovery. Thus, Heeb was rather chagrined to discover that he had to share the small, beige-colored hospital room with another patient — the fifth person to whom he would have to recount his traumas of the evening.

As the nurse wheeled Heeb into the room and helped him climb into his bed, he tried to avoid any direct eye contact with the man sitting up in the adjacent bed. But through his brief glance, upon entering, Heeb noticed that the patient was a handsome-looking man in his late twenties, with a full head of thick, jet hair, blue eyes, manly eyebrows, and well-sculpted cheekbones. He was reading *Entertainment Weekly*. And, like Sammy, he was covered by only a thin, grey hospital gown. He looked up for a moment just after Heeb passed his bed but he couldn't really see him because the nurse was obstructing his view. He looked back down at his magazine.

"The doctor should be here shortly," the nurse said before leaving.

Heeb adjusted his position on the bed a little, and then looked for a magazine to read. He settled on *Scientific American*.

Heeb's hospital roommate looked up from his *Entertainment Weekly* again. He saw Heeb's nearly bald head, chubby figure, and *Scientific American*, and decided to go back to his magazine.

But while moving his head back to his magazine he caught enough detail to notice that his new roommate had some kind of groin injury. He did a double take just to make sure, and then exclaimed, in amazement: "I can't believe it!" He looked directly at Heeb, who was still reading.

"What the hell's going on in this city?" he asked.

Heeb looked up from his magazine just enough to acknowledge that he had heard his neighbor express the same irksome curiosity as everyone else before him. Sammy muttered in response: "Look, I really don't want to talk about it."

"Believe me, I know how you feel…I'll leave you alone," he said, returning to his *Entertainment Weekly*.

169

The reply sounded so sincere that Heeb looked up from his *Scientific American* for a moment. He glanced over at his roommate, who was reading again, and realized that he too had a groin injury.

"Oh my God!" Heeb was now genuinely curious about the calamity that had befallen his neighbor. "What happened to you?"

"I don't want to talk about it...I mean the embarrassment is almost worse than the pain."

"I know exactly what you mean."

They both tried to resume their magazine reading.

A few moments later, Heeb's roommate looked up and said, "Come on, man, it's obvious what happened to you, because the same thing happened to me...And if it happened to both of us, there's really no need to pussyfoot around...No pun intended..."

Heeb looked up, shocked at the precise and specific pun. He stared at their identically bandaged members. The eerie similarity of their circumstances suddenly overshadowed any differences. The distress, fatigue, and painkillers – combined with the uncanny coincidence – made Heeb conclude that his roommate was Melody's mailman, who had apparently suffered a similar fate – perhaps from the night before.

"Was it the black one with you, too?" Heeb asked, wishing he could swing the cat by its tail and hurl it off a skyscraper.

"And don't forget her accomplice."

"Yeah, I would have never thought that they'd do that sort of thing."

"They certainly caught me by surprise."

"I just can't believe she went postal on me," Heeb remarked bitterly.

"Oh, she's definitely a bit loco."

"Believe me, I know...But how could she do it with the mailman, for God's sake?!" Heeb exclaimed, suddenly feeling jealous.

"Why not? She's not exactly discriminating in her line of work."

"Yeah, but having odd jobs doesn't mean you have to do it with any loser who comes your way," Heeb insisted.

"Hey, easy there. You're not getting jealous, are you?"

"What do you expect, after she told me all about you and your mail exploits?"

"Male exploits? What are you talking about? That's definitely not my style."

"So you met her after work?"

170

"Of course. I couldn't do that in the middle of the day."

"But I'm sure there's a mail exploit somewhere, or she wouldn't have mentioned it."

"A good friend of mine had a male exploit…It was so bad that he had to leave his job afterwards."

"Well, I'm sure they fire you, if they catch you doing something like that."

"Don't be silly, this is a free country. But it wasn't really his choice…I mean, he was deceived."

"Deceived?"

"Yeah, the whole thing really fucked with his head…He left his law firm to go recover in an ashram."

"I'm confused."

"So was he."

"I thought your colleague works as a mailman."

"He's my friend, not my colleague."

"So you're not a mailman?"

"No."

"Oh…So maybe she didn't let the mailman lick her envelope, after all."

"Who?"

"Melody."

"I thought her name was Brandy."

"Brandy?"

"Well, I might have misheard her name. The music was loud. And I was a little nervous and distracted."

"Her name was definitely Melody. Melody Katz."

"Hmm….She didn't seem like a Katz, but I guess it's possible that that was her name."

"There's one way to know for sure."

"How?"

"The music that you said was loud."

"What about it?"

"Was it Bach?"

"Are you kidding? It was nothing but hip-hop."

"So that settles it."

"Settles what?"

"I've been talking to myself this whole time."

"Why do you say that?"

"Because I don't have a clue what happened to you, and you don't have a clue what happened to me."

"You mean you didn't get into an SUV with two women tonight?"

"No...Is that what happened to you?"

"I don't really want to talk about it."

"Come to think of it, I don't either," Heeb replied, convinced that his story was probably more embarrassing, since it involved multiple animals, rather than multiple women.

Heeb opened his *Scientific American* to a random article and began reading. His neighbor did the same with his *Entertainment Weekly*.

A few moments later, Heeb's roommate broke the silence again.

"OK, I'll tell you, if you tell me." By now, Heeb was too curious to focus on reading anything anyway, so he was actually relieved at his neighbor's offer.

"OK. You go first."

"Well, I don't really feel like going into too much detail, but let's just say that I'm probably going to need some psychiatric therapy before I can ever enjoy a blowjob again."

"Someone bit you while blowing you?"

"Yeah. Let's just say that she got a little too into it. And I don't know how I'm ever going to trust another woman to go down there."

"But it was probably just an honest accident, so there's no need to – "

"It wasn't an accident...I mean, I...I...I don't want to get into it any more...What about you?"

"What do you mean it wasn't an accident?"

"I don't want to get into it. Now it's your turn. What happened to you?"

"All right...Well, tonight I came across a black cat, and a few hours later, I literally hit the Jackpot."

"What do you mean?"

"The black cat brought me so much luck that I had to smack it off my penis."

"What?"

Heeb really didn't want to explain the whole thing yet again – even to someone who might be able to commiserate. "Look, if you want details you're going to have to reciprocate."

"I said I don't want to get into it."

"OK."

They picked up their respective magazines and started trying to read again.

Heeb's neighbor broke the silence again.

"All right, I got held up by a prostitute at blow point."

"Huh?" Heeb looked up in genuine confusion.

"While she was blowing me – and it was the best blowjob I had ever had until – by the way, what's your name? Since I'm telling you all of this…"

"Sammy."

"I'm Evan. Good to meet you."

"Nice to meet you, Evan. Sorry it's not under better circumstances."

"Yeah. Tell me about it. So as I was saying, it was the best blowjob I had ever had until she turned it into a hard bite. And her accomplice had a gun. She told me that my whole dick would be bitten off if I didn't give up my wallet. It took me a while to find my wallet, with her teeth on my Johnson like that, and I guess I just passed out from the pain and the shock of the whole thing. Next thing I know I'm in an ambulance. Apparently, someone saw me on the street and called an ambulance. They took everything in my wallet except for my health insurance card and some ID photos."

"Good thing they didn't take your health insurance card," Heeb said lightly but sympathetically.

"Tell me about it."

Sammy suddenly began to feel a little better about his situation. His disaster hadn't been caused by a prostitute, and he hadn't passed out from the whole thing. By comparison, he actually felt morally better – even "cooler" and tougher – than his more handsome neighbor, who suddenly seemed to be less of a man for his willingness to pay for sex and for his faint-heartedness in dealing with the attendant risks.

"Now don't get me wrong – I don't ever use prostitutes," Evan began again, as if to clean up the reputation he had just tarnished. "I mean, I'm opposed to the idea of paying for sex. That's actually why she bit me…It's definitely a strategy that she and her partner have used before, and I know for a fact that if I had just been a normal, paying customer I wouldn't be here right now."

Heeb thought that this was a desperate attempt to sugarcoat a base and pathetic scenario, but he was nonetheless relieved to have found a support group of sorts for men who have suffered penis injuries under bizarre circumstances. And, he reminded himself, the premise of any support group is unconditional support and acceptance of the other members in the group.

"Well if it makes you feel any better, I'm going to need some serious psychiatric therapy before I can ever date a woman with pets — particularly cats."

"So what happened exactly? Now it's your turn. Give me the details."

"All right," Heeb began, reluctantly. "My girlfriend — my ex-girlfriend — I should say, had twelve cats in her — "

Heeb stopped because a doctor had entered their room. Doctor Clayton was a tall, forty-four-year-old African-American with round spectacles that accentuated his generally distinguished appearance. Evan also looked up at the physician. It had been a busy night at the hospital, and Doctor Clayton hadn't yet had a chance to read the respective reports for the two patients in the room.

He started to look down at each of their reports, but then realized — from his cursory glance at the two men — that both patients seemed to be suffering from an improbably similar injury. The doctor looked back up at Evan and then Sammy; each man was sitting on his respective bed without any pants and with bandages on his groin area. He raised an eyebrow for a moment as he tried to ballpark the statistical odds of two men, roughly the same age, sustaining groin injuries, at roughly the same time on the same night, in New York City.

He concluded that, in all likelihood, the two were either gay lovers, or that they had been at the same strange swinger party where various forms of rough sex had left both men injured. Since this data was potentially relevant to his diagnosis, and since he doubted that it had been fully disclosed to the hospital staff that had prepared the reports, he decided just to ask the two directly, in the most professional manner he could.

"Did...Did the two of you come here...together?" he asked, with the perfectly suggestive yet non-judgmental tone.

"No!" both patients vehemently replied, in near unison.

"OK. I just needed to check that because it could affect the diagnosis."

"No, not together," Evan added for emphasis.

"Definitely not," concurred Heeb.

"OK. OK. No problem. Now just give me a second to read through your charts here, and then I'll examine you..."

174

Doctor Clayton compared the two charts for a moment and then looked up again.

"Are you Evan Cheson?" he said, looking at Heeb.

"No, that's Evan."

"OK. Apparently you've been here for about twenty minutes longer, so I'll start with you."

*****

Evan tried to read but couldn't stop thinking about the bad news that Doctor Clayton had just given him. He would have minimal scarring, but he would need to be tested for syphilis, hepatitis B, and HIV after twelve weeks, to ensure that any absence of symptoms was not the result of an incubating infection. He would need to stay in the hospital for at least three days. Doctor Clayton advised him not to engage in any sexual activity for at least two months, to ensure complete healing, and thereafter always to use condoms during any kind of sexual activity.

Evan wondered how similar all of these assessments and instructions were to whatever bad news the doctor was discreetly delivering to Sammy, several feet away. Evan correctly assumed that Sammy would be staying in that same dreary, light blue room with him for a few days. Both had injuries that needed to be closely monitored and regularly irrigated by health professionals to prevent the onset of any bacterial infections.

Heeb's injuries were worse. He was checked for rabies, and put on a regimen of special antibiotics to combat Pasturella, a particularly nasty bacterium that lives in cat mouths and can dangerously infect the bloodstream. There was a good chance that he would have three scars from Jackpot's claws and two from his teeth. The doctor couldn't yet tell how large the cicatrix would be, but added that diligent and patient care of Sammy's wounds would minimize their appearance. Sammy could probably be released after five or six days with a good supply of painkillers, and he would have to come back for periodic checkups and cleanings. Doctor Clayton warned him not to engage in any sexual activity before the healing process was complete, and – erring on the side of caution – advised waiting at least three months.

In a discreet, professional whisper, Doctor Clayton had managed to convey all of the necessary information to each patient without the other overhearing any details. But each patient knew that he would tell everything to the other at some point after the doctor left. They both knew that they wouldn't be able to sit there pretending to read their magazines and suppressing their curiosities for days on end. All of the truth would have to come out eventually, just as it had before the doctor's arrival.

The doctor finished his consultation with Sammy, made some notes on his clipboard, and then left the room.

A heavy silence followed. The psychological trauma of their respective injuries was almost greater than any physical pain. Upon hearing from Doctor Clayton that there would be some scarring, each patient imagined the total mortification to be suffered over the rest of his life, as he had to explain to each subsequent woman how his penis had become scarred.

Evan and Sammy each tried to digest the full extent of the bad news, while thinking about whether and how to share it.

Finally, their silence was broken when Evan spoke.

"Mine is really bad."

Heeb didn't reply. He looked as if he was in a bit of a daze, staring blankly in front of him. He feared that with his freakish injury, he may have permanently lost any hope of attaining even the lowest levels of Kojakness.

"Is yours bad?" Evan prodded him.

Heeb remained silent, but nodded his head in answer to Evan's question.

"This is by far the worst night of my life," Evan continued. "I've never felt like such a loser before."

Heeb remained silent.

Evan wasn't quite sure what, if anything, would make Heeb talk, but Evan felt the need to talk.

"The funny thing is that I'm really not a loser. I mean, there's nothing more loserish than having to point that out to someone, but – in all honesty – I'm not as much of a loser as you might think from tonight."

"What do you mean?" Heeb said, suddenly roused.

"You just happened to catch me in a particularly down period in my dating life. But it's not typical for me."

"Oh I see. And this is typical for me," Heeb replied. "But now you're so down that you feel like you've dropped to my level of loserness."

"No, I think you're probably a pretty cool guy," Evan replied.

176

"Come on. Let's be real," Heeb snapped back. "You're just talking with me now because you feel like we're stuck in the same room, with the same injuries, at the same low point in our lives, right?"

"Well it's certainly not because I'd like to take you home with me tonight."

"With the way things look for you down there, I don't think you'll be taking anyone home for a while," Heeb rejoined.

"Like you're one to talk!"

"I know. I know," Heeb said, retreating into a moment of silence. "I'm pathetic," Heeb continued. "And no matter how much you try to insist that you're equally pathetic right now, I'm not going to believe you. Even though you were with a prostitute and that's pretty pathetic in my book."

"Hey, I said I didn't pay her! It was just a challenge. I just wanted to see if I could talk her into a freebie."

"Yeah, well we see how persuasive you were."

"At least it wasn't a cat!"

"All right. Enough. I'm going back to my magazine." Heeb was now feeling more peeved than pathetic, but the only way to give any expression to this indignation was to protest Evan's presence by picking up the *Scientific American* on his bed, which Heeb did rather dramatically, making as much paper ruffling noise as possible.

"Fine. Then I'll go back to mine!" Evan responded childishly, picking up his *Entertainment Weekly* with equal vehemence.

But Heeb couldn't stop thinking about his plight and how limited his protest options were, and he soon went back to feeling more pathetic than peeved. Nevertheless, his pride resisted the idea of making amends after Evan's cat comment, particularly since Heeb was convinced that Evan saw himself as belonging to a cooler category of males. Heeb wasn't about to make any gestures that might reinforce such haughty notions. But he quietly hoped that Evan would apologize so that their relationship might evolve into the highly supportive male friendship that they both so needed now.

Evan sensed Heeb's insecurity and, under ordinary circumstances, he might have dismissed such sentiments as proof that Heeb was, in fact, in a lower category of cool. But these were no ordinary circumstances, and Evan very much wanted the same kind of supportive relationship that Heeb needed.

"All right, I'm sorry about the cat comment," he finally said. "You were still attacked by a pussy, like me. And I'm not gonna lie to

177

you. I probably wouldn't be talking to you if we weren't both here right now. But we are both here right now."

Heeb was still silently pretending to read his *Scientific American*.

"And maybe I need to learn from all of this...Expand my social horizons a little. Question some of my knee-jerk judgments about people...Maybe my people skills need some work... I certainly didn't deal with that prostitute well."

Heeb was still silent.

"Hey come on. Lighten up, man. I said I'm sorry. We're not just gonna sit here in silence for the next few days, are we?"

Evan's repentant self-flagellation finally satisfied Heeb's pride. Heeb put down his *Scientific American*, and moved his head in Evan's direction without making full eye contact with him.

"I'm going to have five scars on my dick forever," Heeb said sullenly.

Then, like a toddler who's been smarting from a bad fall but holding back his tears until a sufficiently private moment presents itself, Heeb suddenly began to cry.

Evan wanted to get off his bed, walk over to Heeb, and comfort him, but the doctor told him to stay put as much as possible for the first twenty-four hours.

"Hey now...It's gonna be all right. I promise," Evan started. "We'll both get over this. I promise..."

"All right?!" Heeb replied, between sobs. "I don't see anything all right about this...Penis...Penis pain for weeks to come...No...No sex for three months....S-S-Scars for the rest of my life...Where's the all right part?"

"Well, the penis pain could have been for months instead of weeks. And you might have lost the whole thing completely. Then you'd have no penis and no sex for the rest of your life."

"Yeah. Things could always be worse. My ambulance could have gotten into an accident that left me a quadriplegic. So you want me to rejoice about that now?"

"I'm just trying to help you look at the bright side."

"You're not doing a very good job."

"Look, we have the same challenge. Let's just be glad we're in this together...It'd be a lot harder if there were no one I could talk to about the whole thing."

"But are you going to have scars too?"

178

"Probably."

Heeb wiped away his tears and began to feel genuinely reassured by the possibility that he and Evan were going to be a team that together confronts the same bizarre set of issues.

"What about the scars? How will we ever be attractive to women again?"

"I'm not so worried about that for some reason."

"Probably because your scarring won't be so bad."

"I won't know for a few months. But even if it's bad, I think that by the time any woman is looking at your dick, you've already won her over."

"You really think that?" asked Heeb, desperately clinging to the hope that Evan might be right about this.

"Yeah. Besides, most women prefer to do it in the dark. It's sexier. And they often have their own imperfections that they want hidden…So chances are it'll be too dark for anyone to notice – especially with a condom on…And I'm never doing anything again without a condom."

"But what if she prefers to do it in the light?"

"Well, you'll insist on doing it in the dark. You'll make up some tender, psychological reason why you need to do it in the dark. You'll promise to please her in just that way she loves, and eventually she'll be cool about it doing it in the dark. And after a few months, you'll feel comfortable enough to show her your scars, if she gets too curious on you. At that point, she's not going to leave you. Trust me. And if she does, then you wouldn't want to keep her anyway."

Heeb was reassured by Evan's surprisingly rational analysis of the situation. "Have you been through this kind of thing before?" Sammy asked.

"Definitely not."

"So why do you seem so calm about the whole thing?"

"Probably because the reality hasn't hit me yet."

"Really?"

"Yeah. I think."

"Reality sure takes a long time to hit you, Evan."

*****

The two exchanged detailed reports of their respective medical conditions, and then drifted to other topics. They spent several hours

179

exchanging life stories, when suddenly, in the middle of Heeb's summary of his early childhood, Evan burst into tears.

"What's wrong?" Heeb said, confused by the timing of Evan's crying.

The reality finally hit Evan too.

"You…You got me thinking about childhood," Evan began, wiping away some tears, "And how we each get a fresh…A fresh start… And what if…What if I have HIV now? What have I done?" he burst into fresh tears again. No longer the cocksure man confronting bad news, Evan now looked like a little boy who had accidentally broken his favorite toy.

"It'll be all right, Evan."

"We don't know that!" Evan said, pessimistically between tears.

"Don't deal with bad news until you have to," Heeb counseled.

"But what if there's bad news? How will I deal with HIV?"

"Magic Johnson does."

"I'm not Magic Johnson," Evan said, with a detached sobriety that accompanied the end of his teary outpouring.

"I'm just saying that it's not a death sentence any more…I mean, you've gotta see the cup as half full."

"It's looking very half empty from here, Sammy."

"We'll get through this, Evan…I know we will…"

"And even if I come out clean, what am I going to tell my future wife if she asks me some day whether I've ever been with a prostitute?"

"I think you can honestly tell her that you never paid for sex," Heeb suggested, putting the best spin he could think of on Evan's story.

"But I was technically with a prostitute…That's lower than low!"

And with that, Evan burst into a new volley of tears. His male pride couldn't bear such a humiliating blemish on his sexual record.

"Well, it was just an experience. You can chalk it up to your experimental youth."

"But I just turned twenty-nine a few months ago."

"So call it your 'experimental twenties.' Besides, everyone's got some skeletons in the closet. Including your future wife. So the two of you will just have to accept each other as is."

"My wife won't have any skeletons!"

"How do you know?"

"Because she'll be perfect," he said, thinking wishfully of Delilah Nakova.

"There's no such thing."

"She'll be perfect I tell you," Evan said, with conviction, wiping away his tears.

"Well if she's perfect, why would she choose to be with anyone less perfect than her?"

"Because she'll have compassion for imperfect fools like me. That'll be part of her perfection."

20. Penilosophy

At 8 a.m. the next morning, over a hospital breakfast of saccharin cereal and salty scrambled eggs, Evan and Sammy began discussing life and women again, but in a much more jocular spirit. They exchanged funny anecdotes of female flubs and follies: from the long list — still in Evan's back pocket — of untried permutations for Sayvyer's forgotten phone number to Heeb's brief foray into nude modeling for art classes.

They continued talking and laughing for a few hours and almost forgot where they were until their light mood was cut short by the arrival of a nurse in her late fifties. It was time for a cleaning. They looked at each other with the same expression of terrified anxiety, exhaled heavily, and took some painkillers.

Despite the analgesics, they both felt occasional flare-ups of soreness that led them to shake their legs involuntarily. In fact, the only thing that made those stinging moments tolerable was humor. They had grown comfortable enough with each other to laugh freely at how ridiculous they each looked in their respective beds, wearing just the baggy, grey hospital gown, with their naked legs shaking and their groin areas covered by loose gauze.

Although the flare-ups didn't usually occur to Evan and Heeb at the same time, the worst incident of that morning was relatively simultaneous.

Evan desperately searched for some levity to relieve their pangs.

"You know the United Negro College Fund?" Evan began, between groans.

"You're thinking of civil rights now?!" Heeb replied in a gasp.

"No…" Evan replied, as he began to moan.

"As long as it's…" Heeb began, breathing through some burning sensation. "As long as it's not animal rights," he continued, to Evan's amusement. "Because the animals…The animals violated my fuckin' civil rights…My prick feels like it's been pricked," Heeb said, gasping for relief. "Like someone put pepper on my peter…"

Evan blurted out a squeal that combined laughter with an achy howl.

Heeb involuntarily gnarled up his face into a comical, exaggerated expression as he tried to contain the smarting sensation. "Damned cat turned my penis into a pain-is."

Evan emitted some more spastic laughs between his wailing. "Painis...That's a good one...I've got a painis now too..." The two switched between laughing and yelping.

"So like I was saying...The United Negro College Fund has a great quote," Evan began again, trying to get the words out faster, to avoid laughing at Heeb's joke again. "A mind is a terrible thing to waste."

"I know there's a relevant connection here somewhere," Heeb replied sarcastically through gritted teeth.

"There is," Evan stammered, between chuckles. "There is...If you'll let me finish."

"Just a sec," Heeb said, taking some more painkillers.

"Good idea," Evan replied, doing the same.

"I used to live by," Evan started and then exhaled some pain away. "By...by the Hugh Hefner version of that quote."

"You mean: a penis is a terrible thing to waste?"

"Yeah," Evan replied, in a moan. "But these days I've got a new version of that quote...A penis is a terrible thing. Period," Evan said, gasping.

"Yes...It really is," Heeb said, in strained agreement. "But the sad irony is that, without it, we'd have no motivation to do anything."

Evan struggled some more with the intense discomfort and then added, "You're so right..."

And as their penile pain began to subside, the two men were able to form more complex thoughts, resulting in a collaborative work: the development of a worldview that might be described as "penilosophy." This reductionist metaphysics posited that the penis is the source of all significant acts – good and bad – produced by men. From the Trojan Wars prompted by Helen eloping with Paris, to the muse that Beatrice was to Dante, to the castration suffered by Abelard for his love of Heloise, Heeb and Evan came up with various examples of how the course of a man's life is determined by the compass of his penis.

Any psychologist would have taken their speculative philosophical foray as evidence that Heeb and Evan had developed a penile fixation in response to their injuries, but the two men were increasingly convinced and excited by the depth of their insight. They concluded that virtually everything done or made by men could be explained in terms of Darwinian survival strategies to perpetuate sperm.

"Even pavement, for God's sake!" blurted out Evan. "Even pavement is there because of the penis."

"Of course it is!" replied Heeb. "There were a lot of penises performing lots of hard labor to create the pavement. And the pavement itself enables a more efficient society, in which penises can more readily travel to vaginas, and vice-versa."

"Good point," said Evan. "And did you know that if you put the word 'penis' into a Google search you'll get six million hits, but if you put in the word 'vagina' you'll get only three million hits?"[3]

"That's probably because there are more men than women surfing the Internet," Heeb conjectured.

"But those men are mostly straight, so why would the websites be about penises?" Evan asked.

"True. But even straight men obsess about the penis. After all, we've established that it's the moving force behind everything."

"But what about the Pet Rock," Evan began, worried that he might have found a powerful counter-example to refute their carefully crafted theory. "I don't see the penis there."

"That's just like bubble gum," Heeb said, without the slightest concern about the soundness of their new philosophy. "The product itself is of no real utility to evolutionary survival, but a penis out there realized that – with some shrewd marketing – the idea could make money. And money is always a great way for one penis to outdo all the other penises, in its competition for the best vaginas out there."

"You have a point there," Evan replied, somewhat relieved. "But what if the Pet Rock was invented by a vagina?"

"I don't think Gary Dahl had a vagina. But that's irrelevant," Sammy concluded.

"Why is it irrelevant?"

---

[3] The reported results were based on Google searches performed in 2003. About a decade later, a search for "penis" produces 226 million results, and "vagina" produces 148 million results, indicating just how much the Internet has grown in the last decade. The exponential increase in web content dedicated to the penis and the vagina is another testament to how much these things matter to humanity. Also noteworthy is how the vagina seems to be catching up to the penis: whereas in 2003, there were only fifty percent as many web pages dedicated to the vagina as to the penis, ten years later the ratio has increased to about sixty-five percent.

"Because these days vaginas also make money to compete for penises. Look at all of the female multi-millionaires out there today."

"You mean to tell me that the Oprahs of the world are pursuing success so they can choose from a better selection of penises?" Evan asked.

"You don't see them dating guys who look like me, do you?" Heeb replied.

"That's just because they haven't discovered your lovely cock yet."

"Hey, that's not funny," Sammy snapped, getting defensive and insecure.

"Coming from me it is! Come on, you can tease me about the same issue. We have to be able to laugh about this, or we'll never get over it."

"All right, but don't get us off on a tangent. Our theory still works," Heeb said.

"What theory?"

"We can still safely conclude that if you eliminated every penis on the planet earth, very little would get done, and the human species would go totally extinct in no more than about a century."

"You mean eliminate men? Or leave the men but eliminate their penises and testicles?" Evan asked.

"The second one."

"And you're assuming that the sperm banks have gone bankrupt?" Evan clarified.

"Yes, take all frozen sperm out of the equation."

"OK, so if all you have is men without their equipment, then you don't have sperm. And then the men have no sex drive, so they have no motivation to do anything significant, and the women's eggs all go to waste, and, as the decades pass, more and more of humanity is gone."

"Right," affirmed Heeb. "And then, no more than about a century after you removed male genitalia from the planet, the last, longest living human has died. And then the roaches take over."

"That's pretty grim."

"It really is."

"God bless the penis," Evan declared.

"Amen. God bless the penis."

The two shared a pause of reflective silence, as if to pay homage to the grand penisophical conclusions they had just reached.

During the passage of this awe-filled, respectful moment, Heeb noticed that his "painis" was now only a mild irritation, and merely noting the improvement was enough to return him to the calamity at hand.

"So I think it's fair to say," Heeb began, breaking their silence, "that we've been injured in the spot that's most important to mankind."

"And to manhood," Evan added, looking over at him.

"How can we get over something like this?" Heeb asked, somewhat distressed. "How can we get over an attack on the organ that is most important to manhood and mankind?"

"We have to."

"We do?"

"Yes. We just agreed that the future of mankind depends on it," Evan remarked.

"Well, that's not exactly accurate. It's not like every other penis on earth has been decommissioned."

"No, but that's how you have to think of it – as if the future of our species now depends on you and me overcoming this terrible penile challenge."

"That could be an inspiring way to approach it," Heeb replied.

"Yes. Remember that we're men. And another prerequisite to being a man is being tough."

"But maybe I'm not tough enough for this," Sammy worried aloud. "And if I'm not tough enough, and my penis is broken, maybe I'm no longer a man."

"Your penis isn't broken!"

"It sure feels that way."

"Just give it a few months. We'll get over this thing, I promise… Look, I'm actually seeing how this could be a good thing for me."

"What?!" Heeb replied, incredulously.

"Well, I haven't told you this yet, but I'm a writer."

"I thought you're a computer programmer."

"I am. But that's my day job. You know, my version of bartending. But I'm really a writer. I've been working on a novel for the last five years. And I've written several screenplays."

"Wow! Were any of your scripts made into movies?"

"I hate that question."

"Why?"

"Because the answer always sounds so loserish. It sounds really hip and glamorous to tell people that I write screenplays. Until they ask if one of my scripts has ever been produced. The answer always takes me from cool writer to unproven wannabe."

"I actually started with the assumption that you're an unproven wannabe," Heeb retorted.

"Yeah, yeah. Anyway, I generally don't tell anyone that I write unless it's some woman I'm trying to pick up."

"Why is that?"

"Because a lot of women think it's sexy – especially those who don't ask annoying follow up questions and just assume that I'm a successful screenwriter."

"See what I mean? I'm becoming a woman. I'm not tough like a man, my schlong is broken, and you're telling me things that you only tell to women."

"Would you stop with that self-pitying crap? My little guy is as broken as yours, and I'm telling you that I'm a writer because you asked how I could view this injury as a blessing."

"Oh. Well excuse me for not seeing the very obvious connection between your creative writing and the blessing of sustaining a dick bite…You know, sometimes I miss these things that are as clear as day."

"Well, we got sidetracked when you asked me that annoying question that everyone asks."

"All right. I'm sorry for not assuming that you're an Oscar-winning screenwriter."

"That's not the point!" Evan protested. "People should think that being a writer is cool. Even if you're just a starving writer. Besides, most great writers were starving writers at one point or another. It comes with the title."

"All right already. I think it's cool that you're a writer. Now would you make the damn connection for me between your writing and your penis injury?"

Evan adjusted himself on the bed a little and exhaled a breath of deep frustration, in preparation for an admission of which he was quite ashamed.

"I've been writing this novel for the last five years…" Evan seemed reluctant to continue the confession.

"What's it about?" Heeb asked, trying to prod Evan along.

"It's about women…Men and women…Five years…Do you know where I am in the novel?"

Heeb shook his head.

"Five years…And I'm on page fifty-nine."

Heeb wasn't quite sure why that was so bad. Fifty-nine pages over five years came to almost a page a month, he figured, and that was far more than he had ever written. But then, again, he had never wanted to write.

Evan saw that Heeb wasn't so impressed with his tragic confession, and proceeded to explain the problem in greater detail, his voice rising in angry self-rebuke. "Do you know where I would be right now – in the novel – if I didn't have a penis?"

Heeb shook his head again.

"I would be done. No. I would be more than done. I would have already cranked out the prequel, and I'd be finishing up the sequel. That's where I would be, after five years. But...But because I have a penis, I'm only on page fifty-nine of the first book. Do you see the connection now?"

"Almost. But I'm still confused. Because you say that you've written several screenplays. So maybe if you were writing only the novel you would have made better progress on it."

"That wouldn't have helped."

"Why not?"

"Because the screenplays had almost nothing to do with women, and I had no problem cranking them out quickly. But the novel is all about women. Women and men."

"So?"

"So instead of writing my novel about women, I would go out and try to meet them, date them, sleep with them. And then I would justify all of that time that I should have been writing as research time."

"But that actually sounds like a very reasonable and scientific approach to your subject matter: collecting raw data before reaching your conclusions."

"I've got enough hard data, Sammy!" Evan was clearly very disappointed with himself. "No pun intended," he added.

"I see. And your excesses in the data collection department are all because you have a penis."

"Exactly....And now we come back to the paradox we started with. If I didn't have a penis, then women wouldn't be such a huge distraction for me and I could finish my novel. But then I wouldn't have as much to write about. And I certainly wouldn't care about actually finishing the novel."

"Why not?"

"Well, for one thing, if I didn't have a penis, women wouldn't be so much more interesting to me than men are, and I wouldn't feel the urge to write about them. And – more to the point – I'd have no desire to impress them with the completion of a great novel."

"Why not finish the novel to impress your family?"

"That would never impress them."

"So you mean to tell me that you want to finish this novel so badly because it'll make you more attractive to women?"

"Basically."

"You can't be serious," Heeb replied, skeptically rumpling his brow.

Evan reflected on Heeb's reaction for a moment.

"You're right," he said in resignation, as if he had finally been caught distorting the truth. "I'm not entirely serious," he continued, introspectively. "There's definitely something deeper going on with this ridiculous compulsion I feel to write...Because there are far more effective ways to attract women than to write a novel about them. After all, who the hell even reads novels anymore?"

"Why do you say that?"

"Come on, let's be honest. Do you read novels?"

"No. Not since college."

"There you go...And you're a Harvard grad."

"Yeah, but I've always been more into math, science, and philosophy." Heeb opened the drawer next to his bed and pulled out the chocolate Snickers bar that he had asked the nurse to bring him.

"That doesn't matter. A few hundred years ago, even the math geeks read novels. Because there was really nothing else in the way of entertainment."

"I'm not so sure about that," Heeb replied, trying to couch his doubts softly, on what was clearly a sensitive topic for Evan.

"Why do I feel the need to succeed in an art form that's doomed to extinction?" Evan asked, in despair.

"Just because I don't read novels doesn't mean they're doomed," said Heeb, as he unwrapped his Snickers bar.

"Look, novels made sense as an entertainment form back in the 1800s, when the closest you could get to a soap opera was Dickens and Balzac. Today, you can get dicks and ball sacks on Internet porn, so even soap operas don't cut it."

Heeb was somewhat distracted by his Snickers chocolate bar now. Compared to the hospital food, it seemed to Heeb as if it were the quintessence of pure and natural food — grown organically from the earth and full of goodness for the body and spirit. His mouth began to salivate, just looking at the large bar of chocolate and imagining beneath it the nutty and creamy filling that would provide his mouth with an instant orgasm.

Somewhat pained by the social obligation of having to offer some of this heavenly treat to his neighbor, Heeb extended the bar out to Evan while hoping that Evan would decline. To Heeb's substantial relief, Evan quickly shook his head, almost irritated with such a frivolous interruption of their all-important discussion.

"You've got interactive games, DVDs, Internet, 3D films, and an ever shrinking attention span," Evan continued, as Heeb proceeded to take an enormous bite of his chocolate bar. "Novels don't stand a chance against such easy and immediate gratification. These days, people just consume whatever gives them the fastest form of amusement, without any concern for the long-term effects that these empty pleasures may have on their constitution."

Heeb blissfully focused for a moment on the easy and immediate gratification of his Snickers bar, as he methodically chewed on the large chunk of candy bar that filled most of his mouth. He wasn't at all concerned about its long-term effects on his constitution.

"Are you listening to me?" snapped Evan, somewhat irked that his neighbor seemed so untroubled by the social and technological trends that would doom literature.[4]

Heeb's mouth was obviously stuffed, but it was clear that Evan wanted an immediate answer.

"You gotta have sex on the cover," Heeb blurted out, rather unclearly, with his mouth full.

"Sex under the covers?" Evan asked, trying to make out what Heeb said.

"No. Sex on the cover," Heeb replied, with his words just as garbled by his glutted mouth.

"Sex undercover? As in, undercover sex?" Evan asked, trying again to decipher what Heeb said, and now impatiently convinced that whatever Heeb was trying to say was going to be an annoyingly irrelevant, inappropriate, or unsatisfying response.

---

[4] Back in 2003, there was no hint that e-book readers would soon arrive and help to produce a whole new generation of enthusiastic readers!

"No." Heeb shook his head and took a few more bites before trying to speak this time. "You just have to have the word 'sex' on the cover."

"What do you mean?" Evan asked, still not sure that he was hearing Sammy correctly. By now, Sammy had finished most of his chewing and could enunciate properly.

"I mean, the book can be about sex on the covers, sex under the covers, or undercover sex. Or anything else really. It doesn't matter, as long as you've got the word 'sex' on the cover."

"You mean the cover of the book?"

"Yeah. Even better: make sex the first word in the title. Like Sex and the City did."

"But that was television."

"It doesn't matter. If it's a novel about racecar drivers, call it 'Sex and Speed.' Or if it's a work of historical fiction set in antebellum Texas; call it 'Sex in the South.'"

Evan looked like a priest hearing sacrilege from a proud atheist for the first time in his pious career.

But the appalled expression on Evan's face only goaded Heeb on more: "Suppose you've written a mystery thriller about an evil scientist who changed his identity into someone totally unknown. Don't just call it 'Unknown'; call it 'Sexual Unknown.'"

"Sexual Unknown?" Evan repeated, incredulously.

"Yeah, that still works."

"How could that possibly make sense as a title?"

"Look, if the disguised scientist is now generally unknown to people, then he's probably also sexually unknown to them."

"You've gotta be kidding."

"OK, maybe that's not a good example," Heeb conceded, before continuing, undeterred. "Take a novel about a man's self-discovery. A good title for it would be something like 'Sexually Searching Self.' You get the idea. Just have the word sex in there, and make it prominent enough so that it's the first thing that people see when they see your book."

"Sammy, you're more full of bullshit than a Texas ranch!" Evan exclaimed, in an agitated, high-volume reaction.

"All right, maybe I'm overstating things a little. Look, I'm a math guy, not a literature guy. So I'm looking at this from a purely statistical perspective: all else being equal, your novel is more likely to sell if it has the word 'sex' in the title than if it doesn't. That's all I'm saying."

"You just stated the same bullshit in slightly modified form... But that doesn't change the fact that what you're saying is still basically bullshit."

"Trust me on this, Evan. I'm telling you that if you have sex in the title, publishers can market your book much more effectively, and people will buy it."

"Please, Sammy!"

"I mean it. Even if you write a novel that has nothing to do with sex and has no sex in it – I'll bet you could still sell more of it by putting sex in the title."

"But that would make no sense. How could you put the word 'sex' in the title of an asexual novel?"

"Easy. How about 'Sex only in the Title?'"

"So a story about a man who escapes from prison but never has sex in the process could be called 'Sex only in the Title?' You can't be serious."

"OK, you're right. There are limits. But if your novel has at least some sex in it, then it can be somehow mentioned in the title, and – "

"This is really depressing."

"What's wrong?"

"Can't you come up with a more plausible or classy way to restore my literary dreams?"

Sammy put his Snickers bar down. It was clear by now that he wouldn't be able to savor the chocolate, caramel, and nuts properly until this particular conversation was concluded.

"I'm being totally serious, Evan. The word 'sex' sells. Just look at ninety percent of the glossy covered magazines on any newsstand... You know what I'm talking about – those trashy frat boy magazines flaunting scantily clad women and tasteless jokes all over the nation's newsstands."

"You mean like *Maxim, FHM, Stuff,* and *Gear?*"[5]

"Yeah, those," Heeb replied, somewhat amused and impressed. "How can you rattle off their names so quickly?"

"I subscribe to all of them."

"You're a writer and you read that crap?"

"Sure. There's some good stuff in there."

---

[5] While all of these magazines existed when this novel was first written, Wikipedia indicates that *Gear* expired in 2003 and *Stuff* merged with *Maxim* in 2007.

"You see what I mean? Sex sells."

"No, I read them for the articles and the pop culture reviews."

"Yeah, that line is as old as *Playboy* itself," Heeb quipped dismissively. "Let's face it, Evan: sex sells. Period. And it even sells to guys like you who are writers and presumably care about intelligent content."

Evan just shook his head and frowned, as if he refused to acknowledge the terrible truth that Heeb was now determined to expose for all of its ugliness.

"And you'll find sex on the covers of classier, more respectable publications too. Like the stuff that hospitals include in waiting areas and patient rooms. Look on your bed there!" Heeb ordered, pointing to the *Entertainment Weekly* by Evan's side.

Evan picked up the magazine on his bed and looked over the titles on the cover until his eyes stopped at the third one from the top: "Sex symbols of cinema."

"Look at this *Vogue* here," Heeb continued, taking the *Vogue* magazine off the stack of publications lying on the table between their beds. "Twenty-three ways to make sex with him better." He put it down and picked up another magazine from the stack. "Or this *Time Magazine*. The politics of sex." He dropped it back on the table and took another one. "Or this *People Magazine*. Sexiest stars of summer." Sammy returned it and picked up yet another magazine. "Or this *Esquire*. What every man should know about sex." Heeb tossed it back on top of the pile. "Look! Even *Scientific American* has sex on the cover sometimes." Heeb read the title aloud in a serious, scientific sounding voice: "Sex in Space? Eager to understand human behavior in space, NASA mulls future studies."

"All right, already. I get the point," Evan replied.

"It's not necessarily a bad thing. Putting sex in the title just helps your novel to compete with all of the other entertainment options out there…You have to entice people with some of the pleasure they expect to get out of films and the Internet or your novel won't stand a chance."

"I just always thought of a novel as being more substantial than that…I can't approach literature as an exercise in marketing to the lowest common denominator…"

"Didn't Shakespeare write for the masses? I seem to recall that piece of literary trivia from my college days."

"He did. But he did it brilliantly, in his own way…And I guess today it just seems so much more crass…"

"But maybe at the time it seemed crass to Shakespeare too," Heeb rejoined.

"But I'll never be Shakespeare, so how can I justify my crassness when I don't have the genius he had to make up for it?"

"Lighten up, Evan. It's just entertainment."

"I guess you're right. It's just entertainment."

"And sex is entertaining."

"It's true," Evan finally agreed, in resignation. "Whether you're in the sixteenth century or the twenty-first century, sex has always been entertaining…Why is that?" he asked rhetorically, as if he had never before thought about the issue. "Maybe it's because dramatic events usually precede sex – and there's usually lots of drama after sex," he speculated.

"I think it's more basic than that," Heeb replied. "We're just hard-wired as a species to pay lots of attention to sex, because sex is part of reproduction – or at least it used to be. And what could be more important to a species – more worthy of its attention – than its own reproduction?"

"So entertainment is just a function of our evolutionary programming?"

"Probably."

This answer didn't sit well with Evan. It violated all of his idyllic and lofty notions about literature, the way that natural selection might upset the perfect worldview of a creationist.

Heeb had no romantic notions about literature and didn't want their conversation to stray too far from his original recommendation.

"Look," he said, "sex is entertaining. It's just a brute fact that you should accept – particularly since you subscribe to all of those trashy sex magazines."

"I never denied that sex is entertaining. I'm just not thrilled about that fact."

"You don't have to be. You just have to put some sex in your work. Or at least in the title. Look, if sex is entertaining, and entertainment sells, then sex sells. QED, as we math geeks say."

"But when Shakespeare used sex to entertain, it was just a minor element of a very complex work. Today sex is the whole show. It upstages everything else."

"Why do you say that?"

"Because it's true. You know, a few days ago, I was a little bored and – out of curiosity – I decided to run some Google searches on various words."

"You're really into these Google searches, aren't you? So let me guess: sex had the greatest number of hits?" Heeb ventured.

"Ninety million," Evan continued, eager to get this off his mind. "Then I tried 'love' and got only Sixty-three million hits. The word 'soul' got twelve million hits. And – get this – 'friendship' got only four million hits.[6] What does that say about us? There's something very sad about that."

"Sex is definitely more common than love, soul, or friendship," Sammy observed.

"And look at music. In the 1950s, Jazz was considered this sexually subversive musical revolution. But by today's standards, the lyrics couldn't seem more innocent."

"Very true."

"When we were in college the top musical hits were about sodomizing your sister's best friend. And it only gets worse each year. Just look at 2 Live Crew's lyrics. So when we go to our twenty-year college reunions, that's what we'll all be singing about – sodomizing our sister's best friend — as we do the white man's shuffle in front of our old college sweetheart, or try to network with our various classmates."

"So?"

"So what do you mean, 'so?'"

"So hip-hop proved that you can get people to chant really obscene things if you just give them a good rhythm to chant to…So what?"

"How can you say 'so what' about that?"

"Evan, at the end of the day, it doesn't make us who we are. It's just music. It just reflects who we are."

"Just music? Reflecting who we are? Our oldies are going to be about sodomizing your sister's best friend for God's sake! If that's what

[6] About a decade later, Google search results for "sex" grew from 90 million to 2.75 billion. "Love" skyrocketed from 63 million to 6.49 billion. "Soul" went from 12 million to 824 million, and "friendship" increased from 4 million to 310 million. So maybe Evan's frustrations were related to an earlier zeitgeist, when the Internet was still in its infancy and "sex" dramatically prevailed over "love." If only Evan had known that a decade later, "love" would emerge victorious on Google.

our oldies are, can you imagine what they'll be singing about fifty years from now? What's left to get explicit about?"

"I'm sure they'll come up with something."

"That's what scares me. I mean, if it's just music reflecting who we are, then who the hell are we? What are we becoming as a species, Sammy?"

"A bunch of psychotically violent, sex-crazed automatons with advanced technology to help us finish the job of global self-destruction," Heeb replied.

"Great...I thought you were a half-full-glass kind of guy."

"I am. I give us another eighty years before we self-destruct as a species."

"So what would be half empty?"

"Half empty would be estimating only forty years before we self-destruct."

"Oh. I see. Thanks for clarifying that one," Evan replied.

"Besides, what ever gave you the impression that I'm an optimist?"

"When you were trying to tell me that I won't end up with HIV."

"I was just trying to cheer you up."

"So you're really a half-empty-glass kind of guy, Sammy?"

"Usually."

"When are you a half-full-glass kind of guy?"

"When I'm getting laid."

"Right...I should have figured."

"So you're not gonna put sex in the title?" Heeb asked.

"I don't know. First I have to finish writing the damn thing."

"Well, at least your penis won't get in the way for a while."

"That's looking at the bright side of things."

21. Love at First Sight

By their fourth night together in the hospital, Heeb and Evan's wounds felt significantly better. The cleanings stung less intensely, and the two had grown somewhat accustomed to the smarting sensation. They were also rather adept at making each other laugh through the worst moments.

The two had spent seventy-two continuous hours in the same room, learning everything about each other, laughing with and at each other, and supporting one another through medical care that was at times painful and embarrassing. Heeb explained to Evan the concept of "Kojakness" and how it sometimes helped him to deal with his insecurities about being bald, and his insecurities with women generally. Evan told Heeb about how he was a late bloomer because his parents had never let him date anyone as a high school student. Evan admitted that this upbringing had made him insecure about his skills with the opposite sex — an insecurity that turned him into a player who was always trying to prove something to himself when it came to women.

Evan couldn't bring himself to understand how anyone could actually love being an actuary the way Heeb professed to love it, and Heeb couldn't understand why Evan felt the need to make it as a writer when he had a perfectly interesting and lucrative career as a computer programmer. But despite these and many other differences, Evan and Heeb had become close friends — an improbability that could have been produced only by the even greater improbabilities that brought them together.

*****

The nurse came in to drop off their lunch trays and then left. Evan and Heeb began sampling their meal of refried beans, yellowish chicken breast, and suspicious-looking, steamed vegetables.

The offensive hospital food had become a regular target of their jokes, although by now Evan and Heeb had grown accustomed to blithely sucking up the slop, as if it were just another unpleasant fact to be accepted as cheerfully as possible alongside their general misfortune.

Two bites into his rubbery chicken breast, Evan blurted out a question to distract them from the taste of their lunch: "Do you believe in love at first sight?"

"I believe in love at first bite," he replied, looking up from his overly salty beans.

"Tell me about it," Evan replied wryly. "As if being injured weren't enough of a punishment…"

"It's not about punishment…It's really about hospitals encouraging the body to heal faster by encouraging rapid departures – it's a way to stimulate the body's natural healing mechanisms."

Evan chuckled.

Heeb cautiously tried his vegetables and then gave his review: "You know these have the shape, taste and consistency…" He paused to finish chewing and tasting. "…Of frozen food that shouldn't be eaten until all other comestibles in the nuclear shelter have been depleted."

Evan laughed in agreement. "But putting the gourmet food aside for a second, do you believe in love at first sight?" he persisted.

"I'm not sure," Sammy replied.

"I'm totally convinced of it."

"You are?"

"Absolutely."

"Hmm…" Heeb thought about something in amusement, as he chewed on his refried beans. "So if there is love at first sight, and I'm a little nearsighted, does that mean that I jump into things too quickly?" he asked.

"You definitely did with Melody," Evan replied, between bites of chicken.

"Hmm…And what about Yumi?" Heeb asked.

"I'm not sure about Yumi. I think most guys would have been blindsided by that one."

"I think you're probably right," Sammy replied, with a pinch of self-pity in his voice. "So what makes you so sure about love at first sight?"

"I've experienced it…" Evan tried some of the block-cut vegetables and was appalled. "You know, this food is worse than eating out a woman with really bad hygiene."

"Much worse. There's no reciprocity – no sexual prize or even praise – waiting for you at the end of the tunnel, to help you get through it."

"It takes talent to make something taste this bad and still have it look like food," Evan added.

"And I doubt there's any nutritional value to this crap," Heeb opined.

"Let's just scarf it down and get the eating over with," Evan suggested. "Think of it as a sports challenge. How fast can you eat really bad-tasting food?"

"You mean, how fast can you join the vomitorium?"

And with that, the two proceeded to eat their food, for the next thirty seconds, as quickly as possible, without taking a bite more than necessary to feel as though they had eaten something for lunch. They looked up at each other, with convoluted brows of disgust and amusement, and then washed the remains in their mouth with some hospital water.

"Uh. I feel like my taste buds were brutally violated," Evan said, with a sour face.

"Yeah, like I need to make it up to them with seven weeks of daily Ben & Jerry's binges," Heeb added.

"So...Now that we got that over with, let's get back to love at first sight," Evan said. "Not infatuation at first sight...Love. With a capital L," he clarified.

"Love?" Heeb asked, playfully pretending not to know the concept.

"Yeah. The real thing. The conviction that if you had this one woman, all other women would become irrelevant. You'd never again be unhappy. And you'd give up anything to have her and keep her."

"You've experienced that?"

"Only once. And I haven't stopped thinking about it ever since."

"Tell me more."

"Sometimes I think that I still chase women just to forget about her. Because I know I can never have her. But I can't seem to forget about her, no matter what girl I'm chasing...No one can possibly compare...."

"Who is she?"

"Delilah," Evan said wistfully.

"Delilah?" asked Heeb, intrigued.

"Delilah Nakova," Evan replied, with a hint of awe and reverence in his voice.

"Delilah Nakova?" Heeb repeated, with dismissive skepticism.

"Yeah," Evan said, looking up reminiscently. "I met her."

"You met Delilah Nakova?" Heeb was still incredulous but very curious.

"Yeah…I met Delilah Nakova…Once."

"Where? How?"

"About a year ago. And I completely blew it…I haven't stopped thinking about her ever since."

"Where were you? What happened?"

Evan sighed heavily, looked down, and shook his head, as if he were experiencing the deep disappointment in himself all over again. He then seized upon a hope-filled fact on which he had clearly reflected many times, and abruptly looked up with newfound optimism. "Do you realize that she's half Czech?!" he exclaimed.

"So?"

"So I'm one-sixteenth Czech. My great grandfather was Czech."

"And?"

"And so was hers."

"So?"

"So that means we have the same heritage."

"That's completely absurd. You don't identify yourself as Czech. Or even a fractional Czech. In fact, this is the first time I've heard you say anything about your one-sixteenth of Czechness. You mentioned French and Italian."

"Yes, and my paternal great-grandfather moved to France from Czechoslovakia, so I'm one-sixteenth Czech. And I'm very proud of that one-sixteenth."

"You can't be serious."

"I even speak some Czech…I studied it for two years in college."

"You were just fulfilling some foreign language requirement. And you probably wanted to choose something that seemed interestingly exotic."

"That's not true."

"Yes it is. Bohemian literally refers to a Czech dialect, and you can't get much more hip than Bohemian, right?"

"I studied it because I'm proud of my Czech roots, and of Czech culture," Evan declared, in a tone that seemed somewhat forced to Heeb.

Heeb rolled his eyes doubtfully and said, "You embraced your Czechness only after you discovered your Delilah infatuation."

"Kafka was Czech," Evan boasted insistently, as if to prove the sincerity of his ethnic affiliation.

"Kafka was Jewish," corrected Heeb, with equal pride.

"He was a Jewish Czech."

"No, he was a Czech Jew."

"Whatever. We can claim joint ownership of the guy, OK?"

"All right, the point is that you think this one-sixteenth gives you some special connection to Delilah Nakova?"

"And she's majoring in political science at Brown. That's my alma mater. And I studied some political science there too."

"Everyone takes a political science course in college."

"And I'm interested in writing for Hollywood. And she works for Hollywood."

"So?"

"So how many people are there who have some Czech blood, speak some Czech, have an interest in working for Hollywood, and studied some political science at Brown? You can't deny that Delilah and I are in a very small class of people, with very similar experiences, values, and interests…We were meant to be together…We're soul mates."

"You're being completely delusional, Evan. The two of you couldn't be more different. She was a girl of mixed race growing up in Eastern Europe. I'm sure that formed her identity and personality far more than any of the stuff you mentioned. You'll never have any idea what it's like to be a girl of mixed race growing up in Eastern Europe."

"But I can imagine."

"And she's only twenty for God's sake. You're twenty-nine."

"So? She's got the maturity of a twenty-five-year-old. And I've got the maturity of a twenty-three-year-old. So that makes us more like two years apart."

"But you've lived a totally different life. She became famous at the age of fourteen, and is a world class actress now with fans flocking towards her wherever she goes."

"I can imagine being that famous. Writers can imagine anything – especially their own fame."

"Well you're definitely imagining this connection you think you have with Delilah Nakova because I just don't see it."

"But I spoke to her in Czech, Sammy."

"You had a conversation with her in Czech?" For the first time, Heeb's tone seemed to acknowledge that Evan might be remotely justified in sustaining some illusions about Delilah Nakova.

"Yes, I did…How many chances in a lifetime does a man get to speak with Delilah Nakova— in Czech, no less? And I blew it. On May 5, 1999, I fucking blew it."

"What happened? How did you meet her?"

Evan had never shared the story with anyone because of how ashamed and frustrated it made him feel. But now a cathartic urge to tell someone overcame him and — at this point in their relationship — Evan and Heeb were comfortable discussing anything. Evan looked down for a moment and exhaled some regret, before recounting to him everything that had happened on that momentous night.

22. The Fiasco at Float

At 10 p.m., on May 5, 1999, in the VIP section of Float, a chichi midtown club, several new media companies threw a gala Internet-Hollywood fete with a Mexican theme to celebrate Cinco de Mayo. The Hollywood guest list was rumored to include five major movie stars, and with all of the fanfare and publicity surrounding the party, it was virtually impossible to gain admission to the soiree. Fortunately for Evan, one of the event sponsors was a CEO who remembered the free software consulting that Evan had provided him a few months earlier.

At 11 p.m., Evan walked right past the hundreds of people waiting outside and flashed the classy key chain invitation that had been mailed to only eighty VIP guests the week before. The large bouncers unclasped the velvet cordon and Evan walked into what was undoubtedly the best party he had ever seen.

The dimly lit club space was illuminated by softly hallucinogenic lights passing lightly over the hundreds of people walking, dancing, and chatting. He saw inviting and indulgent faces. People seemed happy just to be inside the festive and magical ambiance rather than waiting outside in the long line, hoping for the ill-tempered bouncers to respond to a smile.

Sexy House beats occasionally sampled with mariachi themes gently reverberated throughout the dreamy interior. The ornate tables had trays spiraling upwards, full of quesadillas, nachos, guacamole, miniature burrito dishes, ready-made tacos, and a full assortment of sweet desserts. The open bar was serving tequilas, margaritas, and caipirinhas. The seductive music, the posh extravagance, the exclusive and mysterious milieu, the glossy cover faces everywhere, all created the heady feeling that anything was possible that night.

Evan was never one to shy away from women or the dance floor and the music quickly drew him to the pulse of the party. Swaying all around him to the intoxicating beats were gorgeous women of every nationality, slick-haired boy toys of the Latin flavor, groups of young ravers, media executives, dot-com millionaires, and people who made their living from their association with the "in" crowd. In the background, journalists, and photographers were busily documenting the high profile affair.

By 1 a.m., Evan was taking a breather by the bar. He had drunk and danced and flirted and eaten, and was back for some more drinking. The grooving bodies all around him seemed to move more slowly and easily as the tequilas took their toll. He stood by the bar, waiting for his next glass, when a blonde with a lifeguard tan tried saying something to him above the din of the music and club chatter.

"What was that?" he asked, with a tipsy nonchalance.

"Do you know what that line means?" she said, with her index finger pointing upward and moving rhythmically to the music that was playing. "I want to know what that Spanish line means," she said flirtatiously. "You looked kind of Spanish, so I thought you might know," she continued, with a playful gleam in her eyes.

"Hold on. Let me listen," Evan replied. He paused for a moment, pretending to listen to the line in Spanish. "OK, I got it."

"What does it mean?" she asked.

"It means, 'I couldn't be luckier that you thought I was Spanish.' Cool lyrics, huh?"

"You big liar!" she said, taking another sip of her margarita.

"All right. You got me. I'm a big liar. But an honest one," he said, basking in his own silliness.

"So what does it really mean? I never studied any foreign languages…"

"You got me! I was too stupid to study any languages that I could actually use."

"You didn't study Spanish?"

"No, that was far too useful for me to study it."

"So what did you study?"

"Only pointless, impractical languages that nobody cares about or speaks," he said, trying to make her feel better about not having studied any foreign languages.

"Like what?" she said in a giggle.

"Like Czech!"

"Czech?" she said, as if she had never even heard of the language.

"Yeah. Czech!" Her doubtful reaction provoked him into a brief diatribe. "I spent two years in college learning Czech. And who the hell speaks Czech around here?! When was the last time you heard Czech on the streets of America?" The young woman was clearly amused by Evan's unexpected tirade, which only encouraged him to continue. "When was the last time you saw a job that requires Czech language

204

skills? How many English words come from the Czech language? It's a completely useless language!"

And then – out of nowhere – between Evan and the woman he was talking to, Delilah Nakova playfully protested Evan's commentary in Czech. True to Evan's invective, he hadn't heard Czech spoken in almost five years, but he still remembered enough to understand what Delilah Nakova was saying: "How can you say that about my beautiful language?! And how useless does it seem to you now?" she said with a mischievous look – as if she fully expected Evan to be shocked by the stunt she just pulled.

Evan was dumbstruck. No more than two feet away from him stood the starlet herself, in all of her five-foot-six splendor. Her black hair was sculpted into dark tendrils adorning her raised cheekbones. Her impish smile, long dark lashes, and large emerald green eyes looked larger than life. The black satin halter neck top hanging from her nape perfectly complemented her smooth coffee complexion and hinted at her delicately shaped breasts as it hugged her hips. Delilah's tight white pants highlighted her gracefully feminine figure, and ended just above her open toe, silver stilettos.

Evan desperately tried to jog his drunken memory enough to assemble a decent reply in Czech. But the combination of genuine shock, too many tequilas, and too many years since he had practiced his Czech produced only an unimpressive "What…What are you doing here?"

"I have an invitation," Delilah said in Czech, innocently waving her key chain VIP admission, as if she was completely willing to prove to anyone who challenged her presence there that she was legitimately invited to the party. "And I was just waiting in line behind you for a drink," she continued with a coy smile.

Delilah Nakova was so adorably sweet and humble and charming all at once that Evan realized, then and there, that he had fallen helplessly in love with her. But it was for precisely that reason that he had no idea what to say next – even in English – much less in Czech. Instead, he just maintained a stupidly dazed look on his face, oblivious to the fact that the drink he had ordered was waiting for him and that Delilah was actually herself waiting to get a drink.

"I think your drink is ready," she said to him, politely amused that he was still so shocked.

But Evan was paralyzed in a loose, dizzy sort of way. He couldn't bring himself to say anything else, even though his jaw and tongue felt like they could move on command, if he could just think of something to say. The problem was that his mind had been slowed by the alcohol, just as it was being overwhelmed by the emotional intensity of falling in love – of witnessing before him the perfection of a human being whom he couldn't imagine parting with – while fearing that she was just seconds away from fading away forever. He couldn't decide whether to say something cheesy but intelligible in English, or something infantile and possibly incoherent in Czech. And because everything seemed to be moving in slow motion, he felt as though he still had some time to figure out the best course to take.

And then, just as abruptly as Delilah Nakova had appeared, she disappeared. Her entourage of six male friends and four female friends, all in their early twenties, pulled her away and absorbed her into their midst. "The other bar is less crowded!" was all Evan heard someone from her group call out before Delilah vanished with a playful wink. And where Delilah Nakova had been standing right next to him just seconds ago, was now an empty space that might, at any moment, be filled by some lesser specimen of humanity. Evan became so consumed by what just happened that he didn't notice the woman who had been talking to him earlier. She asked him several times to recapitulate the conversation he had had in Czech with Delilah Nakova, but she soon realized that there was no way to get Evan to pay attention to her again. He was now in a deep and lonesome trance for the rest of the night.

He forgot about his drink and the woman next to him, and aimlessly wandered about the club, trying to collect his thoughts, formulate a strategy, and figure out the meaning of what he had just experienced – particularly Delilah's goodbye wink, which he continually replayed in his mind. He still noticed all of the gorgeous women at the club, but their beauty suddenly struck him as vain and vapid. He meandered around with the hope that he might spot Delilah Nakova again, but eventually stopped at a centrally located table with food, where he began mindlessly munching on mini-tacos and guacamole-dipped nachos.

Suddenly everything that he could have said to Delilah began to occur to him, much of it in the Czech language. He could have told her how his great grandfather was born in Brno. He could have said that he really loves Czech culture, from its great writers like Jaroslav Seifert and Milan Kundera, to composer Antonin Dvorak and filmmaker Milos Forman. He could have mentioned how much he loved the architecture of Prague, which he had visited during the summer right after college.

He could have asked her if she was taking any political science courses with any of the professors he had studied under at Brown. He could have told her how Murphy's Law had governed his entire interaction with her, including the fact that she showed up just in time to overhear him belittling the utility of speaking Czech, when, in fact, he was really just trying to make the woman next to him feel better about not having studied any languages, and would actually love it if he found someone with whom he could regularly practice his Czech. And if she could hear him at this moment he would tell her how the proof that Murphy's Law was dictating the night consisted in the fact that all of these thoughts were streaming through his head with perfect clarity only now, as he recited them to the taco he was holding in his hand.

About twenty minutes later, Evan noticed the cumulative effect of all of the tequilas and Mexican snacks stirring in his stomach and felt a sudden urge to relieve himself. He made his way to the unisex bathroom and was pleased to see that, while both toilet stalls were occupied, there was no one else waiting in front of him.

The scatological sounds coming out of one of the stalls were disgustingly loud and explosive – discordant with the swanky style that marked even the bathroom of the high-end club. He began to wonder whether there was something in the food, or the way it was digested with alcohol that caused the person in the stall to have such bowel movements. As he heard the grunts and moans of hard work, he began to wonder whether the same problems awaited him.

After about five minutes, the person who had made all of those offensive noises emerged from the stall. It was a stunning, five-nine, cover girl model. The moment seemed amusingly surreal as she tried to smile politely at Evan for the brief moment between when she opened the stall door and when she moved to the faucet to wash her hands. As Evan moved towards the now available stall, he thought to himself, "Wow…Beautiful women also make those noises…But I'd really rather not know about it…I never did like unisex bathrooms…"

And seconds later Evan was producing the same revolting sounds and noisome odors, as his body discarded much of what he had been feeding it over the last few hours. As Evan sat there, occasionally groaning to ease the process and trying to ignore the bustle and babble of a fast growing toilet queue, he decided that his next move after the bathroom was to survey the club for Delilah Nakova. Now that he knew what to say to her, he would figure out some way to break through the large entourage around her so that he could talk to her.

But just as he thought he was finished with his bathroom business, another embarrassingly loud volley of farts and their solid accompaniments was emitted from below him, followed by a sigh of relief that he couldn't contain. In immediate response to what he had just thunderously accomplished, the large crowd in line erupted into a series of giggles and outbursts like "nasty!" and "ewww!" and Evan felt quite mortified at the fact that he now had a rather large and responsive audience.

Eager to escape the scene, Evan quickly finished up, wiped, flushed, and opened the stall door, only to find Delilah Nakova standing right in front of him, waiting to use his stall. She was looking right at him as he exited the stall, and all around her were the members of her entourage, each of whom looked amused to put a face to the record-breaking sounds that they had just heard.

Trying to avoid eye contact with anyone, Evan wasn't sure whether it would be worse to wash his hands while Delilah's ten friends stared at him, or to walk out right away and leave everyone thinking that he doesn't maintain proper hygiene. He opted for a desperate charm offensive while washing his hands.

"I'm really sorry about that," he said to Delilah and her crowd as he moved towards the faucet. "I think that Mexican food didn't go so well with all of those tequilas."

Delilah took one step closer to the stall to see if it could be used and was immediately repelled by the stench. One of the guys in her entourage yelled out, "You nuked the place, dude!"

"I know…I'm sorry, you guys may want to evacuate the area for a few minutes," Evan said, as he finished washing his hands and headed towards the exit. He felt oddly guilty about leaving them there in the newsworthy fetor of his making, but he would have felt even stranger lingering there any longer. He tried to walk out as nonchalantly as possible, even though all eyes were on him, and the second he was out of the bathroom he heard the crowd urgently fleeing behind him.

*****

Heeb was sitting at the edge of his bed, wide-eyed and completely engrossed, as Evan finished telling the story about his brief encounter with Delilah Nakova.

"That's it? You didn't go up to her again later that night?" Heeb asked, feeling as frustrated and disappointed as if it had all happened to him. "Maybe an hour or so later?"

"No. Of course not."

"Why not?"

"What did you want me to do? Go up to her and say, 'Hi. I'm that guy from the bathroom. Remember me? Did you find a safer place to crap after I left?'"

"Couldn't you try to joke around with one of her friends and get into her circle somehow?"

"Oh, you mean go up to the guy who accused me of nuking the bathroom and be like, 'Hey, that was a pretty funny joke you made about my bowel movements. This Mexican food sure is rough on the stomach, isn't it?'"

"I'm sure you could have come up with something."

"They'd probably be thinking: 'Who is this freak? First he drops the mother of all shit bombs on the bathroom and then he thinks he can turn our collective trauma into a friendship.'"

"That really sucks, Evan."

"It was a fucking disaster, Sammy. A total fucking disaster. And I've been mourning that night ever since."

23. SQ and the Fellowship of the Schlong

A few hours after Evan finished recounting his Delilah debacle, Doctor Clayton returned to inspect both patients. Evan would be able to leave the next morning, but Heeb would have to stay for another forty-eight hours after Evan's release. The brief examination and Evan's pending departure made Heeb insecure about his injury again. After the doctor left, Heeb shared some of his troubled thoughts.

"I can't afford to date randomly for another year before looking for a Jewish wife. That would leave me with only two years for my search, and right now I'm not sure if even three years would be enough," Heeb worried. By now, Evan was well aware of Heeb's plan for a kosher marriage by age thirty. "This dick disaster completely destroyed whatever was left of my SQ."

"What's SQ?" asked Evan.

"Sexual Quotient."

"What's that?"

"Basically, it's your odds of getting laid. Everyone has an SQ. Just like everyone has an IQ."

"I've never heard that term before."

"That's because I made it up."

"That figures. Finally applying your actuarial skills to what really matters, eh?"

"Yeah…It's an idea I had always sort of toyed with, but after I lost Yumi to my boss, I really began to develop and refine it."

"Why is that?"

"Because I started obsessing over why she suddenly dumped me for him. And in the process of figuring that out, I developed the concept of SQ."

"So how does it work?"

"Your Sexual Quotient is really just an attempt to quantify, on some absolute scale, how attractive you are to the opposite sex. In general, the higher your SQ, the more desirable you are."

"So the higher your SQ, the easier it is for you to get laid."

"Right. But your SQ determines a lot more; it effectively defines your bargaining position in a relationship. The lower your SQ, the more likely you are to be dominated by the person you're with," Heeb explained.

"You really think so?"

"Look at me. I always end up being the doormat because of my SQ. But if you look at models — male or female — they generally get away with demanding more and giving less."

"So how do you figure out your SQ?" Evan asked, suddenly eager to compute his own Sexual Quotient.

"Well, your subjective SQ is how attractive you are to a particular person. And your objective SQ is just the average of all the scores you got for all of the people out there."

"So how do I calculate my SQ for a particular woman?"

"It's calculated the way you would calculate your personal income taxes."

"How's that?"

"Various facts cause you to take deductions from the total, although with taxes you want the deductions and with your SQ you obviously don't. Because the lower your objective SQ is, the fewer women you attract, and the less picky you can be. And that's a bad thing. And for anyone who wants to marry a Jew, it's a disaster."

"Why?"

"Because there are only about fourteen million Jews in the whole world, which leaves about seven million for each gender. So let's say I'm willing to date any Jewish woman who's twenty to forty years old. That leaves me with a choice of about two million women in the world. And if we assume that half of those women are already taken, I'm left with a million eligible women roaming about six billion people.[7] And, chances are, the million that's not taken is not taken for a reason."

"A million?"

"Yeah. And if you want to get really precise, we need to shave off at least another three hundred thousand, because I can't date any Chasidic, Orthodox or even Conservative Jews."

"Why is that?"

"Because I'm compatible only with bagel Jews."

"Bagel Jews?"

---

[7] The world population in 2003 was six billion. Eleven years later, it is over seven billion.

"The ones who are Jewish culturally but not religiously. Which leaves about seven hundred thousand."

"That's pretty bad."

"Tell me about it. I lower my standards by at least twenty percent the minute a woman tells me she's Jewish."

"So why do you limit yourself like that?"

"I'm not really sure…It's complicated…Part of it is pressure from my family. Part of it is thinking that cultural familiarity makes it easier to get along with someone."

"But you're not even religious. So what are you talking about? The fact that you can enjoy bagels with your wife?"

"Don't underestimate the importance of bagels," Heeb rejoined.

"OK."

"But it's more than that. It's a shared history. A value system. A kind of humor. And there's also this idea of cultural survival."

"What do you mean?"

"After genocide eliminates one third of a community, the remaining two thirds feels somewhat obligated to replenish the population."

"I guess I never thought about it like that."

"And even if I know very little about my own religion — embarrassingly little — I can confidently say that we must be doing something right."

"Why is that?"

"Because we've survived three thousand years of persecution, and along the way we still managed to spit out Einstein, Freud, Marx, and seventeen percent of all Nobel Laureates."[8]

"Well, you're definitely not a group of slackers."

"Yeah. But I still have my doubts about sticking to Jewish women, given how few of them there are. Especially when I'm competing with all of the other men out there and have to take my deductions."

"What deductions?" Evan asked.

"A man's SQ is derived using a composite formula, based on seven key factors: wealth, social power, age, handsomeness, height, weight, personality, and hair."

---

[8] The percentage of Nobel Laureates who are Jewish rose from about seventeen percent in 2003 to about twenty-two percent in 2012.

"Is that in order of importance?"

"Basically. Although wealth and social power are probably tied in terms of importance, and hair can sometimes outweigh personality, if you're dealing with a shallow hottie."

"And how do these factors combine?"

"It's pretty obvious if you just compare scenarios. For example, between a seventy-nine-year old billionaire and a nineteen-year old billionaire, the vast majority of women would prefer the nineteen-year old, unless of course they're hoping to inherit quickly, in which case you wouldn't want them anyway."

"Very true."

"And if you have two millionaires of the same age, but one has hair and the other doesn't, the one with the hair wins."

"So this is how you deduct?"

"Essentially. You start with one hundred percentage points, which represents a guaranteed lay with any female you approach. One hundred is, of course, a theoretical ideal. No man actually has a one hundred SQ because no man could really have sex with absolutely any woman of his choice."

"Why not?"

"Because there's always this random component to sexual taste."

"What do you mean?"

"Even the hottest, tallest, wealthiest hunk with a full head of hair and the best personality, might still strike out with some female who, for some random reason, would never want to sleep with him."

"Why?"

"Maybe he reminds the woman of her evil stepdad, or some psycho ex-boyfriend."

"Or maybe she just became a nun," Evan offered.

"Right. Or she might have some deep medical or emotional reason to remain celibate. You never know. So you have to account for this possibility with a standard deduction of ten percent. Just like there's a standard deduction for every taxpayer."

"OK...So really, the highest possible SQ is ninety."

"Right. But after the standard deduction you need to apply the itemized deductions for the seven key factors of wealth, social power, age, handsomeness, height, weight, personality, and hair."

"So give me an example of an itemized deduction."

"OK. Take the all-important factor of age. Just like your tax rate depends on which income bracket you fall into, the size of your age deduction depends on what age range you're in."

"So what's the first age range?"

"Fourteen and under. If you're under fifteen, you have to deduct eighty percent from your SQ."

"Eighty percent?!" Evan exclaimed. "So after the standard deduction a thirteen-year-old boy has only a ten percent chance of getting laid?"

"Exactly."

"But I thought Jews consider a thirteen-year-old male to be a man."

"Well, for Bar Mitzvah purposes, but not for SQ purposes."

"Why not?"

"How many thirteen-year-old guys do you know who are getting laid? It's not exactly the age that women are looking for."

"I'm not so sure," Evan objected. "Pop culture is bringing sex to younger and younger audiences, so I wouldn't count on that."

"Look, we can quibble about the cut-off points and percentages later. Let me just finish with the age factor."

"OK."

"So if you're fourteen to sixteen, you deduct thirty percent. If you're sixteen to seventeen, you deduct twenty percent. And if you're eighteen to twenty-two, you don't deduct anything."

"Why is that?"

"Those are your college years. Assuming college guys want to sleep with college women, they couldn't do better in terms of their age, so there's no need for a deduction."

"But what if the college guy wants sleep with an older woman?"

"Then he'll probably need to take a deduction of ten to thirty percent for that older woman, depending on how sophisticated he is and how much of a Mrs. Robinson she is."

"All right. Go on."

"So twenty-two to twenty-nine, deduct ten percent. Thirty to thirty-three, deduct twenty-five percent."

"Whoa! Why does turning thirty bump you from a ten-percent to a twenty-five-percent deduction?" Evan asked.

"Because most guys in their early thirties still want to go after females in their early twenties."

"So?"

"So many of those females think of guys in their thirties as being dirty old men."

"Shit," said Evan, reflecting on the fact that he had only ten months left before his thirtieth birthday.

"Continuing along the age spectrum, if you're thirty-four to thirty-eight, deduct forty percent. If you're thirty-nine to forty-four, deduct – "

"All right, I get the picture. This is depressing me."

"Depressing you? What about me? I'm almost as old as you and we haven't even gotten to the deductions for height, weight, handsomeness, and hair."

"All right, well how do those work?"

"Let's take hair. The more hair you have, the less you have to deduct."

"That makes sense," Evan said, patting the top of his scalp lightly, as he tried to estimate how much longer the slightly thinning hair above would still look like a full head of thick hair.

"In fact, if you have hair at an age when nobody expects you to have hair, you actually add a bonus rather than take a deduction."

"I assume handsomeness is fairly straightforward," Evan said.

"Yes. Handsomeness can add or deduct up to twenty percentage points from your SQ."

"Why only twenty?"

"An old, short, bald, fat guy with no money and no personality who has a very handsome face still isn't going to get very far. And, conversely, a guy with an ugly face who's young, tall, charming, with a head full of hair and a bank account worth millions, should still do pretty well. The face is important, but ultimately limited in its impact on SQ, when you go through the whole calculus."

"What about height and weight?"

"Height is like hair: the more, the better, unless you've hit a freakish extreme.

"Like what?"

"Like a Planet of the Apes look in the hair department, or someone over six-seven in the height department."

"Why over six-seven?"

"At that point, it's going to be hard to find women who are tall enough to feel comfortable around you. Kind of like with too much weight."

"What about personality?"

215

"Personality is an all-encompassing term that includes all of the nonphysical attributes like charm, wit, intelligence, creativity, social skills, etc."

"So personality should be very important."

"In theory. If it's ever fully discovered. But how many parties have you been to, where the woman spots your personality from the other end of the room and comes flirting in your direction?"

"So are you saying that most women are too shallow to get past looks unless they already know your other qualities?"

"Usually. But they're still better than men as far as that goes. I'm the ultimate proof of that, because if women were as shallow as men, I'd still be a virgin."

"So now you're saying that men don't care about personality in women?"

"Men notice female personality even less than women notice male personality."

"I think you're wrong. Personality is very important to me in a woman," replied Evan.

"I'm sure it's the first thing you notice, Evan."

"It definitely affects the way I perceive her."

"OK. How many overweight, unattractive women with personality have you dated?"

Evan was silent.

"Like I said, the fact that women are less shallow than men is the only reason that there's hope for guys like me."

"No! That's not a fair question," Evan protested.

"Don't feel bad about it," Sammy continued. "You would care less about looks and more about personality if you were less attractive. But the fact that you're a good-looking guy makes you feel like you're entitled to date a good-looking woman."

Evan still seemed uneasy about Heeb's analysis, so Heeb went even further.

"Hey, if I looked like you, I'd also feel entitled to date more attractive women."

"But why does a preference for attractive women mean that I don't care about personality? Why can't I date an attractive woman with personality?" Evan asked.

"That's like a woman asking why she can't date a rich man with personality."

"Well why can't she?"

"She can. And she will — which also proves how women are smarter."

"How does it prove that?"

"Because a man's superficiality just gets him a nicer-looking woman. A woman's superficiality gets her a nicer life."

Evan thought about Heeb's observations, and furrowed his brow, somewhat troubled by everything he was hearing. Heeb saw that he was clearly having an effect on Evan, and this only encouraged him to expound further upon his ideas, so that he could — for a little longer — relish the guru power that he seemed to hold over Evan now.

"That's why wealth is such an important factor in a man's SQ — and arguably even more important than his age. Think about it: a multibillionaire — whether he's sixteen or eighty-two years old — can still attract a vast number of women, because women have their eye on the ball. It's their evolutionary survival instinct. They're looking to find the most plentiful and resourceful environment for their offspring."

Evan started fretting about his net worth. He owned a small, unimpressive studio, with a large mortgage on it. He calculated that his net worth was about sixty thousand dollars. Then he started thinking about how long it would take him to be worth eight million dollars, and whether that would be enough to guarantee him the SQ that he wanted.

"And the nice thing about wealth," Heeb continued, "is that it's always true that more is better. It's not like weight or height or even hair. At some point, if you get any more of those things, you hit an unattractive extreme. You start to look like a blimp, a skyscraper, or the Planet of the Apes. But that's never the case with money. In fact, with enough money, you can actually make up for any freakish extremes or deficiencies you might have."

"You don't even need personality."

"Nope."

"So would you give up your personality for a few billion dollars?" Evan said.

"Of course not."

"Why not?"

"Because I can't give up who I am. Besides, personality includes IQ, and if I give that up, then I'd quickly lose all my money — on bad investments, idiotic purchases, and fraudulent schemes that exploit my stupidity."

"That wouldn't be good."

"No, it wouldn't. Then I'd be a short, bald, overweight, twenty-seven-year-old idiot with no cash and no personality."

"Yeah, that would be bad."

"You can't lose perspective, Evan. SQ isn't everything."

"I guess it isn't."

"Unless, of course, you haven't been laid in a while."

"Right."

*****

The next morning, the nurse gave Evan some medications and cleaning material to care for his wound at home and gave him some pointers to keep in mind until his follow up visit in one month. Evan happily took off his hospital gown, put his regular clothes back on, and then thanked the nurses and doctors who had helped him during the last four days and nights.

Heeb was secretly a little envious of Evan. Irrationally, he even felt a tad betrayed by Evan for being so happy about leaving. Heeb knew, deep down, that he and Evan had bonded in a deep and lasting way. But the fact that he would now be alone for the next forty-eight hours made him reflect on how both his injury and his SQ were worse than Evan's, and how these differences could mean that their close bond might be as temporary as the circumstances that united them.

Fortunately, the two had grown so attuned to each other's emotional states that Evan quickly felt the awkward tension and unspoken questions surrounding his imminent departure. He walked over to Heeb's bed.

"Sammy, thanks for making this whole thing so much more bearable."

"Don't mention it."

"In some sick way, I'm going to miss our hospital room days together."

Heeb's face lit up. "Me too," he replied. "Particularly since I'm still here for another forty-eight hours."

"You're gonna be fine. Ten years from now, this will just be another funny anecdote from your past."

"What are you talking about? It's already a funny anecdote."

"Yeah, but you better not tell anyone!" Evan said sternly but with a smile.

"Don't worry, our time here is not exactly something I'm putting on my resume."

Heeb got up from his bed to embrace Evan and say goodbye. But he felt somewhat ridiculous standing barefoot on the lukewarm hospital floor with nothing on him but the grey hospital gown, looking up at the taller and fully clothed Evan.

"Just remember what Nietzsche once said," Evan began, trying to offer some inspiring words of fortitude for Heeb's remaining time in the hospital. "Anything that doesn't kill you will make you stronger."

"In our case it's more like: Anything that doesn't castrate you could still ruin your sex life."

"Tell me about it," Evan replied, suddenly retreating from his bravado. "I don't even want to think about what this did to our SQ."

"Dick-bite scars are at least a ten-percent deduction."

"No. That's too much."

"At least that, if not fifteen percent," Heeb insisted.

"Like I said before, if a woman is getting anywhere near your dick scars, you've already won her over."

"True, but you can always scare her off at the last moment."

"Keep the lights dim and it won't be more than a two-percent deduction, Sammy."

"You know, I thought of a way for us to possibly compensate for the SQ loss."

"How?" Evan asked.

"At the end of the day, finding women comes down to odds. Like everything else in life. And I've been thinking that our odds would improve significantly if we formed a posse of four or five guys."

"A posse of players, eh?"

"You bring in Narc and Trevor, and I'll bring in Carlos."

"That's gonna be really tough."

"Not tougher than Carlos. He's happily married, for God's sake."

"Yeah, but Narc and I had a falling out. And Trevor could be impossible."

"Trevor needs to be rescued anyway," Heeb insisted.

"You're right. He's gotta get over that incident."

"Look, I don't know for sure if Carlos will join, but it's certainly worth a try. We have nothing to lose. And there's a huge potential upside."

"Like what?" Evan asked.

"First of all, a posse would produce a certain Spice Girls effect."

"It's funny because I never did think those girls were that cute as individuals, but there was definitely something sexy about them as a group."

"Exactly. With a posse, the whole is sexier than the sum of its parts," Heeb said, happy to elaborate. "And it makes each of us look like we're socially well adjusted enough to have lots of friends."

"Women definitely prefer guys who seem normal," Evan agreed. "And the more friends you have, the more normal you seem." Evan thought of another advantage. "And if you're seen as a group of normal guys, it probably tempts women to start speculating about the members of your group, comparing them, following their individual stories – like what happens with boy bands," Evan added.

"Yes! And if you get rejected, it just becomes a group joke rather than a personal failure," Heeb added.

"There's strength in numbers, as they say."

The two spontaneously clasped each other's hands on the proposition. Sammy wanted to embrace Evan, but it would have felt too strange getting so close to him with his convalescing Hebrew National dangling freely below.

"I'd hug you, but – " Heeb looked down, and Evan laughed a little.

"That's all right. I'll consider myself hugged."

"Hugging just seems like the right thing to do after you've formed the fellowship of the schlong," Heeb gushed.

"Well, consider yourself hugged too," Evan reassured him lightly, still holding Heeb's hands.

"Long live the fellowship of the schlong!" Evan cried out, raising their clasped hands even higher, as if to formalize an important military alliance between two neighboring medieval tribes.

"Amen!" Heeb added.

They looked at each other, smiled, and released their hands. Evan started towards the door of their shared room and Heeb accompanied him. When they arrived at the door, they stopped.

Like a prisoner of war about to escape an enemy prison on his own and sadly unable to bring his fellow prisoner friend with him, Evan turned to Heeb and said solemnly, "I'll be back for you. I promise."

They shared a smile and a thumbs-up, and Evan turned around and left.

24. Operation Repulsive

During the three months that followed their serendipitous introduction, Heeb and Evan helped each other through the persistent difficulties and insecurities that accompanied their injuries. The bad news for Evan, which he discovered about two weeks after his release from the hospital, was that he had contracted syphilis. The good news was that he was spared the uglier effects of the disease by promptly obtaining treatment. Within one month, he was completely cured of the disease and no longer infectious. However, the fact that he had contracted the STD increased his anxiety about the HIV and Hepatitis B tests that he would have to take three months after his fellatio bite.

Aesthetically, Evan's member seemed to be healing well, and he was hopeful that within six months, the scarring would be relatively minor. Heeb's injury also saw substantial improvement, but it wasn't nearly enough to restore Heeb's confidence to where it had been before he hit the Jackpot.

"It's not like my SQ wasn't already really low to begin with," Heeb remarked, a few weeks after his hospital discharge.

"At least you didn't get syphilis with a chance of getting HIV or Hepatitis B," Evan replied.

"Why is that supposed to make me feel better about having a scarred penis?" Heeb asked.

"Because things could be worse. A lot worse. Hell, you could have gotten rabies on your dick."

"True. But things could always be a lot worse."

"They could be. You could be dead."

"But then I wouldn't know the difference."

"Yeah, but you'll get there anyway. So you might as well enjoy the ride along the way as much as possible."

"OK. But why do others get to enjoy a better ride along the way?"

"Others? Like who?"

"Like all those guys who have a penis without scars, a scalp full of hair, and a bank account with millions of dollars in it. Can't I be depressed about the fact that I don't have those things?"

"Look, the scars will improve with more time, you're on way to becoming a partner at your actuary firm, at which point you'll have millions of dollars too. And science is working on a cure for baldness. Isn't that close enough?"

"I guess it'll have to be."

"How about this: if we can still get you laid with a hottie, will you feel better about things?"

Heeb grinned and they shared a laugh, acknowledging that virtually any worry or woe could be cured by a beautiful woman. "You realize that it's a contradictory idea. What you're really asking me is: would I feel better about having such a low SQ if I had all the benefits of a high SQ?"

"But that's not totally absurd," Evan insisted. "People can still have very successful lives despite relatively low IQs. So maybe they can have very successful sex lives despite relatively low SQs."

Evan decided that he wouldn't pursue women again until his hepatitis and HIV test results arrived in early December 2000; if they came back negative, he would jump back into the game. Until then, he decided that he would focus all of his free time exclusively on his novel, because he couldn't be sexually involved with anyone for several months anyway, and – more importantly – because a best-selling novel was the only way he thought could compensate for the injury-related drop in his SQ. Quite apart from his injury, he concluded that he had no more than ten years with a full head of hair and therefore needed to be rich and/or famous by then to compensate for the additional drop in SQ that would follow. Ten years struck him as very little time to become rich and the Internet certainly wasn't getting him there.

But because it had taken Evan five years to write fifty-nine pages, he didn't exactly trust himself to enforce this new resolution to finish his novel over the next few months. Thus, he adopted some drastic practices that he believed would make it easier for him to stay disciplined. He stopped shaving or grooming himself and dressed in the most stylistically inept and unattractive way he could imagine, so as to minimize the odds that any female might cast a favorable glance in his direction. As if this measure weren't enough, Evan also began eating large quantities of garlic and onions throughout the day, to quickly stave off any woman who miraculously managed to get past his outdated, mismatched, and generally disheveled appearance.

"How's 'Operation Repulsive' coming along?" Heeb would ask, during their daily phone call.

"I've been happily hunkered down in my place as if it weren't, in fact, a tiny, roach-infested, light deprived, slovenly hole in the wall."

"How have you managed to overlook the many charms of your apartment for such extended periods of time?"

"I don't know, but it's amazing. I'm on my third straight week of solid writing. No female distractions whatsoever, and I've written one hundred more pages. Can you believe that? Three weeks of writing without thinking about or talking to women gets me twice as far as five years of writing with women in my life. Of course, being unemployed is also a big help."

"Not to take the wind out of your sails, but what if it turns out that you're just writing a bunch of crap?"

"Now why would you want to take the wind out of my sails like that?"

"I'm sorry."

"Look, every writer has to contend with the haunting thought that what he's writing is really just a bunch of crap. That's what makes this solitary art form so damn painful and why every writer has to convince himself that he's writing a masterpiece, even if in the end everyone hates it."

"So you work under a narcissistic fantasy as a way to stay motivated?"

"Exactly. And this whole process has also made me realize a basic writing truth."

"What's that?"

"If there's always the chance that what I'm writing is really just a bunch of crap, I'd rather write it in a few months than in a few years."

"You got a point there. Better to produce a bunch of crap quickly than slowly."

By the seventh week of Operation Repulsive, Evan had barely seen the light of day: he had been writing for forty-two consecutive days, spending an average of fifteen hours per day on his novel. He was on page 240, had covered about two-thirds of the story in his novel, and was convinced that he was writing a masterpiece.

But Evan's unprecedented forward momentum came to an abrupt halt on October 18, 2000, at 11:29 p.m., when he had to leave his apartment and go to the corner store for some toilet paper and toothpaste, both of which he had depleted almost sixteen hours earlier. He was in the most revolting condition ever – far worse than what he had looked like after the all-nighters he had pulled as a college student at Brown, cramming for finals. The last two days he had barely slept, after being possessed by the muse like never before. His scraggly beard, thoroughly tangled hair, tired and bag-ridden eyes all appeared to be part of the same lifestyle choices behind the dirty, wrinkled, and clashing clothes that covered his body. Evan had even exhausted his clean underwear and was down to the last pair in his "reserve" pile (which, thanks to age, had developed some built-in ventilation). Daily sandwiches of canned sardines, raw garlic, and uncooked onion all but ensured that his breath could be weaponized, if produced in highly concentrated form.

In this veritably frightful state, Evan emerged from his writing lair to stock up on some basic supplies at the local twenty-four-hour Duane Reade drugstore. With his head still thoroughly immersed in the alternate reality that was his novel, Evan's brain was floating far too much to take any notice of the white stretch limousine parked in front of the Duane Reade. In zombie-like fashion, he began strolling the aisles of the store looking for toothpaste and toilet paper. Some late night drugstore patrons noticed Evan walking by them and eyed him with a mixture of disgust, bewilderment, and either fear or pity. Evan was largely oblivious to these people, but after a few minutes of wandering about the store he had become somewhat more conscious of his surroundings, to the point that when he walked past Delilah Nakova, he suddenly realized that there had been a white stretch limousine outside.

A jolt of adrenaline suddenly snapped down Evan's entire back as a stream of panic-stricken questions seized him: Was it really Delilah? What was she doing in this particular Duane Reade at 11:47 p.m.? Had she recognized him? If so, were his dreams of Delilah forever doomed now? If not, could he quickly clean himself up enough to talk to her? Maybe even in Czech? Could this be a divinely delivered first chance to make a second impression? Or could it even be a second chance to make a first impression, if she miraculously forgot about their prior encounter about seventeen months ago at Float and didn't recognize him in his current state?

Having had virtually no contact with the outside world for the last few weeks, Evan had temporarily forgotten the social norms governing shopping conduct or approaching celebrities in public. Nor did Evan have the time to reacquaint himself with such trifles. Instead, he became singularly focused on quickly cleaning himself up enough to approach Delilah before she got back into her limousine and disappeared forever. He spotted some toothpaste on the shelf and hastily opened it and squeezed some into his mouth, and put the rest into his shopping basket. As he chewed on the toothpaste, he spotted some mouthwash and quickly took a swig, gargled for a few minutes, and then — not having anywhere to spit out the sharp, powerful alcohol-based liquid — he spat the liquid and the toothpaste back into the bottle of mouthwash, which he then put in his shopping basket. Afraid that Delilah had already been out of sight for too long, he ran to the end of the aisle and across the back of the store, until he spotted her looking up and down the shelves where the chocolate "energy" bars were located.

He ran back to the neighboring aisle, spotted his disastrous-looking hair in a store mirror, and hurried to the next aisle to get a brush and some hair gel. In a mad rush, he squeezed out an enormous gob of gel and began padding it down on his tangled and disheveled hair. He frantically brushed his hair in various directions, trying to achieve something interesting, if not respectable. Realizing that he was running out of time, he finally gave up on the hair, thinking, "Maybe she likes the edgy, scruffy look." But then he realized that his body odor smelled akin to hazardous waste. He threw the brush and gel into his shopping basket and ran to another aisle, looking for deodorant. He grabbed the first deodorant he found and began liberally spraying his entire body, from head to toe, as well as under his shirt and undershirt. He was far too fixated on the mission at hand to notice the disapproving stares his behavior had elicited from nearby shoppers. He dropped the deodorant in his shopping basket and rushed back to the aisle where he had last seen Delilah, only to discover that she was no longer there. In a panic, he ran across the back of the store, looking up the aisles, until he realized that she was probably already at the checkout counter.

From the end of the last aisle, he spotted her at the front of the store, chatting amiably with the young cashier. Evan dashed in their direction, and as he approached them, he could see from the cashier's delighted expression that the universally beloved movie star had made her night. As he quickly came closer to Delilah, who hadn't yet looked in his direction, he suddenly panicked, as he realized that he didn't have a clue what to say to her. But at that point, it was too late, because the cashier and Delilah had already turned their attention to this scruffy, disheveled man with a strange hairdo who had just finished sprinting over to them for some reason. The twenty-nine-year-old man was

225

slightly out of breath, and wore a red plaid felt shirt with olive green sweatpants, brown loafers and white tube socks pulled over the bottoms of his pants, and seemed to carry with him the odd smell of mouthwash, hair gel, garlic, old spice, body odor, and sweaty gym socks. Evan could feel all the pressure of both women waiting for him to explain his presence and bizarre appearance. But all he could think of as an opener was, "Hi."

"Hi," they replied, sharing an amused look with each other before looking back at him. Evan noticed that Delilah's security guard was standing just outside the exit to Duane Reade, looking at him suspiciously.

"I...I...just came here to say...Well, I wanted to thank you for representing Czechoslovakia so well..."

"Thanks, but it's actually no longer Czechoslovakia. It's now the Czech Republic."

"Oh right, of course. I knew that they split from Slovakia in," Evan was drawing an excruciating blank.

"In 1993."

"Right, in 1993...I'm sorry, it's...it's...I'm a bit tired."

Evan felt like a complete idiot at that point, but was now compelled to ride the train wreck to its final destination. There was no hopping off gracefully.

"Oh that's OK. Lots of people still make that mistake," Delilah said, good-naturedly.

"Well, I wanted to thank you for representing the Czech Republic so well."

"I'm also American," she said warmly.

"Well, I...I think you represent America and the Czech Republic really well." Evan was praying that someone – the cashier or even Delilah's security guard – would save him from himself. He was sure that if Delilah was nice enough to continue talking to him, the stupidity of his lines would only get worse.

"Thanks," Delilah said, with a smile. She was about to walk off when Evan suddenly remembered how to say something in Czech.

"I think the Czech language is very beautiful," he said in Czech.

"I do too," she replied in Czech, turning gracefully around a little, with a look of pleasant surprise. "Have a nice night."

The delusional optimist in Evan saw the last part of their conversation as encouraging. He was tempted to follow her and give her his phone number, but she was already too close to her security guard, and there was no way she'd ever call him anyway, he figured. He breathed a heavy sigh of resignation. He couldn't fathom what he had done to deserve such a lovely coincidence – particularly when he was so ill-prepared for it. Evan also had no idea what Delilah Nakova was doing in his neighborhood Duane Reade that night. "I guess movie stars need supplies too," he thought, at which point he realized that he was still missing some essentials.

As he went back through the aisles looking for toilet paper, his step felt a little lighter – as if he had just tasted a piece of heaven. He was also delighted at the fact that Delilah apparently didn't connect him to the man she had met almost a year and a half ago at Float. "Thank God she meets too many people every day to keep track of them all," he thought. Evan was also grateful for the fact that he looked and smelled so atypically bad during their brief encounter. He reasoned that – if by some miracle – he could ever see Delilah Nakova again, he would seem unrecognizably different on that next, divine occasion of their meeting, such that the follies of their Duane Reade encounter wouldn't necessarily have to follow him.

For the next seventy-two hours, Evan wrote absolutely nothing. His mind was fixed exclusively on Delilah Nakova. He replayed in his mind, over and over, the first time he met her at Float and then their second encounter at Duane Reade. He daydreamed of countless future coincidences in which they were randomly reunited, all over the city, at sidewalk intersections, on the subway, at VIP parties, in elevators, and at restaurants. He imagined all of the lovely conversations that they would have together, in both Czech and English, each time that serendipity brought them together. "Isn't it odd – even supernatural – that we keep running into each other like this?" he asked her.

"Yes, I think it's a sign," she replied. "I wonder what would happen if we actually planned to meet some time," she said playfully.

"Maybe if you gave me your phone number, we could find out," Evan replied. "I really do promise to call. Not like I did with that Sayvyer woman. And by the way, that wasn't my fault. I honestly forgot her phone number. But I'm going to write yours down on paper, and then I'll tattoo it to both of my arms," he said. Delilah Nakova laughed lightly and freely, as if the world were just perfect in his presence. And then she wrote out for him her email, her cell phone, and her parent's home number.

Between two of his daydreams, Evan went out and purchased several Czech language textbooks and tapes and began reviewing Czech grammar, vocabulary, and pronunciation. He read every Delilah Nakova fan website and magazine he could find and even devised an elaborate plan to bump into her accidentally on the Brown campus. Evan also cleaned himself up and straightened out his place, just in case Delilah happened to walk into his apartment unannounced. He had to be prepared. Operation Repulsive was officially over.

Four days after his Duane Reade encounter with Delilah, which he had recounted to Heeb in painstaking detail at least seven times, Evan began to descend into a mild despondency. The reality was beginning to sink in: there was no way he was ever going to talk to Delilah again except by some elaborate scheme that would seem thoroughly contrived and calculating to her, and this didn't bode well given her known preference for genuineness.

"Forget about her, Evan," Heeb advised, when Evan shared his depressing conclusions with Heeb over a pizza dinner. "She has millions of fans around the world who worship her just as much you do. It's a complete fantasy to think that you could date her."

"But she spoke to me. She was sincerely nice to me."

"She's like that with everyone. That's her reputation. That's one of the reasons everyone loves her so much. You've gotta get over her, Evan."

"But I can't. I'm totally in love with her."

"You mean you're totally obsessed with her," Heeb corrected.

"What's the difference?"

"The difference is that you don't even know this woman, for God's sake! Like her other obsessive fans, you think you know her from all of the fan material you've been devouring, but you don't actually know her at all. And she knows you even less. The whole thing is completely absurd, Evan."

"I need a plan, Sammy. A real plan that will reunite me with her again."

"You need a shrink."

"I'm serious, Sammy. I need a plan."

"What ever happened to your novel?"

"I lost my steam, ever since I bumped into Delilah. It just seems so unimportant by comparison…Nothing seems to matter next to seeing Delilah again."

"You've totally flipped out, Evan."

"But haven't you ever been in love?"

"I don't know, but I've definitely never obsessed like this about anyone."

"I need a plan."

"How about your novel?"

"I just told you."

"No, I mean, why not use your novel to get to her?"

Evan's face lit up at the suggestion.

"Sammy Laffowitz, you're a fucking genius! Of course! If Evan cannot come to the mountain, then he will make the mountain come to him. With the novel. Delilah loves literature. I'll develop a character in the story that she'll fall in love with, so that she'll want to turn it into a film project that she stars in." And with that, Evan got up, said goodnight to Heeb, and rushed back to his apartment to finish his novel, which he resumed with a newfound urgency.

But during the next two weeks of writing, Evan realized that it was going to be much harder than he had assumed to create and integrate into his novel a compelling character for Delilah to play. He worked diligently and continuously but his progress was hindered by his frequent doubts concerning the exact nature of the Delilah character. These were the most critical details, as they would provide the hook that would help him to ensnare his love. Thus, he found himself consuming every book and film she had ever mentioned as a favorite, and learning everything else he could about her life and her psychology to fashion the perfect Delilah character for his novel.

As Evan struggled with the difficulties of word-wooing Delilah, he also became more realistic about his prospects with her, due to Heeb's substantial counseling efforts. Heeb even managed to persuade Evan to reverse his decision "to go exclusive" with Delilah Nakova and to start "seeing other people." By the third week of rewriting his novel for her, Evan acquiesced to the fact that it would take him several more weeks to complete his rewrite and that, in the meantime, he should be open to dating other women.

In early December 2000, when Evan learned that his HIV and hepatitis test results were negative, he felt as if he had been given a miraculous second chance. He resolved never again to "play a contact sport without a helmet," as he put it. The euphoric relief that Evan felt also translated into an impulse to celebrate and start going out again. He called Heeb's office to share the happy update and bring him out for an after-work drink at the pool hall they frequented.

During their game of billiards, Evan affirmed that he was, in fact, willing to date other people until his novel was ready for Delilah. Worried about how much Heeb had become a hermit, Evan began making the case for why it was time for them to resume their dating lives. "The longer we wait to jump back into the fray, the more it'll erode whatever's left of our confidence on the female front."

"You seem to have plenty left, since you think you can actually date Delilah Nakova."

"Everyone's entitled to some fantasies, Heeb. Besides, it's motivating me to make my novel better. But there's no denying that our SQs have suffered serious blows."

"Mortal blows," Heeb corrected him.

"Serious, not mortal...But if we stay out of the game for too long, they'll become mortal. It's been three months now," Evan said, sinking another billiard ball. He walked around the table to angle for his next shot. "We've gotta get back out there or we're gonna forget how it's done."

"I'd rather stay home and watch the Discovery Channel...I just don't feel up to it yet. Besides, on my last checkup, Doctor Clayton recommended that I let things heal for a few more weeks."

"I think I'm going to give it a few more weeks as well. Just to be safe. But that won't be a problem."

"Why not?"

"Because the strategy will be to flirt without any intention of scoring."

"Huh?"

"I mean it. Psychologically it's a very empowering approach."

Evan sent a yellow three ball spinning across the pool table and into a corner hole.

"Empowering?" Heeb asked skeptically. "Because there's no pressure to score or because we know that we won't have to reveal our scars?"

"Both," Evan said, positioning himself to sink the eight ball. "But there's an even bigger benefit."

"What's that?"

Evan was bent over the pool table at just the right angle to sink the eight ball and win, but he suddenly forgot about the game and began delivering an inspiring call to arms: "If you have no intention of scoring, then rejecting becomes much easier. And the power to reject will make you a man of self-esteem, high standards, and untouchable

230

confidence," he said, gradually standing back up. "Because when you exercise the power to reject, you dictate the terms of your destiny!" Now upright with his chest high, Evan held his pool stick as if it were a scepter and he were Pericles addressing ten thousand Athenians preparing for battle with Sparta. "The power to reject shifts the burden of proof from the pursuer to the pursued. Women you once thought were out of your league become women you reject. And you become that elusive, unattainable man every woman wants because no woman can have him!"

Heeb was suddenly and hopefully intrigued by the idea. The power to reject could bring back his Kojak, he thought. In a big way.

"It's true," Heeb said, looking upward as if to marvel at the epiphany at hand. "Women have only as much power as you give them. If you go in with every intention of ultimately rejecting them, then you take away all of their power." Heeb looked into Evan's eyes and beamed.

"Let the fellowship of the schlong begin!" Heeb announced, clasping Evan's hand.

"Yes. Let it begin!" Evan declared triumphantly, raising their bonded hands.

25. The Posse Forms

The official recruiting process for their posse began. Because Carlos, Narc, and Trevor each had high SQs, Heeb and Evan reasoned that adding the three to their group would raise the average SQ of each group member (much the way that colleges recruit individuals with higher test scores to increase the average test scores of their matriculated students). Heeb would have to persuade Carlos to join the group of single men even though he was happily married to his dream woman. Evan would have to make amends with Narc and then the two of them would have to bring Trevor back from his ashram.

Given the tall task at hand, Evan and Heeb agreed that they would divulge their injuries to underscore their real need for a supportive male group, even though Narc and Carlos would have no equally embarrassing stories with which to reciprocate (unlike Trevor). Evan and Heeb also figured that, in a tight-knit group, some reference to their injuries might eventually slip out anyway.

Heeb visited Carlos in his Fifth Avenue penthouse. It was Saturday afternoon and Carolina had just left for her gym workout, which gave the two friends a good ninety minutes to speak privately. The former college roommates had spoken a few dozen times since Heeb's arrival in New York City, but it had been five months since their last in-person visit.

Heeb discovered that even the idyllic marriage between Lucky Chucky and perfect Carolina had its share of problems. Carlos hadn't mentioned their marital issues before because they had never seemed significant enough. But now that he and Carolina were having their first dangerously important disagreement (whether to have children, and when), all of their minor differences seemed magnified. Carlos believed that people have children for purely selfish reasons (namely, to see variations of themselves continue) and that the morally right thing to do, given the planet's overpopulation and its many parentless children, is to adopt a child rather than create a new one. He was also ambivalent about irreversibly adding so much more stress and responsibility to his life at the age of twenty-seven.

Carolina, on the other hand, had always taken it for granted that she would have children, and — at age thirty — she worried about how many fertile eggs she had left. As far as Carolina was concerned, she wasn't fully a woman until she gave birth. For her, creating life was an essential part of a fully and richly lived existence as a woman. She had traveled the world, completed her PhD, and proven herself a phenomenal business success. She had already made far more money than she would ever need to retire comfortably, at the time of her choosing. And while she shared Carlos's concerns about overpopulation, she was convinced that their baby would inherit such phenomenal genes that its unique talents would represent a net gain for the world.

Carolina and Carlos still loved each other and the magnetic attraction that they had felt upon their initial meeting in Carolina's office was still present to an unusual extent, relative to other five-year couples. But such a fundamental issue – on which there was no obvious compromise – loomed large over their shared life. This unresolved difference created an uncertainty in their relationship that had never existed before Carolina's thirtieth birthday sent her into a mommy-panic. The problem amplified the intensity and significance of their lesser quarrels, whether they concerned spending decisions (Carlos, who never forgot his humble immigrant beginnings, preferred frugality), charitable giving (Carolina favored helping children's organizations, while Carlos thought environmental charities were far more neglected) or neatness (Carlos was obsessed with tidy organization, while Carolina preferred a "more relaxed" approach, as she called it).

All of this came as a surprise to Heeb, who – despite his general cynicism – had always clung to the example of Carlos and Carolina as evidence for his romantic belief that perfect relationships could exist, at least for a few extraordinarily lucky people. Initially, the news also made Heeb ambivalent about inviting Carlos into the posse, since such an invitation might somehow hasten the demise of his marriage. But as he heard Carlos recite the litany of things that he loved about his wife, he recalled how absurdly choosy Carlos had always been, and concluded that his inclusion in the posse would only make him value Carolina more. He decided to continue with his plan to recruit Carlos.

"Meeting new women will just show you how lucky you are to have her," Heeb explained.

"I can't, Heeb. Our marriage is already under too much pressure as it is."

Heeb realized that this tack wasn't going to work, and decided instead to resort to Carlos's sympathy.

233

"There's another reason I'd like you to join us…I actually came here to tell you that I've got a serious medical condition…Permanent damage…I don't know how it will affect me long-term, but I just wanted you to come out with us a little, while I'm still going out," Heeb said cryptically.

"What is it? What do you have?" Carlos asked anxiously, his face and voice suddenly full of concern. It sounded to him as if Heeb might be terminally ill or something. But Heeb couldn't yet get himself to disclose anything about his penis scars; Evan was still the only friend who knew.

"I've got halitosis and alopecia," Heeb said, soberly. It was all he could think of to stall for a moment.

"What's that?"

"It's very serious."

"What is it?"

"Halitosis is bad breath and alopecia is male pattern baldness."

Carlos shook his head and rolled his eyes. He was both relieved and annoyed.

"Pinchi pendejo!" he exclaimed, cursing Heeb in Spanish. "Don't scare me like that!"

"All right, I'm sorry. I do have something more serious than that. It's not life threatening or anything…But I've permanently lowered my SQ, even though I used to be sure that it couldn't get any lower."

"What happened?"

By the time Heeb had finished recounting the tribulations that he and Evan had endured, Carlos committed himself to joining the posse for up to three nights out per month, for the next few months, and possibly longer, if Heeb was still having trouble meeting women at that point.

*****

Until their quarrel, Evan and Narc had enjoyed almost a decade of good times and reliable friendship, despite their considerable differences.

Evan replayed their fight in his head several times, soon after it happened, trying to understand how what started as a casual discussion about work-related discontent deteriorated into something so much worse. Whatever the explanation, he knew that the longer they didn't speak after such an inconsequential quarrel, the more consequential it could start to seem to them. Thus, Evan tried to make up right away. But when Narc rebuffed him, Evan's pride prevented him from trying again, although he occasionally still wondered what had happened between them.

After Heeb happily reported that he had persuaded Carlos to join their group, Evan put the posse before his pride and felt emboldened to approach Narc again. As it turned out, reconciling with Narc would prove much easier than he had expected, in part because of the dramatic decisions that Narc was contemplating. Narc was happy to hear from Evan, with whom he hadn't spoken in about eight months. He suggested that they meet for Sunday brunch at the same Chinatown restaurant where the two had broken the bad news about Charlene to Trevor. The preferred locale suggested to Evan that Narc had some personal things to tell him.

"Thanks for keepin' it real, yo," Narc said, as they waited for their food. "You were right to call it like you saw it."

"Yeah, but I could have used more tact. So I want to apologize for the way it all came out."

"It's all good, bro. You were just trying to help me realize that I needed to make some changes in my life." Narc looked up at the waiter transferring the food to their table.

"You realize that I haven't had any booty in almost three years?" Narc said, as if he himself could scarcely believe or accept this fact.

"That's not as bad as my sex life has been, Narc."

"You haven't been getting any?"

"Not only that, I've got some permanent damage that's going to make it harder to get some in the future."

"What do you mean?"

Evan then expounded on the concept of SQ and recounted everything that had happened to him and Sammy. Narc was genuinely shocked and deeply sympathetic, as if his own crown jewels had been attacked twice, in two separate and traumatic incidents. Evan concluded by pitching Narc on the idea of forming a posse.

"I'm totally down with that, bro. We should go upstate for Trevor too. I'm worried about that kid."

"Yeah, I haven't spoken to him in ages," Evan agreed.

The waiter came by to clear their empty plates.

"I haven't even told you about the big decision that I reached, since we last spoke. And you're partly responsible for helping me to get there, because I needed someone to bust my chops about my work situation."

Evan's face lit up at the news that his former college roommate might finally be doing something to improve his life. "What did you decide?" he asked.

"I'm quitting."

"Really?"

"Before they fire me."

"They're going to fire you?"

"My midyear review is in two weeks and I know they're going to fire me, so I'm gonna fire them first. Next week."

Evan assumed correctly that Narc still, on occasion, used drugs recreationally.

"Did they spring a drug test on you or something?"

"No."

"So why would they fire you?"

"They know I hate my job. The quality of my work shows it. Especially the last few months. And I've done some pretty bold things since we last spoke."

"Like what?"

"You know that asshole partner, Edward, who always talks to me about work while I'm pissing? Well, one time I cut him off and told him that I really just wanted to piss in peace."

"You didn't!"

"Oh, it gets much better."

"Really?"

"Yeah. As you know, my sex life has been nonexistent for so long that I've become totally addicted to Internet porn. And since I'm always in the office, which has a great T-3 broadband connection, that's where I do some of my best surfing."

"No!" Evan said. "You didn't!"

Narc nodded mischievously. "Do you know how they found out?"

"The IT guys checked your Internet browsing history?" Evan ventured.

"Yup. I have a friend in the IT department who gave me the heads up that the management committee had requested my browsing history. But what made them ask for it in the first place? I do have my own office, you know, and I always close the door first."

Evan thought about what might have made the firm suspect that Narc was surfing porn but he couldn't come up with anything. He shrugged his shoulders.

"One of the documents that I was marking up for Edward had some physical evidence on it…Accidentally of course…"

"No!" Evan couldn't believe his ears.

"I didn't realize it. And when I gave Edward the document he asked me what the liquid was. I tried to pretend that I had sneezed. He was in a mad rush to meet a client deadline or he probably would have asked for a new print out. But before he went back to work, he looked down at my pants for a sec with this look of disgust. And as soon as I left his office, I saw that there was some on my pants too."

"No!"

"Yeah. That's how it happened. But the best part is that I'm not gonna be a passive observer any more. I'm gonna be an active participant being observed."

"What do you mean?"

"Instead of just watching porn, I'm gonna make it…I've finally decided to go for it…It's the only way to make up for the last three years of no sex."

With his mouth agape, Evan looked increasingly shocked by the second. Amused by Evan's predictably stunned reaction, Narc kept speaking nonchalantly as if he weren't reporting anything extraordinary.

"I just realized that I have to try it at least once. Maybe it'll really suck and I won't want to do it anymore, although I kinda doubt it. I just have to spend a few weeks getting rid of all this fuckin' fat I put on during the last four years here, so I got a gym membership."

Evan still looked dumbfounded.

Narc continued: "Hey, I know you've got your issues with pornography. But I'm living proof that people go into porn out of their own free will. And I know deep down that you wish you had the balls to do it too. But don't worry, I'll send some hot honies your way."

Evan finally managed to respond: "But…But what about your parents?"

"I know…I know…That's the one thing that's always held me back all these years. But I've spent the last seven years living for them. Life is short, bro. Too short. Gotta take chances to get what you want. If I'd been born Michael Jordan I'd be the happiest man alive. I'd give anything to be Michael. But that's just a fantasy. Like joining the NBA. But becoming a porn star is actually doable."

"So you're going to tell them?"

"Fuck no! But I figure that the odds of them finding out are nil. They barely watch TV, they don't even know how to connect to the Internet, and none of their Chinese friends watch porn. So how are they ever gonna find out?"

"I guess…But what are you going to tell them about your law job?"

"The truth: that I need to take some time off and want to explore a career in film. You know, some porn stars actually transition into legit films, so I'm technically telling the truth. Anyway, it'll give me more time to help them with their business, so they'll be happy about that."

"What are you going to tell people at your Columbia Law School and Brown alumni reunions?"

"I don't plan on going to those."

"What if one of your classmates recognizes you in a porn?"

"They'll probably envy my lifestyle. I'll be making more money and fucking more hot women than they'll ever have in their lives."

"I guess," said Evan, skeptically. "God…You've definitely made some bold decisions since we last spoke."

That Saturday, on the bus to Trevor's ashram in upstate New York, Evan asked Narc some more questions that were on his mind.

"What about your dignity? I mean don't you feel weird about total strangers seeing your pecker and how you use it?"

"Nah. I'm proud to be a well-endowed Asian-American. Just like you told me in college: my family name is 'Wang' for a reason. If more guys like me went into porn we'd probably eliminate that fucked-up stereotype. I think it's good for people to see that Asian men can be physical and sexual, and not just a bunch of science nerds."

"I guess. But is this really what you want to do with all of that education and intelligence?"

"I'll do anything but corporate law."

"But most lawyers don't transition into porn when they burn out on corporate law."

"Well, I'm not most people. Besides, people should do what they like. And what they're good at. And I love sex. And women have always told me that I'm good."

"I remember from college; your happy customers would call you 'Big Everlast'," Evan said reminiscently.

"Word. I mean, not to brag about my goods too much, but I'm a legit eight-incher, I got great stamina, and it doesn't take me long after an orgasm to get hard again. Where else but the porn industry can I be rewarded for these virtues? Where else but porn and the NBA can I get paid to do what I love?"

"There's definitely some method to your madness...It's just hard to imagine such an educated person becoming a porn star."

"Like I said, this isn't a lifetime career decision. I'm just tryin' it out."

"Aren't you worried about STDs? Believe me, they're no joke."

"The production company I'm gonna work with uses condoms on all of their films, and contractually makes everyone get tested before they work on any film...They told me that there's still some small risk there, but I'm willing to take it."

"You always talked about how you grew addicted to this expensive lifestyle and that's why you couldn't leave your law firm salary."

"I've got enough saved up to live in New York for two years. And if I stop livin' so large, I could easily stretch it out to four years. Don't get me wrong, it'll be an adjustment, unless I become huge overnight...But it's worth it, bro. Hell, I should be payin' them! Even back when I knew how to be smooth and had the patience to date honies properly, they were never as fine-lookin' as the honies I'm gonna be fuckin' on camera. And I'll get to have orgies with four hotties at once. I could never pull that off unless I was a legit NBA playa."

"What'll you tell women you meet?"

"I'll tell 'em I work in film. Besides, I won't exactly need to pick up women while I'm workin' as a porn star."

"You're not trying to back out of the posse now are you?" Evan asked.

"Nah. I'm down with you fellas."

"So you really don't think there's a social stigma?"

"Thanks to Howard Stern, porn is now very mainstream. Porn stars are known as 'professionals' who 'work' with each other, and they get interviewed like real stars. Some of them even go into legit Hollywood productions. So lotsa people want to become porn stars. And everyone either watches porn or lies about it."

"I don't watch porn."

"Then you lie about it."

"I really don't."

"Whateva."

"And I'm definitely not going to watch it now that I know I might see you up there."

"Yo, I'm expectin' you to head up my fan site," Narc said, with a playful elbow jab.

The bus pulled up on the dirt road that extended half a mile into the ashram. Evan and Narc exited the bus.

When they reached the end of the road, where the grassy, gated entrance to the ashram stood, Trevor walked up to greet them. His towering head hovered strangely above the top of the gate, and was totally shaved as always, but now he was wearing a plain peasant garb rather than his usual chic New York clothes. Happy to see his two friends, Trevor gave each of them a warm hug.

"You must be totally knackered and peckish from that long bus ride," Trevor said. "Come inside for some grub."

They followed Trevor into a large eating hall and sat down for a tofu-based lunch with sweet milk and raw vegetables.

Over lunch, they caught up on the last eight months of each other's lives, and Narc quickly resumed his playful imitation of Trevor's British accent. Trevor seemed relieved and delighted to revert back to such a familiar and intimate mode, since it was the first visit he had had from anyone he knew since his arrival at the ashram. He laughed hysterically at Narc's work story with Edward, and felt less embarrassed about his own past with Charlene after hearing from Evan what had befallen him and Heeb. Trevor told his visitors how he had discovered the joys of meditation and a pure lifestyle, but conceded that it was a bit boring at times, although nothing as bad as law firm tedium.

"We actually came to bring you back, bro," Narc said.

"I know. I can feel that in your energy. You really are a good bunch of mates. I'd be lying if I told you that I didn't occasionally doubt my decision to come here. But my time here has been spiritually fruitful and I've learned many things about myself through meditation. A part of me would like to assume the challenge of applying those lessons in an environment that is less conducive to Zen thought — in a place like New York City, where the mind is so easily distracted by so many stimuli...But a part of me still feels the need to be cleansed here."

"You're clean, bro," Narc reassured him. "You were squeaky clean before you got here. By now you're so clean I could install you on my windows as an air filter."

Trevor laughed a little. "But you really don't know what it's like to live in constant purity."

"And you really don't know what it's like to live in constant sin," Narc rejoined.

"Trevor, Narc almost has a point, in a twisted sort of way," Evan added. "You learned whatever lessons you had to learn from this place and the experience that led you to come here. But this is ultimately an escape like any other. You have to deal with your life. In the real world. Not in some ashram."

"Evan's right. If anything, this experience will make it harder for you to accept your mistakes because it's only going to reinforce your sexually conservative outlook."

"It wasn't a mistake, Narc."

"What do you mean?"

"Mates…I have to tell you something…"

"What is it?" Narc, asked, expecting something grave.

"One of the things I've learned here is that I just have to accept who I am, as much as I have to accept the laws of nature, and the interrelationships among all things in the universe."

"That's cool, yo. No one's telling you to be different than who you are…We just want you back in the city. So that you can explore a more liberal lifestyle now, for some balance."

"That's just the problem…You see, I was mistaken about Charlene's gender at first, but I eventually learned that Charlene is, in fact, a man."

"Everyone makes some major mistakes. My penis injury is a testament to that fact."

"But that's my point, mates. I still slept with Charlene after I discovered the mistake."

Narc and Evan looked blankly at their friend, trying to understand the full import of what he just said.

"You see, the Charlene incident made me realize who I really am…And that, by itself, was hard enough to deal with…There was no bloody way I was going to explain to the two of you that I'm actually drawn towards men…"

Narc and Evan just sat at the dining table, speechless.

"I guess coming here was an escape from all of the social consequences of realizing who I am… I just didn't want to face the fact that my friends might no longer accept me…It was just easier to come here and meditate about the world and nature."

There was some more silence, and then Narc finally spoke.

"Are you sure that you're...that you're a homosexual?"

Trevor solemnly nodded his head. "Believe me Narc, I've had lots of time to think about it here."

An awkward silence returned.

Narc finally spoke again.

"Well, the gay scene in New York City is a lot better than this little house on the prairie," Narc added with a playful grin.

Trevor smiled a bit at the joke. "But, Narc, ironically enough, that's exactly what I find so unsettling about going back to the city...All of my friends are straight, and there's this whole gay community and gay culture in the city that I know bugger all about."

"Well, who says you have to change circles like that, yo?"

"Well, I just assumed that...well...that...."

"That what?" Narc replied. "Evan and I came to bring you back...Gay or straight."

"Really?" Trevor asked, surprised and relieved.

"I mean, don't think that this shit didn't catch me by surprise, or that I'm not buggin' out about it a little right now...But whateva, yo... We're forming a posse, and we want you in it..."

"Do you really mean that?" Trevor asked, in disbelief.

"We do," Evan chimed in, now that he was finally sure how he felt about the whole thing.

And with that, Evan and Narc began lobbying Trevor to join their posse.

After a few hours, they finally persuaded him to return to New York City and join their group, at which point the discussion turned to practical problems.

"Not to worry about the blatant, but what will I do in the way of employment now?" Trevor asked. "If I'm just going to be sitting about on my bum, I might as well stay here."

"That's exactly the danger I was beginning to worry about," Evan replied. "You could forget how to deal with the real world. Finding jobs, dating women – I mean, men. You know what I mean: taking care of business. But you'll be fine. I've been talking to someone at the UN Development Program for you. A friend of a friend. The position you were interested in was taken, but there's another one that opened up. And I can get you an interview."

"Really?!" Trevor's face lightened up. "That's brilliant!"

"Yeah, we'll just have to make some shit up about what you've been doin' for the last eight months," Narc added. "But it's all good. We'll figure somethin' out."

"And what about my flat? I've already sublet it for another six months."

"You can stay with me until you find a sublet," Narc replied. "Just don't start touchin' me while I'm sleepin' and shit."

"Don't worry, mate…You should know that I think of you only as a brother."

"I know…But I just had to say that…I mean, it's definitely a little strange for me…But it's all good, yo…There's a first for everything…You're still ma' main man….We'll just need to find you an extra large futon for your stay."

"Thanks for being such great friends," he replied. He reached across the table, offering his hands in thanks, and Evan and Narc reached across and clasped his hands for a moment.

"Hey, are you gonna try to get back together with Charlene?" Narc asked.

"Not a chance. Not after the sex operation."

"Sex operation?" Evan asked.

"She sent a letter and some pictures to my address, and the guy subletting from me forwarded it here."

"So no transgender types for you?" Narc asked.

"No. I'm interested only in men who want to continue being men."

"But you're still cool with joining our posse, right? Even if we're chasing women? I mean, you can chase men all the same…We'll help each other out…"

Still not sure about how easily he could be integrated into their posse, Trevor smiled in delighted relief at how tolerantly two of his close friends had received his new identity.

"So you're in?" Evan asked.

"Yes, I suppose I am," Trevor said, in wry resignation. After a moment's hesitation he added, "But I would really rather not tell the rest of your posse about what happened with Charlene."

"There are no secrets in the posse," Evan replied. "Besides, what happened to Heeb and me is arguably just as bad, if not worse. You just really discovered what you should be doing with your penis. But we practically lost ours…And now you know all the ridiculous details. So Heeb should get to hear your story too. It's only fair."

"And my story with that fucked up partner Edward ain't exactly somethin' I'm telling everyone I meet. Or the fact that I'm going into porn."

"I still can't believe that you're really doing that!" Trevor remarked.

"Evan is dyin' to join me. He just won't admit it."

Evan rolled his eyes in amused denial.

"And you'll be doin' gay porn before you know it!" Narc continued.

"Purity, Narc. Purity."

"Sin, Trevor. Sin."

"Balance," Evan interjected, as if to resolve the dispute. "Balance."

26. The Posse Goes on the Prowl

The unlikely group that resulted from the union of five diverse characters in their late twenties operated with surprising harmony. This cohesiveness could be attributed to two factors: 1) everyone's issues and embarrassing pasts were plainly disclosed prior to the gang's formation and 2) the clan had been expressly conceived as a male support group. Carlos's unusual charm and good looks ensured his quick and easy acceptance by Narc and Evan; Trevor and Carlos hit it off particularly well, given their shared interest in Buddhism, good style, and vegetarianism. Heeb and Trevor got along naturally thanks to their shared love of irony. Heeb particularly appreciated Trevor's British style and articulate intelligence, and his gentle and accepting manner; he was also sensitive to Trevor's potentially awkward and lonely status as the only homosexual in the group. Narc and Heeb were perhaps the only mismatched pair in the posse, but any impulse Narc might have had to reject Heeb for his lack of looks or athletic inclinations was overridden by his knowledge of how close Carlos and Evan were with Heeb. Similarly, any tendency Heeb might have had to dismiss Narc's porn star decision, his continuing NBA fantasies, his occasional ghetto talk, and his narcissistic obsession with fashionable clothing and looking good, was checked by his awareness of Narc's close friendship with Trevor and Evan. After some initial adjustments, Narc and Heeb eventually embraced each other as friends and equally important members of the group.

The posse was a collection of handsome single males over six feet tall (except for Heeb's looks/height and Carlos's married status). They each belonged to some ethnic minority: Mexican, African, Jewish, Asian and Czech (Evan now proudly identified himself as Czech). Walking down the street or waiting on a subway platform together, they easily drew attention as a group, thanks to their intriguing and attractive diversity and their collective stature (capped by the Tower).

It was also a group of highly intelligent and professionally diverse young men: a software developer turned novelist, a top actuary for a large insurance company, the president of a real estate development company, a corporate lawyer turned porn star, and a corporate lawyer turned project finance associate for the African development program at the UN (Trevor got the job). Carlos and Heeb were the busiest members of the posse. Those with the most time were Evan, who could freely determine the intensity of his novel-writing, and Narc, whose film production schedule occupied no more than a few days each week, for a few weeks at a time, followed by several weeks of no work.

Despite his newly embraced homosexual identity, Trevor felt surprisingly at home in the otherwise heterosexual posse, if only because such a group felt far more familiar to him than any gay group would have felt at that time. While Trevor secretly admired Carlos, he accepted that the Latin hunk was married and – in any case – "straight as a ten dollar bill," as Carlos once jokingly described himself to a burly gay man who had hit on him in front of Trevor. Ultimately, the benefits of the posse still outweighed the costs, as far as Trevor was concerned. While he occasionally felt awkward in the group, it afforded him the company of smart, good-looking men whose collective presence attracted the interest of homosexuals whom Trevor could then very naturally approach without any competition and lots of moral support. The other members of the posse also felt occasionally awkward about Trevor, but they too concluded that the gang was better off with him as a member, because he added a rather interesting look, sound, and feel to the whole group. Above all, women were still very intrigued by him – particularly when they learned that he was gay – and, for this reason alone, everyone believed that he was an essential member of the clan.

Because Carlos had the most to lose from his membership in the posse, it convened entirely according to when his wife was supposed to be out of town or unavailable for several hours. On a few occasions, a planned posse prowl was cancelled or continued without Carlos because Carolina's meeting ended sooner than expected or her plans changed and she wanted to see Carlos. This flexible arrangement, which was fully understood and accepted by the others, prevented Carolina from realizing that her husband regularly joined a band of single men on the hunt. Carlos felt some guilt about joining such a group and then hiding it all from Carolina, but he rationalized these actions as a subtle protest against her insistence on having children. When he went out with the posse, he forgot his marital issues and just enjoyed the fleeting freedom of feeling single again. Nevertheless, Carlos always left his marriage ring on, which generally had the paradoxical effect of making women want him even more.

One concrete indication that Evan and Heeb had successfully assembled a fraternal team to take on the city collectively was the fact that, after just a few occasions out together, a shared vocabulary had already begun to emerge within the gang. The combination of Trevor's British expressions, Narc's hip-hop talk, and Heeb's inventive witticisms ensured that a rich and eclectic new language accompanied the posse's evolution.

Trevor began frequently employing the term "gaydar," which was already in fairly common use in Manhattan. He also innovated a derivation of this word for Heeb's marital mission: "Jewdar." In reality, Carlos had the best gaydar (perhaps because homosexuals always noticed him), and Evan's Jewdar was almost as accurate as Heeb's (because, according to Heeb's explanation, Evan had grown up in Manhattan).

Heeb introduced the first two terms to be unanimously adopted by the group: "SQ" and "Kojak" (including its variations, "Kojaking" and "Kojakness"). He also popularized the concept of flying different classes of airline service as a way to describe the kind of woman (or man, in Trevor's case) one could realistically approach. Heeb always flew coach, Carlos always flew first class, and everyone else flew in business class, unless an exceptionally good hair day was involved. Related concepts were "trying to upgrade without enough miles" and "insufficient mileage" – applicable to any posse member who was hitting on someone out of his league.

Narc popularized the term "Whiplash Libby"[9] to describe any member of the posse suffering from attention deficit disorder in a situation where the failure to focus on a single prospect – out of the many present – left the guy empty-handed with a neck sore from whiplash. Narc and Heeb introduced several other important terms after scoping out a potential female of interest for Heeb at Sounds of Brazil ("S.O.B."), the Latin dance club where the posse was lounging one night. As Narc returned from the scouting operation, he signaled to Heeb the findings by waving his hand in front of his nose as if there were a putrid stench he was fanning away. Narc's signal only confused Heeb, but the two were still too far apart to discuss anything. Two

---

[9] The term is short for "Whiplash Libido" and Narc first applied it to Evan when they were college roommates and Narc tried to claim that Zoe dumped Evan because of his Whiplash Libido (and not because of Narc's porn-watching habits).

minutes later, when Narc arrived back to where Heeb and the others were standing, he clarified.

"No good, yo. Waving the hand like that means she's got BF, and you should keep moving."

"BF? What's BF? Body Foulness?" Heeb's guess was based on the hand gesture. Narc shook his head.

"BF is the opposite of FB."

"So what's an FB?"

"A fuck buddy," explained Narc, who seemed a tad amused that Heeb didn't know.

"Oh I see. So BF would be a boyfriend."

"Word; a BF is really just an FB, but with obligations and restrictions."

"That's BS."

"What is?"

"The fact that the order of the letters makes such a huge difference."

"I guess," Narc conceded in amusement.

"But it gets worse. Look at God, live, star, and stun. If you spell those words backwards you get dog, evil, rats, and nuts."

Narc looked at Heeb as if he were from another planet.

"Sorry. Didn't mean to be a nerdy SOB who elaborates on linguistic BS in the middle of a club called SOB," Heeb added delightfully.

"Naw, you're just bein' a CB right now," Narc replied.

"What's that?"

"A Cock Blocker."

"A Cock Blocker?" Heeb asked, somewhat confused.

"You know, from that Kool G rap song?"

"Oh, because we should be focused on ladies rather than linguistics."

"Word."

"Well, getting back to the ladies, I'm very bummed that that TH has a BF."

"What's a TH?"

"A Traffic Hazard," Heeb clarified.

"Oh you mean because the woman is so hot she'll take your eyes off the road?" Narc confirmed.

"Exactly."

"She's definitely a TH – a TH with a BF. But that's why we're in a club, Heeb. So you can keep on moving when that happens."

"I hear you. But she was the one for tonight, I think."

"Well – I don't recommend this – but if you're really feelin' her, I could try to get friendly with her man and pull a legit CB. You know, get him away from his lady long enough for you to get her digits."

"No. I can't do that," Heeb protested.

"Why not? It's doable if your game is good."

"No, it's against my ethics – like hitting on married women… That's being a home wrecker. And I'm a firm believer in home improvement."

"True 'dat. And home wrecking can get her man vexed," Narc observed.

"Yes. Collapsing homes can cause severe bodily harm to those in the immediate vicinity."

Heeb and Evan benefited differently from the posse. For Heeb, the group was the largest circle of reliable, good-looking, and "cool" male friends he had ever had, and consequently provided a tremendous boon to his badly damaged male ego. For Evan, who had enjoyed male packs of almost comparable size and quality in many prior years, the posse provided more literary inspiration than SQ elevation. While Evan was, in spirit, every bit a member of the posse as the others, his heart remained reserved for Delilah Nakova, no matter how much he tried to tell himself and others that he was "free to see other people."

Although Evan never missed a posse adventure and always contributed whatever charm and risk-taking the night called for on his part, he increasingly viewed everything that happened and everyone they met as potential fodder for the novel that would unite him and his love. One time, Trevor confronted him about the issue after he caught him jotting something down immediately after Trevor had answered his question.

"What are you always writing there, mate?"

"It's for my novel."

"You're not nicking my words are you?"

"Just noting the noteworthy."

"I've got to be careful what I say around you."

"Afraid of the unflattering exposure, are you?"

"You know, you really should give people their Miranda rights when they first meet you so that they have fair notice. Something like,

'You have the right to remain silent or walk away. Anything you say or do may appear in my novel."

"Do you mind if I quote that joke in my novel?" Evan asked.

Trevor rolled his eyes and shook his head in amusement.

And so the other posse members came to expect that Evan would always be documenting their time together. His ever-present pen and paper also provided pretexts for various openers by him, and sometimes even by forward females wondering what he was writing. This advantage, as far as the other members were concerned, was enough to justify whatever oddity the posse stenographer represented.

27. Sex in the Title

By late January 2001, the clan had been out seven times together (although they celebrated New Year's without Carlos, who was with Carolina), and Evan had finally finished the novel that was entirely designed and destined for Delilah. As he was printing out the first draft, he called Heeb and put his cordless phone near the noise made by his printer.

"You hear that?" Evan asked. "That's the sound of completion, my friend!"

"That's great, Evan. But do you have a good title yet?"

"Would you stop carping about the title? It's the body that counts. That's where the sleep is lost, the hair is pulled, the sardine dinners are eaten, and the schizophrenia is developed."

"You're definitely right about the schizophrenia part."

"Are you dismissing the five-hour discussion I had last night?"

"With whom?"

"The two main characters in my novel."

"Yeah, yeah. Very funny. So did you come up with a title for it? Preferably with the word sex?"

"Delilah's too sophisticated to like a novel just because it has the word 'Sex' in the title."

"You're making a huge mistake, Evan. Trust me on this."

"I can't believe you're serious about this." Evan began to pace around his apartment restlessly. He was in the mood to celebrate wildly and receive enthusiastic congratulations but was encountering stiff resistance from his good friend over trivial details.

"Evan, it doesn't matter what else you've written if you can't get her to the first page. And sex is the best way to do it. Look at you: you read those cheesy frat boy rags with sex plastered everywhere on them."

"But she's so much better than me, Heeb."

"Evan, unless she's Mother Theresa, the word sex will still intrigue her the way it does everyone else."

"So what do you want me to call it? Sex With Delilah? Or should I be truer to life and call it 'Sex Without Delilah.'"

"They both sound too much like a stalker's confession…How about "Sexy Delilah?"

"That's too direct. And too sycophantic. I need something more subtle," Evan said, now sounding genuinely troubled about not having a suitable title.

"How about Sex and Sexuality?" Heeb suggested. "You know, a kind of play off of 'Sense and Sensibility'?"

"Sex and Sexuality? That sounds like the title for some biology book. Or some mildly pornographic guide to lovemaking."

Evan began to pace more nervously. "Just let me think for a sec," he said, to curb Heeb's distractingly bad suggestions. There was a long silence as Evan walked wildly all over his tiny apartment with the cordless phone in his hand, feverishly brainstorming for just the right title with the word "sex" in it.

"I got it! I got it!" Heeb declared triumphantly.

Evan stopped in the middle of his kitchenette to hear Heeb's idea.

"Sex in the Title."

"Yeah, that's what you've been saying I need."

"No, that's the title: 'Sex in the Title.'"

"You want me to call my novel 'Sex in the Title?'"

"Yeah. Isn't it great?"

"To quote that bimbo model from last Saturday night, that's the most retardest thing I've ever heard."

"You don't like it?"

"It's completely idiotic. That title makes no sense at all. It's the worst thing you've come up with yet."

"It was a joke, Evan."

"Oh."

"I mean, what better way to tease you about your title troubles than to state them in the title itself?"

"All right, but now you've got me obsessing about the title."

"I'm sure you'll come up with something good."

"Let me think for a second."

Heeb patiently waited in silence for a few moments.

"The funny thing is," Evan began, "as I think about it some more now, there's actually something kind of appealing about Sex in the Title."

"You can't be serious."

"I kind of like how the incoherence – or rather the suggestion of coherence – is unshakably intriguing to the mind."

"It was a joke, Evan."

"But I kind of like it."

"It's totally asinine. Ask the characters in your novel. They'll tell you."

"I just did. We had a brief conference during that last silent pause. And they all agreed that it's a good title."

"So they're just as whacked as you."

"Pretty much."

"Well, don't come crying to me if the manuscript comes back to you unread."

"With cheerleaders like you, Heeb, who needs book reviewers?"

"Forget me and the book reviewers. You have a much bigger problem."

"What's that?"

"Getting it to her."

But Evan had already worked out an elegant solution to that problem. He explained to Heeb how his strategy was premised on the unfortunate fact that nothing would happen in Hollywood if it weren't for the exploited assistant. "Shame on Hollywood for using its glamorous aura to milk starry-eyed newcomers like that!" Evan exclaimed, as if his plan were some Marxist plot to rectify the injustices of Hollywood. Deviating from his usual naysaying, Heeb had to admit that Evan's plan just might work.

One week later, after several rereads and polishes, Evan finalized the manuscript, and was ready to send it to Delilah Nakova. His prior research had uncovered that she was represented by the International Artists Agency, a prestigious Los Angeles talent agency also known as "IAA." After some additional research and a few anonymous inquiries (using his best imitation of Trevor's accent), Evan was able to determine the names and numbers of several assistants who worked with Delilah's main agent.

The next day, Evan called IAA at 7 p.m. Pacific Time, when he knew that most of the agents were likely to be wooing new clients over cocktails, while their assistants were still laboring away at the office. He tried several extensions until he reached Mike Yuvalov, a fresh UCLA college graduate working at IAA as an intern "assisting the assistant" of a top Hollywood agent.

"Hi Mike. My name is Evan."

"What can I do for you, Evan?"

Evan chatted him up for a while, developed some trust, made him feel important, and got him talking about life on the exciting inside track to a glamorous Hollywood career. After about ten minutes of rapport building, Evan felt comfortable discussing his proposal.

"Mike, you seem like a nice guy. How would you like to do me a personal favor and make infinitely more money than you make now?"

"One dollar per hour is infinitely more than I make now, so that's not necessarily such a tempting offer."

"See that? You're smart and witty and probably better at math than your boss, and yet you're getting paid nothing. That's just scandalous. A moral outrage!"

"Tell me about it."

"I'm offering to do more than tell you about it. I'll pay you some real money if you can just help me out with something."

"How much are we talking?"

"Up to two thousand dollars."

"Are you serious?"

"Yes. I am. But since I don't know you that well and I have no way to verify whether you actually do this personal favor for me, I have to incentivize you properly."

"What do you mean?"

"I'll give you five hundred dollars upfront. And then fifteen hundred dollars on the back-end."

"If you're talking about net profits, I know they don't exist, so I'm not into back-end compensation."

"You're good, Mike. Sharp and quick-witted. I like you. This little transaction could evolve into a nice friendship between us."

"I somehow doubt that, since I don't really know you."

"I know you don't know me. But this phone call is changing all of that. So here's why the back-end is legitimate in our little situation here. You see, I've written a novel that could be a perfect film adaptation project for Delilah Nakova. And I just need to get her the manuscript now. Which is where you come in. All you have to do for the five hundred dollars is put the manuscript which I mail to you into an IAA envelope, include whatever cover note – on IAA stationary – you think will make her read it, and then you're done."

"That's it? You're offering me five hundred dollars to stuff an envelope and include a cover note?"

"Yup. And that's five hundred dollars more than your boss pays you to do the same thing every day."

"Sad but true."

"So what do you say?"

"I say it sounds good, except for the part about me losing my job afterwards."

"You're worried about losing a non-paying job?"

"Well, I'm just weeks away from being promoted from intern to paid assistant."

"Fair enough. But you won't lose anything if you don't mention your name anywhere. Besides, if she ends up loving the manuscript and her agent gets credit for sending it to her, do you really think he's going to fire anyone? At that point you could probably confess your crime and get a promotion for secretly trying to advance the agency's interests."

"You may have a point there."

"Of course, I have to take the leap of faith that you won't just pocket the cash and use the manuscript for toilet paper. But you seem like a nice, honest guy, and my manuscript paper isn't exactly soft, so I'm willing to take that chance."

"What about that back-end you mentioned?"

"Ah. The back-end. Here's how it works. The back-end is your little fifteen hundred-dollar bonus if Delilah likes the manuscript enough to contact me directly. So you may want to encourage her a little. You can mention that you thought this story would be perfect for her next project. And you can suggest that she get in touch with me directly. That should significantly improve your odds of getting the back-end."

"But how can I trust that you'll actually pay the bonus if she does get in touch with you?"

"That's where a little bit of trust will have to come into play, Mike. Just like I'm going to have to trust you with that first five hundred dollars. And, you see, if she contacts me, I'll know that my trust in you paid off. And I'll be in such a good mood about the beauty of trust that I'll want to send you an extra, pre-agreed thank you. Besides, I may need you for other favors in the future, so I wouldn't want to ruin all of that beautiful trust we'd have going on, if you know what I mean."

And with that, Evan sold Mike on the plan. Mike would forward Evan's novel to his agency's top celebrity client, with an IAA note attached that would induce her read it.

28. The Posse Takes on a Snobby New York Club

The successful start to Evan's scheme sent his confidence soaring to new heights, as if he had no scars in strange places and it hadn't been over seven months since he last had a girlfriend. Suddenly, it seemed as if his creative ingenuity could propel him into a whole other league, which – until that phone call with Mike Yuvalov – had always seemed elusively inaccessible and otherworldly.

The whole posse knew that Evan's head was in a new place. Happy to have finished his novel, Evan no longer diligently collected story details on paper and was now an active participant in the gang. But his attitude towards meeting new women evolved into the aloof indifference that marked Carlos's style. Lucky Chucky would flirt with women primarily to persuade them to meet his friends. Only on rare occasions, when a particularly stunning and charming female was involved, would he flirt on his own behalf, just to see if he still "had it." Just as Carlos believed – as a matter of objective fact – that no woman could compare to Carolina, Evan was utterly convinced that no woman could even approach Delilah Nakova, and so he rarely bothered to take any flirtation too seriously. It was only when a posse member reminded him that he and Delilah weren't even communicating yet, much less dating, that he sometimes mustered the motivation to get a phone number.

The bulk of Evan's renewed self-esteem was now spent boosting Heeb and sending women his way. In mid-February 2001, Heeb finally decided to try to seduce a woman with the goal of becoming sexually involved with her, in a real relationship or otherwise. Doctor Clayton had reassured Sammy, over a month earlier, that his penis was totally healed and that he could resume a normal sex life. But Heeb still harbored deep insecurities about his injury and wanted the scars to shrink a little more. He had also grown accustomed to "the power to reject" and the reassuring thought that he wasn't really interested in taking anyone home with him anyway. So, on the posse's tenth night out, when Heeb faced the prospect of rejection for the first time since the group's formation, he was more insecure than usual. And because Evan could so easily empathize with Heeb's situation, he made even more of an effort to encourage and reassure him.

That night was a brutally cold one. The biting February frost made it particularly hard to motivate Carlos, Evan, and Heeb into leaving their warm apartments, but Trevor and Narc rallied the troops after Narc mentioned a swanky VIP party on Thursday night at a posh Chelsea lounge called Bungalow Eight. By 10:30 p.m., everyone but Carlos was waiting at the door to get in.

Christophe, the doorman at the club, was a homely Parisian waif with thick glasses, a sloppy hairdo, and clashing fashion choices that seemed more contrived than creative. In his right hand, he held a clipboard containing the club guest list, which he wielded like a royal scepter. Christophe took obvious pleasure in his fleeting supremacy over the shivering patrons, many of whom were begging to be admitted more for the warm shelter than for the exclusive party inside. The list was really just a power prop because Christophe rarely consulted it and, in any case, needed no particular justification to reject anyone. He often refused individuals on a whim, just to feel better about himself and the club. He genuinely savored his own rudeness, as if it to highlight the fact that his power – embodied in the large bouncers at his command – rendered his weak physique, ugly appearance, and humorless attitude irrelevant for that precious moment that people needed his approval.

While Trevor, Narc, and Evan were among the most attractive and well-dressed men in the crowd gathered around the velvet ropes, Christophe summarily dismissed them upon discovering that Heeb was in their group and that they were unaccompanied by women. "If you don't have girlz weet you, don't waste my time. Pleez. Go home," he said in his thick French accent, eyeing Heeb with particular condescension.

As others pushed their way in front of the posse to test their odds, Heeb was tempted to throw in the towel.

"Louis the Sixteenth seems to have overlooked my modeling credentials," Heeb remarked.

"This asshole wouldn't let himself into the club if he was trying to get in," Evan affirmed, his breath billowing like dragon puffs in the cold.

"Guys, you'll never get in with me here. Why don't you go ahead without me?"

"No way, Sammy. You're not getting out of this!" Evan protested.

"Sorry I can't party in Antarctica…I mean, it's been ten minutes since I last felt my nose."

"It should be slammin inside, Heeb. Just hang tight," Narc said.

"Carlos'll be here any minute," Evan added. "We can't just bail on him now...Just think of this as a subway dilemma."

"What's that?" Trevor asked, as he rubbed his frozen hands together.

"A subway dilemma occurs when you've waited ten minutes past the time you expected the subway to arrive," Evan explained. "At that point, you already feel painfully invested in the next train, and you're afraid that if you give up, you'll not only lose the time you invested, but you'll just barely miss the train, because the longer you've been waiting for it, the more likely it is to arrive right after you give up and leave."

"Subway dilemma...I like that," Trevor said.

"But there's a flaw with your subway dilemma analogy," Narc objected.

"What's that?"

"Sometimes the longer you've been waiting, the less likely the train is to come, because the longer wait could mean the train just completely broke down and it's gonna take hours to fix."

"Narc makes an excellent point," Heeb added. "This train's not arriving any time soon," he said, looking around them, as if to highlight all of the glamorous club-goers standing nearby, vying for entry.

"Hold on a sec. Carlos is calling." Narc answered his cell phone.

"Whassup Carlos? No, we're still outside...Where are you? Oh, cool. We're right in front. See if you can round up some TH."

"Tell him he has to bring at least five TH or we're going home," Heeb said insistently.

"Heeb said you gotta bring five or we're going home...No...It would definitely help...It looks very good inside...I don't know...He's definitely getting impatient...OK...Word. Hey, do you know if..."

Narc suddenly stopped talking into his cell. He looked up at the others.

"Damn. Chucky hung up on my ass."

"You know he hates talking on the cell," Heeb reminded him. "He worries about the brain cancer risk."

"So what did he say?" Trevor asked. "Is he on the way?"

"His cab's two blocks away," Narc replied. "I don't know how he'll come up with five babes, but I told him to try."

"That's all you had to do," Heeb replied, looking somewhat encouraged. "Now there's hope...Remember, this is Lucky Chucky we're talking about."

And sure enough, on Tenth Avenue and Twenty-seventh Street, just as Carlos was getting out of his cab he spotted a bevy of beauties getting out of the taxi right in front of him and heading towards the club, about 150 feet away. The five stunning women had each clearly calculated that they would be better off waiting two minutes in the bitter cold wearing sexy, skimpy outfits, than waiting ten minutes in the same cold wearing warmer but less revealing clothes. Their seductively rhythmic, stiletto-tipped walks were another indication that they knew the norms of New York nightlife.

Carlos approached them from the side, as smoothly as lightly melted butter spread across a warm piece of toast. With a slight smile, a cock of his dark eyebrow, and an aplomb that suggested he was the owner of the club, he approached the apparent leader of the group, a long-legged brunette cover girl and said, "Hey there. My friends and I have a table reserved inside. You want to join us?"

She almost replied with her canned rejection to street overtures but when she looked at the cool, dark, six-foot-one Adonis smiling mysteriously her way, she could say only, "Um...OK." Her four friends immediately drew closer as he led them all to where Heeb and the others were standing in silent awe.

Heeb threw an amused glance at Narc, as if to say, "What did I tell you?" Narc smiled back an acknowledgement. The posse played it cool, as if they weren't at all flabbergasted by how easily Carlos had just produced a set of stunners out of thin air, and approached the doorman with them. The crowd by the velvet rope noticed Carlos and his five femme fatales. Even the doorman looked impressed when Carlos went up to him and said, "They're with me."

Christophe tried to suppress his smile of amazement and automatically unclasped the velvet rope, as if this were a common occurrence at the snobby club. But Carlos didn't advance and held the women back as his four buddies approached the area. "So are they," he added. Christophe shot a glance at the men he had rejected earlier and then looked back at Carlos disapprovingly. Carlos just stared back at him nonchalantly, as if there were ten other elite parties on his list of options for the night.

Christophe backed down and proposed a compromise. "You can go in weet everybuddee but zee short guy," he said, clearly referring to Heeb.

"Either we all come in, or we all go to Pangaea," Carlos replied, with debonair equanimity.

Carlos's challenge surprised Christophe, who was unaccustomed to being declined in the one situation where he normally did the declining. Christophe stood silently, unsure how to respond.

"It's no problem. Have a good night," Carlos said, graciously, as he began to turn away with his crowd. Carlos and his gorgeous gang of girls were prepared to prove — in front of the large queue watching the showdown — that they considered Heeb cooler and more important than Christophe, and the doorman preferred to avoid such a humiliation.

Christophe stopped him: "OK. Come on."

A vindicated joy lifted the posse, as they walked into the warm and festive club with five hotties alongside them and Carlos leading the pack. The many attractive people at the glitzy soiree suddenly seemed like mere background scenery for the charming story of five men meeting five women, thanks to Lucky Chucky. They checked their coats and then Narc, who knew the club well, brought them to a more secluded seating area upstairs where the two groups of men and women could mingle. As they followed Narc, the men and women began to pair off. A few minutes later, they were all seated upstairs.

Narc had already begun talking to Jade, a twenty-one-year-old model of Thai-Swedish extraction. They chitchatted for a while, and, after a few drinks, Narc confessed that he had dated only a few Asians in his life, much to his parents' disappointment. "I think it's the rebel in me…So my parents would probably view a Eurasian as major progress," he noted with amusement.

"I never cared about race," she said. "And if my parents did, I wouldn't even exist. But they're very liberal. They were pot-smoking hippies in the sixties. Speaking of which, do you have any weed?"

"As a matter of fact, I do," Narc replied with a playful grin. As he pulled out some marijuana from his blazer pocket.

"You know you still haven't told me what you do for a living," Jade remarked lightly, as if she'd been cheated out of some vital information. Narc had been subtly and effectively evading the question.

"I'll tell you about my early mid-life crisis after we finish this," Narc replied with a mischievous smile.

Next to Narc, Trevor was getting acquainted with Dawn, a redheaded artist who was, at five feet eleven inches, the tallest of the five women. "Do you come here often?" Trevor asked, despite his aversion to such safe and boring conversation starters.

"Let's make a deal," she began, with an ironic smile. "Why don't we avoid all topics that don't have something to do with politics or religion?"

"Why is that?" Trevor asked, grinning with surprised relief.

"Because when I'm not painting I work as a cocktail waitress at expensive banker parties, and I'm supposed to just look pretty and make small talk the whole time. They actually tell you to avoid religion and politics in any conversations that come up. So that's exactly the sort of thing that you and I need to talk about right now."

This was divine music to Trevor's ears, as was the revelation that she – like Trevor – had studied history in college and was now exploring different eastern philosophies. Within minutes, they were discussing Zen Buddhism, yoga, and meditation. After about ten minutes, Trevor also mentioned his newly discovered homosexual identity, in order to avoid misleading Dawn.

"Just my luck!" she said, rolling her eyes ironically. "Oh well... Hey, I actually have the perfect guy for you!" she added, taking Trevor by the arm and leading him away from the group and towards the bar. "He's a total hottie, almost as tall as you, built like a Michaelangelo sculpture, and an amazing painter...We met at my yoga studio...He's bartending here tonight."

When they reached the bar, Dawn introduced Trevor to Luigi, an Italian male-model type who was every bit as handsome as Trevor had imagined him to be. Luigi was a few years older than Trevor but had all of the boyish flamboyance of an adolescent youth – a flare that came out in everything he did, whether it was pouring a drink, flirting playfully with everyone around him, or moving energetically to the rhythm of the music playing in the background. The gracefully muscular Luigi wore black, tight-fitting clothes with an earring in each lobe. He had his black hair closely cropped to his skull, except for an ice cream swirl of hair that was gelled to peak at the left corner of his head. Dawn could tell that the two men were drawn to each other physically and conversationally, and she slipped away soon after her matchmaking services were complete.

Back upstairs, Carlos was seated next to Raquel, the Brazilian model he had approached outside of the club. Her eyes were fixed on Carlos, who was speaking to her in Portuguese about his perfectly magical year in Brazil. In keeping with his strictly healthy diet, Carlos never had more than one glass of wine when he went out. Raquel sipped her second caipirinha.

Evan sat next to Jess, a twenty-three-year-old blonde bartender by night and aspiring actress by day. Upon learning of her ambitions, Evan shared his unusually in-depth knowledge of every film in which Delilah Nakova had had any role. Jess and Evan had a nice enough rapport, but within a few hours, he informed her that he and Delilah had plans to get married in six months. This was, he explained, why he knew every detail about her personal biography and her Hollywood career. He was just out to support the boys, and, if Jess could encourage her roommate, Angelina, to show more interest in Heeb, he would talk to Delilah about introducing Jess to her talent agent at IAA. The combination of alcohol and the powerful delusions guiding Evan's convincing act led Jess to believe Evan and eventually encourage Angelina to show more of an interest in Heeb.

When everyone had first entered the club and begun to pair off, Evan asked Heeb to indicate his preference between the only two women who had not yet started talking to someone. Heeb chose Angelina. At five-eight, she was the shorter of the two roommates and his Jewdar concluded that she was not a member of the tribe. As he introduced himself to the first fashion model he had ever spoken to (without the deceptive benefits of online dating), a thousand insecurities ran through his mind: "She's thinking how she's a full inch taller than me…My bald spot looks so shiny she could use it to fix her makeup… Even if a miracle happened and she somehow wanted to sleep with me some day, I'd have to tell her that my penis was attacked by a cat. What am I thinking? I have zero chance with this woman. How can I get out of here?"

"Do you come here a lot?" she asked.

"Every now and then, when there's a good party," Heeb replied, trying to sound as if he belonged to some "in crowd." Angelina remarked that she had never seen him there before and then went on about the clubs and restaurants she frequents. "Why is she still talking to me?" Heeb asked himself. "She's probably just being polite. She doesn't want to ditch her friends, who all seem to be hitting it off with the rest of the posse. Because if she ditches the ugly guy, they'll all look bad. That's the only reason she's still talking to me. I have to get out of this somehow."

They started up the stairs with the others, who were following Narc to a more secluded area in the club. Heeb's thoughts continued: "How do I escape? The guys won't let me out now. Maybe I can just turn around on these stairs, and pretend that I got lost in this crowd of people coming down. But I'd look like the biggest wimp. I'm finally going out with a fully functional penis that I'm prepared to use, and I chicken out." He forgot his worries for a moment to appreciate the perfection of the figure walking up the stairs right above him. "And look at that. How can I just leave that? Evan and Chucky would be beyond pissed, if I just bailed out after they got me this far. I can't just bail out. I have to Kojak it somehow. I have to be funny. Keep her laughing. Women like a sense of humor. They're evolutionarily programmed to seek comfort, and laughter creates a feeling of comfort in this crazy world, even if it's totally baseless comfort. I just have to be funny. Make the most of the strongest factor in my SQ. Make her laugh so hard she goes blind and can't see bald spots any more. That's my only hope."

After they were seated with the rest of the group and Heeb and Angelina had downed a few drinks, Heeb loosened up a bit, and became increasingly bold with his humor strategy.

"I really love this city. There are so many beautiful women here…My dating life has never been better."

"Are you popular with the ladies here?" Angelina asked, trying to conceal her surprise.

"In fact, I am."

"Why is that?" she asked.

"Well, it's a commonly known fact that the world is run by forty-seven Jews. Not the guys with the black hats running that famous camera store on Forty-seventh Street, which – by the way – is the only street in Manhattan that was named after the forty-seven Jews running the world. No, the world is run by forty-seven Jews who look just like me. So when women discover that I'm Jewish, they realize that I'm one of those forty-seven guys running the world."

"Really?" Angelina chuckled.

"Yeah. So if there's anything you need – a new landlord, a green card, a change in American foreign policy, an increase in the Federal reserve rate, a change in French fashion trends, a cover story on *Time Magazine* – just let me know and I'll talk to my forty-six buddies about taking care of it."

"That's fabulous. I'm so glad I met you. Do you guys like Italian Catholics? Will you look out for us?"

"We luuhhhvv Italian Catholics!" Heeb proclaimed with élan. "Especially the ones like you who want to launch a fashion label. We generally have a real soft spot for models trying to make career moves. And we luuhhhvv Italy."

"Really? Have you been?"

"I took a vacation in Florence a few summers ago. The problem was that I couldn't take anyone seriously."

"Why?"

"Because everything was like a Hollywood movie. Everyone was beautiful, the food was incredible, the language was beyond charming – even though I didn't understand a word…I mean, you could sit there and read me the phone book in Italian and I'd get turned on." Angelina laughed, which was music to Heeb's ears. "So when the Florence traffic policewoman is trying to tell you that your rental car is illegally parked, you just can't take her seriously. She looks gorgeous. She sounds like she's singing the most irresistibly seductive song you've ever heard, and really what she's saying to you is that you're going to get towed and fined if you don't leave that spot."

Angelina's giggles came with increasing ease, as the cumulative effect of all the laughter and the alcohol made everything seem irresistibly funny.

"See that? You're laughing so hard that you've forgotten that you ended up with the fat ugly bald guy in the group," Heeb said. Angelina burst into chuckles. "And by the way, I've got more than enough hair on my back to make up for the scalp." She burst into more laughs. "And if that's not enough, there's some in my ears too. They keep my eardrums warm in the winter, and in the summer they make for great earlobe accessories."

She was now convulsively in stitches.

"Speaking of body decorations, I luuhhhvv your belly piercing!" Heeb said, looking at the gold ring in the center of her slim, tan waist. Despite the arctic cold, Angelina had opted for a skin tight, black tube top that ended just above her belly, on the assumption that a warm cab, a winter coat, and a short wait to get into the club was an adequate frosty weather strategy. Heeb was still reverently staring at her belly when Angelina finally caught her breath from laughing.

"Do you really like it? You're just saying that so that you can check out my belly!"

"And what's so bad about that? I mean, didn't you get that belly piercing so that people would check out your belly?"

"No. I just thought it would look cool…Do you have any piercings?"

264

"Actually, I do," Heeb replied.

"Where?"

"My appendix."

"Huh?"

"I wanted to be the first guy with a pierced organ. And the appendix is a totally useless organ anyway, so I figured why the hell not?"

"That's pretty original," she replied, amused.

"Oh yeah. I've outdone every piercing fanatic out there. The only problem is when I have to go through metal detectors at the airport."

Angelina burst into laughs again, and then managed to say, "Don't you have to take it out occasionally for a cleaning?"

"Nah. I figure I'll just get it removed when my appendix bursts. It'll be a two-for-one operation, if you know what I mean."

"Ewww!" she said, in entertained disgust.

"I'll bet your last date didn't have a pierced appendix!"

"No! And he didn't pay for my drinks either! Cheap bastard," she added, in amusement. Heeb was now immensely hopeful: Angelina didn't object when he had impliedly conferred "date" status on their situation by comparing it to a prior date of hers. "And he was some rich investment banker guy," she added.

"Oh, that's not just right. The man should always pay."

"Do you really think that?"

"It's the male tax."

"The male tax?"

"Yeah. The tax that men have to pay for not having to menstruate every month. Or risk getting pregnant. Or deal with the physically stronger sex in a macho world...Women have to put up with all of that stuff, so the least we men can do is pay the male tax and get the tab."

"You are so sweet, Sammy! What's your sign?"

That question made Heeb certain that he was getting somewhere. No woman cared to ask about a man's sign unless she had some interest in him.

"You don't actually believe in that astrology stuff, do you?" he playfully asked.

"It's the only real science out there, Sammy."

"I guess three billion women can't be wrong."[10]

Angelina laughed, until she was interrupted by Jess, who said that it was time for a ladies' break in the bathroom. "Oh, OK. I'll be right back," she said to Heeb.

Upstairs, not far from where Heeb was waiting for Angelina to return, Narc and Jade had finished the marijuana and were regularly breaking into silly, boisterous laughs. "All right, so when are you gonna tell me…" she asked, between giggles.

"Tell you what?" Narc asked hysterically.

"What you do for a living."

"You really want to know?" Narc said, cachinnating. "Really really bad?"

"Yeah. Really, really, really bad!" she chortled some more at their silliness.

"All right, I'll tell you," he said, laughing anew. Gasping between more giggles he added, "I fuck."

"You fuck for a living?" Jade convulsed even harder. "That's really, great," she said, between laughs. "Is your employer taking resumes?" Narc burst into laughs even more, as if he was realizing for the first time how absurd his life had become. Narc's guffaw prolonged Jade's laugh attack.

"No, we don't use resumes. Only dimensions," he replied with amused delight.

"Oh…Well how are mine?" Jade said, perking up her small breasts a bit, as she broke into hysterics.

"I think I can get you an interview on the casting couch," he reassured her, and they both started laughing stupidly.

Jess and Angelina returned from downstairs.

"Come on, let's go downstairs and groove a little," Angelina said to Heeb, as Jess walked back to Evan and gave him a wink.

While Angelina's suggestion confirmed Heeb's optimism about the night, he wasn't thrilled about the prospect of dancing downstairs. Despite Yumi's patient tutoring and all of his dance lessons in New York, when Heeb danced his body usually jerked in odd directions, a few beats too late. This fact would be all the more painfully conspicuous at Bungalow Eight, which didn't have a club license that permitted

---

[10] In 2003, there were about 3 billion women. Ten years later, women have increased their numbers by about half a billion (much to the relief of the roughly 500 million men who also joined the world).

266

dancing, and consequently had only a few people dancing in a rather central location, when the bouncers weren't enforcing the no-dancing rule. Even worse, Heeb would have to move in the midst of competing males with far higher SQs, and they would undoubtedly think that Angelina was easy prey, dancing with that uncoordinated nerd.

Fortunately, their dancing was cut short by a fortuitous encounter. But unfortunately, the encounter was even more embarrassing for Heeb than the dancing.

"Oh my God, I know you! I know you! I swear to God we've met," a cute Indian woman exclaimed to Heeb, as he was doing his signature boogie-woogie movements alongside the graceful, rhythmic motions of his gorgeous dance partner.

Heeb stopped to look at her. She did look vaguely familiar, but the dimmed lighting, the alcohol, her different hairdo, and the fact that he had last seen her about eight months ago made her difficult to place. Still dancing, Angelina took some interest in the situation, since the young Indian woman was very pretty and seemed convinced that she knew Heeb, who was also struggling to recall how they knew each other.

"I remember! I remember!" she declared, clearly proud of her good memory, despite her own tipsy state.

"How?" Heeb asked, now genuinely curious.

"You were that nude model for that painting class I took, last spring!"

Heeb's face reddened. "I don't know what you're talking about."

"It's you. You were that nude model. And you got this erection while we were all painting you, remember? And then you tried to pick me up at the deli across the street after class...You don't remember?"

"No. You must be thinking of someone else," Heeb said, even redder, and worried that Angelina believed her.

"I swear it's you."

"No, I've never done anything like that."

"Yes you have. It's you! I know it's you! It's just so funny to see you here, of all places!"

"Look, I don't know what you're talking about...I know you're just trying to be friendly, but I'm here with someone and there are lots of other people to meet here, so why don't you make like a newspaper and circulate a bit, OK?"

And with that, Heeb grabbed Angelina's hand, and led her away into the crowd. He was mortified.

Once they joined their group upstairs, back in Heeb's comfort zone, he took a shot of vodka and was able to relax enough to start joking about what just happened. Angelina was undecided as to whether Heeb was embarrassed because the Indian woman's recollection was accurate or because he had just found it awkward to reject someone vying for his attention.

"Can you imagine?" he said, with affected disbelief. "Me as a model? That's the most ludicrous thing I've ever heard."

"It is pretty funny," Angelina agreed.

"And the other forty-six Jews running the world would never allow it. It's just not a part of the job description, when you apply for a position with the conspiratorial cabal."

"Maybe she just thought you were cute," Angelina suggested playfully.

"Yeah, it must have been my dancing."

Angelina burst into laughs.

At 1:30 a.m., Angelina asked Jess if she wanted to share a cab back to their place. Jess frowned, thinking this meant that Angelina wasn't going to show any further interest in Heeb.

"I've got a photo shoot in eight hours," she explained.

"So? I have one in ten. What's the big deal?"

"You can stay. But I'm wiped. And I've had too much to drink. I need to rest."

"OK...We'll go," Jess agreed reluctantly.

Angelina gave Heeb a smooch on the lips, and he delighted in the fact that it was longer than a peck. She wrote down her email for him. "Use it. I'll be waiting for your email."

"Don't worry. I'll use it. But in case I lose it before I can use it, here's my info." Heeb wrote out his work, home, fax, pager and cell phone numbers, as well as all three of his email accounts. She chuckled in amusement at the two napkins of information.

"That's just in case you weren't sure whether I want you to stalk me," Heeb said.

She laughed and gave him another kiss on the lips.

Jess gave Evan her cell phone and email address, even though he was marrying Delilah Nakova in six months. Evan, of course, had no intention of ever calling Jess, unless it could somehow help Heeb out with Angelina. As stunning as Jess looked, she was – next to Delilah Nakova – a mere mortal without a fraction of Delilah's brains, charm, or gracious humility.

As the two beauties turned around and left, Heeb dreamily watched Angelina walk down the stairs. He meditated on the fact that he had never before had such a gorgeous woman kiss him or hang out with him for so long. Evan and Heeb talked excitedly for a few minutes, exchanging notes on the night.

Twenty minutes later, the two women were in a cab heading home.

Besides Trevor, who would remain by the bar until closing, Narc and Jade were the only ones left from the initial group. Carlos had left around midnight, to ensure that he was home in time for Carolina. As Raquel walked him out of the club, she realized from Carlos's unexpectedly early goodbye that the wedding ring actually meant something. Her heart sank a little. "All the good ones are taken," she thought. If Carlos could rebuff the sexual advances of a twenty-two-year-old runway model in order to stay faithful to his thirty-year-old wife, she wanted to have him that much more. But he wouldn't even take her number much less give her his. He just squeezed her hand good night and kissed her cheek.

At 2 a.m., Narc and Jade went back to Narc's place. They made out for the whole cab ride (between stoned laughs) and were half-naked by the time they stumbled out of the elevator of Narc's building. Outside Narc's apartment door, they kept kissing and giggling as he fumbled with his keys. He finally got the door open, and they slipped inside. They resumed their action once the door closed, and removed the rest of their clothing.

The marijuana made everything seem slow and light, even as they handled each other with raw and carnal impatience.

"Show me the real thing," she said, with an adventurous smile. "I've never been with a real pro."

During the two hours of sex that followed, Narc — true to his reputation — gave Jade an orgasm in each of the four rooms of his apartment. Employing virtually every position and every technique in his arsenal, Narc also climaxed several times. The grand finale — as measured by the loudness of Jade's moans — occurred on the large marble bathroom sink, on which she sat with her legs open to receive Narc's talented tongue, which lapped away with verve while warm water from the faucet behind her trickled down her lower back.

The next morning, however, when Jade kept asking whether Narc really "fucked for a living," Narc finally had to confirm the ugly truth.

"Yup. I do."

"Stop lying."

"I'm not lying. I'm a porn star."

"I don't believe you."

"I'm being serious."

"No, you're trying to be funny."

"All right," Narc said, walking over to his big screen TV and pushing some buttons. "I wasn't planning on doing this, but since you don't believe me, I've got some videos to prove it."

A giant image of Narc fornicating with some silicone-breasted blonde appeared on the screen.

Jade's hand involuntarily rose to cover her mouth as she stood there, speechlessly appalled.

She was disappointed in herself for not extracting such a basic fact about Narc before getting stoned with him. And she was furious at Narc for so smoothly skirting the issue until it was effectively too late. On her silent storm out, she pushed Narc's TV and VCR so that they came crashing down onto his apartment floor in a shattering thud.

There was nothing Narc could do to save his beloved big screen TV, on which he had watched so many basketball games and pornos. He could only stand there and watch it fall, as if it were some slow motion sports replay. The large video image of himself and the busty blonde gradually collapsed into an ever-acuter angle that then became hundreds of pieces of glass.

The thud of his smashed TV was followed by the slam of his front door.

29. Obsessed and Depressed

Prior to the mid-1800s, the most one could hope for from a love interest was the relatively rare occurrence of a letter or an unannounced, in-person visit. In the mid-1800s the telegraph arrived, followed soon thereafter by the telephone. In the 1980s, the fax came about, and the 1990s ushered in pagers, cell phones, and emails.

By the year 2001, with so many people communicating so many times per day with so many devices, every cell phone call, voicemail, email, and pager represented a potential sign from one's budding infatuation. This greatly expanded universe of communication made any silent treatment from one's crush all the more unbearable: it increased the number of disappointments per day exponentially from the horse and buggy days. Yet the emotional mechanism for handling letdowns had not evolved with the technologies that caused them.

Heeb's coping techniques were particularly unprepared to handle the week of psychological torture that followed his night with Angelina. Evan felt partly to blame for this because he had encouraged Heeb to email Angelina the next day.

"But what about the rule from *Swingers?* The Vince Vaughn character said that you're not 'money' if you don't wait at least six days," Heeb replied, in response to Evan's recommendation.

"Yes, but don't forget what happens in that movie. The Jon Favreau character ends up with the girl who called him the day after they met. She calls him. Without waiting."

"That's Hollywood, Evan. Stuff like that never happens to me in real life."

"Heeb, the bottom line is: you're always better off calling sooner. If you're both interested, you can get started that much sooner. And if you're not both interested, then you can move on that much sooner."

Evan felt especially confident about this advice because he was sure that Jess would lobby Angelina to respond to Heeb promptly. He didn't think that she would get on the Internet and thoroughly research all of the latest gossip on Delilah's love life, and discover that she has been single for several months with no mention of any fiancé or upcoming wedding – to Evan or anyone else.

Throughout each of the six days following Heeb's first email to Angelina, he obsessed over why she wasn't getting in touch. "Why doesn't she call?" he would ask.

"Heeb, you're sounding like a girl! Just chill out," Evan would say. "She'll call."

After three days of fruitless waiting, Evan decided it was time to remind Jess about the big Delilah Nakova opportunity. But Jess always let his call go to voicemail, even when Evan blocked his caller ID. So Evan began to obsess about Jess almost as much as Sammy did about Angelina. But after five days, Evan wrote her off, noting that he couldn't have dated her anyway, given his solemn commitment to Delilah Nakova.

"Sammy, you really should learn to juggle more," Evan advised him, as if he didn't need to follow the same advice. "You've gotta have at least three or four prospects that you're talking to at the same time, or you could get too hung up over one female. And if she ever does call you'll sound way too desperate."

"But I really hit it off with her," Heeb protested.

"Heeb, she's not nearly smart enough for you, and she's not even Jewish when you're just a few months from starting your Jewish dating phase…Why are you so obsessed with her now?"

But Heeb couldn't imagine meeting or starting with anyone else because he was now gripped with self-doubt. Not only did he doubt his charms, he doubted his very ability to interpret female behavior accurately. He repeated in his mind, over and over, how Angelina had laughed so hard and so often at his jokes, how she seemed to think he was more of a gentleman than some of her other dates, how she invited him to go dancing downstairs, how she kissed him twice on the lips, and how she wrote down her email for him and said "Use it. I'll be waiting for your email."

Six days after his first email to her, the cumulative pain of phone calls and emails and voicemails from everyone but Angelina felt like a slow but ever-worsening chest ache. Every new incoming call and every new email in his inbox produced a gnawing moment of unbearable suspense and fear that it was not Angelina. Heeb would hesitate nervously each time he had to answer the phone or check his email; yet the ever-present possibility that it might finally be Angelina compelled him to accept the risk of deepening the slow psychological sore that was festering within him. He was also painfully aware that if she ever did call, he couldn't let on that she had won the game of brinkmanship. He couldn't reveal that — while she had played it cool — he had come ever closer to "caving in" and calling her roommate's number (which he had taken from Evan, on the seventh day after his email to Angelina, when he thought he was losing his mind).

On the eighth day, just as Heeb was about to call Jess and ask to speak with her roommate, he got an email back from Angelina. As he opened it, he was overcome by a mixture of relief and dread.

"Hey Sammy. Sorry it took a while to email you back. Thursday was fun. Maybe I'll see you around some time. Angelina."

That was Angelina's tactful way of telling him that she wasn't interested, but Heeb was too obsessed by this point to read between the lines. So he had to email her back and ask her when they could see each other again. After four days passed with no reply, Heeb sent her another email asking what the story was and what her honest thoughts about him were.

Two days later, he received the following reply: "There is no story between us. I think you're pretty funny, but you're just not my type…I like a guy with hair, and I like guys who are five to six inches taller than me. I'm sorry there isn't a nicer way to say it, but if I said something like 'I just don't think it'll work between us' or 'there really isn't any chemistry there' you'd probably want more details. So I figured I'd just give you the details now. Sorry. Good luck to you."

Heeb was devastated.

He forwarded the email to Evan with a simple "Need I say more?" and descended into a deep depression. At the office, where he was normally a star performer, he became apathetic. After work, Heeb didn't want to see or talk to anyone. He lost all interest in going out with a posse that he thought was exponentially out of his league. His appetite for food shrank significantly, and he began to lose weight.

During the first three weeks following Angelina's last email, each member of the posse had left Heeb several unreturned voicemails, each trying to cheer him up and get him to come out. On the two nights when they went out in his absence, they spent most of their time together worrying about how to help Heeb, until Carlos realized that it was time to get Titus involved.

Sammy hadn't spoken to his old blind friend from Boston since a few weeks before his injury, and a call from him turned out to be a good idea. Speaking to Titus, who had lived a rich and varied life despite countless obstacles, always gave Heeb a dose of perspective on things. Titus, who was now seventy-two, embodied optimism itself. He

emanated an indomitably positive spirit that refused to let anything —
whether it was racism or blindness or life's hard knocks — diminish his
joi de vivre. There was also something compellingly simple about his
approach: "It's just hair, son!" he would stress, whenever Heeb
complained about balding.

"Now look out your window and describe for me the
Manhattan skyline. It's been a long time since you gave this old geezer a
treat like that." Titus had the wisdom to know that such a request would
comfort and restore some of Sammy's self-esteem. Returning Sammy to
the familiar and intimate routine that marked their friendship over the
years would remind Sammy of how much he could brighten the lives of
others.

"Go on now. Don't make me wait…Give me my favorite
nighttime view…"

During the day, Titus liked the view from Heeb's bedroom, and
at night, he preferred the living room view.

"All right, hold on…I'm going there now," Sammy said, already
feeling better.

Heeb walked over to his living room.

"All right. I'm here."

"What do you see?" Titus asked impatiently.

"On the left side of the window you can see all of the cubicle
lives of New Yorkers, lit up in the dark, like a bunch of yellow boxes
stacked up on top of each other from the ground up to towering
heights."

"And what are they doing?"

"One guy's watching TV. The woman above him is talking on
the phone. To the right is a couple having dinner together. Above them
are two people kissing. To their left is a woman running on her
treadmill."

"Now what about on the right side of your living room
window?"

"If you move your eye away from all of those miniature people
you get the perspective of the entire city, so that it's not just a few
hundred lives stacked on top of each other, but millions and millions of
lives sharing this same night with us under the same sky. And you
wonder how all of those individuals actually fit into this tiny city – this
city that's a whole little world unto itself, made up of populated needles
standing atop a slender island."

"Keep goin' Sammy. That's beautiful…Now as you move your eye across that Manhattan skyline, tell me about the building that your eye wants to cling to the most tonight – among all those populated needles, competin' for your attention."

"Tonight it's the Chrysler Building."

"All right. Tell me about the Chrysler Building."

"It stands there so simply and majestically. Its small lit triangles each pointing upwards in a triangular formation towards its sharp spire, like the angelic sparkles of a tiny flame in a bright shining candle."

"Ah…The Chrysler Building…I remember those small lit triangles well…From my many trips to New York City…Ain't that somethin', Sammy…New York City! Ain't nothing like it in the whole world."

"It is a sight to see, Titus."

30. The Posse Prevails

From late February until mid-March 2001, with a few more calls from Titus, Heeb gradually became interested in his professional life again. The complex and monumental work project he had completed just before his funk, involving the estimation and management of risk variables for the airline insurance industry, received kudos from several prestigious industry groups and publications. But his social confidence was still far too damaged for him to consider meeting any women or rejoining the posse for anything more than a meal in Narc's favorite Chinatown restaurant (where there was an infinitesimal chance of meeting any English-speaking women of interest).

Meanwhile, Evan's confidence was also beginning to suffer. Nearly six weeks had passed since Mike Yuvalov confirmed that he had sent Evan's manuscript to Delilah Nakova. Just as it took everything in Heeb's willpower to avoid emailing Angelina more frequently than he had, Evan virtually exhausted his self-restraint by calling Mike only once every two weeks to see if there were any promising developments. Evan's entire self-esteem was riding on the assumption that Delilah would fall in love with his novel, and soon thereafter with him, and that the two would end up living together happily ever after.

Evan badly needed something to distract him from his anxiety about Delilah and whether he had any hope of making his living as a writer. He began actively looking for a job as a computer programmer, and became even more determined to save Heeb from his lingering social doldrums.

On Saturday, March 31, 2001, there was a loud knock on Heeb's door.

Sammy Laffowitz wasn't expecting company and was surprised that the doorman hadn't informed him of any visitor. He quietly crept over to the door to see who it was, but the peephole was covered by the visitor's thumb. The knock became louder.

Fearing the worst, Heeb walked over to the kitchen, pulled out a large steak knife, dialed 911 on his cell phone without pushing "send," and walked back over to the door.

"Who is it?" he asked nervously. "What do you want?"

"I want you!" answered the muffled voice.

"What do you mean? What's going on?" he replied anxiously, his thumb ready to push the "send" button on his cell phone at any moment.

"Open up!" bellowed the voice.

"Who are you? I'm calling the police if you don't identify yourself!"

"I'm here to get you!"

"To get me for what?"

"For the posse! You've been neglecting us for far too long!"

The voice now sounded somewhat like Evan's, and the reference to "the posse" reassured him. He put the knife and cell phone down.

"Evan, is that you?"

"Of course it's me. Now open the damn door already."

Heeb exhaled a sigh of relief and opened the door.

Evan, Narc, Carlos, and Trevor, filed into his apartment, each wearing a Giorgio Armani tuxedo and black "Ranger" sunglasses by Dragon Optical. Most startling of all, the top of each man's head was shaved off so that the resulting hairdo looked identical to the large bald spot on the top of Heeb's head; Trevor had even allowed the hair on his head to grow out a little so that he could shave only the top off. He also had a drum strapped to him, on which he rattled off a drum roll, as he used to do regularly over a decade earlier, when Trevor participated in his high school marching band.

"Your presence is requested tonight, for a festive night out with the posse," Evan said with charmingly affected formality, using his best imitation of Trevor's British accent. Outstretched over both of Evan's hands lay a garment bag containing a Giorgio Armani tuxedo with Heeb's measurements. A pair of Ranger sunglasses rested atop the garment bag. Trevor produced another drum roll after which Evan extended his hands towards Heeb, as if to offer him the tuxedo as part of some knighting ceremony. Evan drew closer to Heeb and declared, "Please, Sir Heeb, your raiment is waiting to be donned. And your posse awaits you for a night of revelry, in which the charming company of lovely ladies shall be sought."

Heeb slowly took the tuxedo and sunglasses from Evan, as the rest of the posse broke into a hearty standing ovation.

"I…I…don't know what to say…"

"You were not asked to say anything, Sir Heeb. You were asked only to don your raiment so that we may proceed with the evening's festivities. Tarry not in search of eloquent speeches or elaborate excuses, Sir Heeb, for life is to be lived more through actions than words...Indeed, the fruits of life are to be enjoyed – above all – in the ripened present, rather than in the spoiled past or the unsown future." Evan had no idea what he was spewing, but it all sounded good with that impersonation of an Oxford University president delivering a commencement speech.

Heeb, who was completely nonplussed, had no choice but to join them. He was informed after another drum roll that downstairs a white stretch limousine was waiting for them, so he needed to put the tux on quickly.

The elongated Cadillac, equipped with a full bar, a powerful stereo system, and every amenity, boasted an unusually large sunroof that was large enough for all five men to stick their torsos out at once. The perfect, vernal weather on that last night of March meant that more people were outside and in a good mood. As the posse prowled about the city, hopping from one hunting ground to the next, the five men turned heads everywhere they drove. The driver blasted a compilation, prepared just for the occasion, featuring the best of Bach and Beethoven mixed in with pop hits like Prince's 1992 hit song "Sexy Mutha Fucka," Right Said Fred's 1991 success "I Am Too Sexy" and a collection of salacious hip-hop songs that only Narc could have compiled.

There was something irresistibly delightful and cinematic about seeing five half-haired adult men in sunglasses and tuxedos, sticking out of a stretch limousine, moving in synch to the eclectic music mix resounding from their vehicle. Women always smiled, whistled, waved, laughed, or wildly praised the zany limousine clan as it passed by; some even chased after it for a few blocks, as if it were full of rock stars or teen idols.

Walking the streets, with Carlos leading the slick and eccentric-looking pack, the men turned every head and attracted random followers. And the posse was admitted to every club, lounge, and bar they visited, as if they had innovated a fashion statement that was not to be reckoned with. Never had the posse shared so many laughs, provoked so many female smiles, and turned so many heads. And never had Heeb had such a good time. Luigi, now Trevor's boyfriend, even took some time off work that night to follow a portion of the posse's procession.

The group's gesture of camaraderie and support for Heeb didn't end with that night. The next day, which started at around 2 p.m., the posse reconvened at Columbus Circle, in front of the Maine Monument of Central Park. This time each member wore the same sunglasses, navy blue jogging pants made out of fine knit wool, and a slim-fitting white cotton canvas navy v-neck sweater. More importantly, each man had an Afghan Hound on a leather leash. These eccentrically aloof-looking dogs stood out for their aristocratically projected necks, their exotically attenuated snouts, their long silky topknots, and their unusual coat patterns.

The uniform dress (and dog) code created an enhanced "Spice Girls effect" as good as the one from the previous night. Everyone – especially women – stopped to look at or chat with the group. They were frequently asked if having hair only on the sides, with the top totally shaved off, had any religious significance or was connected to any cultish group. Naturally, the posse's various members took much delight in answering this question with ever more absurd forms of creativity – particularly since it was April's Fools' Day. And virtually every female stopped to pet the dogs – a fact that amazed Heeb. "I just don't get it," he said to Narc, who contributed the dog idea. "Dogs repel pussies, yet they attract women."

"Dogs are the oldest chick magnet in the book, yo. And I've seen plenty of single honies use dogs to get men talking to them," Narc said.

"But it doesn't make any sense to me, this whole New York dog phenomenon," Heeb insisted. "Why the hell would anyone date me for my dog? It's not like we could bring the dog to restaurants or art museums with us. I mean, the woman can't exactly date my dog. And then there's the whole dog shit problem. What's so romantic about that?"

"But your choice of dog says a lot about your style. Like your clothing," Evan tried to explain.

"But my dog could die at any moment. So does my style die at that point? Would I automatically get dumped when the dog croaks?"

"By then you'd probably get sympathy from her. And you could always go out and buy another dog."

"Well that raises another point! She could always just go to a store and buy a dog for herself. She doesn't need to date me to get the dog…I'm telling you it's the most irrational thing I've ever seen."

"They appeal to the maternal instinct," Evan chimed in, offering his own explanation. "Like babies, they're warm and cuddly and need lots of attention."

But after hitting the Jackpot, Heeb was not a fan of any animal.

"Look, they may be warm and cuddly, but they've got sharp teeth, they shed hair, and they shit."

*****

The unforgettable weekend with the posse was enough to make Heeb rejoin the clan in earnest and resume his pursuit of females with true Kojak confidence.

A few days later, by an overwhelming majority, the posse decided that its members would shave off all of the hair on their heads, because, the majority concluded, this looked substantially better than leaving hair on the sides with nothing on top. The only vote against the measure was from Heeb, who vociferously objected to eliminating the little hair that he had left to enjoy.

"I've never shaved it all off," he protested.

"That's probably been a part of the problem," Narc said.

"Narc's right, Heeb. I think you'd look a lot better if you shaved it all off," Evan agreed. And so the measure was passed and implemented. The posse embraced Kojakness like never before.

Evan's elaborate charm offensive to bring Heeb back into the posse involved strenuous persuasion and a variety of promised favors to ensure participation from every member of the clan, given the significant sacrifice involved. As wild and entertaining as it all was, the plan had a variety of repercussions on each member of the group. The stunt's impact was the least severe on Trevor and Narc, and the most taxing on Evan and Carlos.

Trevor was actually relieved when he could finally shave off all of the hair on his head, as he was accustomed to doing. Luigi had objected vociferously when Trevor began growing out his hair for the morale-boosting event on Heeb's behalf. So — as a consolation prize to Luigi for having to tolerate Trevor's new hairdo for a few weeks — and because he didn't have room in his apartment for two dogs — Trevor gave an Afghan Hound to Luigi, who absolutely adored the pet. Trevor had ended up with two dogs because Heeb refused to sleep in any apartment containing any animal. After his calamitous experience with Jackpot, Heeb not only became a bona fide ailurophobe, but also developed a general paranoia about sleeping near any living thing that was not a human or a plant. So Trevor kept the dog for him and brought him out whenever the posse wanted to hound around together.

After a few weeks, though, Trevor decided to give the dog to Luigi, on condition that he let Heeb walk it whenever the posse got together for a day in Central Park.

Narc was happy to keep his new pet, but would have to take a two-month hiatus from his budding pornography career so that his hair could grow back enough to resume production. For the sake of consistency, the various producers he worked with didn't want to change his look so dramatically. They figured that, after two months of hair growth, the difference wouldn't be too significant on camera. And Narc had already made six films over the last three months, so he didn't mind taking a break and spending more of his time helping his parents with their laundry business.

31. Carlos Gets Busted

Carolina, who had been away on business for a few days, returned home to discover Carlos's dramatic haircut and the new Afghan hound running around their penthouse. She feared that her husband's new hairdo signaled his conversion to some kind of ultra-religious Buddhist. During the five and half years since she first met Carlos, she had quit smoking and become an aspiring vegetarian. But she wasn't about to become any more Buddhist than that, even if she liked the religion as a philosophy.

"What's with the hair and the dog?" she asked.

"I did it for some friends," Carlos said. "It's a long story."

Carolina furrowed her brow suspiciously.

Later that night, she strategically resumed her interrogation in the midst of Carlos's blissful post-coital languor. "So tell me about these friends of yours, mi amor."

Carlos knew, as a general matter, that there is no worse time for a man to answer probing questions from a woman than two minutes after she has sated him, when her soft cheek is resting on his warm chest. But he was so tired and happily carefree at that moment that he thoughtlessly dropped his guard, figuring that he would have to tell her everything sooner or later, and the longer he waited, the worse her reaction would be.

So he came clean about his group of friends. He told her about each posse member, and some of their nights out together.

"You're not upset are you, mi amor?" Carlos asked her afterwards, caressing her delightfully smooth and curved lower back.

"Not at all," she replied calmly.

"Do you trust me?" he asked.

"Yes."

"Are you jealous?"

"Of course not," Carolina answered, in a perfectly relaxed and matter-of-fact tone. "But it's a shame because now we can't have sex until I'm sure that you've been faithful to me."

These shocking words – uttered with such pedestrian nonchalance – roused Carlos from his post-orgasm indolence. He sat up and looked at her, his face beginning to panic.

"What do you mean? What's wrong? I didn't do anything with those guys...I just joined them because of Sammy," he began to explain, repeating the group's original raison d'être and how Sammy had been disconsolate.

"And how would you feel if I joined a woman's group like that? If I frequented the city's bars and clubs with four single, horny women and kept it a secret from you for almost half a year?"

Carlos silently tried to imagine his reaction for a moment. The hypothetical definitely provoked jealousy in him but he immediately began searching for some way to claim that it was irrational and unjustified jealousy. Carolina continued on the offensive. "So there you have it. You would be jealous too, which is why – "

"But I didn't say that, mi amor, I just – "

"You didn't need to say it...It was all over your face as you searched desperately for some justification." She looked away for a moment, as if to leave her husband alone in the spotlight, where some invisible audience could behold his shameful loss in the discussion. "But don't worry," she continued, looking back into his eyes. "There's an easy solution to all of this."

Carlos began caressing her shoulder and arm, "What is it, Carolina? How can we fix this?"

"We can have a child."

Carlos stopped caressing her and took a hard swallow.

"Why does everything have to come back to that these days? I've already told you that I'm not ready yet."

"Because you hurt me with this posse thing, Carlos. And you would be hurt if I did it to you. And because I want babies. With you."

"Babies? How did we go from a singular child to plural babies?"

"Yes, plural. I want several babies. At least three. With you. And if you're the father of my children you'll be too busy being a daddy to go out with your single buddies, flirting with other women, shaving your head and buying exotic dogs for our apartment."

"I can't just become a daddy now, mi amor. I need more time. You just have to patient."

"But I've been patient, mi amor. And my biological clock is ticking faster every day."

"I'm just not ready at twenty-seven to be a father. And I'd rather adopt. It's the moral thing to do."

"We can have three babies of our own and then adopt some more."

Carlos rolled his eyes.

"You really do want me to be a full time daddy."

"I've been wanting it for a while now."

"Since you turned thirty."

"You know it's not that!"

"Well I'm not thirty yet, and I hate it when people try to round me up from twenty-seven."

"I'm not rounding you up."

"And I'm not having kids yet."

"How do I know you're not cheating on me with those guys?"

"You'll just have to trust me."

"No, you'll just have to convince me, unless you don't mind going celibate until you decide to have kids with me."

Carlos turned away for a moment, looked up at the ceiling, and then looked back at Carolina, exhaling in stressful frustration, like a squirrel cornered by a pack of wolves.

"All right. You win. How do you want me to convince you?"

"First, I want you to describe for me, in lots of detail, every night that you've gone out with this posse."

"Every night?"

"Si, mi amor. And then I want you to answer any follow up questions I have about those nights. And we're going to video tape all of our discussions, for handy reference later."

"Video tape?"

"Si, mi amor. And then I want a private interview, as long as necessary, with each member of this posse of yours."

"Private interview with each member?"

"Si, mi amor. And I'm going to ask each of them individually whatever questions occur to me. Of course, the information that you will have supplied beforehand will be helpful in formulating my questions."

"You're going to depose my friends?"

"Si, mi amor. And then, if there are any particular interview portions that don't quite match up with what you told me, you and I can watch that portion of the interview together. And then you'll have a chance to try to explain away the discrepancy."

"Explain away the discrepancy?"

"Si, mi amor. And after that, if there are no unexplained discrepancies, we can start having sex again without having babies."

"Without babies?" he repeated, with some relief.

"Well, no babies for another five months or so," she clarified. "Then we can revisit the issue properly."

Carlos was silent for a moment. He felt overwhelmed, trying to imagine the days and weeks ahead. "I can't believe this...Is this really the only way to reassure you?"

"Well there is one other way."

"What is it, mi amor?"

"I start joining you on every posse outing, and you start joining me on each of my visits to married couples with children...And you sign up with me for some parenting 101 classes, and we start babysitting for my friends, so that we can get a little taste of parenthood together."

Carlos took a moment to envision the second alternative. He quickly concluded that he would be powerfully pressured into paternity within a matter of weeks and there would really be no escape at that point. He told Carolina that he needed a few days to reflect on the options she had laid before him.

After explaining his predicament to the posse, he opted for the inquisition.

32. Big News Makes Evan Elated but Panicked

Evan's apartment was a little small to be shared with an Afghan Hound, but he and his new pet were slowly adjusting to their cramped coexistence. The real challenge for Evan was accepting his new haircut. Two days after he and the posse had shaved everything off, Evan was beginning to feel OK about his appearance. But on Wednesday night, April 5, 2001, the third day of his Kojak look, Evan came home to two unexpected messages on his answering machine.

Message one was an invitation to be interviewed for a full-time position as a neural network developer for the financial modeling division of a prestigious but stuffy investment bank. This was the first promising interview he had obtained after three weeks of sending out resumes, and he wasn't thrilled about trying to impress a notoriously conservative corporate employer with his totally hair-free head. As he jotted down the details of the message, he wondered whether he could somehow postpone the interview for a month, so that his hair could grow back into what would then look like a military-style crew cut.

The second message, however, was the one that truly made Evan panic about having zero hair for the coming weeks. Indeed, message two was so dramatic that he would end up forgetting to follow up about the job interview offered in message one.

"Hi, I'm trying to get in touch with Evan Cheson," the voice began. "We've never spoken before and I don't know if you were expecting a call from me, but this is Delilah Nakova...I'm calling you because my agency sent me your novel, and I just finished reading it. And I guess I'm calling to tell you that I really enjoyed it...In fact, I think it's one of the best novels I've read in a very long time, and I don't know if you've given much thought to the possibility of adapting it into a film, but I personally get very excited just thinking about it. I hope you don't think it's too forward or random of me to contact you like this, but I'd love to meet the person who wrote this novel, and I'd also like to talk to you about adapting it into a screenplay."

And then she left her cell phone number and email and said that she really hoped to hear from him soon, noting that she would be in New York City for a week starting tomorrow.

Evan began to hyperventilate from elation and nearly passed out. He replayed the message to himself seven times, thinking that he would eventually believe his ears. When he finally convinced himself that the message was real, he made three backup recordings of it. Then he called Heeb and replayed it to him several times. Then he played it for Trevor, Narc, and Carlos. A little later, he realized that he had just inadvertently disclosed the movie star's contact details to four people, so he had to call everyone back to confirm that no one had made a note of her private details. He extracted solemn promises from each friend not to use or divulge her information if it somehow popped back into memory.

Evan couldn't stop thinking about how April 5, 2001 was without a doubt, the greatest day of his life. And he repeatedly thanked the divine powers behind this miracle for timing its occurrence while he was away, because – had he been home to pick up the phone – he would have surely made a complete ass of himself from the mere shock of the call.

For fifty minutes, Evan obsessively examined his hairless scalp in the bathroom mirror from various angles while talking to Heeb on his cordless phone for the fifth time that night. "But she wants to meet tomorrow and I don't have any fucking hair!" he exclaimed.

"Now you know how I feel every day," Heeb replied.

"Can't you at least acknowledge that the fellowship of the schlong has required some very heavy sacrifices on my part?"

"What about that unconvincing reassurance you always give me?" Heeb replied.

"You mean that she might be into bald guys?"

"That's the one!" Heeb said, delighted that the tables were finally turned for a change.

"Heeb you're not helping."

"OK, why don't you look at the bright side?" Heeb said.

"What bright side?"

"You've substantially lowered the odds that she'll recognize you as the guy from that wild Mexican party at Float, who first belittled her beloved Czech language and then nuked the unisex bathroom just as she was trying to use it. And she also won't recognize you as the guy from the Operation-Repulsive encounter at Duane Reade, six months ago."

Evan was silent for a moment as he thought about this.

"You know, I think you may have a point there…But what will I do once my hair grows back and she sees me looking like I did on one of those two incidents?"

"I don't think you'll ever again look like you did during Operation Repulsive. That was too good even for Halloween. And the Float incident was two years ago…I really doubt she'll remember that. Unless, of course, you're stupid enough to remind her somehow."

"Given my record with Delilah Nakova, we really can't discount that possibility."

33. The Posse's Problems

During the month that followed the momentous message from Delilah Nakova, the posse was confronted with a few challenges. Trevor became more serious about Luigi, who began insisting that he be allowed to join him when he went out with his gang. Carolina subjected each member of the guy group to her rigorous tape-recorded interrogations, and Carlos had a difficult time making it up to his buddies.

After three weeks of no sex and rigorous questioning, Carolina finally and correctly concluded that her husband had been admirably faithful, given the many opportunities he had had to cheat on her with very desirable women. Carlos was so thrilled to be having sex with his wife again, and so relieved to be absolved of her accusations that he became increasingly loath – even uninterested – in joining his friends for a night out unless Carolina could come along.

The posse was genuinely torn about whether to admit the two individuals who were actively applying for membership rights. Most of the posse members were especially uncomfortable with having Carolina accompany them after having recently squirmed under her piercing depositions.

Even more threatening to the posse's continued viability was the situation with Evan. On April 6, one day after the message that sent him into a euphoric tailspin, Carolina tried questioning him on videotape. She became frustrated with how little he could focus on her questions, and how he kept seeking her advice with respect to Delilah Nakova. After two hours of mostly fruitless investigation, she concluded that he had no useful information for her and released him. That was the last that anyone had seen Evan for four weeks, although a week after his interrogation he did resume regular phone communication with everyone during his absence.

The posse did manage to meet twice in Evan's absence, and on several other occasions Heeb and Narc were forced to prowl without the rest of the crew, unless they were prepared to invite Luigi and Carolina to join them. So the two briefly mulled the possibility.

"Chicks are chick magnets," Narc pointed out. "And Carolina is smokin' hot. So it wouldn't necessarily be a bad thing for her to come along."

"I just feel weird going out with the Grand Inquisitor," Heeb replied.

"Word. Well, what about leaving Lucky Chucky and Carolina out, but we take Trevor and Luigi?"

"I guess we could do that, but that would change things too much...And it's just not the same without the others."

"I hear ya'," Narc said.

And so Narc and Heeb decided to go out on their own a few times. As they considered the fortunes and circumstances of each member, they speculated about how much longer the group would last, but assured each other that they would continue going out together as long as they were both single.

34. Evan and Delilah

Evan totally forgot about the posse because of the unforgettably surreal experience with Delilah Nakova that began on the night of April 6, just a few hours after Carolina's deposition ended. At 8 p.m., Evan closed his front door and approached Delilah Nakova's limousine, parked outside of his apartment, as if it were some exotic space ship that was about to take him to another world. Inside the limo was Delilah Nakova, in all of her graceful beauty and down to earth charm, sporting a mysterious, Asian look. Her black hair was neatly and tightly folded against her head and wrapped into a chignon secured by wooden hairpins. She wore an elegant red and black peony cheongsam made of silk. Her radiant face, long dark eyelashes, mocha-colored skin, and elegantly feminine figure seemed almost surreal to Evan as he stepped into her limousine and closed the door.

"I'm sorry for calling you like that rather than ringing your doorbell," she started. "I just prefer to avoid being seen in public whenever possible because of the paparazzi."

Evan was speechless and could only nod in approval of her explanation. And then he suddenly started fumbling in a panic: "I'm sorry about the shaved head...I don't usually look like this...I just lost a bet with a friend, and – "

"Oh it's cute...I kind of like it," Delilah said reassuringly. "We're going to a very comfy restaurant," she continued, as her limousine drove off. "I hope you like Greek food," she added. "This place is delicious."

"Sounds Greek to me. I mean, sounds great to me," he said nervously.

Delilah laughed a little at Evan's awkward deadpan. Evan actually wasn't sure if he had intended the pun but was glad that Delilah found it funny.

Over a sumptuous, candlelit dinner, Delilah began gushing about Evan's work.

"It was such a wonderfully memorable novel...I'm actually reading it for the second time now. I really like the lead female character and would love to play her in a film based on your book."

"Really?" Evan asked, nearly choking on his food.

"Are you artistically comfortable with the idea of making it into a film?"

"It would be a dream come true," he said, barely containing his ecstatic astonishment.

"It's really exciting to think about, isn't it?" she beamed. Her intensely green eyes twinkled with warmth and promise. "By the way I absolutely love the title!"

"Sex in the title?"

"Yes! It's perfect. Cute. Sexy. Mysterious. Even profound for what is says about our society. I love it!"

Evan was in heaven. He had to keep reminding himself that this was all happening to him by looking around the restaurant. Every now and then some nearby couple would sneak a peak in the direction of his table, at which point he would imagine them wondering why Delilah Nakova was possibly having dinner with that completely unknown bald guy.

"Well if you can find that kind of inspiration for your screenplay then we may be able to make some magic together," she said, unaware that she had just given Evan another taste of Elysian bliss. "Do you have any experience with screenwriting?"

"Actually, I do," Evan replied, trying to collect himself. "I've written several scripts."

"That's wonderful...Have any been made into movies?" she said, inadvertently asking that follow up question he so detested.

"Um...No...Not yet," he said uneasily. Then he hastily added, "But I'd feel very comfortable writing the adaptation of this novel."

"Wonderful," Delilah replied. Evan was relieved that she still seemed to have total confidence in his abilities. "Perhaps we could talk a little about what the vision would be for the screenplay," she said. "If you don't mind my input, that is."

"Oh no...Not at all...It's...It's quite an honor...And the vision for a movie script is everything."

"OK, well please don't take this the wrong way, Evan, because I truly loved your novel...What I'm about to say is just something to keep in mind when you're writing the screenplay version."

"What is it?" said Evan, cringing a little at the looming criticism.

"Well, the concept of your novel has great commercial potential. And there's a lot of witty and clever dialogue in there, and some hysterical scenes that I'd really like you to keep if you can. But there are far too many subplots going on for a movie."

"What do you mean?" Evan asked.

"I just think it could be hard for the audience to follow so many different stories and characters that jump around in time so much."

Evan watched the waiter clearing their dishes and replacing them with the next course while trying to sneak occasional glances at Delilah.

"Audiences generally like one or two lead characters with a fairly straightforward plotline in a single genre," Delilah said. Accustomed to unsolicited attention, she remained focused on Evan and oblivious to the waiter's occasional looks. "If it's a comedy, then it should stay a comedy and not venture into drama territory, if you know what I mean. There are some exceptions, but they're very tough to pull off."

"I completely agree," Evan said cheerfully, even though he was clueless about how he would respect Hollywood parameters when it came to adapting his own novel.

"And you've got some great observations on human psychology and society, but these are really far too profound for Hollywood, and audiences will either get bored or confused by them."

"Maybe that's why none of my screenplays have gotten anywhere," he replied, feeling a twinge of self-doubt.

"Evan, you're a very talented writer with a wonderful imagination, but you just need to be discovered," Delilah said gently. "Which is why I'm so excited to be here talking to you like this. Because I know that someday, you're going to be recognized as a top writer. And if I contributed in some way to helping you get discovered, it would be wonderful…I know how hard it can be for new artists."

These words sent Evan back into the stratosphere.

"Another thing to keep in mind for the adaptation is that your sense of humor is a little inconsistent. Sometimes it's very low humor, with jokes that involve scatological slapstick, and other times it's very subtle and ironic, or witty."

"Thanks, I think."

"Well it's definitely a compliment for your novel. I think that gives it a much broader appeal. But in film, it might not work. And you may have to dumb down the language a bit."

"What do you mean?"

"Well in your novel the language is also inconsistent. Sometimes it's very high brow with complex thoughts and sophisticated vocabulary, and other times there's a lot of simple dialogue."

"But that mirrors life, I think," Evan said, trying delicately to defend his creative decisions. "At times things are very complex and profound. And at other times, they're very simple. Whether you're talking about human interactions, the way people communicate, or how they think, there are always going to be moments of incredible simplicity – even stupidity – and other moments of unparalleled insight and eloquence. Like this sentence I just said now. That's probably the most articulate and profound thing I've said all night. The rest was mostly blather."

Delilah chuckled at his observation. "Evan, I think you're absolutely right about the varied complexity mirroring life. And please don't take any of this as a critique of your novel, which I really do love. It's also not the way I prefer to see films made. I'm personally a fan of more complex cinema. Independent art films and such. And I would like to start doing more of that, which is one of the reasons I'd like us to work together, Evan." Each time she said his name she elevated him to a higher region of cloud nine. "And I'd really like to see an all star cast attached to your script."

"That would be amazing."

"But that also requires a script that follows the Hollywood rules."

"Why is that?"

"Because an all star cast means a bigger budget. Twenty to fifty million at least. And that's with me doing the film without any upfront compensation. So we'd need a major executive producer to back the project."

"I see."

"And having worked with enough producers, I can tell you that they would basically give us the same script notes that I just gave to you."

"OK."

Delilah smiled encouragingly at Evan, as if to soften the blow of everything she had just told him.

Evan smiled back nervously.

"I think I can get you a script that reflects the suggestions you've made," Evan said, without having a clue how he would actually manage to do this.

"Really?" Delilah's face suddenly lit up in delight. She put her naturally bronze hand across the table onto his and repeated her favorite word. "That's wonderful, Evan!" He felt her soft hand touch his. As he absorbed her warm green eyes, his pulse quickened dreamily.

"I can't wait to read it," she said, her hand still on his. "How soon do you think you could have a first draft ready?"

"Uhm...How about in a week?"

"Wow, that's really fast...But it would be perfect, if you can do it! I'm taking a lighter course load at Brown next year, so that I can work on more projects...I honestly don't want to rush you with this script, because it really deserves to be done right...But there's a small window open in my production schedule this winter, so if we could get a final script ready in the next few weeks, we could maybe get financing in place by early summer, with a cast ready to go for production this winter."

"A few weeks sounds very doable," Evan said, trying to focus on the immortal being commanding his next moves rather than on the feasibility of her commandments.

"Evan, I really don't want you to feel as if I'm just going to disappear after dumping some impossible assignment on you."

"That's unbelievably sweet of you," Evan replied, enchanted by her kindness.

"But I'm being totally serious. In fact, you're welcome to stay in my loft and just work on the script while I'm in town...It's in this quaint little spot in SoHo. A great workspace if you need a place to concentrate. And if you run into any problems or you want to talk through any scenes, I'll be right there to try and help."

Evan couldn't believe his ears. He might as well have been hallucinating.

"I'll be in town for a week, and then I have some meetings in LA for four days, but I'll be back after that for a good month, except for a few short trips to Providence for college stuff."

Evan kept staring at her, as if in a trance.

Delilah was amused by the stupefied expression on Evan's face. "Are you OK, Evan?"

He snapped out of his daze. "Yes, I'm fine. Sorry about that... When you mentioned Providence I just started thinking about my college days."

"Did you go to Brown?" Delilah asked excitedly.

"Yes, I did. Class of '93."

"How funny! What a small world!" she exclaimed.

They spent the next forty minutes discussing courses and professors at Brown, the various bars and hangouts in Providence, and how their respective college years had been similar yet different.

Over dessert, Evan brought out his ace in the hole: "You probably didn't guess this, but I'm also part Czech."

And with that Delilah's face lit up again. "Really?" she said in Czech. "Say something to me!"

"My Czech is a bit rusty," he began in Czech. "I studied it for just two years, but I love the language and wish that I had more opportunities to practice it…" In the two years since he first ran into Delilah at Float, Evan had been regularly brushing up on his Czech language skills with a variety of grammar books and language tapes. "I spent the summer after Brown in Prague and really want to go back," he continued.

"That's so wonderful!" she replied in Czech. "The Czech-Brown-College film-making team must celebrate!" she said, full of verve and joy. Evan could not have been more elated by how well his two years of preparation were paying off. "Do you need to be anywhere tonight?" she asked.

"No," he replied, once again amazed at how unpresumptuous the starlet was about her importance to anyone else.

"Would you like to join me for some cocktails at my place? I'd love to hear more about your Czech roots and your time in Prague… Maybe you could even read me some pages from your novel, too."

Barely able to speak, and stiffening his entire body as much as possible to avoid exploding ecstatically all over the restaurant, Evan answered with a simple, "Sure."

During the next week, Evan practically moved in to Delilah's enormous, stylish loft, except for a few hours, when he went back to his place to hand his Afghan Hound over to his neighbor and pick up his toiletries and some clothes. He worked on her computer incessantly, taking breaks only to join her for a meal occasionally. He slept in a guest room, even though Delilah had invited him to cuddle after their third night together. From their first meeting at the Greek restaurant, it was clear that Delilah liked Evan. During the days and nights that followed, when they were at her place, she often let her arms or hands come to rest on his shoulder, arm, or leg, as he read his work aloud to her or they talked about one thing or another. Such unexpected contact made Evan's heart jump each time, and left him tongue-tied. Still insecure about his bald hairdo, Evan produced a recent picture of himself with hair. "You're very handsome even without hair," she told him.

But despite their comfortable and increasingly intimate rapport, Evan could bring himself to do no more than lightly kiss Delilah on the lips or her hold her hand. He suffered from what psychologists might term "idol impotence": the inability to become sexual with that which one deifies, for fear of disappointing or defiling it. His unqualified apotheosis of Delilah Nakova, which only intensified as he spent more time in her presence, also ensured that he could never truly be himself around her. He was always, in one way or another, in awe of her and unsure of himself.

She, on the other hand, couldn't figure out what she was doing wrong. At the age of twenty, with a fairly conservative upbringing followed by a protected celebrity existence, she had had only two boyfriends in her entire life. But neither of them, nor any of her thousands of suitors, had ever showed such difficulty displaying physical affection for her. This unintended refusal by Evan only made Delilah desire him more. Suddenly, she was around someone who didn't seem to respond to her as a sex symbol and who was apparently – and actually – unattainable. No matter how obvious she made her interest in him, he continued to behave in a sexually indifferent and somewhat distant manner. Evan had unwittingly but rather effectively exercised "the power to reject."

The difficulties produced by idol impotence naturally complicated Evan's progress on the screenplay he needed to write for her, and this made it even more difficult for him to concentrate. He knew that their relationship was severely imbalanced, but he had no idea how to correct the problem and was terrified of openly admitting that he felt so inadequate in her presence, lest she start to believe him. He thought his mortal inferiority was already painfully obvious every time she introduced him to her friends, most of whom were Hollywood VIPs and celebrities.

"This is Evan Cheson," she would say. "He's a brilliant New York novelist and he's writing the screenplay for my next project. It's a wonderful story and I've never been so excited about a script!"

"That's fabulous, Evan! Congratulations!" the person would say. "What have you published?"

"Nothing…Yet," he would answer reluctantly.

"Oh, OK. And how's the script coming along?"

To which Evan would have to reply, with a stiff throat, "Very well, thanks. It's definitely a work in progress, but I'm hoping to finish it in a few weeks."

"Wow. That's impressive," they would add, before moving right back to Delilah. And as the conversation turned to a possible movie deal, a big charity dinner, a great newspaper review, a potential TV interview, or any number of other items of interest in the life of a movie star still in college, Evan's thoughts soon focused on how the only reason that anyone thought anything of him was the fact that Delilah Nakova was waiting for him to finish a screenplay that he had no idea how to write.

35. The Porn Star and Relationship Expert

During the four days that Delilah was in LA, Evan called each member of the posse for advice. Everyone was wowed that Evan was practically dating Delilah Nakova, and reassured him that things would work themselves out in time. But Evan realized that these discussions were more for venting and sharing than getting any useful advice, since no member of the posse had ever been in a similar situation. Evan did, however, cling to the faint hope that Narc might have some helpful tips, since he was the most sexually uninhibited member of the posse and he had some understanding of what it was like to be a film personality.

Narc had even been hit on recently by a Japanese expatriate in New York who had recognized him after watching one of his porno films with her underperforming boyfriend. Narc's popularity would only increase during his hair-growing production break. His six porn titles, each released in late March, were already winning a substantial audience among Tokyo couples, where his films were first introduced in English with Japanese subtitles. Narc's catchy, pseudonymous actor name "Tiger Dong" sat well with Japanese viewers and his most popular film was "Sushi Love." Specifically targeted to the Japanese market, the film featured Narc's exploits at a sushi bar, where he played a straight-laced employee who takes sporadic breaks from preparing sushi rolls to commit a bewildering variety of sexual acts with every colleague and customer, all of whom are, naturally, comely women happy to spread their legs next to raw fish.

On several Japanese porn sites, Tiger Dong is hailed as "the new, stunningly handsome, American hope for Asian porn stars" and his films are reviewed as "excellent arousal material for couples with troubles." But one man's website review warned fans that if their wives watched Tiger Dong's movies with them, they risked being made to feel inadequate by comparison to the images of the long lasting and well-endowed Tiger Dong. To Narc's delighted surprise, female college students from Tokyo and Hong Kong began sending him fan mail with naked pictures of themselves attached.

So it was no surprise that Narc, who was beginning to feel like something of a celebrity himself, couldn't exactly understand what was holding Evan back when it came to Delilah Nakova. "Why don't you just bone her and get it over with, yo?" he asked.

"Please, Narc. Don't use the term 'bone' when you're referring to her."

"What's the big deal? She's a honey like any other. A smokin' hot honey, but a honey no less."

"Narc, this is Delilah Nakova we're talking about. She's not a smokin' hot honey. She's heaven on earth. A living angel."

"You need to chill out on that, bro. 'Fer-real. Just get it over with and you'll see that she's human like the rest of 'em."

"But I can't. I can't just do that. Sleeping with her would somehow put her in the same class as the scores of women before her."

"Yeah, it would mean that you liked her enough to sleep with her, just like with the others. Whasso bad about that?"

"But that's just the point...I like her infinitely more than that... To the point that she's no longer within my sexual reach."

"You are buggin' out, Evan."

"I know...I know...I've got problems," Evan said, pacing wildly in his apartment with his cordless phone.

"Why don't you try smokin' some herbalz with her? That'll chill you two out some."

"I can't do that, Narc. And what if I didn't perform up to her expectations? It would be a disaster for our relationship, and for me. I mean, what if the sex is bad?"

"Just plug in one of my videos bro. It seems to be working for a lot of other couples, so I don't see why it couldn't work for the two of you."

"Narc, you're completely fucking warped. How the hell did we stay friends all of these years?"

"Basketball and booty."

"All right, but can you just try to understand my situation here?"

"I'm tryin'. I think the bottom line is that you've got this girl on a mile-high pedestal."

"No, I don't, Narc. This has nothing to do with what I think of her. It all really stems from the indisputable fact that she's the most beautiful, kind, charming, and intelligent woman walking the earth right now."

"She's just a honey, Evan. Like all the others you've been with."

"No she's not, Narc. And that fact is constantly staring at me in small, everyday ways."

"Like how?"

"Like the fact that we take her limousine everywhere and are always ditching the paparazzi."

"What else?"

"Like the fact that she'll call me up from some major film meeting at some snooty ass restaurant like Lotus, inviting me to join her for dinner. I mean, I never dated anyone who even ate regularly at a place like Lotus for God's sake. And then I can't even fuckin' get in because there's a twenty-minute line monitored by doormen with more attitude than a room full of fashion editors. And then her cell phone doesn't get reception inside so that she doesn't know that I've been waiting for her outside for fifteen minutes, while some big producer tries to cap her upfront acting fee at five million dollars for her next blockbuster."

"I hear you, bro. And, now that I'm thinking about it a bit more, with all of that context you just gave me, I think you should just dump her."

"What do you mean?" Evan asked in alarm.

"You know these celebrity relationships almost never work out. And given that she's the celebrity in this relationship, she's gonna be the one dumping you. So I suggest you take the initiative and be the dumper. Before you become the dumpee."

"You're suggesting that I dump Delilah Nakova?"

"And look at how impressive it sounds! Doesn't it sound so much better to be the guy who dumped Delilah Nakova than the guy who got dumped by her?"

"This is crazy."

"But I still think you should bone her first. I mean, talk about bragging rights! You'd deserve a PhD yo'."

Evan's voice grew angry and insulted. "What did I tell you? Don't ever use the word 'bone' again when Delilah is involved. Understand?"

"Yo, I got a lil' loose with the language. Sorry, bro'. But chill out a little. Have a joint."

"You're high right now, aren't you?" Evan asked, still annoyed but more forgiving, after realizing that Narc had been stoned throughout their call.

"A little puff or three, nothing major. Bro, you could really use some too. With her. It's the only way to make it happen with all of this baggage you've got. Just trust me on this and smoke up some herbalz

301

together, and it'll be all good. Who knows? Maybe you won't need to dump her after all, although I really think that's your best long-term move, given her celebrity status."

"Thanks, Narc. You've been really helpful," Evan said, as he rolled his eyes and hung up the phone.

36. Lost…

The seventeen days that followed Delilah's return from LA were a torturous and depressing hell for Evan.

He had become convinced that the only way he could possibly be worthy of Delilah Nakova was if he wrote her a screenplay that she absolutely admired. So he wrote feverishly and incessantly, sixteen hours a day, for all seventeen days, trying to produce just the right draft for her to read. Each morning, at 9 a.m., he would quickly review the screenplay that he had finished at 3 a.m. the prior night, and conclude that it was garbage and not true to his novel or what Delilah wanted. And then he would proceed to crank out an entirely new version of the same screenplay so that Evan effectively wrote seventeen versions of the same screenplay in seventeen days. He slept only six hours per day, leaving only two hours per day of "quality time" with Delilah.

When Evan joined Delilah for a private meal, a ride in her limousine, or, on rare occasions, a more public activity, he reassured her that he was making good progress and didn't need any help working through anything. He did his best to conceal his chronic distress, fearing that she might conclude that he wasn't up to the task. On the seventh day, when he snapped at her for asking to see his work, she gently offered to have a friend of hers, who was a top Hollywood screenwriter, help him out, or even join the project as a co-writer, if it would help Evan's progress at all. But that suggestion went to the very root of his insecurity: the fear that he just didn't have the necessary talent to be truly worthy of Delilah.

And the more he labored under this conviction, the more impossible the challenge seemed, and the less worthy he felt of her. Meanwhile, Delilah was gradually willing to risk being seen with him in public, as she grew into the idea that he was her boyfriend. After all, she reasoned, she really did like him, she had no other male interest at the moment, he was effectively living with her and working intensely on her passion project, and they did occasionally hold hands or kiss lightly. This, she assumed, qualified him as her boyfriend. Evan, on the other hand, was terrified of being seen with her in public, fearing such exposure would prompt people to question why she was with a "nobody" like him, which would, he assumed, cause her to second-guess her decision to be with him.

After Evan's tenth day of work on the screenplay, Delilah again asked to read what he had written so far. He managed to convince her that he couldn't let anyone read a work of his that was still in progress. "It just completely stifles my imagination," he explained. "I get into this self-censoring mode, because then I start anticipating everything the reader might say to me...Just trust me. I can't show it now. But I promise. I absolutely promise to have a first draft for you in one week."

"OK, honey. Whatever you're comfortable with," she replied, somewhat concerned but unsure how to deal with the unpredictably complicated psychology of a writer at work.

The night before his promised delivery of a first draft, Evan stayed up all night, downing coffee like water and cranking out the seventeenth version of the screenplay. But by 7 a.m., he was only on page fifty-five, and had serious doubts that it was any better than the previous sixteen drafts.

At 7:45 a.m., when Delilah was still soundly asleep, Evan finally printed out a single page for Delilah to read when she woke up: "Dearest Delilah, I can't be with you anymore. Please don't call me. I'm sorry."

He signed his name at the bottom of the note, left it on his pillow, took his belongings, and quietly crept out of her loft.

37. ...And Found

Every human relationship begins with a coincidence. Even the most fundamental relationship – that of parent and child – begins entirely with a coincidence. The child is produced by whatever serendipity brought its parents together, and the fact that the child was born to its particular parents instead of to another couple is pure happenstance. Thus, children have no choice over the relationship that is most important to their existence.

By contrast, friends and lovers choose each other, but even these choices are reactions to whatever random coincidence made the resulting relationship possible. And despite the undeniable fact that all human relations are partly or wholly created by chance, the initial meeting of two lovers always seems more magically coincidental than all other relationships. This feeling may be nothing more than the relief that two lovers share at the fact that they acted wisely when they could have just easily failed to transform luck into love.

And so it was on May 10, 2001, at 8:15 a.m., when Heeb met Hila.

It was a typically cramped subway commute to work that morning. Sammy was wearing his best suit and tie and needed to exit at the Fulton Street stop (rather than his usual Grand Central stop) for an important presentation at his Wall Street client's corporate headquarters.

From the time Heeb boarded the five train at Eighty-sixth Street until the moment it stopped at Grand Central, he intensely skimmed over fifty pages of notes and summary charts for his presentation, while leaning against a train pole. He made some additional notes to himself in the margin, using his awkwardly large briefcase as a hard surface for writing. At Grand Central station, Heeb almost got off the train by sheer force of habit, but caught himself and remained on the train. He noticed a petite, young woman, five feet two inches tall, with dark curls flowing down to her girlish shoulders. She was standing sideways relative to him, so that he could see only her left side, which had the poise and smoothness of a porcelain ballet doll. She weighed no more than 110 pounds and wore dark sunglasses and a light, cotton pastel green dress.

Heeb looked at her for about twenty seconds before remembering, when the train started to move again, that he had to use every available commute moment to prepare for his presentation.

A few minutes later, as the train was leaving the Fourteenth Street station, a loud, garbled, and largely indecipherable message blasted over the train's intercom. Heeb looked up, annoyed at the distraction.

The petite woman next to him turned towards Heeb with a confused frown and said, in a light, quasi-French sounding accent, "Do you know what they just said?" Now that her face was turned towards Heeb's, he could admire her full lips, delicate chin, and ruddy cheeks. He couldn't resist flirting with her for a moment.

"You mean you don't speak subway intercomese?"

"I'm sorry. I don't understand what you mean."

"It's one of the hardest languages to grasp phonetically."

"You mean what they say on the subway speakers?"

"Yes, it's really the only foreign language I speak. My friend Evan speaks some Czech. My friend Titus speaks some Hebrew. My buddy Narc is fluent in Chinese. And I speak subway intercomese…It's actually very useful. They say formal instruction isn't enough and that you really have to live in New York for at least five years to become fully conversant in it, so I'm still learning it."

"You're funny," she said, with an innocent smile.

"I'm totally serious. I was thinking of opening up a school for people who are new to New York and need a crash course in better understanding subway announcements."

"Well, can you tell me what they said?"

"Oh yes, I'm sorry. They said that they were skipping the Brooklyn Bridge stop because of repair work. I mean, New York just wouldn't be the same adventure if it had a truly reliable subway system. So you just have to embrace the fun surprises as they come."

"But that's the stop I need," she said, with a girlish frown.

"I'm sorry. Well I guess you'll have to get out with me at the next stop, which is Fulton."

"OK." She frowned again. "Thanks for your help," she said, and looked away so that he again saw only her profile.

Heeb took that as his cue to leave her alone, and a vital reminder that he needed to get back to preparing for his presentation.

As he began to look back towards his notes, he noticed that just beyond her stood two muscular youths, covered with tattoos and gold jewelry. They each looked down at Heeb, as if to mock his inferior height and chubby physique. They looked him in the eye, daring him to keep staring.

Heeb moved his eyes back down to his work, but a few minutes later, he heard them laughing obnoxiously. Seconds later, he snuck a peek and saw that they were whispering some kind of tasteless comment about the petite woman next to him. Unable to concentrate on his work, he let his eyes shift about the subway car for a neutral spot that still gave him a peripheral view's warning of whatever they were up to.

They continued their rude and rowdy joking amongst themselves until the subway train stopped at the Fulton station.

"You should get off here," Heeb reminded the small woman.

She turned towards him and smiled. "Thank you...Can you just help me off the train?" she asked.

Heeb noticed her walking cane for the first time and his heart sank a little. "Of course. Come this way," he said, taking her arm and helping her to step down from the train and onto the platform.

"Do you know the way to get back to Chambers Street?" she asked.

Sammy looked anxiously at his watch. He had to be at his presentation in exactly ten minutes. He was about to ask someone else to help her out for him, because he was so running late, but he couldn't bring himself to do it. Sammy took a hard swallow and resigned himself to fate.

"So where are you from?" Heeb asked, trying to make friendly conversation as he walked her to the platform for the uptown train. He knew that he was too linguistically challenged to accurately place a foreign accent.

"I'm from Israel," she answered, as they walked, with her cane tapping the floor a few feet ahead of them. "That's where my funny accent is from."

Heeb took another hard swallow.

"Very cool," he finally said. "You know, in addition to speaking subway intercomese I can actually say two things in Hebrew. My blind friend Titus taught me."

"What can you say?" she asked.

And then, in Hebrew, with an atrocious American accent, Heeb said, "You're a beautiful woman." And then, after a moment's pause, he added, "Can I kiss you?"

"Hey that's pretty good!" she exclaimed. "I see you tried to learn the important stuff."

"Yeah, well this is the first time I've actually used those phrases with anyone other than Titus," he admitted, somewhat embarrassed.

"My name is Hila, by the way," she said, with a timid smile.

"Oh. Nice to meet you, Hila. My name is Sammy. But you can call me Heeb," he replied, all too eager to report his common ethnicity.

"Heeb? How did you go from Sammy to Heeb?" she asked, amused.

"Heeb is short for Hebrew. My friends used to tease me with the name 'Heeb' when they learned that I wanted to date only non-Jewish women until I turned twenty-eight, at which point I was going to date only Jewish women, so that I could be married to a Jewish woman by thirty."

"Really? And how old are you now?"

"I actually turned twenty-eight last week..."

"So no more shiksas now?" she asked in amusement.

"I know...I know what you want to say. That it's a totally crazy idea."

"No, that's not what I wanted to say."

"Oh. So what did you want to say?"

"It's not the idea that's crazy, Heeb, it's you," she said, giggling.

"Yes. I know. I'm finally beginning to accept my own wackiness."

She laughed.

"So what brings you to New York, Hila?"

"I'm going to see a world-famous eye doctor. I was blinded six months ago in a terrorist attack in Jerusalem."

"Oh...I'm so sorry to hear that."

There was an uncomfortable silence as they kept walking. The only sound Heeb could hear was Hila's cane, rhythmically tapping the ground ahead of them like a metronome in synch with the slow and rhythmic swing of his right arm carrying his large, heavy briefcase.

Hila finally broke the silence. "Well I was lucky, you know...I could have been on the bus....Then I would be dead...I was just nearby, so some of the exploding glass injured my eyes."

"I guess that's looking at the bright side of things," Heeb said meekly, feeling terribly ashamed at every complaint he had ever uttered about his own life.

"Well, it's been difficult to learn how to live without eyes," she said. She stopped for a moment and turned her face towards Heeb at an angle that was slightly off. "But what choice do I have?" she said. "There is still much to live for, you know," she added, with a small smile.

Heeb swallowed again, harder this time.

"And you came all the way here from Jerusalem by yourself? Without any help?"

"No, my aunt came with me, so that made the travel much easier. But she got really sick and had to stay in bed today."

"You're staying in a hotel?"

"No, hotels are really expensive here. She found us a sublet for two weeks."

"And you couldn't change your appointment until she got better and could take you?"

"I tried. But the next appointment with this doctor was in four months, so I had to go on my own today."

They walked in silence for a bit. Heeb's eyes were now watering and he wasn't thinking much about where they were going or his presentation or any other particular detail. His thoughts flitted about uncontrollably to a thousand sad, angry, ashamed, and confused places, as they continued walking.

Suddenly, their private moment was awakened by the hubbub of the two youths from the subway, laughing and yelling wildly as they ran towards Heeb and Hila.

For a moment, Heeb thought that they would just dash past them on their boisterous, immature way, but the shorter one skidded to the floor mischievously, about a foot in front of the next tap of Hila's cane. His coconspirator approached Hila from her left side, with a callous, lewd look in his eyes. Heeb, who was walking on her right side, stopped her from walking over the stumbling block that the youth on the floor was about to become.

But the hoodlum coming at Hila from the left side grabbed her arm and began feeling up her chest, saying "Come here little ho'! I'm gonna give you a taste of Brooklyn's finest!" while his coconspirator rose from the floor to participate in the crime.

At that moment, Heeb forgot about his important work presentation. He forgot about the important papers in his hand that went falling to the floor. He forgot about the fact that he was shorter and weaker than the two cruel thugs in his midst. He forgot about the fact that he had no practice whatsoever in physical combat. He forgot about all of these things as he instinctively slammed his heavy briefcase across the head of the hoodlum who had gotten up from the floor, so that he was knocked back down to the ground, where he remained, badly dazed and bleeding.

Seconds later, the larger ruffian groping Hila landed a solid, powerful punch in Heeb's nose, sending him stumbling backwards, as blood started to gush down his mouth and chin and all over his nice suit. Leaving Hila for later, the thug advanced towards Heeb, who was still recovering. As he approached for a second punch, Heeb landed the hardest kick he could muster in the youth's groin, making him buckle over. Blood still dripping all over himself and his whole face swollen and stinging, he thrashed the hoodlum hard on the head with his briefcase, so that he too fell to the subway floor, writhing in pain.

Heeb could hear Hila crying and afraid behind him, but he wasn't finished.

"Listen, you piece of shit," Heeb began, with a solid kick into the larger youth's ribs; the youth groaned in pain. "Didn't your mother ever teach you not to place stumbling blocks in front of the blind? What's your fuckin' problem, asshole? Is this what makes you feel tough?" Heeb kicked him again in the ribs. "You feel tough now, asshole?"

Heeb took a pen out of his shirt pocket and pressed it painfully up against the youth's neck, right on the jugular, until any further pressure might puncture it.

"You think you're a real badass because you and your asshole friend can attack a blind women half your size, when she's accompanied by a nerd like me, eh? Well watch the fuck out, punk, because this is that movie called 'White Collar Warrior Strikes Back.'" The thug was still groaning in pain and now raising his hands as if to surrender so that Heeb would stop pushing the pen into his neck.

"Oh does that hurt? Well it's gonna hurt even more if you don't apologize to that lady for what you just fuckin' did."

The ruffian squirmed a bit and then said, "Sorry M'am."

"That's not enough," Heeb yelled, pushing the pen a little harder into his neck. "Say sorry I was such a brutish and inhumane asshole to you."

"Sorry I was such a brutish and inhumane asshole to you."

Heeb got up, picked up his papers, and walked Hila out of the subway system and into a cab. There was no way he was going to make it to that presentation. He was now quite late, his face was a mess, and his suit was stained with blood and subway dirt.

But it didn't much matter, because he needed to take his wife to the eye doctor.

38. The Posse Dissolves

Later that night, Evan showed up at Heeb's apartment to see him in person for the first time in about a month.

"What happened to you?" he exclaimed, seeing Heeb's swollen, broken-looking nose.

"I'm taking Kung Fu now...You know, to defend myself against the hazards of actuarial work."

"You got into a fight?" Evan asked, surprised.

"Yeah. But there's a bright side."

"What? You get a nose job now?"

"Even better. I met a woman who doesn't think I need one."

"Wow. That is better...Are you serious?" Evan asked, genuinely happy for his friend.

Heeb smiled. "More serious than you can imagine... Her name is Hila...And she may be the only gorgeous woman who can't see how scarred my dick is, how bald my head is, or how short my height is. And even if she could, I don't think she'd care."

"Really?" Evan said, in disbelief. "So this one doesn't care about SQ?"

"Oh, she still cares about SQ, but I think she weights the factors very differently than most."

"Wow..."

"Crazy, huh? In fact, I may end up losing my job, but I found my future."

"Really?"

"Evan, I've finally experienced love at first sight – with a blind woman, ironically enough...."

"A blind woman? Doesn't that mean she has a seeing eye dog?"

"She needs to get one. I think she wants a Labrador retriever."

"But that'll never work! Look what happened the last time you slept in a room with an animal."

"Don't be silly. That was a cat. This is a dog."

"But you wouldn't even take the Afghan Hound."

"This is totally different, Evan."

"It's beginning to sound like it."

"The whole thing's really one big miracle that would have never happened if any one of a million details had played itself out any differently."

"Like what?"

"Like the fact that I was getting off at a different station today. The fact that she couldn't get off at her station because of train problems and had to exit at my station. The fact that I decided to help her and miss my presentation. The fact that she's here from Israel to see some top eye specialist. And then, on top of all of that, the fact that she happens to be Jewish when I'm in the Jews-only phase of my dating life."

"You're crazy, Heeb."

"That's what she said. And you know what else? I realize that I don't really like tall women…I don't care what all of the damn fashion hype says. I like a short, petite woman. Like Hila."

"Really?"

"I feel like more of a man around her…And I guess that's another thing that's so perfect about Hila and me: I feel like she needs me at least as much as I need her."

"You've had a rather deep and insightful day, haven't you Heeb?"

"I definitely have…But what about you? I feel like I haven't seen you in ages…"

"I'll tell you. But I need a beer."

Over a cold six-pack in Heeb's living room, Evan told Heeb all about his torturous three weeks with Delilah Nakova and how they ended.

"You took relationship advice from a porn star?" Sammy asked in shock.

"Well, not exactly. I mean, I tried to ignore what Narc said for a while but it kept creeping back into my thoughts when I realized that I'm completely insecure about this woman."

"But I thought one of the reasons you're so in love with her is that she doesn't have a Hollywood A-list ego."

"She doesn't. But she still has a Hollywood A-list life."

"And for you, that meant that she would inevitably dump you, so you dumped her first?"

"Sort of. I mean, I don't care about Narc's bragging rights or his other immature notions like that. But I was just convinced that I could never really enjoy a normal relationship with her."

"Do you even know what one of those feels like?" Heeb asked playfully.

"Probably not...But I was convinced that I could never have any kind of normalcy with Delilah. Because of her celebrity lifestyle but mostly because of my own insecurities..."

"So you haven't communicated with her in eight days?" Heeb asked.

"Seven days, if you count the note I left her as communication. But I don't think it counts because I told her not to call me and then she called me that same morning, so I obviously didn't communicate successfully...In fact, she left me six voicemails over the next three days."

"Six voicemails?! And you didn't call her back?"

"No, I just couldn't handle it then. I didn't even know what to say...I was gonna have a nervous breakdown, Heeb. But on the fourth day after leaving that note, I woke up in a cold sweat about the whole thing...I finally got a grip and decided to call her. But then she wouldn't take my calls."

"Can you blame her?"

"But Heeb, I've left her twelve voicemails since then, including three today. And she won't call me back."

"You better cool it on those voicemails, or she'll start to think you're some psycho stalker. And believe me, it wouldn't take long for the police to grant Delilah Nakova a restraining order."

"Yeah, you're right. I've gotta stop. But what am I gonna do, Heeb? As usual, I totally screwed up with her – but much worse than the last two times. And now the posse's completely dissolving on me just when I need it most." Evan looked down for a moment. "Unless you're still willing to come out," he added, as a hopeful plea.

"What about Trevor?" Heeb asked.

"We caught up by phone today. He and Luigi are completely in love," Evan replied. "Luigi introduced him to all of his gay friends, and now Trevor feels much more comfortable in that community."

"But he could still join you once a month for a few hours, no?"

"Heeb, the guy's totally whipped. He and Luigi are taking yoga lessons together, for God's sake. And some weekly night course on African art. And they take off on these weekend getaways. Forget it. He's totally out. Might as well be married."

"What about Carlos?"

"He is married."

314

"Right," Heeb replied. "Speaking of which, he may be having kids in the next year or so."

"What?!"

"Yeah, we spoke a few days ago. I think the posse was really good for his marriage."

"What do you mean?" asked Evan.

"Meeting all of these other women when he was out with us just reminded him how special and irreplaceable Carolina is. And the jealousy it caused in her made them both realize how much they care for each other. They've done a lot talking since then, and it looks like they reached a compromise on the kids issue."

"Wow…I can't believe it! Carlos is definitely out now."

"What about Narc?" Heeb ventured.

"You didn't hear what happened to Narc?" Evan asked.

"No. I haven't spoken to anyone other than Carlos in about a week."

"So I guess Carlos hasn't heard yet either."

"Heard what?" Heeb asked.

"Trevor told me that Narc moved up to that ashram where Trevor had spent eight months meditating," Evan said.

"What?!"

"So get this. Narc goes over to Jersey to help his folks with their laundry business, and then, in the middle of the day, Mr. Wang calls his son into his office for one of those you're-in-really-deep-shit kinda talks. Turns out that his parents had seen him in that 'Sushi Love' porn flick he did."

"What?!" Heeb was dumbstruck. "Narc's parents saw their own son in a porno?"

"Isn't that insane?! Can you imagine the shame and humiliation?"

"Not in my worst nightmare."

"Well shortly after that awful chit chat with pops, Narc called Trevor to talk, because he was pretty shaken up by the whole thing. He had apparently even thrown up at his parent's place. According to Trevor, Narc was traumatized on several levels. First of all, he didn't even know that his parents actually had sex. Apparently, he had the wrong idea about their 11 p.m. rule, when their bedroom door was locked and they were not to be disturbed unless there was a major emergency in the house."

"What do you mean?"

"Narc always just assumed that after 11 p.m. his parents wanted privacy to take care of family matters or stuff related to their laundry business. He never imagined that his parents were actually having sex. That thought alone completely freaked him out."

"That's a little extreme, don't you think? I mean parents are people too."

"Narc's an extreme kind of guy in his own extreme ways. But it gets crazier."

"It does?"

"Yeah. Apparently, Narc's father started off by excoriating his son for leaving his prestigious law job in exchange for work that would bring shame to the entire Wang family. But after he was done berating poor little Yi, his dad began critiquing his son's sexual technique, saying things like 'Didn't anyone teach you how to have sex with a woman? I just assumed they covered that stuff in school or I would have sat down and taught you when you were entering manhood.'"

"That is crazy."

"So, in one fell swoop, Narc discovers that his parents still have regular sex, that they sometimes watch pornographic films to spice things up, and that they watched a porno that he starred in. And to top it all off, he discovers that his father thinks he's got terrible technique in bed and that all of those women that Narc was fucking in the movie were just faking their orgasms."

"Wow…That's a lot to discover in one sitting," he agreed. "I'd definitely be heading for the ashram."

"Yeah, Trevor thinks the posse should go back for him in about half a year. He recommended six months to Narc as a minimum cleansing period. Trevor could totally relate, I think. In a strange way, they were both confronted with very dramatic discoveries that shook them up, even if they were totally different revelations."

"What a crazy nine months this has been," Heeb said.

"It really has been," Evan agreed.

They reflected for a moment on everything that had happened since they first met in the hospital.

Evan returned to the more pressing issue at hand. "So you see, you're really my last hope for the posse at this point."

"I've finally found true love at first sight, and you want to make me risk it all so that you can go out and find a replacement for the dream girl you stupidly lost? Clearly you have no idea what real love is, Evan."

316

"That's not true!" Heeb's accusation animated Evan into an impassioned defense. "Look at where I've been, Heeb. I used to be a complete womanizer — always hounding about insatiably for the next woman. Whiplash Libido, as Narc used to call me. And ever since I ran into Delilah Nakova, no other woman has really mattered to me. To feel true love, even the inveterate womanizer must be willing to forget all other women for the sake of the one he can't betray."

Heeb looked unimpressed with Evan's histrionics, which only goaded Evan into more of an emotional outpouring.

"Love has only the sacredness, meaning, and intensity that you give it. And the more you forfeit for love — including other women, or particular personal freedoms — the more you have invested in that love, and the more subjective meaning that love will possess. And ever since I ran into Delilah Nakova on May 5, 1999, she has occupied my mind and heart more than anything else. There isn't a thing that I wouldn't do for her — just like with you and Hila."

"OK. Fine. So I misspoke," Heeb conceded. "You are in love with her. But you didn't have the courage to keep that love."

Evan's eyes watered a little.

Heeb continued: "You failed to communicate your deepest feelings to the person you wanted to get closest to. You were so in love that you were afraid to have your heart broken. But that fear cost you the very love you so passionately wanted to possess."

Evan was silent for a minute, as he looked at the empty beer can in his hand. He finally looked up. "You're absolutely right! I was a coward. And I let myself worship Delilah to the point where I couldn't even communicate with her properly. How the hell did I forget that she's as human as you and me?"

"Well, she is Delilah Nakova, Evan."

"So what? I was living in her loft, for God's sake. She had invited me to come into her world. And I was too afraid to enter it with anything but half steps. I'm such a fool!"

"Somehow I doubt my performance would have been any better."

"I should have just been honest with her about my fears. Even if she dumped me afterwards, at least I'd know that my love was based on illusion."

"It's such a shame that you're not saying all of this to her instead of me."

"I know. But she won't call me back now. And why should she, after the way I behaved?"

"Evan, you're just going to have to wait this out, and have enough confidence in yourself to try again. She obviously really cared for you, so she'll eventually call, once she gets over herself."

"I don't know…I think it'll take more than that…"

Heeb felt genuinely sorry for Evan. He wished that he had some easy cure for his friend's ills. Now that Sammy had found love, he wanted the same for Evan.

Then an idea suddenly occurred to Heeb. "There is one way you could probably get her to talk to you again."

"How?" Evan asked, his eyes tired but still hopeful.

"I mean, it's not the easiest solution, but it's the only one that comes to mind."

"What is it?"

"Write her another novel."

"Another novel?" Evan asked, full of dread.

"Yeah."

"About what?"

"I don't know, but I have the perfect title for it."

"What?"

"Sex in the Sequel."

THE END

About the Author

Zack Love graduated from Harvard College, where he tried to create a bachelor's degree in Women. With the bachelor portion of that degree in hand, he settled in New York City but — to afford renting his bed-sized studio – found himself flirting mostly with a computer screen and stacks of documents. Determined not to die a corporate drone, Zack decided to sacrifice sleep for screenwriting, an active social life, and Internet startups offering temporary billion-dollar fantasies.

To feed his steady diet of NYC nightlife, he regularly crashed VIP parties in the early 2000s and twice bumped into his burgeoning crush, a Hollywood starlet. But — much to Zack's surprise — neither of those awkward conversations led to marriage with the A-list actress. Zack eventually consoled himself by imagining fiascoes far worse than those involving his celebrity crush. In the process, he dreamed up a motley gang of five men inspired by some of his college friends and quirky work colleagues. And thus was born *Sex in the Title*. But the novel is not autobiographical: Zack never had his third leg attacked by any mammal (nor by any plant, for that matter). In fact, keeping his member safe has been one of Zack's lifelong goals — and one of the few that he's managed to accomplish.

After publishing *Sex in the Title*, Zack developed the SQ Calculator (www.SQCalculator.com), an app that uses "crowd-sourcing" to measure how sexy someone is.

Some Shameless Self-Promotion

(hey, if not here, then where?)

First of all, thanks for making it this far. You've got stamina. Hopefully you enjoyed the ride. If so, please take a moment to give this novel an awesome review on Amazon and Goodreads.

Maybe you can even buy the book as a fun gift for someone you may know in one of the following categories:

1) disgruntled lawyers
2) Asian men with a bad-boy side
3) funny bald men
4) writers
5) basketball players who read fiction
6) men trying to trying to understand or laugh at themselves
7) women trying to understand or laugh at men
8) New Yorkers
9) oversexed men (i.e., men)
10) anyone else who could use the same laughs and nonsense you just enjoyed.

In case you needed any more encouragement, if this novel does well enough, I will write a sequel. To sign up for any sequel-related updates, visit www.SexInTheSequelBook.com.

In the meantime, feel free to connect with me on Facebook (www.tinyurl.com/FBSITT) or through my web site (www.SexInTheTitleBook.com), where you can also sign up for my newsletter to receive my latest blogs/musings and news about other releases. There is also a *Sex in the Title* fan group on Goodreads (www.tinyurl.com/SITTfan).

CPSIA information can be obtained at www.ICGtesting.com
Printed in the USA
BVOW04s2016131214

379216BV00016B/494/P